FORTUNE'S WORLD

MICHAEL COLLINS
(Photograph © Melendez)

FORTUNE'S WORLD

Michael Collins

with an introduction by
Richard Carpenter

Crippen & Landru Publishers
Norfolk, Virginia
2000

Cover design by Deborah Miller

Crippen & Landru logo by Eric D. Greene

ISBN (limited edition): 1-8859941-45-5
ISBN (trade edition): 1-885941-46-3

FIRST EDITION

10 9 8 7 6 5 4 3 2 1

Printed in the United States of America on chlorine-free, acid-free paper

Crippen & Landru Publishers
P. O. Box 9315
Norfolk, VA 23505
USA

Email: CrippenL@Pilot.Infi.Net
Web: www.crippenlandru.com

TO BOB RANDISI
Thanks for being a good friend to Dan Fortune
and his creator all these years

CONTENTS

INTRODUCTION
By Richard Carpenter

This collection of Michael Collins stories, ranging over a period of some thirty years, is aptly named *Fortune's World*. For its narrator-protagonist, Dan Fortune, is at the center of events in each of the fourteen stories, despite their wealth of diverse characters and situations. He is the sole "post of observation," in the words of Henry James, and the fulcrum on which the events of the stories turn. Until he comes on the scene, digging around, stirring things up, the crimes and misjudgments of the cases would rest in the archives. The wicked would get away with murder, the unfortunate would be made to suffer for what they did not do.

This is, of course, the world of every private detective, from Poirot to Hetty Wainthropp, the essential difference in these stories being in their tone. These are not puzzles — although they are often puzzling enough — to be elegantly solved with the little gray cells; they are gritty tales of arrogance and greed, misery and desperation. They take place in the real world in which we all live, whether or not we are aware of it, seen from its underside. Dan is the center of this world.

He might well have gone in the same direction as the people whose lives he is investigating, for he, the only one-armed detective in mystery/crime novels [Ed. Note: This may not be true any longer.], lost his left arm while attempting to hijack a German freighter, the escapade of a juvenile delinquent, in his own words, and a possible first step on the path of crime. This great disaster for a boy of seventeen he eventually turned to his advantage. Without his handicap he would probably have become a policeman like the father who deserted his family when Dan was young, or more likely in the mode of Captain Gazzo of the NYPD, the man he most respected.

This avenue closed to him, he adopted the profession of private eye where his real talents could be best put to use. The empty left sleeve is not only his burden to bear but also his advantage. Ironically his misfortune becomes his good fortune. No doubt his tenacity, his courage (he really has guts) and his natural capacity for observation and analysis would have been there anyway, but his handicap tends to lead the people he is investigating to underestimate his intelligence and his physical ability. He asks no favors, expects no sympathy, would spurn it if it were offered.

His ability to observe and interpret is, of course, also the stock-in-trade of all great fictional investigators from Holmes to Dalgleish. They focus on details that to others are insignificant or simply completely overlooked. Dan similarly notices everything, even the absence of the expected — one thinks of Sherlock Holmes's dog that did not bark in the night.

This perception of clues and their possible import, is not, however, the most important quality of Dan's observations, and here he begins to go well beyond the usual detective. Like Simenon's Inspector Maigret he has a gift for intuitively understanding the inner personalities of the actors in each case: What they are concealing; what they fear or hope. From their manner, their clothes, the furnishings of their homes, their responses to different kinds of questions, he gathers impressions which build up a complete picture for him of what kind of people they are, and what they might have done. Unlike Maigret, he supplements this intuition with a patient and almost incredible pertinacity. As Karen Parker points out in "Angel Eyes," he'll keep "...digging, hammering at you until it gets in the way of your work ..." In short until he finds out what he is looking for.

Beyond the hard data, Dan's psycho-social antennae are constantly alert, sensitive to all the nuances of the situation wherever it may be. Sometimes this intuition becomes the principal element in the story, as in the experimental "Killer's Mind" where he outdoes Maigret in imaginatively re-creating how the murderer planned and executed his crime, showing us in passages of interior monologue the precise processes of thought that must have taken place.

Dan needs this congeries of abilities in order to function in the unusually wide arena of his cases. Most detectives, whether private or police, stick pretty much to one territory and investigate a rather narrow spectrum of society: Morse stays in Oxford; Warshawski in South Chicago; Brother Cadfael in Shrewsbury or close by. Dan ranges much farther afield. Although the centers of Dan's world are the Chelsea district of Manhattan, where he lost his arm long ago, and Santa Barbara in Southern California where he lives now, many of the stories are set in a wide variety of places from the crashing surf of the Mendocino coast to the bleak and grimy wintertime streets of Syracuse, New York. In "Long

Shot" he even goes to the hot and dusty towns of a composite Central American country, and the plot that began in Chelsea finally works out some thousands of miles away.

Wherever the case takes him Dan creates for the reader not just some vague background but the contours, the sights and sounds, the very feel and ambiance of these milieus. The physical environment becomes an integral part of the seamless web that Collins is weaving so that the reader feels completely involved in each situation, no matter how far removed it may be in time and space from another story just read. Few, if any mystery/crime short stories bring as vividly to life both the California coast and the seamy atmosphere of Irish Johnny's in Syracuse.

The reader who takes this book from the airport rack looking only for a "good read," a complex mystery solved by a clever and unusual detective, will not be disappointed. An astute and determined detective; complex plots that render up their meaning bit by bit; intriguing clues that have to be properly interpreted; vividly realized settings of great variety — these ingredients of the best mysteries are manifestly here. However, and this is a very big "however" indeed, the mystery/crime dimension of these stories is only an aspect, and not the most important aspect the reader should pay heed to.

As Collins has said, he writes not so much pure mysteries as crime-based "socio-dramas" where the "inside forces" of arrogance, greed, rage, hate, misery, desperation combine with the outside forces of the culture to produce violence and crime, or, sometimes, as in a few of the best stories here, simply tragic misjudgment.

If the reader should ask, why bother with crime at all if the real interest is social problems, the answer would have to be that crime provides not escape from societal problems but a powerful lens for understanding them and their wider implications. When an abortion doctor is shot, a respectable gay man brutally beaten to death, we see through the glass, not darkly, but face to face. This is our culture. Crime focuses our view in a way no other means can.

Collins tackles a veritable galaxy of these problems in most of these stories. The outside forces of ideology, ethnic discrimination, economic inequality, societal alienation, stoke up the inner forces to bring about the crime which is Dan Fortune's job to investigate. In "A Matter Of Character," for example, he digs into what the NYPD has concluded is the

open-and-shut case of a gay man in the wrong place at the wrong time —
murdered by a 14-year-old male prostitute in a flea bag hotel. But the dead
man's long time partner insists it could not have happened that way, and
Dan's judgment tells him to dig deeper. In "Family Values," when Della
Keene, a pregnant Modoc teenager in rural Tulare County, kills her
boyfriend the town agrees it was to be expected. But Dan, in Tulare on
another case, becomes curious when he notices two respectable
townspeople showing great interest in Della before the murder.

The tone of those two stories is a kind of white-hot anger, but other of
the socio-dramas have a tone more of sadness than anger. "The Chair,"
"Culture Clash," and "A Death In Montecito" are stories of this sort, with
"Angel Eyes," the story Collins thinks is the best he ever wrote,
particularly melancholy. With its interweaving of four themes, "Angel
Eyes" is a most unusual and powerful story.

In the end we probably must ponder what the general import of these
socio-dramas can be. Obviously, they are not conventional crime/mystery
stories in the usual mode: Dan is a long way from Poirot or Lord Peter
Wimsey. Yet they are also different in emphasis and attitude, from the
"hard-boiled" school of crime tales, whether those of Marlowe or V.I.
Warshawski. In these stories, in the words of F. Scott Fitzgerald, the
American Dream seems to have gone "belly up in the sun."

Does Dan, and therefore Collins, want to change society with these
tales? The answer has to be no and maybe. Dan is not a reformer; he is a
revealer. As a detective his job in life is to uncover the evil that men do,
the mistakes they make; to turn over the rocks so that we can see what
lies underneath.

Collins has written that "the detective and the writer are the same,"
and what both he and Dan want to do is, in the words of Joseph Conrad, to
make us *see*. The world he wants us to see is the real world. What we do
with what we see, is up to us.

*RICHARD CARPENTER, professor emeritus of English at Bowling
Green State University, Ohio, is the author of* Thomas Hardy, *1964, and
articles on Joseph Conrad, Kay Boyle, and many other authors.*

This second anthology of Dan Fortune stories contains all those not published in Crime, Punishment and Resurrection (Donald I. Fine, 1992). *Because the book completes the cycle, I decided to run them in chronological order, starting with "Scream All The Way," which was actually written in my last years in New York without Dan Fortune, or even his precursor, Slot-Machine Kelly. After the success of* Act Of Fear, *I rewrote it, and it became the second Fortune story. The genesis was the observation you'll find as the key to the tale. I read it somewhere. I now have no idea where.*

In the late Sixties, because the pay might be only $50, you wrote a story in one draft, and then rewrote if necessary after rejections. Three or four rejections — that's how many mystery mags there were depending on the given year or even month — and you filed it for a better day. I got lucky with this one, sold it to Alfred Hitchcock's Mystery Magazine *for nearly what they pay today.*

I have cleaned the text a bit, but left everything that doesn't make me wince, and the piece is essentially unchanged.

SCREAM ALL THE WAY

If I have a nightmare, it always concerns my falling from some great height, screaming helplessly all the way down into the abyss. I wake up in a shivering sweat, my missing arm aching where there is no arm to ache.

I light a cigarette.

I don't go back to sleep for some time. I'm afraid of the vision of falling to my death.

That's why I remember so well what Captain Gazzo called The Sussex Towers Case.

★ ★

It walked into my office on a hot Monday in August, in the person of a small, dapper man wearing a gray tropical suit and an aloof manner. The heat that oozed through my one window must have made him think he was in a swamp, because he moved as if his feet were in mud to the ankles.

He saw that my arm was missing. "You're Daniel Fortune?"

The tone of his voice, and the look in his eyes, denoted silently: *You? A cripple?*

I was tempted to tell him that he would get his money's worth because I had two heads to compensate for the arm, but, no matter what they show in the movies, humility gets more work than wit.

"Yes, sir," I said humbly. "What can I do for you? "

"You're a licensed private detective?"

"They'll give anyone a license these days," I said. So much for humility and good business manners.

Luckily, he had other matters on his mind. He sat down without even a thin smile at my wit. "My name is Wallace Kuhns. I'm an attorney. I have a job: two men to guard $250,000 in cash, five P.M. to nine A.M. for five days. Fifty a day for each man."

"Fifty isn't much," I said, ready to bargain.

"Oh, damn," Wallace Kuhns said, and he transformed before my eyes. The starch went out of him. He slumped in the chair, stretched out his legs, reached for a cigarette, and looked ten years younger. "This whole thing is a pain. Listen, Fortune, I know that fifty is peanuts. If Ajemian weren't a big client, I wouldn't be here at all."

"Who's Ajemian?"

"Ivan Ajemian, president of Tiflis Rug and Textile Company. Factories in New Jersey, North Carolina, and Connecticut. Offices on East 26th Street. Real headquarters in apartment 16-A, The Sussex Towers. That's his apartment."

"He has the $250,000 in cash there?"

"He does. He's a modern businessman, but with some quirks. One of the quirks is that once a year, during the annual sales meeting in August, be hands out bonuses personally to the best salesmen. They come to his apartment one at a time. He gives them one drink, a pep talk, and the cash bonus."

"The insurance company doesn't like it?"

"You guessed it," Kuhns acknowledged. "Two weeks ago the apartment was broken into. The insurance boys are howling. They want two guards. Ajemian says okay, but no more than fifty a day per man."

"What was stolen two weeks ago?"

"Nothing. The police think Ajemian came home and scared the thieves off. The insurance people think the thieves were after the bonus money, and made a two-week mistake."

"Why guards only at night?"

"Ajemian says two company men can guard during the day and save money. At night they'd get overtime."

"When do I start?"

"Tonight. Can you get the other man?"

"Yeah. Pay the fifty in advance for each of us."

★ ★

That's how it began. After Kuhns had gone, I called Ed Green. I'd worked with Green before, and he'd take the fifty.

We arrived at apartment 16-A, The Sussex Towers, at 5:00 p.m. Green was grumbling about the heat and the lousy fifty bucks.

"I hope it's at least air-conditioned," he said.

It was. It was cool, and big, and bizarre. Ivan Ajemian went in for ornate furniture from a shah's palace, heavy decoration, velvet drapes, Oriental hangings and Persian rugs — all in one of those old "depression" apartments for the really-rich that had rooms they couldn't even find.

"The detectives?" Ajemian said when we were ushered in by an Oriental houseboy. "With one arm? What was Kuhn thinking of?"

"I'm small," I told him, "but I'm sneaky."

"Spare me the humor," Ajemian said. "I need protection, not comedy. I've got a lot of cash, I'm not especially brave, and my nose tells me that last so-called burglary might have been an inside job."

"What tells your nose that?" I asked.

"Follow me."

We followed him to the back door that opened into the kitchen from a service stairway. He was not what I had expected. Kuhns had made Ajemian sound old, but he wasn't a day over fifty. A big, calm-looking type. No matter what he said about his bravery, he moved with power, had sharp eyes, and looked like he could take care of himself.

"There," he said, "look at the lock."

I looked. So did Green.

"It's scratched," Green said, "but it could be a fake. What about it, Dan?"

I studied those scratches. They might have been made by a picklock. They were certainly intended to look like the work of a picklock or a jimmy, but they could have been fake scratches, too.

"I'm not sure. Somebody could be trying to make it look like entry from outside without a key."

"That's what I think," Ajemian said. "I want the doors watched carefully, you hear? Now, people come and go here, and I don't want them bothered. Keep out of the way. The money is in my study safe. Stay in the study, or at the doors. Nowhere else. Is that clear?"

I turned for the door. "Let's go, Ed."

Green nodded and started after me. Ajemian watched us.

"All right," he said, "I'm impressed. What do you want?"

I turned back. "We decide what we do, and how we do it. Take it or leave it. I can always sleep."

Ajemian laughed. "Touchy, eh? I always said a handicap makes a man tougher. Very well, but try to keep out of my way. I happen to have a friend who comes here often. Understand?"

Ajemian winked at me. I understood.

"We'll check the money now," I said.

"Check the money? Why?"

"I've been hired before to guard what turned out to be an empty safe from the start."

I thought he was going to turn purple, but he controlled himself and started for the study. Green followed him.

"I'll count," Green said. "You check the layout."

I checked the layout. It was simple, a lot of rooms but only two doors. The front door opened into the main corridor with the elevators. The back door opened from the kitchen onto a landing of the service stairs. The study where the money was had two doors, one from the living room and one from the kitchen. Nothing but a fly could get in through the windows, even though there was a ledge outside the study windows.

"Money checks," Green reported.

"The only entry is through the two doors, and there are two of us," I said. "It's a vacation with pay if we stay awake."

Green agreed with me. I took the living room door, and he parked at the kitchen door. Ajemian worked in his study with the cash. It looked like a quiet week ahead.

★ ★

It wasn't.

About ten o'clock I heard a key turn in the outer door. Ajemian had already gone to the living room. I jumped to the wall on the far side of the front door, my ancient revolver in my hand. The door opened, and one of the trimmest shapes I ever saw came into the room from the corridor.

"Ivan, honey!"

She was small and wore a blue summer suit she filled beautifully. She saw me behind her, and my jaw must have been hanging. She smiled, preened for me, and then saw my empty sleeve.

"Goodness! What happened to your arm?"

"Do you have a couple of days to listen?"

She giggled. "I bet you were a soldier."

"Who are you, miss?"

"Mary Kane. Isn't Ivan here?"

This, then, was the reason for Ajemian's wink. She had no handbag, and she couldn't have hidden a razor blade under the suit without it showing clear against her curves.

"He's back in his bedroom."

She tripped off toward the bedrooms, calling again, "Ivan! Honey?"

I went back to my chair. Mary Kane had a key. I wondered who else had a key to the apartment? It was a nervous thought. The next visitor didn't have a key. At least, he didn't use it. He knocked, lightly.

Since there was a doorbell, I approached the door with care. The knock had the sound of someone checking to see if anyone was in the apartment. I opened the door quickly, my pistol in my solitary hand.

A tall, thin man stared at the gun.

"In!" I snapped. "Back away. Easy."

He came in, backed away, and I leaned out and checked the corridor. It was empty. I closed the door and faced him.

"Who are you?"

"Max Alvis." He was thin and nervous. "Executive VP of Tiflis Rug Company. Are you one of the detectives?"

"Yeah. Dan Fortune."

"You're alone?"

"My partner's around."

"You always remain separate?"

"We don't do anything always. We mix it up."

"I see, yes. Quite clever."

"No," I said, "standard routine."

Alvis nodded. "Kuhns seems to have hired good men. It's an annoying situation all around. I wish the insurance company had never found out about the earlier burglary attempt. We've gone along without guards for years. That stupid attempt was probably of no importance anyway." He glanced around. "Isn't Mr. Ajemian here?"

"In the bedrooms."

"Alone?"

"No."

"Ah," Alvis said. "Well, I suppose it can wait."

The executive VP wheeled around, strode to the door, and went out. Green appeared behind me.

"What was that all about?"

"I don't exactly know. I guess he decided to change his mind, if he had any real reason to come here at all."

"Yeah," Green said dubiously. "At least he didn't have a key. Let's change posts, you're having all the company."

"Ajemian's not working anymore tonight," I told him. "I'll sit in the study."

★ ★

In the study, all was quiet. I opened the door into the kitchen and sat where I could see the rear door. I thought about Max Alvis. What had he really wanted? There was something about my conversation with him that bothered me, but I couldn't place what it was.

I thought about it, and must have dozed lightly, but jerked alert when I heard voices in the living room, a man's, a woman's, and Green's. The man was Ajemian, and he burst into the study with his arm around a tall woman in black. He was all smiles. She wasn't.

"My dear wife needs her blood money," Ajemian said. "I'm opening the safe. You men want to draw your guns?"

"Ivan has such a sense of humor," the woman said. "That's why I left him. He made me laugh too much."

"Two years, Beth, and no divorce," Ajemian laughed. "Admit you miss me."

Mrs. Beth Ajemian wasn't a strudel like little Mary Kane, but a fine figure of a woman. Red-haired and full-bodied, she walked with grace and just enough sway. She was a woman, she knew it and liked it.

"I miss you, Ivan, exactly as you miss me," she said. "Do you perhaps want a divorce to marry your latest little friend?"

"I never claimed to be a saint, Beth."

"I didn't want a saint. I wanted a husband who was sometimes at home with his wife."

Ajemian shrugged. "I guess that's water under our bridge."

He opened the wall safe and took out an envelope. I saw the big bundle of $250,000 still intact. Ajemian handed the envelope to his estranged wife.

"A little extra, Beth. Don't tell my lawyer."

"Thank you, Ivan."

She slowly gazed around the study, as if remembering better days. Or studying the layout to refresh her memory? Then she left the study, crossed the living room and went out without looking back.

"We just didn't work out," Ajemian sighed.

"How come she came for her money at this hour?" I asked.

Ajemian looked at me. "I don't know. She called, said she needed it. Why?"

"Nothing special," I said.

Ajemian went back to Mary Kane in the bedroom. Green resumed his post in the livingroom. I remained in the study, but I didn't like the feel of it. I went into the kitchen and studied that lock again. The marks were still there, and they still could be the work of a jimmy, or the work of someone who wanted to make them look like a jimmy.

I went back to the study and settled in. I didn't doze, but nothing more happened that night.

★ ★

We were relieved at nine the next morning. On our way to the elevators we met the first salesman. He had the gleam of bonus in his eyes.

Green headed for home and some sleep. I didn't. I went across the street and sat on a bench just inside the park, from where I could see both the front and service entrances to The Sussex Towers. Last night had been too busy, too much traffic in that apartment. I sensed it. Ajemian was nervous. So was Max Alvis, and what was it about Alvis' talk with me that rang wrong?

There are only two ways to plan a crime and get away with it: hide it, or disguise it.

Amateurs tend to disguise a crime. They plan it to look like something else, or look like the work of someone else, to prevent anyone looking in the right place for the obvious motive. They have to resort to illusion.

Most professionals hide their crime, but they don't disguise it. They don't care if the crime is known for what it is, as long as they're not caught doing it, or have it proved against them later that they did this particular job.

Both methods have their problems, and both require some planning, so I sat in the park and watched The Sussex Towers. For a few hours I saw nothing more interesting than what looked like more hungry salesmen hurrying into the building; nothing suspicious, no one who looked like pro or amateur casing the place.

Then Max Alvis appeared in a taxi. He didn't get out at the front entrance, but at the rear, then walked into the alley that led to the service entrance. I could see him all the way. He stopped at the service entrance and seemed to study it.

Then he went inside. I waited, but he didn't come out.

A half hour later he did come out — the front — and hailed a cab. Making a quick decision, I sprinted for another taxi. Luckily, The Sussex Towers attracted cabs.

"No wisecracks," I said, "but follow that cab."

The driver muttered, but he followed. We ended up at an office building in the East Thirties. Alvis went inside. I tailed him to the elevators. There was no way to follow him any farther without being spotted, so I checked the building directory. Wallace Kuhns, Attorney, had an office in room 310.

Fifteen minutes later Alvis appeared again in the lobby. Kuhns was with him — and Mrs. Beth Ajemian.

They hurried out into the heat and split up. Alvis took another taxi, while Kuhns and Beth Ajemian walked toward Third Avenue. I had no choice, there were no other empty cabs, so I followed Kuhns and Mrs. Ajemian. I would have followed them, anyway. Kuhns was holding Beth Ajemian's hand — tight.

On Third Avenue they went into a cocktail bar.

Inside there were booths, dim light, and a small bar. Kuhns and Beth Ajemian slid into a middle booth. I sat at the bar and watched them. They had all the aura of lovers, and not new lovers.

Kuhns held her hand while he talked hard and fast. I watched through three beers, then I saw Kuhns dig for his wallet, and I left first. I picked them up as they came out. They went straight back to Kuhns' office.

I headed for home. There was nothing in itself suspicious about Kuhns being close to Beth Ajemian. The wife and Ajemian seemed to have gone their separate ways, and Kuhns would have known the woman for a time. I remembered that Ajemian had said, "Don't tell my lawyer," when he had given Beth Ajemian some extra money last night, so Ajemian knew that his wife and Kuhns were close.

Too, Kuhns had hired me — or was that part of some scheme? I felt more than a little uneasy. At the very least, Kuhns might have been forced to hire detectives against his will. It was something to think about. So I thought about it, and I didn't get much of the sleep I needed.

★ ★

I got back to The Sussex Towers at 4:50 p.m. to find Green already there, the company men on their way out, and Ajemian in a lousy mood.

"I've got two hours of work," Ajemian growled. "Stay out of the damned study, and keep quiet. If anyone comes, tell them I've gone to China."

It looked like the start of a long night. I filled Green in on what I'd seen that day while we waited for the last of the Tiflis Rug Company men to leave.

"We'd better keep a close eye on people with keys," Green decided.

"I hear you loud."

When the last man had gone, and Ajemian was closed up in the study, I double-locked the front door, then went to check all the bedrooms to make sure no one was lurking around. Green took the rear and the kitchen.

I found no one in the bedrooms — not in the rooms, the closets, or under the beds. I had one more room to check when I heard the shot — a single shot that echoed through me like an atomic bomb. From the rear — the study!

I ran with my old revolver in my lone band. I reached the door into the study from the living room, but didn't barrel on through. That way lay suicide. I flattened beside the door, and kicked it open, then jumped through, crouched low, with the old cannon out ahead of me.

Ajemian lay on the floor, bleeding. No one else was in the study. I ran to Ajemian, who struggled up.

"One man. Masked. Tried to stop him," Ajemian croaked. "Waiting for me in here. He got it all!"

"Let's see the —"

"No! Flesh wound. Back door! Get him."

I hesitated a second. No amount of money is worth a life, no matter what the victim thinks, but the wound didn't look bad.

I ran out into the kitchen.

Green lay on the kitchen floor, out cold. An ugly lump on his left temple showed what had happened to him.

The back door was open. I went out onto the service landing. The only way out of The Sussex Towers was down. Even if the thief had gone up, he would have to come down sooner or later. I ran down those sixteen flights as fast as I could, listening all the way. There was no sound below like that of a running man.

In the basement I listened. I heard nothing.

I went out into the alley at the rear. In the hot sunlight there wasn't even a cat. I ran out into the street that bordered the park. At this hour traffic was thick, and if he'd made it this far there was no way to catch him, not if he was a pro.

A woman's high, shrill scream shattered the hot evening.

I looked up toward the windows of Ajemian's apartment sixteen floors above.

For one brief instant the whole evening held its breath in frozen silence. No sound at all. Sixteen floors above, I saw the man seem to hang in space, his face masked, his arms spread, his feet and legs twisted, a black bag floating beside him. All motionless for the one split second.

Then I stood there and watched the man fall the whole long, endless sixteen stories in slow silence, like a grotesque sequence from some old, silent movie.

He hit on the roof of a parked car, and bounced off into the street. Two cars ran over him before they could stop. The black bag hit some twenty feet away, split open, and spilled bundles of money across the street. A small pistol hit near the bag.

I ran to the fallen man through screams and squealing brakes. Blood spread all around him. Two patrolmen were running up, and a cruise car was in sight. I bent over the man. He was still masked. I took off the mask.

It was Wallace Kuhns. He didn't have much face left, but it was Kuhns. I stared at him for a long count of ten, then looked up at the tall building isolated from all the other buildings around it.

I grabbed the police sergeant from the cruise car.

"Put a man on the back and front doors!" I said. "Now!"

"Who the hell are you? What do you know about —"

I quickly showed him my license. "Dan Fortune. Call Captain Gazzo at Homicide. Ask about me, and get him up here fast. But put men on the doors now. No one in or out. No one! You've got to do that."

I was in luck. The sergeant was a good cop who would take no chances. Maybe I was crazy, but he'd find that out later. Meanwhile, maybe I knew what I was doing.

He sent one patrolman to the back door, and one to the front doors; no one in or out until further orders. The windows on the first two floors of the building were barred. It would do. A minute had barely passed since Kuhns had taken his fall.

I went back up to the apartment.

I revived Green and checked Ajemian's bleeding, and by then the doctor had arrived. So had Captain Gazzo. The captain looked at me, at Green, at Ajemian, and got down to business.

★ ★

"Okay, what's the story?"

Ajemian's wound was minor — a deep flesh wound that had bled but wasn't serious. Green had a nasty lump and a headache.

Ajemian said, "He was hiding here in the study when I came in tonight. He was masked. He held the gun on me, and made me open the safe. He heard Fortune lock the front door, and go off to search the bedrooms. He heard Green in the kitchen."

Green nodded. "I was checking the lock on the back door when I heard him behind me. He slugged me good — and that's all I know."

"After he hit Green," Ajemian went on shakily, "I tried to jump him and he shot me. He ran out the back way. Fortune came into the study. You know the rest."

I said, "Didn't you know Kuhns hadn't left tonight?"

"He did leave," Ajemian said. "An hour before you arrived. He must have come back in through the rear and hid in the study."

Gazzo gave me an odd look, and went out. I sat while the doctor worked some more on Ajemian and Green. I lighted a cigarette. Gazzo came back after about fifteen minutes.

"M.E. says Kuhns died from the fall, no doubt," the captain reported. "We found a money wrapper under the window on the service landing outside the back door. There's a ledge out that window. Looks like he tried to hide there while Fortune was chasing down the stairs, only he slipped."

I said, "Nuts."

Gazzo glared at me. "There are fresh picklock marks on the back door, but we think they're fake. Kuhns had keys to the apartment in his pocket. He knew the routine of Green and Fortune, timed it for when they would be separated. If Ajemian hadn't made him shoot he'd have gotten away. He had bad luck."

"Bad luck, hell," I said. "Kuhns was murdered, Captain."

Gazzo nodded wearily. "I figured that's why you called in Homicide and had the doors sealed off. What've you dreamed up this time, Dan?"

"Kuhns didn't fall, he was tossed over. Whoever tossed him didn't have time to get out of the building. There's no way off the roof, so the killer's still inside. Keep the building sealed tight, no one in or out without identification."

"You're saying Kuhns wasn't alone? You want to tell me how you figure all this?"

"No, you wouldn't believe me."

"I'll bet," Gazzo said drily. "Any idea who?"

"Someone who knows Kuhns, this apartment, and where the money was," I said. I turned to Ajemian. "Is there anyone besides your ex-wife Beth, Max Alvis, Mary Kane, and the insurance people who fit that bill?"

"Myself," Ajemian said, "and the company guards we have in the day. The insurance people don't know the apartment."

"Okay," I said to Gazzo, "those are who you look for."

"I'll check them out," Gazzo said, "and a few other things, if that's okay with you? Like Kuhns' actions?"

"Why don't you just do what I'm going to do now, Captain?" I said.

"What's that?"

"Wait," I said, and that's what I did, I waited.

★ ★

Green was carted off to the hospital for observation, and Ajemian and I waited alone in the apartment. Ajemian watched me watching television for two hours before he blew up.

"Are you just going to sit here, Fortune? Do you expect me to pay you for that?"

"What do you want me to do?"

"Work! If you think Kuhns was murdered, go and solve it!"

"It's being solved," I said.

"By the police? Couldn't you help them, for what I'm paying?"

"Not the police," I said. "It's being solved by time. Time will solve it, and I've done my part. The killer is still in the building, for sure. No one gets out now, and sooner or later we have our killer."

"Just like that? It's not very imaginative," Ajemian said.

"Most police work isn't," I told him. "Follow routine, set up your conditions, and wait. That's the way it plays most of the time. Why don't you just go to bed if waiting gets you?"

"With a killer loose in the building?"

"There's a police guard on both doors," I said.

He went to bed.

I sat and waited alone. It was a long night. I began to jump at every noise, and from time to time in my mind I saw Kuhns falling those long, silent, sixteen stories to his death.

★ ★

Gazzo returned at eight o'clock the next morning. I was groggy from lack of sleep. Ajemian had slept fine and was bright as a pin. Gazzo hadn't slept any more than I had, but he was as bright as Ajemian.

"Here it is, Dan," Gazzo said. "Kuhns needed money. He'd lost a few clients, and had a big stock option. Beth Ajemian admits Kuhns wanted to marry her, but she wasn't about to divorce Ajemian until Kuhns had cash. She also admits Kuhns could have copied her set of keys to this place.

"The bag with the money in it was bought by Kuhns yesterday. The pistol is a Tiflis Rug office gun that vanished two months ago. He probably didn't want to hire detectives, but his hand was forced, so he hired two of the cheapest he could get. He probably figured you and Green were dumb. Maybe he was right."

I shrugged. "All circumstantial, and all a setup. Someone wanted it to look like Kuhns was out to rob the place, or maybe force him to rob the place. No one tried to get out of the building yet?"

"No," Gazzo said. "I'm waiting for a call to finish off your little hunch."

"What call, Captain?" Ajemian asked.

"Fortune will find out," Gazzo grinned.

I said, "You know, that first robbery attempt really stinks. If it was unknown thieves, it's too much coincidence. If it was Kuhns, it was crazy; it just drew attention when he knew the money wasn't even here. I figure it was a fake to make everyone think about robbery. All part of a big illusion, only there was a flaw in the illusion that made me think."

Ajemian said, "What kind of flaw, Fortune? Are you sure you're not just dreaming, as the captain says?"

Before I could answer, which I didn't intend to then anyway, the telephone rang. Gazzo answered. He listened for a time, nodded a few times, and hung up with a bigger grin at me.

"That's it, Dan. Everyone is accounted for. Beth Ajemian's been home all night, Max Alvis is in his office, Mary Kane is at her modeling school, the two company guards are at work, and even the insurance men are where they should be. None of them are in this building."

"Right," I said. "Then Ajemian's the killer."

★ ★

The big rug company executive was on his feet, red as fire and spluttering at me.

"Is this a joke, Fortune? I'll have you —"

"No joke," I said. "Simple elimination. I told you time would solve it. No one got out of this building. You're the only one still in the building. So you're it."

Ajemian was so red I thought he would choke to death then and there. He whirled on Gazzo. "Are you going to let him sit there and accuse me? I'll ruin both of you!"

Gazzo said nothing. He was watching Ajemian and me and waiting for my story. I gave it:

"Kuhns never left the apartment." I faced Ajemian. "You knocked him out and hid him in the study. He wouldn't stay quiet long, so you pulled it off as soon as Green and I were alone. You hit Green, opened the rear door, and shot yourself. When I chased after the supposed thief, you hauled Kuhns up on the windowsill and heaved him out with the money and the gun.

"I'd gone all the way down. You saw me down there, and figured it was the perfect touch— I'd *see* Kuhns fall — but that was a mistake. It broke a good illusion."

Ajemian tried a laugh. "You expect anyone to believe all that? An intricate scheme like that?"

"Not so intricate. It almost worked. The groundwork was harder than the killing trick. You had to fix it so Kuhns needed money. You got clients to leave him, and he was your lawyer so you had him take a big stock option for you, but in his name. We'll find he's done that before. The gun was easy, and he'd have bought the bag for you if you told him to. I'll bet we find he had other bags he could have used safer."

"He did," Gazzo said quietly. "Two attache cases we found."

I nodded. "I guess you were really jealous, wanted your wife back. That'll be easy to prove, the motive, or you wouldn't have tried for such a big illusion of robbery. Gazzo should be able to trace those keys eventually. Anyway, a paraffin test will show you shot a gun last night, and with —"

Ajemian waited for no more. He had another gun. He'd been ready. He took a shot at me, missed, and went out the front door. Gazzo picked himself up and went after him. I sat down. I had a cigarette. A one armed man isn't much help in a fight, and I value my skin. Catching him wasn't my job.

After a time I heard shots on the roof. I went to the window. Then I heard the scream, and I leaned out the window to look up. I was just in time to see him fall, his gun still in his hand. He screamed all the way down.

★ ★

I was still at the window when Gazzo came back.

"We didn't have much," Gazzo said. "You know we don't use a paraffin test anymore, it's useless. No court will take it."

"He didn't know that," I said. "It's not the truth that counts, Gazzo, it's what people think is true. He knew he did it, and he had to be a little crazy."

"All right, tell me. I'll believe how you figured it now."

"There was one thing Max Alvis said. He didn't know how the insurance people learned about that first supposed robbery attempt. Only three people could have told them. Alvis didn't. Kuhns didn't. That left Ajemian himself. He wanted the insurance men to know, so they would insist on guards. He needed witnesses for his fake robbery illusion."

"That had to come later, Dan. How did you start to think it was murder in the first place?"

Instead of answering, I asked, "What happened on the roof just now?"

"He tried to shoot it out, slipped, and went over the edge."

"He fell," I said, "and he screamed all the way down."

"So?"

"They always scream, Captain. Or almost always."

"Okay, so they scream. So what?"

"Kuhns didn't scream," I said. "Kuhns fell sixteen floors without making a sound. Even when they jump they usually scream, it's a reflex I guess. Kuhns fell, supposedly by accident, and he didn't make a sound. The only way that could have happened was that Kuhns had been unconscious. He'd been tossed out — murdered."

Gazzo stared at me. "Damn it, Dan, who can prove everyone screams when he falls? Maybe Kuhns was one man who just didn't scream!"

"It doesn't matter," I said. "It was the little flaw that made me wonder. It made me think."

Gazzo groaned. "Dan, you've got too much dumb luck."

"Like I said, it's not what's true that counts, but what a man thinks is true. If you build an illusion, it has to hold all the way. I didn't believe a man would fall sixteen floors without a scream. So I just couldn't believe the illusion."

Gazzo had no more to say. He was a cop, and he'd sweat for days about my shaky reasoning that could have been dead wrong. I won't sweat. Maybe someday I'll find a man who falls sixteen floors in silence, and then I'll be wrong. This time I'd been right, and that's what counts in detective work.

*In the mid and late Fifties my lady at the time was a member of
Actor's Studio in New York, and their unofficial hangout was a bar
and restaurant named Downey's. The tongue-in-cheek fable of how
Jim Downey started his place was printed on the menus. When I came
across a newspaper piece about the consequences of a daring robbery
and escape in South America, I combined it with Downey's yarn and
wrote this story.*

It turned out to be Dan Fortune #3, and also sold to AHMM.

LONG SHOT

Around the Chelsea slums of New York they tell the story of an
immigrant who came here with only the clothes on his back and a dream
of opening his own restaurant. He knew that hard work and saving his
money was the way to achieve his dream, so he worked day and night as
a waiter, and after ten years he had $312.27 in the bank. He thought about
it a while, then took the $312.27 out to Belmont Park and put it on a 100-1
shot. The horse came in, and that's how the immigrant got his restaurant.
Frank Marno knew that story as well as anyone.

★ ★

It was a hot day when Frank came into my office. He was twenty-five,
busy and eager. "You'll handle a job for me tonight, Dan?"

"What kind of job?" I asked. I'd known Frank Marno most of his life.
His father had been Sal Marno, chair number two at Cassel's Barber Shop.
Sal had left Frank that chair as his legacy, but Frank had other ideas.

"Same as usual," Frank said. "You deliver the package out to Kennedy
International tonight. Negotiable bonds, so take your gun, okay? The
client likes to see a gun."

Frank had no education beyond cutting hair, but he had imagination
and energy. He started by picking up whatever he could sell for a profit.
He hustled pool, gambled when he had a stake. He ran messages for
bookies, and worked up to taking small bets. Then he got a franchise from
the top men for his own book, started his legitimate messenger service,
handled a few actions I didn't want to know about, and finally bought a
share of a good liquor store. At twenty-five he was doing fine.

A long time ago, when Frank had been just a kid, Sal saved my life by
hiding me out when some unpleasant types wanted me dead. Sal had stood
up to the muscle and the cops, had taken more than one beating, but had
not revealed where I was hiding. I got out of the country on a ship, the
ones who were out to get me ended up dead themselves, and I hadn't

forgotten what I owed Sal Marno.

When Frank started his messenger service he wasn't flush, and he knew the principle of holding down the overhead, so he kept his staff low. If he needed a bonded man, he hired me. I remembered Sal, and detective work in Chelsea doesn't make a man rich, so I took the work.

★ ★

I picked up the package at Frank's store. That was unusual. Normally I got the package from the client. I didn't think about it then, which shows how careless a man can be when dealing with friends. Frank himself gave me the package and the instructions.

"Get to the hangar at eight o'clock, Dan. The client says not before, and don't be late. Okay?"

"Pay me," I said, "and I fly."

I ate some dinner, had time for a few good Irish whiskeys with Joe Harris, and caught the airport bus from the East Side Terminal. Frank Marno didn't pay enough for a taxi.

At the airport I found the hangar two minutes before eight o'clock. I went in with my big cannon displayed to impress the client. There was a small private jet all warmed up out front.

Two people waited inside the hangar. One was a really beautiful girl. The other was Frank Marno.

★ ★

Frank had a gun in his pocket. He let me see it once. "Hand over the package, Dan."

I gave it to him. "Why, Frank?"

He grinned at me. "You mean why do it like this? I couldn't carry it around, Dan. Too dangerous. I had to cover myself."

"Cover what?"

"Why my delivery was late. I covered okay, but it would've looked funny if I was carrying a big package. He might have wanted to know what was in it, or maybe why I took a package on a date."

"Who might have wanted to know?"

"Mr. Krupp," Frank said. "I had to pick up Angela, and make it look like just a regular date."

I wasn't following him all the way, but enough to have a cold feeling — cold and hard as ice. The girl came up then, and she was maybe nineteen. She held Frank's arm and looked up at him. Every man should have a woman look at him like that once in his life; with adoration, love, and a fierce kind of possession. Frank Marno was a lucky man. He was also insane. I recognized the girl now — Angela Krupp.

She smiled a defiant smile. "Hello, Mr. Fortune. Don't blame Frank, he couldn't tell you. You might —"

"I might have gone to your father," I said. "Maybe I would have, I like living."

Angela Krupp, the only daughter of Mr. Wally Krupp. The apple of

Mr. Krupp's eye, guarded from the harsh world like a vestal virgin. She wasn't in an airport hangar with Frank Marno with the blessing of Wally Krupp. Never.

Krupp had been Krupanski once. I don't think Wally Krupp ever realized the symbolism of his changed name — he wasn't a man given to thinking much about symbolism. But Wally Krupp lived by the gun as much as his famous namesakes had — the gun, the numbers, the dope, and the terror. Second only to Andy Pappas himself in New York. He was polite to Pappas, but to no one else. Racket boss number two, and trying hard.

Frank Marno said, "You didn't know I've been working for Mr. Krupp for over a year now? My own operation in the liquor store? A big take, Dan, and I met Angela. Bingo! That was it for both of us, me and Angela."

"You and Angela and a jet plane, Frank?"

"We're in love, we got a right. I ain't losing her!"

Angela said, "My father hates any man looks at me."

I said, "You're married, Frank."

"To a tramp I dropped a year ago! I'll get a divorce down south, and if I can't, to hell with it. We're in love. You got to grab in this world to get your share."

"What's in the package, Frank?" I asked.

His face was set like steel. "You got to have money, too, Dan. That's what's in the package. One hundred thousand cash. A month's take. I worked it all out. We're gonna live a good life."

I stared. "Krupp's money, too? You are crazy."

"My money!" Frank snarled. "I worked for it, I conned for it, I muscled for it. It's mine, and Angela's mine!"

When you're young, death is far away. The bigger the risk, the sweeter the triumph. Frank would be rich, and loved, and outlast the whole world.

I never was that young. "Krupp'll get you, Frank."

"I can handle myself," he said, proud and tough. "I'll take care of Mr. Wally Krupp and anyone he sends. I can shoot, I know judo, I fly my own plane, and I'm smarter than any illiterate like Wally Krupp."

"One man you can beat, but there won't be only one. Remember all the hired hands who never held any tool except a gun."

"Maybe a year," Frank said, "and he'll quit looking. I got it planned. What's a lousy hundred grand to somebody named Wally Krupp?"

"He can't let you get away with it, Frank, not one of his own men double crossing him. And there's Angela. No punk was ever going to touch his daughter. She was going to marry respectable; maybe a prince. You can't marry her even if he'd let you. He's a moral family man, Wally Krupp is."

"If he won't quit, I'll get him. I mean it, Dan."

"You can't get him. He's invulnerable, and you know it. Behind his hired guns and shyster lawyers he can't be reached. He snaps his fingers, you die, and you can't fight back."

For that one instant I think I got to him. One glimpse of doubt in his eyes, maybe fear. Angela Krupp squeezed his arm.

The fear vanished. "I've got it planned good, Dan."

Then he was gone — with his package, his woman, and his gun. I didn't wait for the plane to take off. I didn't want to be around if Wally Krupp happened to show up. I didn't ever want to see Frank Marno again.

You don't always get what you want.

★ ★

Six months passed. Word gets round in Chelsea; a private detective hears whispers he doesn't always want to hear.

If it had been only money, Wally Krupp might not have looked so hard. Or if it had been only Angela. Money *and* daughter were too much — a big slap in the face of Mr. Wally Krupp, and face and reputation are important to a racket boss. They were laughing at Krupp. Silently, but laughing. Only Frank Marno's blood would stop the laughter.

I heard bits and pieces, but they all added to a story.

A blonde cried in her beer one night only two months after Frank had run. Her man had been shot in Vera Cruz; he had been one of Wally Krupp's gunmen.

An old woman asked the D.A. if he could help her son and another man who were in jail in Caracas. They too worked for Wally Krupp. Only Krupp wasn't helping them much now.

Lt. Marx from the precinct came around to ask if I knew why Rico Stein had been in Peru. I'd known Rico pretty well at one time. Rico had just fallen off a cliff near Cuzco; rumor said he'd been hired recently by Wally Krupp.

Chelsea lowered the odds against Frank Marno. He was proving to have sharp teeth, it looked like, and maybe he would beat Wally Krupp after all. At least, maybe Krupp would give up. How many men could he lose before the troops rebelled? Frank could be the winner.

I knew better. Frank might be winning skirmishes, but the pressure had to be taking a toll, the roses had to be all gone by now. Frank and Angela weren't getting much of the good life — they were running faster and faster, looking over their shoulders, jumping at shadows. They were sleeping with crushed newspaper on the floor and the windows locked, no matter how hot it was where they were.

I knew the law of averages.

★ ★

The averages ran out for Frank and Angela in a place called Rio Arriba down in Central America. Captain Roy from the D.A.'s squad told me. The D.A. was interested.

"Two of Krupp's best men caught them in Rio Arriba," Roy said. "One of the gunmen ended in the bay, the other one's in jail down there on a

murder charge. Frank Marno got away, Angela Krupp didn't. They found
her in the bay, too."

It was a cold day, but not as cold as Wally Krupp's heart. His Angela
was dead, killed by Frank Marno, of course. Wally Krupp wouldn't blame
himself. No, he would tell himself that Frank Marno killed her by eloping
with her, by stealing the money, by not protecting her.

"Krupp'll never quit now," I said to Captain Roy. "Not if it takes twenty
years. Frank's a walking dead man."

"He always was, Fortune. No one escapes Wally Krupp, not this side of
the grave. The D.A. knows you talked to Marno that last day, and—"

My heart nearly stopped. "How do you know?"

"Don't panic, Krupp doesn't know. What the D.A. wants to know is how
much Marno really liked the Krupp girl."

"I don't know, Captain. He's young. Who can say?"

"Enough to want Krupp dead? To want that bad?"

"Maybe."

"Enough to come back here to get Krupp?"

"No one can reach Wally Krupp."

Roy sighed. "I guess you're right, Fortune. The D.A.'s just kind of eager. Marno kills Krupp, and we're rid of Krupp. Krupp kills Marno here,
and we get Krupp."

"Or they kill each other," I said. "That'd be nice."

"Why not?" Captain Roy said, and left my office.

★ ★

They brought Angela's body back to New York. Krupp buried her in
the biggest funeral Chelsea ever saw. I didn't go, but I got some of the
news that came out of the funeral.

Wally Krupp had the word out: no one was to touch Frank Marno. No
one was even to bruise Frank — just find him, and report back to Krupp.

It figured. Now Wally Krupp would handle Frank Marno personally.
It had to be. A family thing now, personal as well as business. A vendetta.
I don't think we Polacks have vendettas, but Wally's lived too long with
Sicilians. Krupp would kill Frank with his own hands. If not tomorrow,
then the next day — or next year.

★ ★

Six more months went by. I was feeling better about my role in Frank
Marno's departure, until I got the letter from Frank himself.

The letter was in a cheap envelope, with no date, no return address, and
a New York postmark. Frank had given the note to someone to mail for
him in New York, a note with his name scrawled, and just three words:
Find me, please!

So scared he couldn't risk telling me where he was in a call for help.
Trust no one. Even if he trusted me, Krupp could be watching me by now,
and Krupp could get to anyone.

Find me, please!

How long ago had the letter been written? Maybe months. What did Frank want — someone to hold his hand? Was his nerve gone now that he was alone, without Angela, the real reason he'd crossed Krupp in the first place?

What could I do for Frank? What could anyone do, even if I could find him?

Nothing.

But that didn't matter.

I owed Sal Marno's son, as I always had, and in Chelsea word gets around when you owe and don't pay. No, I had to go, if I wanted to live and work in Chelsea.

★ ★

Rio Arriba was a typical small Latin-American country capital city with wide streets, marble government buildings on scrubbed green squares, and the shacks of the poor hanging on muddy hillsides. The Ministry of Justice was a skyscraper with a lot of statues. I asked for Captain Guzman, the officer who had handled the shooting — that much the New York D.A. had told me.

Guzman was a tall type in military uniform complete with medals and polished boots. "Señor Fortune," he said, bowing me to a chair. "You wish to speak of the Angela Krupp murder?"

"I'm looking for Frank Marno, Captain."

Guzman nodded. "A tragic young man. Foolish, I think, but strong also. The señorita was most beautiful. His grief was great, but he was a man, a *caballero, si?* I watch, I see he has a stone in him, he will exact retribution."

"Do you know where he is?"

Guzman shook his head. "We investigated closely, of course, but it was clear that the two *pistoleros* had come to kill Marno and Miss Krupp. The weapons were lost in the bay, but the surviving *pistolero* confessed all. Marno acted in self-defense, and we released him. Where he went, I do not know."

"Can you tell me where he lived at the time?"

"Of course."

★ ★

Five minutes later I walked out with Frank Marno's last address in Rio Arriba. It wasn't encouraging: The Hotel San Martin.

The clerk was polite. "No, señor, he left us soon after the tragedy. Alas, I should have known that there was trouble — the señorita was so silent, so afraid, yes? The assassins actually came here!"

"It happened near the hotel?"

"Oh, no. In the slums, at the docks. So terrible."

"He left no forwarding address?"

"No, señor."

Stupid question. Frank wouldn't leave an address.

"I'll take a room," I said. I slipped him a twenty. "Pass it around that I'll pay for any information."

★ ★

I waited around the hotel for three days. No one came near me, so I went out to try the usual routine.

A man must eat, sleep, have some fun. He can change almost everything except his habits. He can even try to change those, but he has to do *something* with the days and hours, and sooner or later he will slip. If you can look deep enough and long enough, he'll eventually give himself away.

I had a photograph. I tried the movie houses, theaters, *jai alai* fronton, racetrack, restaurants and bars. Everywhere I passed out word I would pay. I drew a blank. There were bartenders and waiters who recognized Frank's picture, but they hadn't seen him for months. It looked hopeless, until one waiter remembered one small incident.

"*Si*, they sit in my corner many days," the waiter said. "The pretty señorita is very unhappy. The man he is angry."

"You never saw him alone later?"

"I think two, three times. He talks with Carmen."

I found Carmen at the bar of another café later that night. She was alone, drinking the local cactus drink. White lightning. She shrugged at my question.

"I see many *Americano* men."

"I'll pay for information about this one."

"What information, *caballero*?"

"About where I can find him. He needs help."-

I showed Carmen the letter. She blinked at it. She looked at me for a time, carefully. "Buy me a whisky. Scotch."

I bought her a Scotch. She drank with a deep sigh.

"Sometimes, I dream of the Scotch whisky," she said. She drank again. "This Marno was a sad man. He had lost his woman. He did not talk much. He say sometimes he don't feel so good. He say he will not long be alone."

"You know where he is now?"

"You are his friend?"

"Maybe the only friend he has."

I signaled for another Scotch. She stared at it when it came. As if all her disappointment could be cured by an unending supply of Scotch whisky. Maybe it could.

She drank. "The last time I am with Frank Marno, he take me to where he live. I show you.

We went through the back streets of the city far from the wide boulevards and scrubbed public squares. The place she brought me to was a cheap, dirty rooming house. Frank Marno had not been there for many months. The manageress didn't know where he had gone and she didn't care.

"He is drunk, always alone. Who can care?"

As I left, an enormous fat man came out of the manager's rooms. "Hey, *Yanqui!* Come with me."

The manageress turned on the fat man, spat something in gutter Spanish. The fat man grew red, and snarled at her. She shrank from his anger and walked away.

He nodded to me. "Come inside."

His eyes were sunk in layers of flesh — cunning eyes that counted my money through my clothes and wallet. He sat down inside the filthy back room. He grinned at me. "You wear fine suit. You are a rich man?"

"No," I said, "but I'll pay to find Frank Marno."

"Of course you will pay. But how much, eh?"

"Fifty dollars."

He sighed, and the whole great mound of his body shook. I could smell the greed. Men like him are what make it so hard for another man to truly vanish.

"Señor Marno is generous," he said. "He pay more so I not tell where he go. How can I tell for so little?"

"You're a man of principle," I said.

He shrugged. "A man must live. I sell him to you, but I will not sell cheap, *sí*? I am honest man."

"Like a saint. How much?"

"Five hundred American."

"Good-bye. I like a man to stay honest."

"Four hundred."

"I'll find him some other way."

Under the rolling layers of fat his muscles tensed. His reaction was a surprise. He was anxious, nervous. "Two hundred fifty?"

"One-fifty. Final offer."

"Okay, okay. You are hard man. Pay me."

"Tell me," I said.

He mopped his face. "I do not know where Señor Marno is now, but I know how you find him. Before he leave he go many days to hospital — they will know where he is."

"The hospital?"

"The big hospital for the rich, and the *Norteamericanos.*"

I paid him.

★ ★

The hospital was large, modern, and in the best section of Rio Arriba. The nurse at the night desk said that Frank Marno had been a patient of Dr. Paul Kolcheck, the senior resident. I found Kolcheck in his office. A thin, mousy man who was self-important and hungry for recognition.

"Frank Marno? Why, yes, I remember him well. A tourist from Chicago. Nothing serious. Stomach trouble, but it was mostly nerves."

Nerves I could believe for Frank Marno. "Where can I find him now?"

"I have no idea."

"Can I look at his chart? It might have an address."

"No, you —" His voice rose sharply. He tried to calm it again. "I'm sorry, but his chart was lost."

"Lost?" I watched his face.

"Yes, in a fire. We had a small fire here."

There was a wariness all over him now. I wondered if he happened to be a plastic surgeon. A little side practice? It was something Frank Marno would have considered fully.

I said, "He made many trips here, Doc, I know. You're sure it was nothing serious? You don't know where he went?"

"Quite sure on both counts. Now, if you'll excuse me."

I left on the cue, but I didn't go far. I hid where I could watch Kolcheck's office door. When he came out, he looked around, then hurried along the corridor without looking back. I followed him straight to the Record Room.

When he came out of the Record Room he had a manila folder, I tailed him to the living quarters. He hurried into a room, and came out again empty-handed. I ducked into a room to let him pass, then headed for my hotel to get my picklock.

★ ★

Back at the hospital I didn't enter the front way. Inside, I slipped along corridors to the room in the living quarters. When I was sure I was alone, and that the room was empty, I picked the lock.

It took me five minutes to find the manila folder, and read it. It was Frank Marno's chart, and I knew why he had wanted a friend, and where to look for him next.

★ ★

In the morning I took the train for the fishing resort of Lake Anacapa up the coast. An ancient taxi took me to the hospital there. They said they had never heard of Frank Marno. I told them about Frank's chart. "It lists letters between the Rio Arriba hospital, and the hospital here — letters from Dr. Jesus Rosas."

"Rosas?" The administrator of the Lake Anacapa hospital was astonished. "An American would never go to Rosas' hospital."

"There's another hospital here?"

He nodded. "For the natives. A pesthole that's been here a hundred years. Rosas is half veterinarian. A crime, really, but the peons trust him. He's chief doctor there, and the only licensed doctor. No American in his right mind would —"

I didn't wait to hear more. Frank Marno was in his right mind, and it was just where he would go. He had — three times within the last three months.

★ ★

Dr. Jesus Rosas shook his head sadly. "What can one do? Such a case I see only once before. The last time he stayed here two weeks, then I sent him home. I do not expect him back again, señor."

"Where is home?"

"Santa Ynez. It is inland near the desert and the Sierra Negra. Some go to hunt. There is nothing else there."

"How do I get there?"

Dr. Rosas shrugged. "A car. It takes many hours."

★ ★

Santa Ynez was a dusty misery of a village, a ruin before it began. It had never existed enough to be forgotten. A few hundred Indians, two cantinas, one hotel for foreign hunters, and the desert vast and empty to the distant mountains of the Sierra Negra.

As I drove into the silent town, the only signs of life were the vultures riding thermals above the scorching-red hills of the desert. The police consisted of a *jefe* and two cartridge-draped Indians. They recognized the picture of Señor Marno.

"I think yes," the chief said. "He is much different."

"Where do I find him?"

The chief consulted the stars. "He lives here, there, nowhere. You must look in the cantinas, *si?*"

I didn't find Frank Marno in either cantina. There was nowhere else to look until morning. I took a room at the one hotel, and after staring at the sagging bed decided to sleep on the floor. I'm as antiseptic as the next American.

In the morning I checked the hotel cantina and found Frank Marno. He was alone at a table. The sun wasn't above the huts yet, but he had a bottle of the local agave cactus *mescal.*

I sat down. "Hello, Frank."

He didn't smile or frown, just reached for the mescal. I stared at the changes in him. The assurance was gone; the eagerness and the youth — and fifty pounds. His dull eyes were sunk into an emaciated face. His ragged clothes were filthy, his hands shook, and he looked a drugged-out sixty plus.

His voice was a croak. "Six months, Dan, nothing to do except sit in the dust. After Angela, and the —"

I knew what he'd been going to say — after the hospital — but he stopped, drank, and looked out the open cantina door at the wall of heat that hung over the dusty street.

"Angela's dead, did you know?" he said. "I'm alone in this hole. I—" He eyes looked at me from the hollow shell of his wasted face. "I'm scared, Dan. Booze and pills; pills and booze. I don't want to die, but Krupp — you can't beat Krupp."

I said, "I read the hospital report in Rio Arriba, Frank."

"You read it?" Startled, and angry. "Kolcheck promised he wouldn't show it to —"

"I know how to find things."

He looked outside again at nothing in particular. "What gets you here is the sameness. Not even a cloud, just those vultures. They're waiting, like me. Only they're waiting *for* me, right? Just me. Everyone else here was born dead."

"How long, Frank? A year? You've got a year, maybe?"

For a moment he didn't seem to hear. Then he looked straight at me. "Go away, Dan. I'm dead. Can't you see that now?"

"You sent for me."

He drank. "That was a long time ago. Angela was just… Go back, Dan, I was wrong. Go home."

"I came too far, Frank."

He drank again, and began to giggle. "To help a corpse, yeah. A corpse, Dan, one way or the other! A laugh!" He giggled, drank, and collapsed on the table. It wasn't even ten A.M. yet.

The bartender came to the table. "He do it all the time now." His English was slow, careful. "Very fast. Sick. I take him to room. I am Ortega. His friend."

Ortega picked Frank up like a feather and carried him out. I followed to a windowless hovel where Ortega laid Frank on a pile of rags. He lay as if already dead, and I went out to walk in the sun and dust. Indians watched me from a distance.

Frank woke up in three hours. It began again: the cantinas, the *mescal*, the babbling talk, the telling me to go home, until he passed out once more.

On the third day I sobered him enough to make him shave, and find the one suit he had worn when he arrived at Santa Ynez. I told him I had a car, and the train left from Lake Anacapa. Then I lost him again. He screamed I was fingering him for Wally Krupp. He grabbed the bottle, and ended in a stupor by dark.

After a week I had him sober for almost a day — sober, silent and nervous. He had agreed at least to go back to Rio Arriba. We were settling it all in the hotel cantina, with Ortega hiding the *mescal* bottle, when I heard the car.

A big car out in the late afternoon dust and heat.

Frank Marno heard it, too. The only car in Santa Ynez was the chief's ancient Land Rover. This wasn't a Land Rover, and the deep purr of its motor wasn't ancient. Frank's head jerked up, sobered in an instant, to look fearfully at Ortega. The bartender hurried toward the rear door.

A man in a dark city suit came in through the rear door. He only glanced at Ortega going out. He wasn't interested in Ortega, or anything else local.

It was a hundred in the shade, but the newcomer wore his suit buttoned, and his tie knotted. He just stood there, empty-faced.

Wally Krupp came in the front way.

Krupp's fleshy face sweated in rivers, not used to such heat. His eyes were cool. Two more dark suits followed him in and stood where they could see the whole room. Krupp sat down at a separate table.

"You're a long way from home, Fortune."

I felt a little sick. He wasn't surprised to see me. He knew I'd be there. I'd led him to Frank Marno. Now he looked at Frank for the first time. "Hello, Frankie."

"What took you so long?" Frank Marno said in that croak.

Krupp nodded. "You always were smart, Frankie. You could have gone a long way with me. Too bad."

"Go to hell, Krupp," Frank said, his voice all at once a lot stronger. "I took your money and your daughter. She wanted me, not a prince. My woman, you hear? You killed her."

Krupp's face darkened with his rage. "I know what killed her, punk."

"Do you?" Frank said. "What does it matter? If she couldn't have me, she wanted to be dead anyway. You came to kill me, get it over with, then."

Wally Krupp smiled. "You want to die, Marno?" he said softly.

Frank's sunken eyes were dark. "Why not? You killed my Angela. The money's all gone. Why not?"

"Gone? A hundred grand in a year?"

"I found ways to spend it. You get nothing — no money, no daughter. Go on, kill me. You're the loser."

"I get the fun of it, Marno. I get the respect at home. No one crosses Wally Krupp and lives."

"Not even that," Frank croaked. "Angela's dead, the money's gone. Back home who cares, you got nothing? Kill me for nothing, Krupp."

I watched Frank Marno. Something had changed. He was goading Krupp, asking to be killed. Did he think he could trick Wally Krupp into letting him live by asking to die? A crazy hope to risk his life on — and mine. I had no illusions about my fate. I had to figure my own way out, if there were one.

"So," Krupp said, "you got it all figured out, punk."

I never saw his signal. One of the gunmen was behind me. I had no chance to reach for my gun. The gunman lifted it from me. The second gunman searched Frank Marno. Frank had no gun.

Wally Krupp stood up. "The car. Watch the local cops."

We went out into the wall of heat on the lone street of Santa Ynez. The chief lounged in the shade across the street, mildly interested in us. It was all unreal, as if we were playing a scene in a bad movie. The dusty village, the silent Indians, the comic opera chief, the Indian cops in their cartridge belts . . .

"Krupp," I said. "Listen, I—"

"In the car, Fortune," he said. "You did me a service leading me here, but you shouldn't have tried to help Marno. Bad luck."

I got into the car, and it was then I got the hunch — a crazy hunch. Krupp had followed me here. How had he known to follow me? It had not been that hard to find Frank Marno, not really. A hunch — or was it only a straw to clutch at?

The big car was cool inside, and silent; air-conditioned and solid. We drove, and there was nothing to measure distance by in the desolate land — or time.

We drove along the one macadam road, then off across dirt roads through the low red hills. A thick cloud of red dust hung in the heat behind us. Beyond the dust rising, nothing moved in that desert, nothing existed. Finally we stopped.

"Out," Krupp said.

We were at the edge of a small box canyon among jagged sand hills. Our own dust cloud still hung in the air behind us. Beyond it I saw only emptiness and cactus. Or was there another dust cloud? Very close.

"Walk, Fortune," Krupp said.

We walked deeper into the box canyon in silence. I listened, but I heard nothing beyond the steady crunch of our feet in the red sand. We walked for almost five minutes, the canyon curving deeper into the jagged hills, deserted and almost soundless.

"All right," Krupp said.

He had stopped behind us. We turned. His gunmen stood behind him, alert.

Krupp looked at Frank Marno. "You killed my Angela. Maybe you loved her, but you killed her. You got anything to tell me?"

"No," Frank croaked. His hands were shaking. "Go ahead and shoot. Go on!"

Krupp said, "Maybe I should stake you out, tie you down in the sun and let you die slow."

Frank licked his lips. "You'd never be sure."

"That's right. I have to shoot you to be sure."

"Yes," Frank croaked, then shouted. "Shoot me!"

His words echoed and bounced, loud in the canyon. Krupp's smile was cruel.

Then I saw them. Up on the rim of the canyon, not a hundred yards away, rifles in their hands: the chief and his two bandits. My wild hunch was true.

"Krupp," I said, "it's a trap! He wants you to kill him." I told him about the hospital chart. "He's got maybe a year to live. The local cops are in the hills. You shoot us, they'll kill you, or take you. This is their country — you'd be helpless down here with a murder charge against you. He's dying already, Krupp. He wants to take you with him."

Frank cried, "He's crazy! Why would I —"

Krupp's laugh was cold, nasty, and crueller than any laugh I'd ever heard or imagined. "You think I don't know all about it, Fortune?" He turned to Frank Marno. "Smart boy. The money's gone, and maybe a year you got to live. So you think you'll get even with Wally Krupp, take me with you. Why not? I'd do the same myself if I had the same reason and chance."

He looked up at the hills.

"You think you trap Wally Krupp so easy? That bartender at the cantina, I figured you sent him to the cops. I let him go so I could watch you sweat. I know what Hodgkin's disease means. You'll go slow and hard. Always cold, the book says, even down here. In the end you'll crawl in the dirt, too weak to walk. Look at you already. Why should I kill a dead man?"

His dark eyes glittered in the setting sun. He was enjoying the vision of how Frank Marno was going to die: cold and alone.

He said, "I'm going home, Frankie. I leave a man to watch, to keep you here. Try to leave, you die faster. When my man tells me you're dead, I'll give a party! Everyone in Chelsea comes." He laughed again. "Now you can walk back to that rathole. Maybe the walk helps you die faster."

He turned and walked away up the canyon. His gunmen followed. They hadn't said one word the whole time. Maybe they didn't know how.

When they were gone, Frank Marno's legs gave out. He slumped to the dust and began to cry.

Ten minutes later the chief picked us up. No one spoke all the way to Santa Ynez.

★ ★

I got my bag from the hotel room, then went down to the cantina. For once, Frank wasn't there. I found him sitting on the floor of his hovel, his sunken eyes glittering.

"Just to make Krupp die too?" I said. "You sent me that note — and you sent another note to tip Krupp to follow me. You wanted me to lead Krupp to you, but you had to make it look hard. Krupp wouldn't have fallen for it if it was easy. Get him here, trap him into murdering a dying man."

Marno's croak was dull, "He killed Angela. I had to get him before —" He didn't finish. He didn't have to.

"A slim chance at the outside," I said. "A long shot all the way."

"I've played longer. Damn it, it should have worked. Doc Kolcheck was supposed to lead you here, but hide the chart."

"You knew I'd found out when I came."

"I tried to make you go."

"Because you wanted to save me?" I said. "No! You were just hoping Krupp hadn't found out about your disease, and you were afraid I would tell him if I was still here when he arrived."

He shrugged in that dismal hut. I didn't matter. Not anymore. Nothing mattered. His big scheme to get Wally Krupp had failed.

I said, "You owe me expenses."

"The money's gone, Dan."

"Yeah," I said, "and you need what you have hidden for *mescal.* You might live over a year."

I walked out. It was almost dark, but I didn't care about the dangers of driving in the dark through the desert. I had a drink in the cantina, got my car, heaved my bag in, and started out of the village. As I drove past Frank Marno's hovel, I saw the chief come out with a fat manila envelope. He whistled as he walked away. I didn't see Frank Marno.

★ ★

In the morning I took the train from Lake Anacapa to Rio Arriba and caught the first jet home. All I wanted to do now was forget about Frank Marno and his desperate long shot to "get" Wally Krupp. I tried hard, but I couldn't forget Frank.

Wally Krupp told the story, and in Chelsea they all buried Frank Marno. A dead man was empty space in a busy world. Not to me. I lay awake thinking about it for a whole month. I thought about how close Krupp had come to murdering a dying man; about the chief whistling coming out of that hovel; about a hundred thousand dollars spent in a year on the run; about Frank Marno waiting alone to die.

I thought about it all for a month.

Then I took the jet back to Rio Arriba.

I went to Captain Guzman and told him another story.

Then I took a room in the Hotel San Martin to wait.

I didn't think the wait would be too long.

Six weeks later, Captain Guzman called me. "Marno is dead. In the smaller hospital in Lake Anacapa. The notice is in the newspapers. He will be buried in Lake Anacapa."

★ ★

Guzman drove me up himself. They took Frank from the hospital to the pauper's cemetery in a ten dollar pine coffin. The *jefe* of Santa Ynez came. Dr. Jesus Rosas, Guzman and I, and a silent man who had to be Wally Krupp's watcher. There was no one else.

"He did not want to live, took no care, drank too much, refused the medicine," Dr. Rosas said at the grave. "The end was quick, he did not suffer too much."

In the coffin, Frank Marno had shrunk to an old man. His sunken eyes were closed, his rigid face the color of sand under the heavy makeup of the local embalmer. Dr. Rosas said a few words, and the coffin was closed and buried.

Captain Guzman left with the fawning chief of Santa Ynez. I hired another car and drove alone to Santa Ynez. Once more I arrived just at dusk.

I went to the hovel. It was dark, no one was there. A few pieces of Frank Marno's useless life, nothing more. I went back outside and crouched in the shadow of a low mud wall. I shivered as the night grew colder, but I never took my eyes off the shadowy hovel. It was a mistake.

He was behind me before I heard a sound, the gun against my back. "Turn around, sit down, hands on the ground."

I could see him by the starlight. He had a pale beard, blond hair, glasses, a large nose and wore a light tropical suit. He carried a leather bag, and his gun was steady on me. I would never have known him.

"The money wasn't in the hut," I said.

"Safer out here," he said. "I watched the funeral. No one examined the body. How the hell —"

"On purpose, Frank, so as not to tip you. Guzman and I already knew."

"How?" Frank Marno said from his new face, "How did you figure it? Krupp's not that smart, and neither is Guzman. It had to be you, damn you!"

"I saw the chief leave your place with an envelope. He was whistling. I asked myself: what made the chief happy? A pay off for the trap you arranged with him to kill Wally Krupp. But why would you pay him if your scheme had failed? It made me wonder.

"I went on home, but another question stuck in my mind: If you were so sure I would find that medical chart in Rio Arriba, how could you have thought Krupp wouldn't find the chart too?"

I waited for an answer. He only watched me in the night.

"You knew Krupp couldn't miss that chart," I went on. "So your plan couldn't have been to trap him into killing you. It had to be to make him *think* you were trapping him! You didn't have any fatal disease. You bought Kolcheck, Rosas, Ortega, the chief. The whole thing was a fake to make Krupp come here, and go away leaving you alive! You played us all like fish. Especially me. I was the convincer for Krupp."

He smiled. "A good act, eh, Dan? I didn't eat much or sleep much for months. I never washed, and I watered the mescal. I looked dead even to you. I had to test it all on you first."

"Good act," I said. "Krupp might have shot you anyway. It was a million-to-one shot."

He shrugged. "Sooner or later he would've gotten me if I kept running. One big risk to be rid of him was better. The odds weren't that bad. I know Krupp. It was a plan he'd believe. All I had to do was make him dig it out, and add you for scenery to make it real. Like he said, he believed because he'd have done it himself."

A long shot, sure, but played on knowledge. Frank had used Krupp's own cunning against him — Krupp's kind of trick.

The old confidence was back in Frank's voice. "Down here I could buy anything. Those people in Rio Arriba; Doc Kolcheck to fake the chart; Doc Rosas in Lake Anacapa; the chief; Ortega the barman to fake the drinking and dying; the undertaker to get a body and slip on a mask of my face. New papers, Dan, a new face, a new life. With fifty grand still left. I'm free of Krupp, rich, and no one hurt."

I said, "And Angela?"

"Angela? What about Angela?"

I said, "I made Guzman look closer at the shooting in Rio Arriba, Frank. He doesn't have the gun, but he has the bullets. Angela, it seems, was shot with the same gun that killed Krupp's gunman that night. The gunman in jail swears it wasn't one of their guns. Wrong caliber. I'd guess it's the gun you've got in my back right now."

"They can't prove anything!"

"They're simple people," I said. "They won't believe your scheme. They'll ask themselves: *What better way for a killer to escape than by pretending to die?* They'll convict you."

His eyes were steel, the eyes of the boy who wouldn't settle for the barber shop where his father had lived and died.

"She turned on me, Dan. She was going back to Daddy. She said I didn't have a chance this side of the grave. That gave me the whole idea, but I couldn't do it if I let her go back. She'd have known it was a fake." He shrugged again. "I guess we hated each other by then, and I had to make Krupp hate me enough to come after me himself"

Kill Angela to make Krupp hate him enough. It worked.

He said. "Take half the money. I don't want to kill you."

"You won't. Guzman is watching the front of your hut. The chief and his bandits are watching the back. A shot brings them. Hit me, I'll yell. Where can you go?"

He shrugged. "The desert. The Sierra Negra."

"You couldn't make it. No chance."

"There's always a chance," he said.

"The long shot again?"

Another shrug. "When you're born poor in a rich world, and you don't want to work behind chair two in a crummy barber shop all your life, all you've got are long shots. Give me a half hour, Dan?"

"No."

He nodded. "You know, I'm sorry about Angela, I mean that. I pulled it all to have her. Kids in love. It didn't work, Dan, pressure changes people. She got to hate me, and I had to stay alive any way I could. That changes a man, too — the thinking of nothing except staying alive."

I said nothing. What was there to say?

He went on, "Maybe Krupp really did kill her. If he'd let us go, who knows? We started in love, but he didn't let us go, and we broke, and I pulled the trigger. It happened like that. Who knows how it would've been if it had happened some other way?"

He was gone, fast and silent in the cold night. I didn't move. Simple caution. I heard a car engine start out in the desert. I was safe, but I still didn't move. Why?

Maybe because some of what he said was true — he had done it all, but not alone. Others had a share of the guilt, even Angela herself in a way, and even the world that had taught Frank Marno how to survive.

Or maybe because he'd lived his short life on the illusion of long shots. He had no chance in that desert, but he'd try. Maybe I wanted him to have that much to the end — the hope that the long shot would come in.

I waited half an hour, then I went and told Guzman and the chief.

He nodded. "We will look tomorrow. No hurry, Señor Fortune. Out there is only heat, empty mountains, no water, hungry Indians and animals. His car will not go far, and no man has ever reached our border on foot."

They found the car, but not Frank. Guzman blocked all roads and sealed the borders, just in case. He rounded up the bribe takers. After two weeks I went home.

★ ★

It was two years before I got the letter from Captain Guzman. They had found Frank Marno's bones. Not in the desert, but in the mountains beyond the desert. The money was beside the bones. Captain Guzman was impressed that an American had gotten so far alone.

After writing crime stories for many years between the mid-Sixties to 1970, I stopped doing stories. There was more money in novels, and I had to support a young family.

But in 1984, Bob Randisi asked me to write a Dan Fortune piece for his first PWA anthology, The Eyes Have It. *I'd always wanted to rewrite a piece I'd written much earlier. It was the next to the last Slot-Machine Kelly story. The Kelly stories started out as something of a spoof, and, despite a growing core of seriousness, they remained light-hearted. But by the time I got to the last two they were neither spoofs nor light, and really called for a different approach and a different detective.*

The last became the first Dan Fortune novel, Act of Fear. *But the next to last remained in limbo. Randisi's request gave me the chance to rewrite it as a Fortune, and that's what I did.*

So here it is: a story first written in 1964 in New York, rewritten twenty years later in Santa Barbara.

EIGHTY MILLION DEAD

We have killed eighty million people in eighty years. Give or take a few million or a couple of years. Killed. Not lost in hurricanes or famines or epidemics or any of the other natural disasters we should be trying to wipe out instead of each other. From 1900 to 1980. The Twentieth Century.

That's a hell of a way to begin a story, except in this case it could be the whole story. The story of Paul Asher and Constantine Zareta and me, Dan Fortune, and I want you to think about those eighty million corpses. Most of those who killed them were fighting for a reason, a cause. A lot of those who died had a reason, a cause. You have to wonder what cause is worth eighty million ended lives. You have to wonder what eighty million dead bodies has done to the living.

I know what those eighty million deaths had done to Paul Asher and Constantine Zareta. Those were the names they gave me, anyway. They weren't their real names. I'm not sure they knew their real names anymore. It was Paul Asher who walked into my second floor office/apartment that rainy Monday.

"You are Dan Fortune? A private investigator?"

He was tall and dark. A big man who moved like a shadow. I hadn't seen or even heard him come in. He was just there in front of my desk:

dark-haired, dark-eyed, soft-voiced, in a dark suit. Colorless. Nothing about him told me anything. Only his eyes that looked at my missing arm proved he was alive.

"I'm Fortune."

"I am Paul Asher. I wish to hire you."

"To do what, Mr. Asher?"

"You will deliver a package."

He had an accent. One I couldn't place, and not exactly an accent. More a kind of toneless and too precise way of speaking English that told me it wasn't his native language.

"You want a messenger service," I said. "You can use my telephone book."

"I will pay one thousand dollars," Asher said. "I wish that the package is to be delivered tonight."

No one makes a thousand dollars a day in Chelsea, not even today. Most still don't make it in a month. It was a lot of money for delivering a package. Or maybe it wasn't.

"What's in the package?" I asked.

"I will pay one thousand dollars because you will not ask what is in the package, and because Zareta is a dangerous man."

He said it direct and simple, expressionless.

"Zareta?" I said.

"Constantine Zareta. This he calls himself. It is to him you will take the package."

"Why not take it yourself?"

"He would kill me."

"Why?"

"I possess what he wants."

"Blackmail, Asher?"

"No, I ask no money. You will take the package?"

I shook my head. "Not without knowing what's in it, and why you want to send it to this Constantine Zareta."

Paul Asher thought for a time. He seemed to look again at my empty left sleeve, but his face remained expressionless. He wasn't angry or even frustrated. I had presented him with a problem, and he was thinking about it. As simple as that.

He made his decision. "The package contains documents, nothing more. I am giving them to Zareta. They are of no value except to Zareta. For him they are of great value. The papers are not a danger, simply of value to Zareta. He would kill me to get them, I am tired of danger. When he has the documents I will not be in danger. Until then, I am not safe from him. I cannot take the documents myself, so? You will take them?"

"Let's see the package."

Asher produced a flat package from an inside pocket of his dark suit.

It was about as wide as a paperback book, twice as long and thick. I took it. They make bombs smaller and better every day, but the package was much too light for even a plastic bomb. It felt like a package of documents and nothing else. Even a deadly gas has to have a container. I could feel the edges, the folds, the thickness of heavy paper.

"How did you happen to pick me, Mr. Asher?"

"From the telephone book."

For the first time I didn't believe him. Too quick? Something in his voice that wasn't quite toneless this time? I'm in the phone book, but I didn't believe him. Because he wasn't the kind of man who trusted to chance? Maybe and maybe. But if it hadn't been the telephone book, how and why had he picked me out of all the detectives in New York?

"I take the package to Zareta," I said. "What do I bring back?"

"Nothing."

"Who pays me? When?"

"I will pay you," Asher said. "Now."

He took a thin billfold from his inside pocket, counted out ten hundred dollar bills. He wasn't telling me the truth, not the whole truth, but I knew that. Warned of the danger, what could happen that I couldn't handle? If anything looked a hair out of line I'd toss the package and walk away.

I took the ten bills. Crisp and new, straight from the bank. Maybe I wanted to know why he had picked me for the job. I wanted to know something.

"What's the address?"

"It is on the package."

"How do I contact you later?"

"You do not. You are paid. I will know if you do not do what you have been paid to do."

"Anything else?"

"Yes," Paul Asher said. "You will deliver the package at midnight. Precisely midnight."

He walked out. I tilted back in my chair. I was a thousand dollars richer. Why didn't I feel good?

★ ★

The address was on the East Side up in Yorkville, far over near the river. Asher's instructions had been definite — midnight — and the slum street was dark and silent in the rain when the taxi dropped me. There was no one on the street. No one in sight anywhere, but I felt the eyes. When you grow up near the docks, start stealing early because you have to eat even if your father ran out long before and your mother drinks too much, you learn to feel when eyes are watching.

I walked slowly along the dark street in the rain and knew that I wasn't alone. I sensed them all around. The address was an old un-renovated brownstone with the high front steps. Two men appeared at the far end of the street. They leaned against a dark building. Two more appeared behind me where the taxi had dropped me. Two stood in the shadows on another stoop across the street. Shadows of shadows all around in the dark and rain. The glint of a gun.

I went up the steps to the front door and into the vestibule. There was only one mailbox and doorbell. I had my finger on the bell when I saw the man outside on the steps. He stood two steps below the vestibule with an automatic rifle. A short, powerful man behind a bandit mustache. There were two more behind him at the foot of the steps. They had guns too. They stood there doing nothing. Too late I knew why, felt the inner vestibule door open behind me.

An arm went around my throat, a hand went over my mouth, another hand held my arm, and I was dragged back into the dark of the entrance hall. I didn't resist. The short one with the bandit mustache and automatic rifle followed us in. They dragged me into a small room, sat me in a chair, came and went in rapid groups. They barely glanced at me. They were busy. Except two I felt close behind me keeping watch.

"What's going on?" I tried.

"Do not talk!" He was the short, powerful man with the automatic rifle. He seemed to be the leader, sent the other men in and out with the precision of a drill sergeant. They spoke some language I didn't even recognize.

I didn't have to know the language to know what they were doing. They were all armed, and they were searching the street outside and the neighborhood for anyone who might have come with me. It was half an hour before the mustachioed leader sat down astride a chair in front of me. He still carried his automatic rifle, and the package Paul Asher had sent me to deliver.

"Your name is Fortune. What do you want here?"

"I came to deliver that package."

"Who are you?"

"You've searched my papers."

"You came to deliver this package to who?"

"Constantine Zareta. Is that you?"

"What is in the package?"

"Papers. Documents."

He studied the package a moment, turned it over in his heavy hands. Then he gave it to one of the other men.

"From who does the package come?"

"Paul Asher."

"We know no Paul Asher."

"It's the name he gave me."

"Your papers say you are a private investigator. We know what that means. A man who will sell his weapon to anyone. A hired murderer. An assassin. You came to kill Constantine Zareta!"

"I came to deliver a package," I said. "I don't have a gun. I don't even know who Zareta is or what he looks like."

"Of course not. They would not tell you who you kill or why. They have hired you only to kill. Do not lie!"

"If someone is trying to kill Zareta, go to the police. That's their work."

I had been watching all their faces as I talked. They were grim, unsmiling, and they didn't look like hoodlums. They were nervous and armed, but they didn't act like gunmen. They looked like soldiers, *guerrillas*. And as I watched them I saw their faces come alert, respectful. Someone else had come into the room somewhere behind me. A low voice with good English.

"The police could not help me, Mr. Fortune."

I felt him standing close behind me. His voice had that power of command, of absolute confidence in himself and what he did. Constantine Zareta. I started to turn.

"Do not turn, Mr. Fortune."

I looked straight ahead at the mustachioed man. "Maybe the police can't help you because you want to kill Paul Asher."

The mustache reached out and hit me.

"Emil!"

Emil glared down at me. "He's another one, Minister. I can smell them."

"Perhaps," Zareta's slow voice said. "Let us be sure."

"We cannot take the chance, Minister. Kill him now. If they did not send him, what does it matter?"

There was a silence behind me. A chair scraped. I felt hot breath on the back of my neck. Slow breathing. Zareta had sat down close behind me. That was fine. As long as I could feel his breath I was ahead of the game. As long as I could feel anything.

"A man sent you to me at this address."

"Yes."

"Why did he pick you?"

"Out of the telephone book."

"Do you believe that?"

"No."

I could almost hear him nod.

"What was his reason for not coming himself?"

"He said you'd kill him."

"Why would I kill him?"

"Because he had what you wanted. Documents, not dangerous to you, but so important you'd kill to get them."

"And these documents are in the package?"

"Yes. He said he was tired of danger, wanted to give them to you, but was afraid to come himself."

It was strangely unreal to be talking straight ahead into the empty air of the dark room, the silent face of Emil.

"This man's name was Paul Asher."

"Yes."

"I know no Paul Asher, but that does not surprise me. You will describe him."

I described Paul Asher down to the flinty calm of his dark eyes, his silent movement despite his size.

"I do not recognize him, but that does not surprise me either, Mr. Fortune. I do recognize the type of man you have described. It sounds true. You have saved your life, Mr. Fortune. For now."

Emil did not like my reprieve. "The risk, Minister."

"I think we can take some risk, Emil," Zareta said, his breath still brushing the back of my neck. "Mr. Fortune could be lying, but I think not. This Asher sounds like all the men we have known, yes? Mr. Fortune has acted exactly as he would have if his story is true, and you found no one else who could have been with him. Then, he clearly does not know what was in the package he brought to us, or he would have told a better tale, yes? And he has no weapon of any kind."

That seemed to stop Emil. I've said it before, most of the time a gun does nothing but get you in trouble. Sooner or later you'll use it if you have to or not, and someone else will use theirs. If I'd had a gun this time I'd probably be dead. I wasn't dead, and I wondered what had been in the package that would have made me tell a different story if I'd known.

"Why?" Zareta said. "I cannot understand what reason this Asher had to send you to me. That makes me uneasy. Tell me everything once more. Leave nothing out."

I told him all of it again. I was uneasy too. Why had Paul Asher sent me if the package wasn't the reason? Or was it Zareta who was conning me now? Lulling me to get me to lead him back to Asher? If that was his scheme he wouldn't get far. I couldn't lead anyone to Paul Asher.

"I do not understand," Zareta said when I finished the story again, "but you have done me an important service. I know now what this Paul Asher looks like." The chair scraped behind me. "Take your money, Mr. Fortune, and go home. Forget that you ever heard of Paul Asher or me."

There was a silence, and then a door closed somewhere in the dark brownstone. The troops began to disperse. The boss had spoken. Emil's heart wasn't in it, but Zareta was boss.

"Tonight you are a very lucky man," Emil said.

I looked around. I saw no one who looked like a boss, but I saw the package I'd carried lying on a table. It was torn open to show — a stack of folded papers. Just what Asher had said it was. Only there *was* something wrong, something odd about the package. Not quite right. What? They didn't give me the time to look longer or closer.

They hustled me out into the dark hall. Then I was alone on the street where I'd started. I walked to the nearest corner without looking back. I didn't run, that would have been cowardly. I waited until I was around the corner. Then I ran.

By the time I got down to Chelsea and my one room office/apartment I felt pretty good. I had no more interest in Asher and Zareta and their private feud, whatever it was. I was a thousand dollars richer and still alive. I figured I was home free. I should have known better.

★ ★

I awoke in the pitch dark to a violent pounding on my door. My arm was aching. The missing arm. That's always a sign. It's what's missing that hurts when the days become bad.

The pounding went on. Cop pounding. As I got up and pulled on my pants, a gray light began to barely tinge the darkness. Captain Pearce himself led his Homicide men into my office area. The men fanned out to look behind the doors and under the beds. Pearce sat down behind my desk.

"What's it about, Captain?"

"Paul Asher," Pearce said.

"Nice name. Is there more?"

"Asher is enough," Pearce said. "He was a client of yours? Or was there some other connection?"

"Was?" I said.

"Asher's dead," Pearce said. "You should give him his money back."

Pearce doesn't like any private detective much, but especially me. I was too close to old Captain Gazzo. Pearce took Gazzo's place after the Captain was gunned down on a dark city roof. One of the new breed, a college man, and he doesn't like me bringing Gazzo's ghost with me. But he's a good cop, he does his job first.

"We found Asher an hour ago," Pearce said. "Dumped under the George Washington Bridge. Shot up like Swiss cheese. Any ideas?"

The George Washington Bridge is a long way from Yorkville, but that I would expect.

"Constantine Zareta," I said.

I told Pearce about Zareta and Asher, about Emil and all those silent gunmen. Pearce got up, signaled for his forces.

"Let's pick them up."

We went in the Captain's car. He sat silent and edgy as we headed uptown at the head of his platoon of squad cars, drumming his fingers on his knee. He had no more questions. I had questions.

"You said you found Asher an hour ago, Captain. How did you dig up my connection so fast?"

"Your business cards in his pocket."

"Cards?"

Pearce nodded as he watched the dawn city, gray and empty of people but teeming with trucks. "He must have had ten, and your name was in his little black book with a thousand dollars and yesterday's date noted next to it."

Business cards cost money, I don't hand them out without necessity. Asher had found me, there had been no reason to give him a card, not even one. I leave some with uptown contacts in case anyone up there wants a kidnapped poodle rescued, so Asher may have picked up the cards from whoever sent him to me before he came down to my office. Or he could have palmed them off my desk when he walked out. But why? And why ten?

In the dawn the Yorkville street was as deserted as it had been last night. We parked all along the gray morning street. Windows popped open in other buildings, but nothing moved in Constantine Zareta's brownstone. It was as dark and silent as some medieval fortress.

It turned out to be as hard to get into as a medieval fortress. Rings, knocks, shouts and threats failed to open the vestibule door, the building remained dark.

"Break it down," Pearce said.

His men broke the door open, and Pearce strode into the dim entrance hall. The mustachioed Emil faced him. Emil had his automatic rifle aimed at the Captain's heart. Other gunmen stood in the doorways of the rooms and on the stairs. We were all covered. It took Captain Pearce almost a minute to find his voice.

"Police, damn it! Put those guns down. We're the police."

Constantine Zareta spoke from somewhere behind Emil, out of sight in the dim hallway. I knew that slow voice by now.

"You will tell me your name, your rank, and your badge number. I will verify that you are police. You will make no moves, my men watch your people in the street also."

Color began to suffuse Pearce's face. The Captain isn't a patient man, and I wondered how long it had been since anyone had asked him to prove who he was. He opened his mouth, looked around the dark hallway at the silent *guerrillas* and their guns, and closed his mouth. If Constantine Zareta was as tough as he sounded, we could have a blood bath in the dark hallway and out on the morning street.

"Captain Martin Pearce," the Captain said through thin lips, and explained that a captain's shield does not have a number.

In the silent hallway we all waited.

I imagined the scene down at Police Headquarters when they got the call asking about a Captain Pearce, and would they please describe the Captain. It took some time, but whatever they thought down there they must have gone along with it and given an accurate description.

Constantine Zareta appeared in the dim light, and I saw him for the first time — a short, thick man as wide as he was tall, with a shaved bullet head attached to his massive shoulders as if he had no neck. He said something in his unknown language. The guns vanished and the gunmen disappeared.

"Very well, Captain," Zareta said to Pearce. "We will talk in the living room."

Pearce and Zareta faced each other in the same room where I had been interrogated earlier. The Captain stood. Zareta sat on a straight chair, Emil close behind him. Neither Zareta nor Emil had seen me yet.

"Just who and what are you, Zareta?" Pearce said. "Why do you need armed men?" His voice was controlled, but I heard the anger in it. No policeman can tolerate a private army.

"A poor exile, Captain," Zareta said. "My men have permits for their weapons."

"Exile from where?"

"Albania."

That was the language I hadn't recognized — Albanian.

"Was Paul Asher an Albanian too?" Pearce said. "Is that why he was afraid of you? Is that why you killed him?"

For a moment there was a heavy silence in the small living room lit only by a single lamp behind its drawn curtains. Then Emil grunted. Others made other noises. Constantine Zareta leaned forward in his chair.

"This Asher, he is dead? You are sure?"

"We're sure," Pearce said.

Zareta laughed aloud. "Good! He is one we will not have to kill! You bring me good news, Captain, I am grateful. But how did you know that this Asher's death would be something I would want to know? How did you know of Asher and myself? How ... Ah, of course, Mr. Fortune. You have talked with Mr. Fortune. It is the only way." He looked around the small room. "Are you here again, Mr. Fortune?"

I stepped out into the dim light where Zareta could see me, flashed my best smile at the glowering Emil, and missed it.

I missed the whole impossible, monstrous plan.

★ ★

Sometimes I wonder if there is anyone left who hasn't killed. I know there are millions, but sometimes it seems there can't be a man alive who hasn't killed. I've killed, but it always shakes me up, killing and death, and maybe that was why I missed what I should have heard in what Constantine Zareta said when I stepped out where he could see me and only smiled at him.

Pearce wasn't smiling. "You're saying you didn't kill Paul Asher?"

"We did not."

"But you would have."

"If he came here, yes."

"Why?"

"Because he would have killed me."

"Why didn't you ask for protection?"

"The police?" Zareta shook his head. "No, Captain. I am not precisely a friend of your government. I am a Communist. I have no love for your capitalist regime, they have no love for me. In my country the present leaders and I have no love for each other either. They want me dead, *must* have me dead, or someday I will destroy them. Six times they have tried. In four countries. Twice we had police protection. Once the police could not stop the assassin, once they did not want to stop the assassins. Each time I was close to death. I have survived. I have killed four of them, but they will not give up. If I were them I would not give up. One of us must kill the other."

That was when I first thought about the eighty million dead in eighty years. Zareta said the word *kill* the way other men say the word *work* — a fact of life. Neither good nor bad, just a tool. I remember when we used to say that a man who killed for the fun of it was an animal, inhuman, a monster. Today we kill without even having any fun from it. We just kill. A job, a duty, our assigned role. And it has nothing to do with being a Communist. It isn't only the Communists who have swallowed those eighty million corpses like so many jelly beans.

Pearce said, "So you have your own army, trust no one to come near you, not even the police."

"That is why I still live, Captain," Zareta said. "But we do not kill unless we are sure a man is our enemy."

"You knew Paul Asher was your enemy. Fortune told you."

"Yes, but Asher did not come here."

"Someone else just killed him for you. A lucky accident."

"I ask no questions, Captain," Zareta said.

Pearce seemed to think. He glanced toward me. If Zareta or his men hadn't killed Paul Asher, it didn't leave many known candidates except me. I didn't like that much, but I couldn't think of anyone else to hand the Captain. While I was thinking about it, and Zareta and the glowering Emil had relaxed a hair now that they knew Paul Asher was dead. Pearce nodded sharply to his men. They grabbed Zareta, had their guns out before Zareta's men knew what had happened.

"Maybe you didn't kill Paul Asher," Pearce said. "But I need to know more. We'll go to headquarters and sort it out there."

"No!" Emil cried. "The Minister does not go with you!"

The police had the edge now, but if Emil and the rest went for their guns it could be nasty. It was a tense moment in the small, dim room. Zareta broke it.

"Very well, Captain," he said. He had little choice. He was an alien, they were the police, and his own chances of surviving a shootout would be slim. "But not alone. I will take Emil and two other men, yes? A precaution of safety in numbers we who do not come from free countries need."

"Okay, but they leave all their guns. My men will stay around here to help protect the rest of your people."

"Agreed," Zareta said.

"Minister!" Emil was uneasy.

"Come, Emil, they are the police," Zareta said.

They laid their weapons on a table, followed Captain Pearce out of the room.

I was uneasy too. Constantine Zareta would kill any enemy, without anger or remorse. He seemed to draw the line at killing without *some* reason, and that had probably saved me the first time around, but it wasn't exactly high morality. Yet, as I watched them go out with Pearce I was suddenly sure that they had *not* killed Paul Asher.

Zareta wouldn't have waited to be caught if he or any of his men had killed Asher. He would have known that the moment Asher turned up dead I would tell the police all about him and his connection to Asher. No, Zareta would have been long gone before the police could connect Asher to me, and I could connect Zareta to Asher and lead the police to him, and the police...

And I knew the answer. The whole thing.

I knew what had been wrong about the package I had delivered. It was still there, open on the table next to the guns of Zareta and Emil and the other two men. The sheets of folded paper, the *documents*, were blank. I had been paid a thousand dollars to deliver a package of blank paper to Constantine Zareta.

And as I was thinking all this I was out of that room and running along the dark hallway to the gray dawn light of the front door. I thought it all, and grabbed Zareta's own automatic from the table, and was running out the front door into the morning like a racer coming around the last turn.

They had reached the sidewalk at the foot of the brownstone steps. The door of Pearce's black car was open. The man stood in the dawn not ten feet from the Captain's car. A stocky patrolman with an automatic in his hands. In both hands. A long-barreled automatic that was no part of the equipment of a New York city patrolman. An automatic aimed straight at Constantine Zareta.

I had no time to shout or even aim.

Zareta had seen the man now. And Captain Pearce. Emil had seen him. None of them could have moved in time.

I fired on the run. Three shots.

I never did know where the first went.

The second shot smashed a window of Pearce's black car.

The third hit the fake cop in the arm. Not much, a graze that barely needed a Band-Aid later, but enough. The assassin's arm jerked and he missed Constantine Zareta by inches.

Pearce, Emil and five real patrolmen swarmed the gunman under like an avalanche on the Yorkville street.

★ ★

I never learned Paul Asher's real name, or who he really was, or where he came from. No one did. No one ever will.

No one will visit his grave in Potter's Field out on Hart Island in the East River. He's buried out there under a marker with only his false name on it. Nameless, even to his partner in the assassination plot, the phony patrolman.

The fake policeman never told us his real name either. No one came forward to identify him or even visit him. No one ever has or ever will while he serves his time up in Auburn. He never told us who sent them to kill Zareta, or what their cause was, their reason, but he didn't mind telling us the unimportant parts, and that it had been Paul Asher's plan all the way. A plan that had very nearly worked.

"Himself?" Captain Pearce said as we sat in his office.

It was late evening. Somehow it was hard to think that it was still the same day the police had pounded on my door at dawn. A century ago. The Captain looked out toward the distant East River as if waiting for it to rise up and drown us all.

"Himself," I said. "He had himself killed just to smoke Zareta out into the open where his partner could get a clear shot, to lull Zareta into dropping his guard for an instant. He died so Zareta would die."

"To do his job," Pearce said. "And he almost made it."

"Because I missed it," I said. "Missed that package of blank paper, and missed what Zareta really told me. When he asked how you knew about him and Asher, and realized that it had to be through me, I should have understood. I was the only one in New York who could have connected Asher and Zareta, and I brought the police to Zareta. He said it, and I missed it."

"We all missed it then," Pearce said. "Even Zareta."

Six killers had tried for Constantine Zareta and failed. So Paul Asher made his own plan. The fake patrolman told us all about it. He was proud of the plan, proud of Paul Asher.

"He picked you," Pearce went on in the silent office, "because he heard you were especially close to the police through Gazzo. He sent you to Zareta so you'd know where Zareta was, and so Zareta wouldn't be alarmed when you brought the police. He put your cards in his pocket, wrote your name and the date in his book, and had his partner kill him and dump his body under the bridge. So we would go to you, and you would take us to Zareta, and we'd bring Zareta out into the open."

Paul Asher, dead, had sent the police to me, and I had taken them to Zareta where his partner lay in wait. Even a rat fights to survive, but Paul Asher died just to do his job. His life and death no more than a tool in his own plan for his cause.

I said, "Every assassin expects to die if he succeeds, maybe even if he fails, but Asher died without knowing if he would succeed or fail. Anything could go wrong. He died on the chance that his plan would work."

"He wasn't human," Pearce said.

There are people all over this world who will say that Paul Asher was a hero. The same people who can live with those eighty million dead, and maybe eight hundred million tomorrow or the next day, and go right on drinking beer and grabbing for a dollar. The Paul Ashers and Constantine Zaretas kill the way other men swat flies, and we let them. We've become used to it.

"He was human," I said. "That's the horror."

It's not the eighty million dead that really worry me, it's what those piled corpses have done to the rest of us in those eighty years. It's not the dead that scare me, it's the living.

Back in the late Fifties when I was a grad student at Syracuse University, my wife and I frequented a tavern near the tracks. Duke Wiltkowski hung out there. He was a black pimp who insisted to anyone who would listen that he was Polish. He wrote the poem in "A Reason To Die." There was also a gentle numbers boss who lived in the ghetto and was sort of a godfather to the entire neighborhood. The Mohawks worked high steel then and now, and the mural was painted on the wall.

I wrote the night of the poem as a mainstream story, "The Duke And The Beautiful Snow," more or less as it happened, with the focus on the Duke and the professor. Although it was published, it never really worked. It was a vignette, lacked a theme to make it universal beyond itself, as fiction should be.

Years later New Black Mask Quarterly *asked me if I had a story available. I went through all my files of ideas, came across the old piece of the Duke, and realized that, when combined with some other clippings I'd collected over the years, I could make it a crime story with a solid universal theme, and it became the first totally new Fortune I'd written in over ten years. The finished piece was far too long for most mystery mags, but, fortunately for me, not for* NBMQ, *and it was published as the sixth Dan Fortune in their second issue in 1985.*

A REASON TO DIE

There are many kinds of courage. Maybe the hardest is doing what you have to do. No matter how it looks to other people, or what happens in the end.

Irish Johnny's Tavern is a gray frame house near the railroad tracks in Syracuse, New York. A beacon of red and blue neon through the mounded old snow in the dusk of another cold winter day too far from Chelsea. My missing left arm hurt in the cold, and one of the people I was meeting was a killer.

I'd been in Irish Johnny's before, on my first day in Syracuse looking for why Alma Jean Brant was dead. Her mother had sent me.

★ ★

"You go to Irish Johnny's, Mr. Fortune," Sada Patterson said, "they'll tell you about my Alma Jean. They can tell you my girl wasn't walkin' streets without she got a reason, and whatever that there was it got to be what killed her."

"Every girl on the streets has a reason, Mrs. Patterson," I said.

"I don't mean no reason everyone got. I means a special reason. Somethin' made her do what she never would do," Sada Patterson said.

"Mrs. Patterson, listen —"

"No! You listen here to me." She held her old black plastic handbag in both hands on the lap of her starched print dress and fixed me across the desk with unflinching eyes. "I did my time hookin' when I was a girl. My man he couldn't get no work, so one day he ain't there no more, and I got two kids, and I hooked. A man got no work, he goes. A woman got no man, she hooks. But a woman got a man at home, she don't go on no streets. Not a good woman like my Alma Jean. She been married to that Indian ten years, and she don't turn no tricks 'less she got a powerful reason."

"What do you want me to do, Mrs. Patterson?"

Ramrod straight, as thin and rock hard as any Yankee farmer, her black eyes studied me as if she could see every thought I'd ever had. She probably could. The ravages of sixty years of North Carolina dirt farms, the Syracuse ghetto, and New York sweatshops, had left her nothing but bones and tendon, the flesh fossilized over the endless years.

"You go on up there 'n find out who killed my Alma Jean. I can pay. I got the money. You go to Irish Johnny's and ask 'bout my Alma Jean. She ain't been inside the place in ten years, or any place like it. You tell 'em Sada sent you and they talk to you even if you is a honkie."

"It's a police job, Mrs. Patterson. Save your money."

"No cop's gonna worry hard 'bout the killin' of no black hooker. You go up there, Fortune. You find out." She stood up, the worn plastic handbag out in front of her in both hands like a shield. A grandmother in a print dress. Until you looked at her eyes. "She was my last, Alma Jean. She come when we had some money, lived in a house up there. She almos' got to finish grade school. I always dressed her so good. Like a real doll, you know? A little doll."

★ ★

Inside, Irish Johnny's is a single large room with a bandstand at the far end. The bar is along the left wall, backed by bottles and fronted by red plastic stools. Tables fill the room around a small dance floor. Behind the bar and the rows of bottles is a long mirror. The rear wall over the bandstand is bare, except when it is hung with a banner proclaiming the band or artiste to perform that night.

On the remaining two walls there is a large mural in the manner of Orozco or maybe Rivera. Full of violent, struggling ghetto figures, it was painted long ago by some forgotten radical student from the university on the hill above the tavern.

The crowd had not yet arrived, only a few tables occupied as I came in. The professor and his wife sat at a table close to the dance floor. I crossed the empty room under the lost eyes of the red, blue and yellow people in the mural.

I knew who the killer was, but I didn't know how I was going to prove it. Someone was going to have to help me before I made the call to the police.

★ ★

The police are always the first stop in a new town. Lieutenant Derrida of the Syracuse Police Department was an older man. He remembered Sada Patterson.

"Best looking hooker ever walked a street in Syracuse." His thin eyes were bright and sad at the same time, as if he wished he and Sada Patterson could be back there when she had been the best looking hooker in Syracuse, but knew it was too late for both of them.

"What made Alma Jean go to the streets, Lieutenant?"

He shrugged. "What makes any of 'em?"

"What does?" I said.

"Don't shit me, Fortune. A new car or a fur coat. Suburbs to Saskatchewan. It just happens more in the slums where the bucks ain't so big or easy."

"Sada says no way unless the girl had a large reason," I said. "She didn't mean a fur coat or a watch."

"Sada Patterson's a mother," Derrida said.

"She's also a client. Can I earn my fee?"

He opened a desk drawer, took out a skinny file. "Alma Jean was found a week ago below a street bridge over the tracks. Some kids going to school spotted her. The fall killed her. She died somewhere between midnight and four A.M., the snow and cold made it hard to be sure. It stopped snowing about two A.M., there was no snow on top of her, so she died after that."

Derrida swivelled in his chair, looked out his single window at the gray sky and grayer city. "She could have fallen, jumped or been pushed. There was no sign of a struggle, but she was a small woman. One push would have knocked her over a parapet that low. M.E. says a bruise on her jaw could have come from a blow or from hitting a rock. No suicide note, but the snow showed someone had climbed up on the parapet. Only whoever it was didn't get near the edge, held to a light pole, jumped off the other way back onto the street."

"What's her pimp say?"

"Looks like she was trying to work independent."

I must have stared. Derrida nodded.

"I know," he said, "we sweated the pimp in the neighborhood. Black as my Captain, but tells everyone he's a Polack. He says he didn't even know Alma Jean, and we can't prove he did or place him around her."

"Who do you place around her?"

"That night, no one. She was out in the snow all by herself. No one saw her, heard her, or smelled her. If she turned any tricks that night she used doorways, no johns are talking. No cash in her handbag. A bad night."

"Who's around her other nights?"

"The husband, Joey Brant. He's a Mohawk, works high steel like most Indians. They married ten years ago, no kids and lived good. High steel pays. With her hooking he was our numeral uno suspect, only he was drinking in Cherry Valley Tavern from nine 'till closing with fifty witnesses. Later, the bartender, him, and ten others sobered up in a sweat lodge until dawn."

"Anyone else?"

"Mister Walter Ellis. Owns the numbers, runs a big book. He was an old boyfriend of Sada's, seems to have had eyes for the daughter. She was seen visiting him a couple of times recently. Just friendly calls, he says, but he got no alibi."

"That's it?"

Derrida swivelled. "No, we got a college professor named Margon and his wife. Margon was doing 'research' with Alma Jean. Maybe the wrong kind of research. Maybe the wife got mad."

★ ★

I took a chair at the table with the Margons. In Irish Johnny's anyone who opened a book in the university above the ghetto was a "professor". Fred Margon was a thin, dark-haired young man in his mid-twenties. His wife, Dorothy, was a beauty-contest blonde with restless eyes.

"A temple," Fred Margon said as I sat down. "The bartenders are the priests. The mural over there is the holy icon painted by a wandering disciple. The liquor is God."

"I think I'll scream," Dorothy Margon said. "Or is that too undignified for the wife of a scholar, a pure artist?"

Fred Margon drank his beer, looked unhappy.

"Booze is their god," Dorothy Margon said. "That's very good. Isn't that good, Mr. Fortune? You really are bright, Fred. I wonder what you ever saw in me? Just the bod, right? You like female bods at least. You like them a lot when you've got time."

"You want to leave?" Fred said.

"No, tell us why drink is their god. Go on, tell us."

"No other god ever helped them."

"Clever," Dorothy said. "Isn't he clever, Mr. Fortune? Going to do great scholarly research, teach three classes, and finish his novel all at the same time. Then there's the female bods. When he has time. Or maybe he makes time for that."

"We'll leave," Fred Margon said.

"All day every day: scholar, teacher, novelist. For twenty whole thousand dollars a year."

"We manage," Fred Margon said.

"Never mind," Dorothy said. "Just never mind."

★ ★

I'd met Fred Margon in a coffee shop on South Crouse after a class. He looked tired. We had coffee and he told me about Alma Jean Brant.

"I found her in an Indian bar six months ago. I like to walk through the city, meet the real people." He drank his coffee. "She had a way of speaking full of metaphors. I wrote my doctoral dissertation on the poetry of totally untrained people, got a grant to continue the research. I met her as often as I could. In the bars and in her home. To listen and record her speech. She was highly intelligent. Her insights were remarkable for someone without an education, and her way of expressing her thoughts was pure uneducated poetry."

"You liked her?"

He nodded. "She was real, alive."

"How much did you like her, professor?"

"Make it Fred, okay? I'm only a bottom step assistant professor and sometimes I want to drop the whole thing, live a real life, make some money." He drank his coffee, looked out the café window. He knew what I was asking. "My wife isn't happy, Mr. Fortune. When she's unhappy she has the classic female method of showing it. Perhaps in time I would have tried with Alma Jean, but I didn't. She really wasn't interested, you know? In me or any other man. Only her husband."

"You know her husband?"

"I've met him. Mostly at her house, sometimes in a bar. He seems to drink a lot. I asked her about that. She said it was part of being an Indian, a 'brave'. Work hard and drink hard. He always seemed angry. At her, at his bosses, at everything. He didn't like me, or my being there, as if it were an insult to him. But he just sat in the living room, drinking and looking out a window at the tall buildings downtown. Sometimes he talked about working on those buildings. He was proud of that. Alma Jean said that was the culture, a 'man' did brave work, daring."

"When was the last time you saw her?"

"The day she died." He shrugged as he drank his coffee. "The police know. I had a session with her early in the day at her house. Her husband wasn't there, and she seemed tired, worried. She'd been unhappy for months, I think, but it was always hard to tell with her. Always cheerful and determined. I told her there was a whole book in her life, but she only scorned the idea. Life was to be lived not written about. When there were troubles you did something about them."

"What troubles sent her out on the streets?"

He shook his head. "She never told me. A few weeks ago she asked me to pay her for making the tapes. She needed money. I couldn't pay her much on my grant, but I gave her what I could. I know it wasn't anywhere near enough. I heard her talking on the telephone, asking about the cost of something."

"You don't know what?"

"No." He drank coffee. "But whoever she was talking to offered to pay for whatever it was. She turned him down."

"You're sure it was a him?"

"No, I'm not sure."

"Who killed her, professor?"

Outside the students crunched through the snow in the gray light. He watched them as if he wished he were still one of them, his future unknown. "I don't know who killed her, Mr. Fortune. I know she didn't commit suicide, and I doubt that she fell off that bridge. I never saw her drunk. When her husband drank, she never did, as if she had to be sober to take care of him."

"Where were you that night?"

"At home," he said, looked up at me. "But I couldn't sleep, another argument with my wife. So I went out walking in the snow. Didn't get back until two A.M. or so."

"Was it still snowing?"

"It had just stopped when I got home."

"Did you see anyone while you were out?"

"Not Alma Jean, if that's what you want to know. I did see that older friend of hers. What's his name? Walter Ellis?"

"Where?"

"Just driving around. That pink Caddy of his is easy to remember. Especially in the snow, so few cars driving."

"And all you were doing with her was recording her speech?"

He finished his coffee. "That's all, Mr. Fortune."

After he left I paid for the coffee. He was an unhappy man, and not just about money or work.

★ ★

The scar-faced pimp stood just inside the door of Irish Johnny's. Snow dripped from his dirty raincoat into a pool around his black boots. A broad, powerfully-built man with a fresh bandage on his face. Dark stains covered the front of his raincoat. The raincoat and his black shirt were open at the throat. He wore a large silver cross bedded in the hair of his chest.

"Now there's something you can write about, Fred," Dorothy Margon said. "Real local color. Who is he? What is he? Why don't you make notes? You didn't forget your notebook, did you, Fred?"

"His name is Duke," Fred Margon said. "He's a pimp, and this is his territory. A small time pimp, only three girls on the street now. He takes eighty percent of what they make to protect them, lets them support him with most of the rest. But the competition is fierce and business is bad this season. He gives students a cut rate, professors pay full price."

"Of course," Dorothy said. "Part of your 'research' into 'ordinary' people. All for art and scholarship." She looked at the man at the entrance. "I wonder what his girls are like? Are they young or old? Do they admire him? I suppose they all love him. Of course they do. All three of them in love with him."

"In love with him and afraid of him," I said.

"Love and fear," Fred Margon said. "Their world."

"Do I hear a story?" Dorothy said. "Is everything a story? Nothing real? With results? Change? A future?"

I watched the scar-faced man come across the dance floor toward our table. Duke Wiltkowski, the pimp who owned the streets where Alma Jean had been found dead.

★ ★

The pimp's office was a cellar room with a single bare bulb, a table for a desk, some battered armchairs, a kerosene heater and water from melted snow pooled in a dark corner. Times had been better for Duke Wiltkowski.

"You sayin' I killed her? You sayin' that, man?" His black face almost hidden in the shadows of the cellar room. The light of the bare bulb barely reached where he sat behind the table.

"Someone did," I said. "You had a motive."

"You say I kill that chippie you got trouble, man. I got me a good lawyer. He sue you for everythin' you got!"

"The police say she was in your territory."

"The police is lyin'! The police say I kill that chippie they lyin'!" His voice was high and thin, almost hysterical. It's a narrow world of fear, his world. On the edge. Death on one side, prison on the other, hunger and pain in between.

"She was freelance in your territory. You can't let her do that. Not and survive. Let her do that and you're out of business."

He sat in the gloom of the cold basement room, unmoving in the half shadows. The sweat shined on his face like polished ebony. The face of a rat with his back to the wall, cornered, protesting.

"I never see that chippie. Not me. How I know she was working my turf? You tell the cops that, okay? You tell the cops Duke Wiltkowski never nowhere near that chippie."

He sweated in the cold cellar room. A depth in his wide eyes almost of pleading. Go away, leave him alone. Go away before he told what he couldn't tell. Wanted to tell but couldn't. Not yet.

"Where were you that night?"

"Right here. An' with one o' my pigs. All night. Milly-O. Me'n Milly-O we was makin' it most all night. You asks her."

One of his prostitutes who would say anything he told her to say, to the police or to God himself. He was that desperate. An alibi he knew was no alibi. He sweated. Licked his lips.

"That Injun husband she got, maybe he done it. Hey, they all crazy, them Injuns! That there professor hangs in Irish Johnny's. Hey, he got to of been playin' pussy with her. I mean, a big-shot white guy down there. Hey, that there professor he got a wife. Maybe she don't like that chippie, right?"

"How about Walter Ellis? He was out in the snow that night."

The fear on his face became sheer terror. "I don' know nothin' 'bout Mr. Ellis! You hears, Fortune! Nothin'!"

★ ★

Now he walked into Irish Johnny's with the exaggerated swing and lightness of a dancer. Out in public, the big man. His face in the light a mass of criss-cross scars. The new bandage dark with dried blood. He smiled a mouthful of broken yellow teeth.

"Saw it was you, professor. That your lady?" He clicked his heels, bowed to Dorothy Margon. A Prussian officer. "Duke Wiltkowski. My old man was Polack." He nodded to me, cool and casual, expansive. An image to keep up and no immediate fear in sight. "Hey, Fortune. How's the snoopin'?"

"Slow," I said, smiled. "But I'm getting closer."

"Yeah." The quick lick of the lips, and sat down at the table, legs out in his Prussian boots. The silver cross at his throat reflected the bright tavern light. He surveyed the room with a cool, imperious eye. Looked at Dorothy Margon. "You been holdin' out on The Duke, professor. You could do real business with that one."

The Duke admired Dorothy's long blonde hair, the low-cut black-velvet dress that looked too expensive for an assistant professor's wife, her breasts rising out of the velvet.

"It's not what I do," Fred Margon said.

Dorothy Margon tore a cardboard coaster into small pieces, dropped the pieces onto the table. She began to build the debris into a pyramid. She worked on her pyramid, and watched The Duke.

The people were filling the tavern now. Coming out of the silence and cold of the winter night into the light and noise of the tavern. They shed old coats and worn jackets, wool hats and muddy galoshes, to emerge in suits and dresses the color of the rainbow. Saturday night.

The Duke sneered. "Works their asses a whole motherfucking year for the rags they got on their backs." He waved imperiously to a waiter. "Set up what they wants for my man the professor 'n his frau. Fortune there too. Rye for me."

Dorothy Margon built her pyramid of torn coaster. "What happened to your face?"

"Injuns." The Duke touched the bandage on his face, his eyes fierce. "The fuckers ganged me. I get 'em."

"Alma Jean's husband?" I said. "The Cherry Valley bar?"

★ ★

The Cherry Valley Tavern was a low-ceilinged room with posts and tables and a long bar without stools. As full of dark Iroquois faces as the victorious massacre that had given it its name. All turned to look at me as I entered. I ordered a beer.

The bartender brought me the beer. "Maybe you'd like it better downtown, mister. Nothing personal."

"I'm looking for Joey Brant."

He mopped the bar. "You're not a cop."

"Private. Hired by his mother-in-law."

He went on mopping the bar.

"She wants to know who killed her daughter."

"Brant was in here all night."

"They told me. What time do you close?"

"Two."

"When the snow stopped," I said.

"We went to the sweat lodge. Brant too."

"Good way to sober up on a cold night. Maybe Brant has some ideas about who did kill her."

"Down the end of the bar."

He was a small man alone on the last bar stool. He sat hunched, a glass in both hands. An empty glass. Brooding into the glass or staring up at himself in the bar mirror. I stood behind him. He didn't notice, waved at the bartender, violent and arrogant.

"You had enough, Joey."

"I says when I got enough." He scowled at the bartender. The bartender did nothing. Brant looked down at his empty glass. "I got no woman, Crow. She's dead, Crow. My woman. How I'm gonna live my woman's dead?"

"You get another woman," the bartender, Crow, said.

Brant stared at his empty glass, remembered what he wanted. "C'mon, Crow."

"You ain't got two paychecks now."

Brant swung his head from side to side as if caught in the mesh of a net, thrashing in the net. "Lemme see the stuff."

The bartender opened a drawer behind the bar, took out a napkin, opened it on the bar. Various pieces of silver and turquoise Indian jewelry lay on the towel. There were small red circles of paper attached to most pieces. Rings, bracelets, pendants, pins, a silver cross. Joey Brant picked up a narrow turquoise ring. It was one of the last pieces without a red tag.

"Two bottles," Crow said.

"It's real stuff, Crow. Four?"

"Two."

I thought Brant was going to cry, but he only nodded. Crow took an unopened bottle of cheap rye blend from under the bar, wrote on it. Close, Brant's shoulders were thickly muscled, his arms powerful, his neck like a bull. A flyweight body builder. Aware of his body, his image.

I sat on the stool beside him. He stared at my empty sleeve. Crow put a shot glass and a small beer on the bar, opened the marked bottle of rye.

"On me," I said. "Both of us."

Crow stared at me, then closed the marked bottle, poured from a bar bottle. He brought my beer and a chaser beer, walked away. The small, muscular Indian looked at the whisky, and then at me.

"Why was Alma Jean on the street, Joey?" I said.

He looked down at the whisky. His hand seemed to wait an inch from the shot glass. Then he touched it, moved it next to the beer chaser.

"How the hell I know? The bitch."

"Her mother says she had to have a big reason."

"Fuck her mother." He glared at my missing arm. "You no cop. Cops don't hire no cripples."

"Dan Fortune. Private detective. Sada Patterson hired me to find out who murdered Alma Jean. Any ideas?"

He stared into the shot glass of cheap rye as if it held all the beauty of the universe. "She think I don' know? Stupid bitch an' her black whore-master! I knows he give her stuff. I get him, you watch. Make him talk. Black bastard, he done it sure. I get him." He drank, went on staring into the bottom of the glass as if it were a crystal ball. "Fuckin' around with that white damn professor. Think she fool Joey Brant? Him an' that hot-bitch wife he got. Business she says, old friends she says. Joey knows, yessir. Joey knows."

"You knew," I said, "so you killed her."

There was a low rumble through the room. The bartender, Crow, stopped pouring to watch me. They didn't love Brant, but he was one of them, and they would defend him against the white man. Any white man, black or white.

Brant shook his head. "With my friends. Not worth killin'. Nossir. Joey Brant takes care of hisself." He drained the shot, finished the beer chaser, and laid his head on the bar.

The bartender came and removed the glasses, watched me finish my beer. When I did, he made no move to serve another.

"He was in here all night, fifty guys saw him. We went to the reservation and sweated. Me and ten other guys and Brant."

"Sure," I said.

I felt their eyes all the way out. They didn't like him, even despised him, but they would all defend him, lie for him.

★ ★

The band burst into sound. Dancers packed into a mass on the floor. A thick mass of bodies that moved as one, the colors and shapes of the mural on the wall, a single beast with a hundred legs and arms. Shrill tenor sax, electronic guitar, keyboard and trumpet blaring. Drums.

"Or did Brant find you?" I said.

The Duke scowled at the dancers on the floor. "Heard he was lookin' to talk to The Duke, so I goes to The Cherry Valley. He all shit and bad booze. He never know me 'n I never knows him. I tells him I hear he talkin' 'bout me 'n from now on all I wants to hear is sweet nothin'."

"You're a tough man," I said. "I'll bet you scared him."

He licked his lips. I watched the sweat on his brow, the violent swinging of his booted foot. He was hiding something.

"I tell him I never even heard o' his broad. What I know about no Injun's broad? I tell him if'n she goes out on the tricks it got to be he put her out. Happens all the time. Some ol' man he needs the scratch so he puts the ol' woman out on the hustle." The swinging foot in its black boot seemed to grow more agitated. His eyes searched restlessly around the packed room, the crowded dance floor. "I seen it all times, all ways. They comes out on the streets, nice chicks should oughta be home watchin' the kids, puttin' the groceries on the table. I seen 'em, scared 'n no way knows what they 'sposed to do. All 'cause some dude he ain't got what it takes."

Restless, he sweated. The silver cross reflected the tavern light where it lay on his thick chest hair above the black shirt. Talked. But what was he telling me?

"Is that when he jumped you? Pulled a knife?"

The Duke sneered. "Not him. He too drunk. All of 'em, they ganged me. He pull his blade, sure, but he ain't sober 'nuff he can cut cheese. It was them others ganged me. I got some of 'em, got out o' there."

"Did you see him out on the street that night, Duke? Is that what you really told him? Why they ganged on you?"

He jerked back as if snake-bitten. "I ain't see no one that there night! I ain't on the street that there night. I—"

He stared toward the door. As if he saw a demon.

Joey Brant stood inside the tavern entrance blinking at the noise and crowd. Walter Ellis stood beside Brant. Which one was The Duke's demon?

★ ★

It was a big house by Syracuse ghetto standards. A two-story, three-bedroom cinder block box painted yellow and green, with a spiked wrought iron fence, a swimming pool that took up most of the postage stamp side yard. Concrete paths wound among bird baths and fountains and the American flag on a pole. Among naked plaster copies of the Venus de Milo and Michelangelo's David.

Walter Ellis met me on his front steps. "The cops send you to me, Fortune?"

He was a tall, slim man with snow white hair and a young face. He looked dangerous. Quick eyes that smiled now. Simple gray flannel slacks, a white shirt open at the throat, and a red cashmere sweater that gave a vigorous tint to his face. Only the rings on both pinkies and both index fingers, diamonds and rubies and gold, showed his money and his power.

"They said you knew Alma Jean Brant," I said.

"Her and her mother. Come on in. Drink?"

"Beer if you have it."

He laughed. "Now you know I got beer. What kind of rackets boss wouldn't have a extra refrigerator full of beer? Beck's? Stroh's? Bud?"

"Beck's, thanks."

"Sure. A New York loner."

We were in a small, cluttered, overstuffed living room all lace and velvet and cushions. Ellis pressed a button somewhere. A tall, handsome

black man in full suit and tie materialized, not the hint of a bulge anywhere under the suit, and was told to bring two Beck's.

"Not that I'm much of a racket boss like in the movies, eh? A small
town gambler. Maybe a little border stuff if the price is right." He
laughed again, sat down in what had to be his private easy chair, worn and
comfortable with a foot stool, waved me to an overstuffed couch. I sank
into it. He lit a cigar, eyed me over it. "But you didn't come about my
business, right? Sada sent you up to find out what happened to Alma Jean."

"What did happen to her?"

"I wish I knew."

The immaculate black returned with two Beck's and two glasses on an
ornate silver tray. A silver bowl of bar peanuts. Ellis raised his glass. We
drank. He ate peanuts and smoked.

"You liked her?" I said. "Alma Jean?"

He savored the cigar. "I liked her. She was married. That's all. Not
my age or anything else. She didn't cheat on her husband. A wife supports
her husband."

"But she went on the streets."

"Prostitution isn't cheating, Fortune. Not in the ghetto, not down here
where it hurts. It's the only way a woman has of making money when she
got no education or skills. It's what our women do to help in a crisis."

"And the men accept that?"

He smoked, drank, fingered peanuts. "Some do, some don't.".

"Which are you?"

"I never cottoned to white slaving."

"You were out that night. In your car. On the streets down near Irish
Johnny's."

He drank, licked foam from his lips. "Who says?"

"Professor Fred Margon saw you. I think Duke Wiltkowski did too.
He's scared, sweating, and hiding something."

His eyes were steady over the glass. He ate the peanuts one by one. "I
like a drive, a nice walk in the snow. I saw The Duke and Margon. I didn't
see no one else. But a couple of times I saw that wife of Margon's tailing
Alma Jean."

"Was it snowing when you got home?"

He smiled.

★ ★

I watched Walter Ellis steer Joey Brant to a table on the far side of the
dance floor. Brant was already drunk, but his startled eyes were wary,
almost alert. This wasn't one of his taverns. The Duke watched Walter
Ellis.

I said, "It's okay, we know he was out that night. He saw you, knows
you saw him, and it's okay. Who else did you see?"

The Duke licked his lips, looked at Fred Margon.

"You writes, yeah professor?"

The Duke looked back across the dance floor to Ellis and Joey Brant. "I means," the Duke said, "like stories n' books n' all that there?"

"God, does he write!" Dorothy Margon said, "Writes, studies, teaches. All day, every day. Tell the Duke about your art, Fred. Tell the Duke what you do. All day every damn day."

"Like," the Duke said, "poetry stuff?" He watched only Fred Margon now. "Words they got the same sound n' all?"

"I write poetry," Fred said. "Sometimes it rhymes."

"You likes poetry, yeah?"

"Yes, I like poetry. I read it."

"Oh, but it's so hard!" Dorothy said. "Tell the Duke how hard poetry is, Fred. Tell him how hard all real writing is. Tell him how you can learn most careers in a few years but it takes a lifetime to learn to write well."

"We better go," Fred said.

I watched the people packed body to body on the dance floor, flushed and excited, desperate for Saturday night. On the far side Walter Ellis ordered drinks. Joey Brant saw us: The Duke, me, Fred and Dorothy Margon. I watched him turn on Ellis. The racket boss only smiled, shook his head.

Dorothy smiled at the Duke. "I'm a bitch, right? I wasn't once. Do your women talk to you like that, Duke? No, they wouldn't, would they? They wouldn't dare. They wouldn't want to. Tell me about the Indians? How many were there? Did they all have knives? Do they still wear feathers? How many did you knock out? Kill?"

The Duke watched Fred Margon. "You writes good, professor?"

"You see," Dorothy said, "we're going to stay at the university three more years. We may even stay forever. Isn't that grand news? I can stay here and do nothing forever."

The Duke said to Fred, "They puts what you writes in books?"

Dorothy said, "Did you ever want something, wait for something, think you have it at last, and then suddenly it's so far away again you can't even see it anymore?"

"I'm a writer," Fred said. "A writer and a teacher. I can't go to New York and write lies for money."

Dorothy stood up. "Dance with me, Duke. I want to dance. I want to dance right now."

★ ★

She opened the apartment door my second day in Syracuse, looked at my duffel coat, beret and missing arm.

"He's out. Go find him in one of your literary bars."

"Mrs. Margon?" I said.

She cocked her head, suspicious yet coy, blonde and flirtatious. "You want me?"

"Would it do me any good?"

She laughed. "Do we know each other, Mr. — ?"

"Fortune," I said. "No."

She eyed me. "Then what do you want to talk to me about?"

"Alma Jean Brant," I said.

She started to close the door. "Go and find my husband."

I held the door with my foot. "No, I want you. Both ways."

She laughed again, neither flirtatious nor amused this time. Self-mocking, a little bitter. "You can probably have me. Both ways." But stepped back, held the door open. "Come in."

It was a small apartment: a main room, bedroom, kitchenette and bathroom. All small, cramped. The furniture had to have been rented with the apartment. They don't pay assistant professors too well, the future of a writer is at best a gamble, so without children they saved their money, scrimped, did without. She lit a cigarette, didn't offer me one.

"What about that Alma Jean woman?"

"What can you tell me about her?"

"Nothing. That's Fred's territory. Ask him."

"About her murder?"

She smoked. "I thought it was an accident. Or suicide. Drunk and fell over that bridge wall, or jumped. Isn't that what the police think?"

"The police don't think anything one way or the other. I think it was murder."

"What do you want, Mr. Fortune? A confession?"

"Do you want to make one?"

"Yes, that I'm a nasty bitch who wants more than she's got. Just more. You understand that, Mr. Fortune."

"It's a modern disease," I said, "but what's it got to do with Alma Jean Brant?"

She smoked. "You wouldn't be here if someone hadn't seen me around her."

"Her husband," I said. "And Walter Ellis."

The couch creaked under her as if it had rusty springs. "I was jealous. Or maybe just suspicious. He's so involved in his work, I'm so bored, our sex life is about zero. We never do anything. We talk, read, think, discuss, but we never do. I make his life miserable, I admit it. But he promised we would stay here only five years or until he published a novel. We would go down to New York, he'd make money, we'd have some life. I counted on that. Now he wants to get tenure, stay here."

"So he can teach and write?" I said. "That's all? No other reason for wanting to stay here?"

She nodded. "When he started going out all the time, I wondered too. Research for his work, he said, but I heard about Alma Jean. So I followed him and found where she lived. Then I followed her to see if she'd meet him somewhere else. That's all. I just watched her house, followed her a few times. I never saw him do a damn thing that could be close to cheating. At her house that husband of hers was around all the time. He must work nights."

"Did you see her do anything?"

She smoked. "I saw her visit the same house three or four times. I got real suspicious then. I hadn't seen Fred go in, but after she left the last time I went up and rang the bell. A guy answered, but it wasn't Fred, so I made some excuse and got out of there. She was meeting someone all right, but not Fred."

"Any idea who?"

She shook her head. "He wasn't an Indian, I can say that."

"What was he?"

"Black, Mr. Fortune. One big black man."

★ ★

Through the mass of sound and movement, bodies and faces that glistened with sweat and gaudy color and melted into the bright colors and tortured figures of the mural on the walls, I watched Joey Brant across the dance floor drinking and talking to Walter Ellis who only listened.

I watched Dorothy Margon move lightly through the shuffle of the massed dancers. Her slender body loose and supple, her eyes closed, her lips parted, her face turned up to the Duke. I could see a man she denied turn to someone else. A man who could not give her what she wanted, turning to someone who wanted less.

Her hips moved a beat behind the band, her long blonde hair swung free against the black velvet of her dress and the scarred face of the Duke. I could see her, restless and rejecting, but still not wanting her man to go anywhere else.

"I can't tell the dancers from the people in the mural," Fred Margon said. "I can't be sure which woman is my wife with The Duke, and which is the woman chained in the mural."

He was talking about himself: a man who could not tell which was real and which was only an image. He could not decide, be certain, which was real to him, image or reality.

"Which man is The Duke on the dance floor with my wife," Fred Margon said, "and which is the blue man with the bare chest and hammer in the mural? Am I the man at the ringside table with a glass of beer in a pale, indoor hand watching The Duke dance with his wife, or the thin scarecrow in the mural with his wrists chained and his starving face turned up to an empty sky?"

He was trying to understand something, and across the dance floor Joey Brant was talking and talking to Walter Ellis. Ellis only listened and watched The Duke and Dorothy Margon on the dance floor. The Duke sweated and Dorothy Margon danced with her eyes closed, her body moving as if by itself.

★ ★

Walter Ellis sat alone in the back of his pink Cadillac. I leaned in the window.

"A black man, she said. A big black man Alma Jean visited in a house in the ghetto."

"A lot of big black men in the ghetto, Fortune."

"What was the crisis?" I said. "You said going on the streets was what ghetto women did in a crisis."

"I don't know."

"You offered to pay for whatever she needed money for."

"She only told me she needed something that cost a lot of money."

"Needed what?"

"A psychiatrist. I sent her to the best."

"A black? Big? Lives near here? Expensive?"

"All that."

"Can we go and talk to him?"

"Anytime."

"And you didn't give her the money to pay him?"

"She wouldn't take it. Said she would know what it was really for even if it was only in my mind, and she didn't cheat on her man."

★ ★

The Duke said, "There was this here chippie. I mean, she's workin' my streets 'n I don' work her, see? I mean, it's snowin' bad 'n there ain't no action goin' down, my three pigs're holed up warmin' their pussy, but this chippie she's out workin' on my turf. Hey, that don't go down, you know? I mean, that's no scene, right? So I moves in to tell her to fly her pussy off'n my streets or sign up with The Duke."

I said, "The last time it snowed was the night Alma Jean died."

Dorothy Margon built another pyramid of torn coasters on the tavern table and watched the Saturday night dancers. The Duke mopped his face with a dirty handkerchief, a kind of desperation in his voice that rose higher, faster, as if he could not stop himself, had to talk while Fred Margon was there.

"I knows that there fox. I mean, I gets up close to tell her do a fade and I remembers that chippie in the snow."

I said, "It was Alma Jean."

He sweated in that hot room with its pounding music and packed bodies swirling and rubbing. It was what he had been hiding, holding back. What he had wanted to tell from the start. What he had to tell.

"Back when I was jus' a punk kid stealin' dogs, my ol' man beatin' my ass to go to school, that there chippie out in the snow was in that school. I remembers. Smart 'n clean 'n got a momma dresses her up real good. I remember, you know? Like, I had eyes for that pretty little kid back then."

The band stopped. The dancers drifted off the floor, sat down. A silence like a blow from a hammer in the hands of the big blue man in the mural.

"I walks off. I mean, when I remembers that little girl I walks me away from that there chippie. I remembers how good her momma fixes her up so I walks off 'n lets her work 'n I got the blues, you know. I got the blues then 'n I got 'em now."

"Everybody got the blues," Dorothy said. "We should write a song. Fred should write a poem."

"It was Alma Jean, Duke," I said.

★ ★

Walter Ellis stopped to say a few low words to the tall, handsome doctor, while I walked down the steps of his modest house and out into the ghetto street. The numbers boss caught up with me before I reached his Cadillac.

"Does that tell you who killed her?" Ellis said.

"I think so. All I have to do is find a way to prove it."

He nodded. We both got into the back of the pink car. It purred away from the curb. The silent driver in the immaculate suit drove slowly, sedately, parading Ellis through his domain where the people could see him.

"Any ideas?" Ellis said.

"Watch and hope for a break. They've all got something on their minds, maybe it'll get too heavy."

He watched the street ahead. "That include me?"

"It includes you," I said. "You were out that night."

"You know what I've got on my mind?"

"I've got a hunch," I said. "I'm going to meet the Margons in Irish Johnny's tonight. Why don't you come around and bring Brant, friend of the family."

We drove on to my motel.

"The Duke hangs out in Irish Johnny's," Ellis said.

"I know," I said.

★ ★

"I writes me a poem," The Duke said. " 'Bout that there chippie. I go home 'n writes me a poem."

The scarred black face of The Duke seemed to watch the empty dance floor as he told about the poem he had written. All through the long room the Saturday night people waited for the music to begin again. Across the floor Walter Ellis talked to those who came to him one by one to pay their respects. Joey Brant drank, stared into his glass, looked toward me and the Margons and The Duke.

"Do you have it with you?" Fred said.

The Duke's eyes flickered above the scars on his face and the new bandage. Looked right and left.

"Did you bring it to show me?" Fred Margon said.

The Duke sweated in the hot room. Nodded.

"All right," Fred said. "But don't just show it to me, read it. Out loud. Poetry should be read aloud. While the band is still off, get up and read your poem. This is your tavern, they all know you in here. Tell them why you wrote it, how it came to you, and read it to them."

The Duke stared. "You fuckin' with me, man?"

"Fred?" Dorothy Margon said.

"You wrote it, didn't you? You felt it. If you feel something and write it you have to believe in it. You have to show it to the world, make the world hear."

"You a crazy man," The Duke said.

Dorothy tore another coaster.

"Give it to me," Fred said.

The Duke sat there for some time, the sweat beaded on his face, his booted foot swinging, while the people all through the room waited for Saturday night to return.

"What happened to Alma Jean, Duke?" I said.

Fred Margon said, "You wrote it, give it to me."

The Duke reached into his filthy raincoat and handed a torn piece of lined notebook paper to Fred Margon. Fred stood up. On the other side of the dance floor Joey Brant held his glass without drinking as Fred Margon walked to the bandstand, jumped up to the microphone.

"Ladies and gentlemen!"

In the long room, ice loud in the glasses and voices in the rumble of conversation, the people who waited only for the music to begin again, Saturday night to return, turned toward the bandstand. Fred Margon told them about The Duke and the street walker working his territory without his permission. The Duke alone in the night with the snow and the woman he remembered from grade school because her mother dressed her so well.

"The Duke remembered that girl. So he let her work free on his streets, went home and wrote a poem. I'm going to read that poem."

There were some snickers, a murmur of protest or two, the steady clink of indifferent glasses. Fred called for silence. Waited. Until the room silenced. Then he read the poem.

> Once I was pure
> as a snow but I fell,
> fell like a snowflake
> from heaven to hell.
>
> Fell to be scuffed,
> to be spit on and beat,
> fell to be like
> the filth in the street.
>
> Pleading and cursing
> and dreading to die
> to the fellow I know
> up there in the sky.

The fellow his cross
I got on this chain
I give it to her
she gets clean again.

Dear God up there,
have I fell so low,
and yet to be once
like the beautiful snow.

Through the smoke-haze of the crowded tavern room they shifted their feet. They stirred their drinks. The musicians, ready to return, stood in the wings. A woman giggled. The bartenders hid grins. Some men suddenly laughed. A murmur of laughter rippled through the room. The Duke stood up, stepped toward the bandstand. Fred came across the empty dance floor.

"I like it," Fred Margon said. "It's not a good poem, you're not a poet. But it's real and I like it. I like anything that says what you really feel, says it openly and honestly. It's what you had to do."

The Duke's eyes were black above the scars and the bandage. The Duke watched only Fred, his fists clenched, his eyes wide.

"It's you," Fred said. "Go up and read it yourself. Make them see what you saw out there in the snow when you remembered Alma Jean, the girl whose mother dressed her so well. To hell with anyone who laughs. They're laughing at themselves. The way they would have laughed if Alma Jean had told them what she was going to do. They're afraid, so they laugh. They're afraid to know what they feel. They're afraid to feel. Help them face themselves. Read your poem again. And again."

★ ★

The Duke stood in Irish Johnny's Tavern, five new stitches in his scarred face under the bandage, and read his poem to the people who only wanted Saturday night to start again with the loud blare of the music and the heavy mass of the dancing and a kind of oblivion. He read without stumbling over the words, not reading but hearing it in the smoke of the gaudy tavern room. Hearing it as it had come to him when he stood in the snow and remembered the girl from grade school.

There was no laughter now. The Duke was doing what he had to do. Fred and Dorothy Margon were listening and no one wanted to look stupid. Walter Ellis and Joey Brant were listening, and no one wanted to offend Mr. Ellis. So they sat, and the band waited to come back and start Saturday night again, and I went to the telephone and called Lieutenant Derrida.

★ ★

Walter Ellis moved his chair and I sat and faced Joey Brant across the tavern table. "High steel pays good money, but you haven't been making

good money in a long time. You were home whenever Professor Margon
went to talk to Alma Jean. You were home when Dorothy Margon
watched Alma Jean. You haven't been working high steel for over a year.
That's why she went out on the streets. You even had to sell Alma Jean's
jewelry to buy whisky at Cherry Valley Tavern. One of those pieces
wasn't hers, though, and that was a mistake. It was the cross The Duke
gave her the night she was killed, the one he wrote about in his poem. You
knew someone else had given it to her, but you didn't know The Duke had
given it to her that night, and it proves you killed her. You grabbed it
from her neck before you knocked her off that bridge."

Lieutenant Derrida stood over the table. The room was watching now.
The Duke with his poem in his hand, Walter Ellis sad, Fred and Dorothy
Margon holding hands but not looking at each other.

Derrida said. "It's the cross The Duke gave her that night, has his
initials inside. Your boss says you haven't worked high steel in over a
year, just low-pay ground jobs when you show up at all. When the bartender, Crow, saw we had proof and motive he talked. You left the tavern
when it closed, didn't get to the sweat lodge until pushing three-thirty
A.M. You brought the jewelry to Crow after she was dead."

Joey Brant drained his whisky, looked at us all with rage in his dark
eyes. "She didn't got to go on no streets. We was makin' it all right. She
got no cause playin' with white guys, sellin' it to old men, working for
black whoremasters. I cut him good, that black bastard, 'n I knocked her
off that there bridge when she was out selling her ass so she could live
high and rich with her white friends and her gamblers and her black
pimps! Sure, I hit her. I never meant to kill her, but I saw that cross on her
neck 'n I never give her no cross 'n I hit her and she went on over."

I said, "Her mother said she would only go on the streets for a big
reason. You know what that was, Brant? You know why she went back on
the streets?"

"I know, mister. Money, that's why! 'Cause I ain't bringing home the
big bucks like the gambler 'n the professor 'n the black pimp!"

"She wanted to hire a psychiatrist," I said. "You know what that is,
Joey? A man who makes a sick mind get better."

"Psychiatrist?" Joey Brant said.

"A healer, Joey. For a scared man who sat at home all day and drank
too much. An expensive healer, so she had to go out on the streets to make
the money she couldn't make any other way."

"Shut up, you hear? Shut up!" His dark face was almost white.

I shook my head. "We know, Joey. We talked to the psychiatrist and
your boss. You're afraid of heights, Joey. You couldn't even go to the edge
of that bridge parapet and see where she had fallen. You can't go up high
on the steel anymore, where the big money is. Where a brave goes. Up
there with the real men. You became afraid and it was killing you and that
was killing her and she had to try to help you, save you. She needed money

to take you to a psychiatrist who would cure you, help you go up on the steel again where you could feel like a man."

"Psychiatrist?" Joey Brant said.

"That's right, Joey. Her big, special reason to make big money the only way she knew how."

Joey Brant sat there for a long time looking at all of us, at the floor, at his hands, at his empty whisky glass. Just sat while Lieutenant Derrida waited, and everyone drifted away, and at last he put his head down on the table and began to cry.

★ ★

Derrida had taken Joey Brant away. The Duke had stopped reading his poem to anyone who would listen. I sat at the floorside table with Fred and Dorothy Margon.

Out on the floor the Saturday night people clung and twined and held each other in their fine shimmering clothes, while in the mural the silent yellow women and bent blue men frozen in the red and yellow sky watched and waited.

"Dance with me, Fred," Dorothy Margon said.

"I'm a bad dancer," Fred Margon said. "I always have been a bad dancer. I always will be a bad dancer."

"I know," Dorothy said. "Just dance with me now."

They danced among the faceless crowd, two more bodies that would soon go their separate ways. I knew that and so did they. Fred would teach and write and go on examining life for what he must write about. Dorothy would go to New York or Los Angeles to find more out of life than an assistant professor, a would-be writer, could give her. What they had to do.

The Duke has one kind of courage and Fred Margon has another. Joey Brant lost his. Fred Margon's kind will cost him his wife. Alma Jean's courage killed her. The courage to do what she had to do to help her man, even though she knew he would not understand. He would hate her, but she had to do it anyway. Courage has its risk, and we don't always win.

★ ★

In my New York office/apartment Sada Patterson listened in silence, her worn plastic handbag on her skinny lap, the ramrod back so straight it barely touched my chair.

"I knew she had a big reason," she said. "That was my Alma Jean. To help her man find hisself again." She nodded, almost satisfied, "I'm sorry for him. He's a little man." She stood up. "I gonna miss her, Alma Jean. She was my last, I always dressed her real good."

She paid me. I took the money. She had her courage too. And her pride. She'd go on living, fierce and independent, even if she couldn't really tell herself why.

*By 1985 my crime novels were changing, moving closer to the
techniques and social/philosophical concerns of my mainstream
work, and the short stories, of course, followed the same path.*

*"Killer's Mind" is essentially about a crime that arises directly
from the psychological pressures, and the personal psychologies,
produced by the stresses and aspirations of a capitalist society. Again,
a newspaper clipping of an actual crime was the immediate impetus,
but the key to telling it was finding the right technique. When I came
up with the idea of presenting both killer's and victim's thoughts and
actions through Dan's putting himself inside their minds, the story
was off and running to be bought for* New Black Mask #6.

KILLER'S MIND

We had an hour before they brought the woman to Captain Pearce's
office, so we went over the whole scheme. Pearce himself, Lieutenant
Schatz from the precinct, and me. The Captain had an open mind. Schatz
didn't. Schatz doesn't like theories, and he doesn't like private detectives
because they have too many theories.

Pearce asked, "Castro planned to kill Roth from the start?"

"It was all that made sense."

Schatz made a noise. "You've got no proof Castro planned anything,
Fortune. How about some facts?"

"All right," I said. "Fact one: three years ago Roth was Castro's junior
partner. Fact two: almost overnight Roth had a big contract that should
have been Castro's, was in business for himself, had stolen Castro's wife,
and Castro hated him."

Schatz shook his head. "Three years is too long to wait."

"Castro didn't wait," I said. "That's fact number three—when I started
to investigate the killing I found out Castro had been working hard to ruin
Roth's business as soon as he realized what Roth had done to him."

"But murder?" Pearce objected. "After three years? In hot blood,
maybe. But Schatz's right. A smart, educated man like Castro should
have cooled down by then."

"Revenge," I said, "and his ex-wife back, and his sons."

"You think he really figured the wife would go back to him after he
murdered Roth?" Schatz said.

"Yes," I said. "She's a practical woman."

Schatz shook his head. "Theory, Fortune, and crazy theory."

"Theory," I agreed, "but all I had. No clues, no evidence, no real facts. From the start I didn't have a damn thing to go on except the theory and my imagination."

From the moment the company hired me — Dan Fortune, Private Investigator — I had nothing to work with except a hunch about Maxwell Castro. No facts, no evidence. Nowhere to even start to prove it all, except to get inside Maxwell Castro's mind. Try to think the way Castro had thought. Become Max Castro — successful architect and bitter man — wrestling with his hate...

He had to kill Norman Roth.

If he was to get his wife back, keep his sons, it had to be murder. There was no other way, not any longer.

He understood his ex-wife. In the end she'd go to the winner. Three years ago it had been Norman Roth, the sure winner. So she had divorced him and married Roth. It was what she would always do.

"You were good for me, Max, but Norman's going to be better." Susan had smiled. "You're getting old. Why should I settle for an old rich man when I can have a young rich man?"

He'd wanted to kill the son-of-a-bitch right then, but three years ago murder was too big a risk. He'd be the first suspect. There were safer ways to stop Norman Roth, and get Susan back. But that was three years ago.

Susan was a woman who shaped her own present and future. He'd always admired that, knew it was the reason she'd married him in the first place. A lot of men had wanted her, and he'd been no more than a small architect getting near middle age in a large firm. It was Susan who had convinced him to strike out on his own, used her contacts to help him, pushed him relentlessly.

It made him proud even now to realize that Susan had expected him to succeed from the beginning. He had been the winner she had to have, each partnership bigger than the last. He smiled as he remembered his climb over partner after partner to build one of the largest architectural firms in the city, the state, maybe the whole damned country.

Until he had taken on Norman Roth as his junior partner.

Young, handsome Norman Roth. Outsmarted by a cheap stud like Roth! That was almost worse than losing his wife and sons, worse than the loss of the Shea contract itself. To be beaten by a fucking pretty boy not even thirty years old.

Castro tossed sleepless in his solitary bed in the large, empty apartment when he thought of that moment three years ago when Norman Roth had his contract and his wife. Of two years ago when Norman Roth, Architects had more business than Castro & Sons. Of...

The frustration and rage squirmed through Max Castro's mind. The rage and defeat inside the mind of a man accustomed to success. A man who knew he was superior. A different breed from normal men. I sensed that rage, that frustration. Felt it inside me as I put myself in his place from the start.

Captain Pearce studied the copy of my report to the company. It detailed Maxwell Castro's actions over the last two-plus years.

"So Castro took hold of himself," I said, "began his fight to destroy Roth. A good architect and a super businessman, he worked hard, took big financial risks. He worked for almost no profit just to get contracts. For a time he actually lost money, but he almost had Roth beaten, on the ropes."

Schatz said. "So why suddenly switch to murder? It doesn't make any damn sense, Fortune."

"His sons," I said. "About three months ago his ex-wife called him, suggested he take her out to lunch. She had a real surprise for Castro."

I saw her, too. Susan Roth, once Susan Castro. She was young, beautiful. Sat there across the white linen and silver of Max Castro's table in the exclusive lunch club after almost three years. Castro looked at the woman he still wanted, who had called so unexpectedly, who smiled at him. I imagined Castro smiling back . . .

"Face it, Susan, you made a mistake. Maybe the first mistake of your life. Admit it, come back where you belong."

The almost soundless waiter brought their drinks. Her martini with a dash of *fino* sherry, his beer: Sierra Nevada Ale brought from the West Coast just for him. She sipped her martini.

"I don't make mistakes, Maxwell," Susan said. "If you did ruin Norman, I probably would come back to you. I admit it because it won't happen. I never back a loser, you know that."

"We all make mistakes, Susan," Max Castro said.

"I don't," Susan said. "You're a winner, Max, up to a point. Norman's going to be a bigger winner." She sipped. "He's younger, more exciting, a lot better in bed. You're all you're ever going to be, Max. It's not enough. I want more."

Castro wanted to hit her right there in the hushed club with its immaculate whites and silvers. Tear her clothes off, show her how wrong she was, but his mind became wary. Did she know something that he didn't know?

She said. "But I didn't come to talk about me. I came to talk about the boys."

"The boys?"

"Norman wants them to be ours, Max, you understand?"

He stared at her. Understand? Understand what?

"We've started proceedings to legally adopt them. You'll be notified in a day or so, but I thought perhaps we could agree on it amicably. Why give the lawyers money?"

"Adoption?"

His mind seemed to be a block of ice. The boys?

"They would, of course, take Norman's name."

Her voice came from across a vast distance, a glacier, the empty Antarctic. *His* sons! Named Roth? *Roth!* The sons of Maxwell Castro to be named *Roth!*

"Never! You hear! Never!"

"I'd really rather not fight about it, Maxwell. But — ?"

The maitre'd turned to look at them. Castro took a deep breath. No court would let a stepfather take children away from the natural father without his consent. It was another trick of hers. He waved for a new bottle of his ale.

"It won't work, Susan," Castro said. "I'm going to ruin your playboy genius. You can't blackmail me with the boys. No court would go against the natural father, and that's me. In case you don't remember where the boys came from."

Max Castro grinned at his ex-wife. She didn't grin.

"The court will back us, Max," Susan said, "but I'd rather stay out of court. The boys are so very young. They'll probably have half brothers soon. They already wonder why they have one name and we have another. We'd really like your consent."

Stunned as he was, he smiled and tried to hide his turmoil and fury behind some light sarcasm. "My consent? Yes, I expect you would like that. Make it all a lot easier, eh?"

"It would, Maxwell. Especially for the boys."

He nodded, looked serious. "A court battle would be very hard on them at their age."

"Then you will sign the papers?" Susan said, just a little too quickly. "Give Norman the boys? Let them take his name?"

His name! The rage welled up inside Castro again. He fought hard to keep it down, hide it. Pretended to consider the impossible idea while inside he boiled. First his contract. Then his wife and his boys. Now his name!

"I'll consider it, Susan." He would not consider it. His mind could not even begin to consider it. But he needed time. He needed to have her think he would, in the end, agree.

"Norman can give them much more than you ever will. You must know that by now."

It was the breaking point. He began to shout in the elegant club, his ale forgotten. The other elite diners turned to look.

"My sons are mine, you hear? I'll never consent, and no court will take them away from me!"

The maitre'd hurried over. Could he help monsieur? The other diners, monsieur. Max Castro sat pale, his fine, honey-like ale forgotten. Susan drank her martini, looked past him.

"The court will back us, Maxwell," she said, her voice soft, almost gentle. "Norman has the best lawyers, influence in the city. We'll prove you're an unfit father. A child-beater. Even a child molester. We have witnesses. You remember that maid you fired? Josie? Those babysitters you threw out of the apartment for smoking pot? There's my mother, my sister. Then the boys themselves. The way you gave them baths, dressed them. Innocent, but when we coach the boys —"

Max Castro sat in the fine club with its white cloth and crystal glasses, shining silver and dark green walls, the silent waiters. He had always loved to eat lunch here, the elegance of it, the privilege, the power. Now he barely knew where he was. Her voice soft as a snake gliding into his ears.

"I can do it, Maxwell. You know me. Think how horrible for the boys. For you."

He would die and his business would go to his boys, and then Roth would have his business too. They would have it all. He had to fight. But would he win? If she told the court he . . . If witnesses said he . . . molested . . . battered . . .

Susan stood up. "You really have no choice, Maxwell. We'll get the boys in the end, with or without you."

Maxwell Castro sat in the lunch club long after his ex-wife had left. A taste of ashes in his mouth. His sons! She was so sure. His stomach was tight, painful. Sure of her lying scheme to steal the boys from him, and of what else? What had happened, or was going to happen, to make Susan so confident?

He went to work, checked all his information sources. It took three days, and then the reports came to him. Roth wasn't ruined. His campaign had failed. Roth was not only unhurt, he was moving upward again. Bigger and better contracts. Roth would succeed, and Roth would get his sons.

No.

Norman Roth would not get Maxwell Castro's sons. This time Susan was definitely wrong. He had a choice. A very clear and obvious choice. He would kill Norman Roth.

I heard Max Castro's inner voice. He would kill Norman Roth as he had really wanted to from the first moment Roth had stolen the Shea contract and Susan. A voice of hate, of fury, of panic at the loss of everything that belonged to him, that whispered over and over in his mind: Kill Norman Roth! Kill Norman Roth!

We still had half an hour before the woman would be brought into

Pearce's office.

"Castro named his company Castro & Sons as soon as his second boy was born," I said. "The adoption threat did it. And the failure of his plan to ruin Roth. I located the confidential reports Castro got after Susan Roth's visit. Roth had been awarded the big Haskins Urban Redevelopment Project contract. General architect, the works. It would save Roth and a lot more. Roth had floated a large loan, had already advanced money to a lot of suppliers. Roth was safe, moving ahead again. With Susan's lies, witnesses, he would get Castro's sons."

Lieutenant Schatz wasn't convinced, paced the office behind its drawn shades. "Okay, he had a motive. But he had to have known he'd be the first man we'd suspect. We'd be down on him before Roth got cold, Fortune. He'd have to have been crazy."

"Most killers are crazy," I said. "But Castro knew he'd be the first suspect. He planned it with that in mind."

I tried to plan it exactly as Maxwell Castro had, our minds a single mind. The pattern was clear as I thought it out with Castro. Alone in his office, smoking cigarette after cigarette, he worked it all out as he would have worked out some delicate problem in architecture. Careful. Logical . . .

Max Castro knew that damn few premeditated murderers went uncaught. It was a fact, and it was precisely *why* murderers were caught — *because they knew that murderers were almost always caught!*

The killer planned, complicated, made an intricate scheme to turn away any shadow of guilt. All possible dangers prevented, all possible suspicion diverted.

The killer attempted to hide his homicide by disguising it as something else. An accident. A senseless killing by some insane night prowler. The panic murder of a startled burglar. Sometimes he worked out a crazy plan to make the murder look like death from natural causes, relied on a shaky verdict of suicide.

He beat his brains out to hide his motive. He planned on an unsolved murder! The police would give up in the face of his cleverness, file the crime away to gather dust and be forgotten.

Or, the most certain of all to fail, the killer laid false trails that would be sure to lead the police to someone else, but that, in the end, always led to him.

The killer, aware of danger, planned a crime so intricate and complicated it was all but inevitable he would be caught.

He, Castro, would not do that.

What a killer could devise, the police could detect. What one man could hide, another man could find. Max Castro would hide nothing.

The answer was simplicity. Exactly like the clean, simple, lines of a modern building. A simple line for a building, a simple plan for a murder.

An obvious murder. A murder that pointed straight to only one murderer. Himself.

Because it isn't enough for the police to know that a man committed murder. They had to prove it. Not that he had wanted to commit murder, but that he actually had committed murder.

He, Castro, would be the logical suspect. He would have no alibi. Definitely no alibi.

The stupid, iron-clad alibi. Stupid, because no alibi could be iron-clad since it was, in fact, an alibi, and not the truth. It was a lie, something that had not happened. The smallest unexpected accident, and the alibi was broken. And once broken, the alibi itself, the carefully constructed lie, became the most damning evidence against the killer.

No, when Norman Roth was dead, the police would come straight to him, Castro. He would say, "Yes, officer, I often thought of killing him myself. I'm glad he's dead. As a matter of fact, I was very near where he was killed at just the time it happened. It's my normal routine to walk past there at that time. I certainly could have killed him, but I didn't. Can you prove that I did?"

Finally, he would not confess. That last and most fatal flaw in any killer's plan. The weakness of guilt that made a man break down under pressure.

Castro would feel no guilt at all. Not for killing one thieving son-of-bitch young stud.

He would not break under questioning.

He was a man of position and wealth.

He could protect himself.

And he would not be forced to confess to save an innocent person. He would be the only real suspect. Susan would have an alibi, a real alibi, and the scene would be completely deserted.

Castro, thought, planned ...

In Castro's mind I felt his excitement as his plan took its final, utterly simple shape. The last little thought — the old criminal adage: If you are innocent, always take a judge alone for your trial. If you are guilty, take a jury. A carefully selected jury. Reasonable doubt, no proof, and a good lawyer.

Captain Pearce chewed on his lip. "So he just walked up to Roth as bold as you please?"

"It has to be," I said. "I've studied his actions, put myself into his mind. There's no other answer."

Lieutenant Schatz swore in the smoky office. "No fingerprints, no useable footprints, no bloodstains, no hair or skin under the fingernails, nothing dropped, no physical evidence at all. A thousand other bricks just like the murder weapon all over that building site. Castro walked past the place at that time every Monday, Thursday and Friday for months."

"All part of his plan," I said. "Those were the days Susan Roth had her alibi. Thursday, the day it happened, was her usual Junior League meeting."

Pearce shook his head. "And Castro planned it all, Dan?"

"Every detail," I said. "As simple as he could make it. Just walked onto that deserted building site and straight up to Norman Roth inside the shell of the unfinished building where no one could see them together."

The perfect place—I heard Castro thinking it. I walked with Castro past the building site of Roth's new job. He couldn't have selected a better site if he had gone to Roth and told the bastard just what he needed for a simple murder. And Roth, good at his work, made a point of visiting his various building sites after the day's work was finished. As Castro knew he did. After all, it was Castro who had taught the younger man to always do just that. You never knew what would pay off in the end.

He watched and waited. The building site was in a downtown business area deserted after six o'clock. It was hidden from view on three sides. The foundation and basement level was already in, the walls just rising.

He began to walk from his office to his own site by way of Roth's building. He bought a newspaper at the same stand each day. People would remember him, yet would not really notice him.

Who really notices a plainly dressed man on a city street in the evening twilight day after day? Who actually remembers the precise time they saw the man if he strolls often along that same city street? They would remember that he walked that way regularly, but would forget the exact day or time when they had last seen him. Was it Wednesday or Thursday? Perhaps Friday?

He chose a drugstore not far from Roth's building site, and stopped there regularly for a soda. The same soda each time, and talked to the boy behind the counter.

"You make a very good cherry soda, son."

The boy grinned. "Thank you, sir."

"Castro," he smiled. "Max Castro. You look like a smart kid. Too smart to be working behind a soda fountain. You should better yourself. Ever consider architecture?"

"Yessir, I sure have!" the boy said. "Architecture's what I want to study in college when I get enough money."

Every murderer needs a little luck.

"Good," he said. "It happens to be my profession. I'm on my way to one of my buildings now. An ex-partner of mine, Norman Roth, has a building going up only a few blocks away. I stop there too, to see how I'd do it better."

He laughed at his own joke, hinted some help might be arranged for the boy, and tipped too much.

"Thank you, sir!"

He made small purchases, browsed among the paperback books and magazines. The browsing was so that the owner of the store would also remember him, and the small purchases did two things. First, they involved him more in the store, increased the chance of being recalled as a regular by customers. Second, they helped his innocent appearance. Who buys a bottle of aspirin, or a tube of toothpaste, on his way to commit murder?

He talked to the boy about Norman Roth. "You go and look at Roth's building, son. Three blocks straight up on this side of the street. His name is on the sign. He's not much of an architect, but he's a publicity whiz."

He talked a lot about Norman Roth. That would look good. Why would a man who planned to kill talk so much about his intended victim to a stranger who would be sure to remember?

He even brought the boy some books. "Read them, they'll help you with the mathematics, help you understand architects and architecture, feel the pull."

"I was always real good at math," the boy said.

"That'll help a lot," he encouraged.

At the actual building site he stopped whenever Roth himself was there. The workmen and Roth's associates noticed him. He made sure they saw him and Roth together, talking.

"Go away, Castro," Roth said. "Anything you have to say to me you can say in court."

"I like to study your cheap work," Castro smiled.

"Stay away from me, you hear? You can't hurt me," Roth sneered. "You're a loser, Castro. Work and women."

"I walk where I please," Castro said, but inside his teeth clenched, and he could barely hold himself from attacking Roth then and there in front of everyone.

He continued his routine, made sure he passed the site just at twilight. Sometimes Roth was there, sometimes he wasn't. Usually he had to wait for Roth to drive up from one of his other sites. Roth wasn't always alone. But most of the time he was.

Twice in July Roth was alone at the site in the late twilight. The first time a group of young boys would not leave the site even when Roth himself tried to chase them away, swore at them in fury as they defied him.

The second time Castro was sure it was the moment. As he walked up the empty street Roth was alone. The younger man went inside the unfinished shell out of sight from the street. Castro moved quickly to the opening without a door. He bent to pick up the brick. Roth suddenly came out of the building again.

Roth was too young, too big. Castro couldn't attack when Roth was facing him. So he smiled, talked to Roth casually as he had done before, then walked away along the street as usual.

His heart pounded, and his head throbbed. But he calmed himself again. He had to wait, be sure...

I felt the blood pound in Max Castro's head, heard his voice tell himself he had to wait. In his killer's mind I heard him say it over and over: wait ... be patient. Haste, that was the greatest danger. Impatience. I heard his mind tell himself day after day: slow, careful, don't panic, don't rush it, slow and careful and wait and there'll be no mistakes...

All the weeks I'd spent digging, checking Castro's routine and route past Norman Roth's building, were on Captain Pearce's desk.

"He could have gone along other streets," I said. "He could have driven. But he was a known walker, and the route was logical enough. Stopping at that drugstore became a routine. He talked to Roth whenever Roth was at the site, casual and hiding nothing."

Pearce nodded. "They all remember seeing him often."

"But not one damned person is sure they saw him the day of the killing," Schatz said.

"He planned it just that way," I said.

"He walked right onto that building site and straight up to Roth," Pearce said. "And no one saw anything. Reasonable doubt all the way. Any jury would buy it."

I felt Castro's mind that last day. Eager, the adrenalin pumping. Time pressed in on him. The day had to come soon. Would it be that day? He couldn't hold himself back much longer, the adoption proceedings would be before the judge soon. I felt the thin thread of tension, his mind fighting...go slow...follow the routine...

He dressed for the twentieth, thirtieth, *nth* time in the cheap suit, checked the buttons again to be sure they were on tight. His fingernails had been cut and filed to the quick for months. He left all his jewelry in his office once more. His hair had been washed every day, all the labels had been removed from his clothes long ago. He carried nothing on his walk past Roth's site that could be dropped, not even his cigarettes or matches.

In the drug store he browsed, bought a new razor, had his cherry ice cream soda. He talked to the counter boy about the books he had lent the boy. That, he thought, was an especially good touch. A smart lawyer could make a lot of the books, with his nameplate in the front, as a sure sign that he couldn't have been planning a murder that day.

A noisy group of juveniles slouched into the store and engaged the counter boy with multiple orders. He was held up a few minutes with dusk settling outside. He didn't think it would be serious, Roth always remained at the site at least five minutes to make his inspection, usually longer, but he decided not to stop and talk to the owner this time as he paid his check.

On the street he walked a little bit faster. He bought his newspaper, spoke briefly to the newsstand man, and continued briskly on to the site. Fast, but not so fast as to attract any attention, and it was just dusk as he reached Roth's building.

The street was deserted as usual, the other buildings dark, the twilight gloomy. The site itself silent. He stood back in the shadows and waited. His plan had always been rigid: walk away instantly if even possibly seen by anyone, and, if unseen, five minutes wait and not a second more.

He had one minute to go when the car drove up. Norman Roth stepped out, seemed to search the twilight for a moment. Castro tensed, ready to follow the younger man into the empty building shell. Roth leaned back into the car to speak to someone.

The car was Susan's car! She was dropping Roth off on her way to her Thursday Junior League meeting. Not even Roth's car would be on the street to attract anyone's attention!

Roth leaned in for a kiss, turned and walked across the sidewalk and the dirt to his partly finished building.

Susan drove off around the next corner.

The street was empty.

It was at just that stage of dusk when it is harder to see than in full night, and no one was in sight anywhere.

Castro hurried across the debris of the building site. As he neared his enemy he slowed, became casual. He made a small smile play across his face. Roth heard him, turned.

"Don't you ever give up?" Roth said.

"No, Norman, never," Max Castro said.

"Go away, Castro. You're beaten," Norman Roth said. "I'm getting the boys, there isn't a fucking thing you can do."

With a gesture of contempt, Roth turned his back and walked into the interior of the unfinished building.

The hate surged through Max Castro. He looked around once more. He was totally alone in the dusk, all but invisible.

He bent, picked up the brick, stepped through the open doorway into the hidden interior of the unfinished building. He looked for Norman Roth, the brick raised.

Norman Roth struck viciously.

Pain hammered through Max Castro's head.

Something dusty, smothering, covered Castro.

The brick in Norman Roth's hand smashed ... smashed ...

I felt the crushing pain as Norman Roth bludgeoned Max Castro with the brick. The shock, and the fear, and the horror, and the final agony of all — the moment of realization that he, Maxwell Castro, had, after all, lost. A loser.

A dead man. The horrible agony as Castro realized he was not the hunter but the hunted. Not the predator but the prey. Outwitted. Dead . . .

I sat in Captain Pearce's dim, silent office behind its drawn shades that seemed to make the city outside light years away.

"It was the only way they could have gotten Castro to that building site under those conditions at that time. He would never have gone there alone, at dusk, unarmed, unprotected, unless *he* was planning to kill *Roth.*"

"Theory, Fortune," Schatz insisted. "Fantasies. That's all you've got."

"It's the only possible answer," I said. "Castro set up the conditions, and Roth and his wife used them to murder him. They manipulated him like Pavlov's dog, goaded him until they were sure he would decide to kill Roth. That was *their* plan, and Castro walked into the trap like a sheep to the slaughter."

Pearce said, "Roth waited inside that building shell." His voice had a tone of wonder. "He hit Castro once with the brick, covered him with a canvas tarpaulin, and hit him four more times. No blood except under the canvas. No witnesses. No fingerprints on the brick or canvas. No clues. The debris on Roth from the building site is useless, he went there every day. Only not that day, he says, and we can't prove he did. No evidence at all."

"Except," I said, "Castro's little mistake."

Schatz shook his head in even more wonder. "Both of them, Castro and Roth, stripped of everything. No labels, no jewelry, no hair or skin under fingernails, nothing. Zero."

"Yeah," I said, "that's what got me thinking. Castro had nothing in his pockets — not even cigarettes, and he was a smoker. No labels. A cheap suit. Fingernails cut to the quick. With Castro the victim, those things made no sense. But if Castro had been the killer, then it made a lot of sense. So I put myself in his mind, dug into what had made him decide to commit murder. Then I did the same for Roth and the woman, imagined how they planned to make Castro try to kill Roth, how they rigged it."

I had been inside one killer's mind, Castro's, and now I put myself inside the minds of two killers. Saw the scene between them, Norman Roth and his wife. Susan Roth once Susan Castro.

Norman Roth lay naked in the giant circular bed of the luxury condominium high above the city. Tall and muscular, lean in the hips, looking up at himself in the mirrored ceiling of the bedroom. "He's going to beat me, Susan. He's a fucking devil in business. He's taking losses, cutting corners, ruining me."

"I like a winner, Norman," Susan Roth said.

Roth stared at her. She was still slim, curved. Her breasts reflected full in the ceiling mirror. She touched Roth in the bed. Her fingers played with his belly, stroked his chest.

"If he beats you, I'll go back to him," she said. "I can't live without what success brings, Norman. Big success. I never lied about that. I'm a practical woman, Norman."

"I'll never let him take you back!"

"Then stop him," Susan said.

"I've tried. I'm almost to the wall. The only way I can stop him now is to kill him."

"All right," Susan said. "Kill him."

Roth blinked at her. "Kill — ?"

She kissed his neck, his throat. Her tongue flicked over his chest as she slid softly against his body.

"He'd kill you," Susan said. "But we'll kill him first."

"How can we kill him? The police would guess at once it was me. Or you. The way he's ruining me, ruining us."

"But they would have to prove it, Norman," Susan said, licked his belly. "We'll make it simple. We'll make Max come to you where there'll be only the two of you alone, and no evidence afterward, and they can't prove you were there when it happened."

"What in God's name would make Castro come to me like that?"

"To kill *you*," Susan Roth said simply.

Roth looked at her, and at her naked body touching him in the big bed. "Why would he kill me? He's already got me ruined."

Her tongue was in his ear now, her breath. "We make him think you're not anywhere near ruined. We convince him you're growing bigger and richer every day, and then we make him have to murder you fast or lose something very important to him."

"Lose what?"

She kissed him, smiled down into his eyes. "The boys, Norman. We start proceedings to legally adopt the boys. We threaten to take his sons from him."

Roth stared, then began to laugh. "*Castro & Sons!*"

"It's the one thing that would make Max commit murder — the loss of Castro & Sons," Susan Roth smiled. "His sons with your name. His business with your name."

Roth laughed aloud. He grabbed her, rolled her over on the bed, kissed her breasts, kissed her mound, kissed ... Stopped.

"The business. It won't work if thinks he's ruining me, and he is ruining me."

Susan Roth stretched and looked up at their naked bodies in the mirrored ceiling. "You've been invited to bid on the Haskins Project. Make your bid so low they must give it to you. They don't reveal details of the bids."

Roth shook his head. "A bid low enough to be sure would lose me a fortune. We'd really be ruined, and for keeps."

"Not with Max dead," Susan said. "A calculated risk, Norman. With Max gone we would get his insurance, his money, and his business. Or the boys would, and that means me. We'd have it all, and you could absorb the Haskins loss."

"I'd need money up front to start the work, make it look good, and no one would give me a loan the way things are now."

"I have my jewels, some securities. We'll get a loan with them as collateral. Maxwell won't know how we got the loan. He'll find you have the contract and the money, are going ahead bigger and better. He'll have to kill you. He's wanted to from the start. You took his contract, his wife, and his male ego. I've known that all along. Now we can use it to save ourselves."

"Will the courts let us adopt the boys without his consent?"

"They will if we can prove Max is an unfit father, a child molester, and we can. Or we'll make Max think we can, and that's all it will take. He wants to kill you, Norman. We'll give him a good excuse, make him tell himself there's no other way."

Roth stared at her, perhaps suddenly a little bit afraid of her. Afraid and excited too. They stared at each other in the giant bed high above the city, Maxwell Castro's ex-wife and his most hated enemy. They looked at each other with the excitement of victory and even of death, and that brought another kind of excitement. An excitement that isn't all that different.

Afterward they began to plan.

They set the business wheels in motion, Susan had her lunch with Max Castro. Then they made Castro wait and wait until he was on the verge of exploding with his hate. When they were ready, they decided on a Thursday, the night of Susan Roth's Junior League meeting.

"I've timed it, Norman," Susan said. "If I drive from the apartment to the Junior League faster than usual, or slower than usual, there is only a difference of five minutes in total time."

Roth nodded. "No jury would convict anyone on a matter of five minutes in city traffic. Not without a lot of evidence."

"And there won't be any. As long as no one sees you with Maxwell at the site, we're safe, and Maxwell himself will make sure no one sees you, eh?"

They both laughed.

"Even if someone notices the car," Susan went on, "it will be just an unidentified car on a dark street for a few moments. It will be far too dark to read the license plate. They'll know we killed him, but they won't be able to prove it."

That Thursday, Roth volunteered to work at the Junior League himself. He told his men that he would not visit the site that night. He told them to knock-off at the regular time.

Roth and Susan went to the empty site. She dropped him off. Castro came. Roth killed him. Susan came back two minutes after Castro had arrived. A minute later Roth walked from the deserted building. Susan held the door open for him, he slipped into the car. Susan ran back around the car to the driver's seat, drove off. Roth looked at his watch.

"Four minutes flat."

They arrived at the Junior League exactly at Susan's usual time. Traffic had been a little lighter than normal. From the numbers, they couldn't have stopped anywhere.

As they worked at the Junior League, they smiled.

I sensed them still smiling when the police came the next morning. They were shocked, horrified, but admitted quite readily that they had hated Castro and were glad he was dead. They admitted they wanted him dead, but they certainly hadn't killed him. They defied the police to come up with a shred of evidence. They knew they had made no mistakes, not one.

In his office above the city, Captain Pearce sighed. "Not one mistake, Fortune. They're right. We've got no real evidence."

"No one else could have done it," I said.

"Or anyone else," Schatz said.

Pearce nodded. "A tramp, a drunk, a psycho, a scared kid surprised trespassing by Castro, and panicked. Some enemy of Castro's we don't even know exists. Roth's lawyer will make hash of a jury."

"Except for Castro's mistake," I said, "and the flaw in the Roths' plan."

Pearce was doubtful. "It's pretty thin, Dan."

"Thin and theory," Schatz said. "No D.A. is going to even go to a grand jury with what you've got, Fortune."

"He won't have to," I said.

They said nothing. They weren't exactly convinced. Neither was I, really, but what I had was all I was going to get as far as evidence was concerned. I hoped it would be enough. I was pretty certain it would be, but it had been a long, hard case and you never know for sure.

"It's funny," I said. "Castro had a perfect plan without a flaw, but he made a mistake. Roth and Susan Roth didn't make a single mistake, but their plan had one flaw — the alibi. They had to have an alibi." I shook my head. "Because their plan had a flaw, and Castro made a small mistake, they're going over."

How do you explain one small mistake? Castro's plan was literally foolproof — if he made no mistakes. What made that one careless moment? I was inside his mind and I didn't know. The waiting? The anxiety to get it done after all those weeks, months? Maybe it was, in the end, only fate, the roll of the dice, working on three lives that last Thursday...

The boy stood behind the soda fountain counter.

"Dead? Mr. Castro's dead?"

"Murdered," I said. "It was in all the newspapers."

"I don't read the papers. I'm studying to be an architect. I liked Mr. Castro."

"Two weeks ago Thursday," I said.

The boy blinked at me, frowned. "Two weeks? Thursday? Gee, maybe that's why I couldn't find him, you know? I mean, it was two weeks ago, sure. Thursday."

"Find him?" I said. "Two weeks ago?"

"He forgot the razor he bought," the boy explained. "We had some loud kids, you know, and he had to wait to pay for his cherry soda and the razor. He walked out fast, forgot to take the package. He was gone maybe three, four minutes when I saw it. The package, I mean. I told the boss, and he let me go after Mr. Castro with the razor. I mean, the boss he liked Mr. Castro too. So the boss took over on the fountain and I went out and tried to catch up with Mr. Castro."

"You went after him two weeks ago Thursday?"

"I knew which way he always walked 'cause he talked to me a lot about going to visit this building of some guy named Roth about three blocks up. I figured he'd probably stop there and I could catch him. Only when I got there, no one was around."

"You went to Roth's building five minutes after Castro left your store, but you didn't see anyone?"

"Not when I got there, and I never did see Mr. Castro. But when I was leaving I saw this big guy come out of the building and get into a car. It wasn't Mr. Castro, and there was only a woman in the car, so I walked back to the store."

"You saw a big man? Could you identify him?"

The boy shook his head. "It was dark. The car was only there a minute. The woman got out to hold the door open for the guy to get in fast. Then they drove off real quick."

"That was all you saw? You're sure?"

The boy nodded. "Except the big guy who come out of the building site had a gray suit, and the woman had a green dress and real dark hair kind of long, and the car was a blue Mercedes four-door."

I stared. "You saw all that in the dark?"

"Sure," the boy said. "When the woman got out of the car I looked close 'cause it might have been Mr. Castro, see? She walked around in front of the headlights to open the door for the big guy and I saw she was a woman. I mean, I saw the guy's suit and the woman and the color of the car because I was looking hard for Mr. Castro."

The boy stands in the dark of that empty street, near that deserted building site, and looks closely at two people for only a few seconds. Because

*he wants to give a package to a man who had forgotten it in his store. A man
who had been nice to him. A man he had gotten to like. So he looks hard,
hoping one of the people is Mr. Castro, but the man is too big and has on a gray
suit, and the other is a woman in a green dress, and the car is a dark blue
Mercedes, and . . .*

In the office Pearce looked at his drawn shades as if he were seeing the
city invisible on the other side. Schatz looked at the door as if he wished
he were on the other side going away.

"Castro didn't need a razor," I said. "So when he was delayed that night
he hurried a little and forgot the package."

"It's not much, Dan," Pearce said

"The boy can't really identify either of them," Schatz said. "He didn't
get the license number of the car, and you got any idea how many dark
blue Mercedes there are in the city?"

"It's enough," I said. "The woman walked in her own headlight beams.
A slim, dark-haired woman in a green dress, and that fits Susan Roth and
what she was wearing according to ten witnesses at the Junior League.
The man fits Roth and what he was wearing. Susan Roth's car is a dark
blue Mercedes."

Pearce shook his head. "I don't know, Dan."

"With what I dug up on all their actions, their motives, my recon-
struction of what happened, it'll probably convince a jury."

"Probably?" Pearce said.

"You want to tell the D.A. about probably, Fortune?" Schatz said.

I said, "Probably is all we'll need."

The interoffice telephone rang. Pearce answered.

"She's here," the Captain said.

The door opened and Susan Roth, formerly Susan Castro, stepped into
the room. She stood tall and poised, a fine-looking woman. Still young and
close to beautiful. Her cool eyes took in each of us in turn.

"Sit down, Mrs. Roth," Captain Pearce said.

"Am I under arrest, Captain?"

"No," Pearce said, "not yet. But Mr. Fortune there has a story we think
you should hear."

Her eyes turned to look at me. She looked at my empty sleeve and my
old tweed sport jacket and cord slacks. Her lips curled faintly. She did not
think much of me, but she sat down, waited, her foot swinging lightly in
its two-hundred dollar pump.

I told my story. From my first hunch about Castro and his murder
plan, through what I had pieced together about Roth and her plan, to
Castro's mistake and the soda fountain boy, and her walking through the
beams of the headlights. She showed no reaction until the soda fountain
boy. At her careless walk through the headlights she blinked. At Roth
coming out of the building site in his gray suit, her foot stopped swinging.

"Castro's company hired me to investigate his murder, Mrs. Roth. They'll do everything they can to convict you and your husband. They've seen my report, they've already hired the best lawyers to work with the D.A. Since you didn't kill Castro yourself, the captain there can offer you a deal to turn state witness. Accessory, five-to-ten years. With good behavior, parole in as little as three years. Maybe less. If you stand up in court with Roth, you could get life without parole."

Her face showed nothing. I was going on my judgment, on everything I had learned, sensed, in the killer's mind of Susan Roth. With both Castro and Roth out of the way, her sons would be rich boys. She would know how to get her share. In prison for life, what good would the money do her? What I had guessed, uncovered, and pieced together might not convince a jury. She might get off. On the other hand, she might not. Say a fifty-fifty chance, maybe a little worse. I figured those odds would be enough for Susan Roth.

"Charge me first," her voice had no emotion, "then I'll tell you how Norman killed poor Maxwell."

It wasn't what should have happened, but it was something. The murder had been mostly her idea, she should have taken the big fall. It's an imperfect world, I got what I could.

The case had been all a matter of getting inside their killer minds. Norman Roth would never make the deal, turn her in. Susan Roth, once Susan Castro, would and did. She was a practical woman.

This is, perhaps, the first Fortune story I was completely satisfied with. The first that presented what I consider an accurate portrait of the world we live in today.

It is another piece that took a long time to develop. Its origin was a small newspaper article about a Puerto Rican boy in New York. Again, I tried for years to write it as a mainstream story, but nothing ever worked to my satisfaction.

Many years later the same small incident between Mexican-Americans and Anglos in Santa Barbara that provided part of the impetus for the novel Cassandra in Red, *gave me the framework I needed to complete the story as a Dan Fortune for the third PWA anthology,* Justice For Hire, *in 1990.*

THE CHAIR

Thin. That was the first thing you saw about him: the scrawny, almost delicate body. The face of a shy young girl on a body not developed enough to be a girl or anything else.

Most of them were thin. With hollow cheeks and bony Indian faces and deep-set dark eyes. One was short and squat like a pre-Columbian Aztec stone statue. One was tall by the standards of the homeland to the south most of them had never seen. But only Molina had the delicate, almost girlish face with the smooth brown skin as the six boys stood sullen before the judge.

★ ★

"His name's Pascual Molina," the deputy public defender had told me when he called. "I have to have something to work with, Dan. It's wrong, I feel it, but I've got nothing I can use."

"You think he's innocent?"

Defense lawyers think all their clients are innocent. Or say they do. That's our system. Thieves, killers and psychos go back on the streets, and that's the risk we take to be sure no innocent man is found guilty. It doesn't always save the innocent or convict the guilty, but it's the best system so far.

"He looks guilty, all six of them do."

That got my attention. A lawyer who said what he really thought?

"But something's missing, and Molina won't talk. He's not like the rest. They're street kids, gang tough. Molina goes to City College at night. He's got a job. His parents are hardworking people who own their home.

Our chief investigator says Molina has no police record at all. The rest have sheets as long as their hair."

"Why don't your investigators follow up on it?"

"We've got six in the killing and it's not our only case. I need special work on Molina."

It's one way a private detective lives. "Okay. Give me names, addresses, everything you know."

★ ★

Now, in court for the reading of the information, I studied Pascual Molina. If he was different, he was trying hard not to show it. As surly and defiant as the rest where they stood in front of the judge who seemed to see them and not see them as he read papers on his high bench and supposedly listened.

Behind the six boys on the hard seats of the courtroom in the fine old Moorish courthouse, the older people sat wrapped in bright colors and black hair and quick Spanish words. The constant whispering and touching of frightened people who understand little of what they are seeing and hearing, but who know that what they are seeing and hearing is important to them. So they shift, and pluck at each other, and talk because they can only wait for someone to tell them what has happened, if it was a time to laugh or a time to cry.

"...on the night of March tenth, about the hour of ten P.M., did commit homicide in the first degree. The victim of said homicide being one Walter Biggs, male Caucasian aged sixteen years. Said homicide did take place in the public park ..."

The droning voice of the information that told in thick legal language how Raul Gonzales, Pascual Molina, Edgardo Montez, Pepe Santos, José Villareal, and José Gonzales, no relation to Raul, did murder one Walter Biggs.

"How do they plead?"

Each, nudged by the deputy P.D., mumbled his, "Not guilty."

The tall one, the oldest, Raul Gonzales aged nineteen, said, "Hey, they gonna lay the gas on us, lawyer man?"

"Keep your clients quiet, Counselor."

Six surly boys remanded to county jail to await trial. The date set. No bail. And loud Spanish wailing went slowly up the aisle of the courtroom and down the polished stone corridors into the city that was named in one language and owned in another.

★ ★

Hands so small and delicate it was hard to imagine them holding a broom handle. Impossible to imagine the smooth brown skin with blood on it, the thin arm feeling the shock of bone as the club struck another human in the dark of a park.

"They want murder one," the lawyer said in the cell. "They say you were laying for white guys. You all planned it and Biggs got killed. Only I don't believe you planned a damn thing. I don't believe you knew what was really going down."

Ankles in the prison pant legs not much bigger than the lawyer's wrists. Chicken legs, a scrawny neck even I could break with my one arm, and a girl's hands. But a club, a knife, a gun are wondrous magic that make a man out of a thin boy, cut giants down to size, grow a delicate kid ten feet tall. A kid who looked at both of us with blank black eyes and said nothing.

★ ★

Detective Sergeant Gus Chavalas is short and dark and everyone thinks he's Latino. He's actually Greek, but if being Latino gives him an edge in the barrio it's fine with him.

"Molina's got no known gang connection until now, and his family's two-hundred percent straight arrow," Chavalas said. "So what, Fortune? He's in a gang now, and we got three witnesses say he was right there laying it on Biggs with a broom handle."

"Witnesses?"

The surprise must have shown on my face. Chavalas laughed.

"The P.D. didn't tell you, huh? We got a transient sleeping under the bandstand, and a smoochy couple with their pants down in the bushes. It was dark, but they saw enough."

"What did they see?"

"Our six Latino guerrillas came into the park looking for trouble. Knocked over signs and benches, ripped up bushes, stomped flower beds. They wanted someone to kick butt on, and Walter Biggs showed up. Not that he didn't feed the fire by being a big-mouth asshole who figured he could handle ten beaners for breakfast. Turns out he was no angel himself, had a record of fights and drunks and drug busts longer than theirs."

"He provoked them?"

"He didn't turn the other cheek," Chavalas said, "but that didn't give them the right to gang him, Fortune. They killed him, and they'll pay for it."

"Molina's studying at City College. He's got a regular job, a steady girl."

"Jack The Ripper was a medical student. Jesse James had a steady girl." Chavalas shrugged. "He went bad. The work was too much for too little bread. School got too tough. How do I know? All we know is Molina was there and in it up to his mustache."

"He hasn't got a mustache," I said. "He can't grow one yet."

★ ★

They were lined up on the flowered couch. The three women and the small boy, stiff and prim, hands in their laps. The father sat apart in a high-backed carved wood chair. No taller than his jailed son but twice as thick, a graying mustache under his straw sombrero, his black eyes were outraged.

"My son is good boy. He work hard, has respect. He does not do what they say. No way."

The small boy was a miniature of his father and his brother. Thin and delicate, wearing a sombrero. The father traditional in the ways of an old country he had probably never seen but claimed as his own because everyone has to claim somewhere.

"Pascual he go to college," the older woman said, "study, know all about America."

The women were somewhere between the country of their language, and the country where they had been born and where they lived. The older woman, the mother, wore a loose print dress proper for a Mexican matron, but American too. The youngest, the sister, sat in a pink party dress with a big bow for company. The third, Molina's girlfriend, was young and slender in a white sheath and low heels, her dark hair short. American clothes and hair, but in the father's house she wore a dress.

A dress and scared eyes. "Pascual couldn't have done what they say, Mr. Fortune. He couldn't hurt anyone."

"What was he doing there that night, Miss — ?"

"Rita Cardenas." She was nervous, and very young, and she didn't look at me. "I don't know what he was doing there."

"He is not where they say," the mother said. "He has good job, goes to the college. He is American."

The father jumped up, his thick mustache bristling. "That is why he is in trouble! He listen to both of you. You make him want to be gringo. You see what is happen?"

There was confusion in the Molina household. To stay apart in your own world — not of the country you were born in, not in the country you are part of — or to cross over into the bigger world? Which one, and what will it do to you?

"When did you see Pascual last before Saturday, Rita?"

"Not for a week ..."

"They go movie Friday ..."

More than one kind of confusion. The two women looked scared as they spoke in unison and said different things.

"Well, what was it?" I said. "A week or the Friday before?"

"We went to the movies," Rita Cardenas said. "I forgot."

"Did something happen at the movies?"

"No."

I looked at all of them. They were scared, that was normal. But they were holding something back too.

"None of you can tell me why Pascual was with that gang?"

"He not there," the mother said.

"I don't know," Rita Cardenas said.

"My son does not do what they say," the father said.

I left them sitting stiff and proper and afraid in their small, neat living room.

★ ★

"The Professor says go on in, Mr. Fortune."

I'd met him at political rallies and militant parties. Officially, he's a Democrat, but he's a lot more radical than that. The FBI keeps an eye on him. He uses his FOIA rights to get their file on him. It's a chess game. They both enjoy it.

"Sit down, Dan. What can I help you with?"

His mustache is as thick as Molina's father's. He looks like Emiliano Zapata. He knows that. It was intended. His eyes are as black as Molina's, and they flashed revolution at me in his nice, comfortable office.

"You don't know what Molina was doing there, Dan?"

He looks a lot more like a Zapatista than a full professor of history and head of the Chicano Studies Department at a major university in the California system.

"He wasn't a gang member, Luis. He goes to college. He has no record. His father and mother are solid, honest people."

"That's the kind it happens to the hardest. The lawyer is right. Something happened. Something that made him see what he'd always really known."

"What had he always known?"

"That the wretched of the earth are that way because the Europeans made them that way. That our society institutionalizes injustice and corrupts human potential to keep itself in power."

"I don't think Molina's read Fannon or Marcuse," I said.

"You never know," he grinned, "but I agree with you. For Molina it was something more immediate, personal. His job is probably bottom menial. At City College he walks around feeling invisible. And something happened to trigger the explosion inside. Like Saul on the road to Damascus. It would have to be some naked trauma. I'd look for a personal kick in the balls."

He has a way with words.

"Thanks, Luis."

He smiled. *"De nada."*

★ ★

It's not as hard as a meet with a Mafia Don or Lt. Col. North when he ran our Latin American policy — Santa Barbara isn't New York or L.A. — but it's hard enough. You have to pass word you want to meet, and maybe you get an answer, maybe you don't. As it does in everything, it depends on what's in it for him.

"You tell the man we don' make this here noise. Raul 'n all of 'em was on they own."

We were at a table in the back of a cantina off Milpas. I'd gotten lucky. The attack in the park had been a private rumble, unauthorized, and he wanted everyone to know that.

"I'll tell them," I said. "How about Pascual Molina? He's not one of your people."

"What you think, man?"

He was another skinny one, but a long way from girlish or delicate. Scars and beard stubble and hard leather. The same hot black eyes, but cold too, with intensity at the edge of sanity. He wore black jeans, a black sateen shirt open to the silver cross in his chest hair, and a black leather jacket like his troops, but he was an easy twenty-two, probably older.

"When did he join?"

"Like, we don' give out that information, right?"

"Why did he join?"

He was half lost in the shadows of the cantina. "Hey, you sees those old movies? Foreign Legion an' all? We don' ask no questions, don' even got to give right name."

"It's a high profile killing," I said. "The good citizens take a bad view of gang kills in their parks, especially outside the barrio. Biggs was an anglo. That's a race riot."

I didn't have to draw pictures for him. He wanted to divert the heat from the killing of Walter Biggs away from the gang. He wanted my voice, I wanted his. Quid pro quo.

In the shadows, he tilted back against the wall. "He come aroun' Saturday mornin'. Raul knows him, he says okay."

"You mean he joined the same day Biggs was killed?"

He shrugged. "José work same place. Molina come aroun' José an' Raul's pad early, say he want to be in gang."

"In the park," I said. "Raul was testing him?"

"No way, man!" His chair legs hit the floor. He leaned across the table. "Raul an' them was high, okay? They go out on they own. Just havin' some fun, you know? This anglo got a gang too, they starts on Raul an' the guys. Raul don' wanna fight, them anglos make 'em. The one guy takes a fall, the others they runs. Cops show, say the bad *cholos* beat up the poor anglo."

He was stating his official position. A communique from the White House, 10 Downing Street, the Kremlin. The explanation of a regrettable but unavoidable incident.

"I'll tell the cops," I said. "You tell me why Pascual Molina came around that Saturday morning?"

"Maybe he just wised up. How do I know? Go talk to Raul."

"Raul would have talked to you," I said.

He stared at me, then tilted back again. "Raul says the kid got in a hassle Friday night. He don' know what, on'y it made the kid wise up, Fortune. He got the real score."

"Yeah," I said. "Look what it did for him."

★ ★

They came out of the high school in twos and threes, to hurry across the wide street deeper into the barrio. Chicanas with their eyes on the ground or watching the older boys who lounged in pickups and low-riders waiting for their girls.

Rita Cardenas came out alone. A few of the lounging Latino lotharios called to her, but she ignored them, walked on looking straight ahead. I caught up with her half way down the block.

"What happened that Friday night, Rita?"

She kept on walking. "Nothing happened."

"The lawyer's helping Pascual. I'm helping the lawyer."

She walked on.

"Those studs outside the school don't think he's coming back," I said. "They figure you're a target chicken now."

She started to cry.

"Is what happened that bad?"

She cried harder as she walked, her head down now. Whatever she knew, she didn't think it was going to help Pascual Molina. She thought it would dig him in even deeper, and she cried all the way to her house. A man came out and watched me. I left.

I walked to Pascual Molina's house. The small boy and the young sister played in the neat fenced yard. The boy vanished somewhere around the house, but the girl stayed to stare at my missing arm. She was older, she remembered me coming earlier.

"Do you know what Pascual and Rita did on Friday night?"

"Go to the movies."

"What movies?"

"Plaza del Sol."

"How come you remember?"

" 'Cause they walk."

"Walk?"

She nodded. "They walk 'cause Pascual only got ten bucks and that's what the movie cost."

"They walked from here to one of the Plaza Del Sol movies, then had to walk back? They must have come home awful late."

"Nope. They don't see the movie. Rita was crying. Pascual was mad."

"When did they get home? You remember that?"

She shook her head. "I was in bed. Maybe ten."

"What time did they go?"

"Maybe six-thirty."

Over a five mile round trip. Two hours to walk there for a nine o'clock show. Two hours back. If they never got as far as the theater, they got close.

"What's your name, honey?"

"Margarita."

"Margarita, did they say anything when they got back? You were in bed, but you listened. Right?"

She giggled. "Rita cried 'cause she didn't see the movie. Rita said Pascual was crazy for a stupid chair. He got real mad. He said Rita should go home if he was so crazy. So she went home. I went to sleep."

"Chair?" I said. "What chair?"

"I don' know."

Stupid chair. The only way was to go out to the Plaza Del Sol and backtrack toward the barrio.

★ ★

There was only one route from the Plaza Del Sol theaters to the distant barrio. A quarter of a mile from the theaters, I saw the furniture out in front of a second hand shop. There were tables, lamps, sideboards, even a hat-rack and an big old refrigerator on the sidewalk. There were no chairs.

A bell jangled as I went in.

"Yeah?"

He was a narrow man in a frayed sweater, worn white shirt with a tie knotted so small it had to have been tied in the same place a thousand times, wool trousers and bedroom slippers. His left forearm was in a cast and sling.

"I was looking for some chairs."

"I got chairs all over, mister," he waved his good arm at the cluttered store, and turned away. "You got bad eyes."

"I didn't see any chairs outside."

He turned back and stared at me, suspicion all over his narrow face. "What's that supposed to mean?"

"It made me wonder if you had any chairs."

He turned away again, grumbling to himself.

"How'd you hurt the arm?"

Now he whirled and snarled. "What the fuck you want here? You some kinda cop? Checking up on me? I got nothin' to hide. I told the hospital and the cop just like it happened."

"Tell me."

Later he could accuse me of impersonating a police officer. But if Pascual Molina had broken his arm, I figured he wouldn't think about it. He'd be too anxious to testify against Molina.

He glared, but he wanted to be sure everyone knew his side of it. "Okay. I'm inside, see, working on some silver. I look up, and there's this goddamn punk Mexican and his señorita out there sitting on two of my chairs. I go out and tell them the chairs ain't there for people to wait for the bus. The little chiquita gets up, but the punk is snotty. He asks me how much for the chairs, you know? I tell him ten bucks. The girl starts crying, but the cholo gives me ten bucks, tells the girl to sit down and then sits down himself and sneers at me, right?"

He looked at me for approval. I said nothing. He growled to himself, went on. "I tell the goddamned beaner the chairs is ten dollars each. He bought one chair. He wants to sit with his bimbo he owes me ten more bucks." Now he laughed. "He ain't got another ten bucks, right? So he says he bought both chairs, I'm a liar. Then I really got mad, told him to get the hell off my chair. I told him to take his fucking chair and get the hell away from my store. Told him I'm going to call the police if he don't take the chair he bought and get away from my store."

He relived his rage like a movie in his mind, his eyes looking right through me. "That's when he hit me. Knocked me down. When I tried to get up he hit me with the chair and broke my arm. I start yelling for the police. The punk greaser and the bimbo run. My wife took me to the emergency. They fixed the arm, I told them and the patrolman just what I'm telling you."

I didn't tell him who I was, or what I was doing. He'd be happy soon enough when he knew the trouble Molina was in.

★ ★

Thin and undeveloped even close on the narrow cell bunk, the girlish shoulders bent, the weak light dim on his black hair.

"I talked to Rita about that Friday," I said. "I talked to the store owner. You broke his arm."

"That guy'll find out soon what's happened," the lawyer said. "He'll tell his story in court."

"It's why you joined the gang," I said, "why you were in the park that night."

He didn't look up. "My old man, he got a big mustache, you know. He's a little guy, but he got this big mustache. Down in Mexico a man always got a big mustache, right? He's real macho, my old man, a big shot in the barrio. Only he works all his life digging holes for the white man."

When he did look up at us, the black eyes were anything but soft. "I never been to Mexico. Maybe I go sometime. Sit on the beaches. Not the good beaches, they're for the rich gringos. Go to the mountains and eat bananas. My aunt she goes once. She don' like it so good. She's got a white boyfriend, right? I mean, he's a dago an' no whiter than me."

His tongue lived in three worlds. Whole sentences from the high school where all boys are created equal. Words from the barrio slums where no one is equal. And the accent of salsa and mariachi and the past of Castillian cavaliers and slaughtered Indians and silent slaves both black and brown.

"Molina," the lawyer said, "you joined the gang only that morning. You should never have been in that park. Give me something I can use. What happened that Friday?"

The black eyes that were neither thin nor like the eyes of a girl studied us. "You got a girl, lawyer? I got a girl. Young, but real nice. She likes movies. All those rich white girls, you know? I got a job all day, an' I go to college three nights, so we don' got a lot of time to go to the movies. There's this real good movie she wants to see. It's out by Plaza Del Sol. Okay, I say. Friday we eat at McDonalds, an' take the bus to that movie. I promise my girl."

Someone was crying in another cell. I always feel buried in a jail or prison, stifled, crushed by the walls.

"Thursday I have a bad day pushing my stinking broom on the job, do lousy at school, get into a crap game late. All I got Friday is fifteen bucks. My girl she says, 'Okay, we eat cheap and we walk to the movie.' All the way to Plaza Del Sol! She says it's a nice day, we start early. So why not, you know? I walked that far before. Only she ain't walked that far, and she got to stop and look in all the stores. I think we never gonna get to the movie she looks in all those stores." He looked at the lawyer, then at me. "Why the chicks got to do that, you know? It makes a guy feel like hell when he ain't got the money to buy all the stuff in them stores."

Somewhere a man whistled the same song over and over, flat and off key. Voices in the silence of the jail told him to shut up. "Hey, man, shut up, for chrissake!"

"We walk and she's thirsty. I tell her we just got bread for the movie. She get hot an' tired. I see this store with chairs out in front. Old wood chairs all beat up. My girl she looks at them chairs, and I say, 'Go ahead, sit down, honey. We're almost there, we got time.' So we sit and, man, it feels good. All the people walk by and look at us, but we don' care, you know? We sit maybe ten minutes. Then this guy comes out of the store yellin' like all hell. I mean, he's yelling like he's crazy. 'Hey! You *cholos* get outta those chairs! Get the hell out of those chairs! What the Christ you dumb beaners think you're doing?' Like that, you know, and all the people on the streets lookin' at us. 'You fucking greasers think you own the city? Lazy fucking bums! Get out of my chairs!'"

Two roaches scuttled across the jail floor. Molina's foot moved suddenly, crushed one. The other wobbled in fear across the concrete and out of sight.

"'You gonna pay me? You gonna buy those chairs, *pachuco*? Who buys them they see you beaners in them? No white man's gonna buy them, *cholo*.'" In the polyglot jargon of a boy with the streets of the barrio under the smooth skin of his unmarked face. "They all looks at us, you know? My girl she jumps up, she's gonna run away. She's scared, and they're all laughin'. I grab her. I say, 'Sit down, baby.' She starts cryin'. I say to that son-of-a-bitch store guy, 'We just restin', mister. *Un momento por favor!*' Jesus, I'm talkin' Mex! The guy laughs, looks at the crowd. They're all laughin'. So I say, 'How much? For the chairs? How much?' My girl she's cryin', she wants to run. The big-mouth bastard's laughin', my girl's cryin', so I say, 'How much you want for the fucking chairs?' "

Down the corridor the man still whistled. Flat and off key and no one shouted now. As if they knew it was really useless to try to stop a man who had to whistle in his jail cell.

"The guy stops laughin', says, 'Ten bucks. For you, *señor*, ten dollar American. Special. You got ten dollar, *señor?*' So I take the ten bucks for the movie and buy the goddamned chairs. I make my girl sit down again, and I sit too. All the people look and they don't laugh no more. The guy he says, 'The chairs're ten dollars each, beaner. Ten more bucks.' I tells him he sold both fucking chairs, he's a fucking liar. He grabs me, yells get out of his goddamned chair and get the hell away from his store. He's gonna call the cops. He's gonna charge me with trespassing and trying to steal a chair. So I hit him. When he gets up I hit him with the chair and knock him down again and he starts yellin' 'Thief' and 'Robber' and 'Police' and me and Rita run. We walk all the way back to my house and she cries all the way and we fight and she goes home. Next day I go find José and Raul and tell 'em I want to join the gang and go get fucking anglos!"

In the silence of the cell, his voice echoed away. His black eyes watched us with the question in them. I didn't have an answer. The lawyer put his papers into his briefcase. The cell smelled of sweat and urine. Molina looked at us, and his thin shoulders moved. A delicate, almost imperceptible shrug, the black eyes flat and empty, the girlish face expressionless.

"They can't get murder one," the lawyer said. "I'll plead you guilty to involuntary manslaughter. They probably won't buy that, but maybe they'll go for voluntary."

I said, "We'll bring in that store owner, put him on the stand. We'll put Rita up there. I'll get the right people to testify you were never in a gang. We'll bring in your parents."

Molina's black eyes had no expression at all.

"*Gracias,*" he said.

A few years ago, an editor on a magazine I'd submitted a story to wrote back to say, "You certainly don't take on pissants." Or words to that effect. She was talking about a mainstream piece that, among other indiscretions, criticized the position the Catholic Church hierarchy has taken on what in Latin America is called Liberation Theology.

I guess this story is another example of that tendency of mine to write about large controversial issues in my fiction. It came directly from a case in California. Even the title is a quote from the sheriff involved in the real case. The story itself, of course, is complete fiction. That's what fiction is: the combination of extrapolation from specific fact, with creative imagination to create what we hope is universal.

Dealing with controversial social issues isn't the most popular way to write fiction, and this story found no publisher in the U.S. In England, Maxim Jakubowski had no problem with it, and bought it for his Constable New Crime I *in 1992. This is its first publication in this country. Maybe it comes at the right time, the subject has been much in the news of late.*

MURDER IS MURDER

"The coroner's doctor ruled he died of cancer."

Outside the old-fashioned high windows of the Sheriff's office, the brown hills of rural California were painted with dark green oaks and ringed by the distant mountains against a cloudless blue sky.

"Coroner's doctors make mistakes, Fortune."

The Sheriff didn't like me. He didn't move a muscle in his weathered face as he said it: Coroners can be wrong. He didn't have any more faith in his local coroner's doctors than he did in private investigators.

"If the coroner sticks to his ruling that Mr. Rainey died of cancer, Sheriff, what can you charge Mrs. Riata with? She didn't use a gun or any other weapon. She didn't threaten that nurse, she only fooled her. If she did anything."

"Depends on the evidence what we charge her with."

"What evidence?"

"The evidence we're going to present to a grand jury maybe tomorrow. You didn't know we had evidence?" The Sheriff smiled. "Shay, that's the smart lawyer who hired you, knows all about it. Probably figures to make a bundle when Shelly Riata gets all her Dad's money."

★ ★

The only high-rise in San Remo, the county seat, is five stories high and seventy years old. Mr. John Shay, Attorney-at-Law, had the biggest office on the fourth floor. An endless view facing east in the late afternoon. Out over the trees and dust of the old cattle town, the rich irrigated farmland, the brown hills and the distant purple mountains.

"If you had the evidence, why send me to the Sheriff?"

"You might have picked up something he's held back. Anyway, I wanted him to know we're investigating."

Shay was blond, handsome, and not that old, with the thick hair and smile of a TV preacher. The best lawyer in the county, and probably the richest. Lawyers don't get rich by defending the complicated and highly unpopular cases.

"You like Mrs. Riata, don't you?"

"I like her," Shay said.

"And her money?"

He leaned back in his high chair, swivelled to his windows. Lawyers do that to impress you with their weighty thought, or to let you know you're out of line, have said something stupid.

"I've known the Rainey's all my life, Fortune. Shelly has always had money, won't get that much more from her father."

"But she gets it?"

He swivelled back to face me. "She gets it."

"A man with Alzheimer's and advanced cancer had to have someone taking care of his money. The daughter?"

"Me," Shay said, "and it's all there."

It was something I could check easily enough about a prominent citizen of a small town, so was probably true.

"Show me the evidence the Sheriff thinks is good enough to go for murder one?"

Shay handed me a file folder from his desk, looked at his watch, stood. "We're due in court tomorrow morning for bail."

★ ★

Central California is essentially a desert.

The sun going down behind the western mountains faded from reds to purples to dark blues and a final long line of pale gold that edged the black silhouette of the Coast Range. Over a Red Tail Ale and a full bowl of peanuts in the motel bar, I read through the file folder.

Testimony of Nurse Ujcic: "*I was on night shift in Mr. Rainey's room. Mrs. Riata come every night to be with poor Mr. Rainey. He didn't talk much, you know, so she talked to me all the time, asked a lot about the life support system. She was so nice, so worried about Mr. Rainey, I thought it'd help keep her mind off everything so I told her how it all worked.*

"*... It was late, way past visiting hours, but we make an exception for the loved ones of terminals, you know? We'd had this emergency, I'd missed my* *dinner, so when she said she'd ring if anything looked wrong I went to get something to eat. I come back in maybe forty minutes, the cafeteria was crowded, you know? I mean, I don't usually take so long to eat, and ...*

"...She was sitting next to the bed right where I'd left her. She was holding his hand and crying so I started to cry myself and comfort her. I mean, I could see he was dead there in the bed, and I was so sorry for her, and then I seen she'd pulled out the whole life support system, everything, and he was dead."

Red Tail is good ale. You only get it in California. It's maybe not as good as Sierra Nevada or that great Belgian Chimay Ale the Trappists make, but it's good. The bartender brought me another. He didn't seem to like me either. I guess he agrees with the sheriff on the competence of coroner's physicians.

> *The letter found in Mrs. Riata's house:*
> *Tuesday. The day after Memorial Day. The day after you.*
> *Shelly sweetheart,*
> *I can't believe I'm writing this, but when I left you last night it all suddenly seemed hopeless for us. I don't think either of us can take much more. The last year was bad enough. Seeing you so little because you had to take care of him day in and day out. Always tired, worn out. What's it going to be like a thousand miles apart the next year or so?*
> *You say you can't come with me, can't leave a man helpless with cancer and Alzheimer's. But I can't refuse this job, and I don't think I can live alone or maybe make once a month visits to that awful house. After how much you were hurt by that bastard Riata leaving you, I hate myself for saying all this, but what else can I do?*
> *Your father could live for years. Now he's on life support, may go any minute, but, honey, I've heard that before. What if he gets better again, the cancer goes into remission, they take him off the life support?*
> *Sweetheart, you have to make a choice. What can you really do for him the nurses and attendants can't? Let go, darling, let go now and come with me, save US.*
>
> > *All my love,*
> > *George*

★ ★

I sensed his bulk behind me before he spoke.

"Seems like maybe she didn't put him out of his misery when she pulled those plugs," the Sheriff said. "She put her new man out of his misery."

"Your own coroner's doctor said cancer killed him, Sheriff." I drank the Red Tail. "You keeping an eye on the out of town snooper?"

"You registered the way you're supposed to, gave the motel address. I just thought maybe you'd like to talk to someone else who can clue you in to the truth."

"What truth? Shelly Riata hasn't denied pulling the plug on her father, has she? He had more than a little problem, and she says right out someone had to solve it for him and she did."

"Maybe she didn't solve his problem, Fortune. Maybe she solved hers."

★ ★

Cynthia Rainey was a slender blonde of forty-plus. In tailored gray silk slacks and a starched shirt that looked like a man's pin stripe button-down but wasn't, she sat and talked to us on the patio of her large ranch house in the cooling night, sipped her margarita.

"I was quite close to my uncle after my father died, and Shelly and I have known each other all our lives."

Margaritas are too sweet after good ale. The silent Mexican maid or housekeeper brought me beer — Bud or something like that. Cynthia Rainey insisted. Before she would talk to us we had to go out to the patio where a small spread was set out, sit on the redwood furniture, and have the girl bring us our drinks. We were guests.

"It's a terrible moment," Cynthia Rainey said, "but at least we can still be civilized."

After a suitable amount of small talk, and the arrival of a second round on the tray of the silent maid, the Sheriff got down to the business of our visit.

"We typed up your statement. While you sign all the copies, Ms. Rainey, maybe you could tell us how you happened to find out about this business deal of your cousin's?"

"I'm afraid Shelly never did have good business judgment, or any other kind of judgment. Anyone could have told her Joseph Riata was a cheat and womanizer before she married him. He walked out on her, and now he comes to her with one of his stupid get-rich-quick schemes."

"Riata lives in town?" I asked.

Cynthia Rainey bent to sign the papers on the redwood table beside the cheese. "No, he left years ago, but she still sends him money. She admitted that when she told me about the great business opportunity he was offering her. She said it was really good, but Uncle Frank's medical expenses, the extra help, had drained her so much she wasn't sure she had enough left to risk."

The Sheriff said, "Her father's estate would bail her out?"

She signed the last copy of her statement. "I can't say that, Sheriff. I have no idea exactly how much money Uncle Frank had. Of course, there is also a large insurance policy. I think I'm a small beneficiary too."

Tears suddenly appeared in her eyes as she looked up at us. "Uncle Frank and I visited and talked each Friday. Now ..."

She shook her head, almost violently.

★ ★

The insurance agent did not appreciate being called on so late.

"I told the Sheriff's people everything there is to tell about Frank Rainey's insurance, Mr. Fortune. Don't know if we pay Shelly or not, never had a murder case. The money got to go to someone."

He wore dirty chino's and a sweatshirt, watched his evening program on TV over my shoulder.

"I represent Mrs. Riata and her lawyer," I said. "Tell me."

His wife hovered behind me ready to trot out hospitality for the visitor from an overstocked refrigerator. The agent ignored her.

"There's nothing to tell, damn it. Rainey took the policy out thirty years ago. Face value of a hundred thousand. Martha is beneficiary with —"

"Who's Martha?"

He gave up on his nightly sitcom, glared at me. "Rainey's wife. She died six years ago, so Shelly automatically became beneficiary with his two nieces and one nephew. The nieces and nephew get five percent each, Shelly gets the rest."

"No sudden, recent, or unusual changes?"

"No way. Frank was out of it with Alzheimer's. John Shay had power of attorney, never did a damn thing about the policy. It was paid up years ago. Standard and routine."

★ ★

Dawn is always grayer in the corridors of a jail. The silence echoes to distant coughs, a weary groan, the heavy shoes of the guards, the clang of metal doors. The lawyer, Shay, was there ahead of me.

"Two days to get bail set," Shay fumed. "They fought me every inch. 'It's for her own good, your honor.' 'We're afraid of what she might do to herself, your honor.' That fucking Sheriff is on a goddamn vendetta." He glanced at the woman with us in the small room. "I'm sorry, Shelly."

She was a small woman who wore her own clothes. Whether they'd never put her in jail clothes, or they'd let her get ready for the preliminary hearing, I didn't know. A simple shirtwaist blue dress, black low heel sling backs, a single rope of pearls, a blue ribbon in her dark blonde hair. She looked older than her cousin Cynthia Rainey, was probably younger. Mid-thirties, and Frank Rainey had been in his late-seventies. Old parents, the daughter too young to handle old age that well.

"You hear much worse than that in here, Mr. Shay."

She smiled at him. It was a tight smile, on edge. The "mister" sounded genuine. If they had anything going, they hid it well, and Shelly Riata didn't look in condition to hide much. Her almost classic oval English face was pale and drawn. Her slender hands gripped a wadded facial tissue and still managed to twist and shake at the same time. She was scared, that was clear in her almost animal eyes as she looked at me, stared at the empty sleeve of my missing arm, but there was something deeper than fear.

"Can you answer questions, Shelly?" Shay was almost gentle.

"Questions?" Her long fingers twined. "What else have I been doing since...since..." She shook her head angrily, looked in that instant almost like her cousin. "Your questions, the Sheriff's questions, the town's questions, everyone else's questions, my own questions."

She was up. And down again. Leaned forward on the hard metal chair in the bare room and stared at her feet, at the floor, at nothing at all. When her voice came again, it was almost a whisper.

"My own, those are the hard questions. Did he want me to do it? He always said he did, but did he really? He was in such pain. The physical was bad enough, but the mental." She slowly pounded her hands on her knees in the silent jail room. "He was a big man, my father, so active, always riding around the ranch, fixing machines at the juice plant. A thinking man. Then he was nothing. A shell. Brainless. He had such pain inside, don't you see? I couldn't go on pretending any longer. He'd made me promise, but did he mean it? Did I do right? Did I?"

She looked up at each of us in turn. We said nothing. She looked down again. "He was my father, I owed him that much."

Shay said, "Can you prove he made you promise, Shelly? Did anyone else hear him? The servants? His brothers?"

"My mother." She shook her head. "She's dead too. They're both dead now." She looked at a bare wall as if she could see them, her old parents. Or see death.

I said, "The Sheriff has a letter, Mrs. Riata. From your boyfriend, George. He —"

"Letter?" She looked up. "Why would George write me a letter? I never got a letter from George. He only lives a mile away. We see each other almost every day. I don't —"

I showed her the letter, read it to her. She watched me the whole time. Sat in the metal chair and watched me. "Was George going to leave town, Mrs. Riata? Leave you? Break up for good? If you didn't get away from your father?"

Her face was drawn, almost dead. "I never saw that letter. George never wrote that letter. He's tired, we all are, but he never wrote that. It's hard on us all, draining us all. But mostly my father. He was so tired, so hopeless. It wore us all out, even George. But he —"

"The letter, Shelly," Shay said. "The Sheriff says he can prove it was written on George's typewriter."

"No!" She stood in the jail room. "I never got any letter. He never wrote any letter. George isn't like that."

I said, "Tell us about your ex-husband's scheme that's going to make you a bundle — if you have enough money to invest. The kind of money you're going to get from your father's estate."

"Fortune..." Shay began.

I ignored him, pressed her. "You were tired, finished. Your boyfriend was leaving you. You had a great deal with Riata but not enough cash to take it. Who knew how long your father might take to die? With him gone you'd be free, have all his money and the insurance on top of it. No wonder —"

Shelly Riata began to shake her head half way through my tirade. And after a time she started to talk, her voice rising over mine until I stopped and just listened to her.

"... all lies! George isn't like that. Joe always has his get-rich-quick ideas. I never listen to him. I send him money, but I'd never invest. I'm not that much a fool. Why are they all lying? Why is it happening? Did I do right? I don't know. I..." Her voice slowly faded away until the room was silent.

Shay began to talk softly to her, tell her she had to get ready to go into court. His voice was calm, soothing.

★ ★

The vast Pacific stretched beyond the great bay as San Francisco International appeared under the wing of the commuter plane. It's the future, the Pacific Rim, but my mind was on today, on what we are, not on what we might become.

It was past eleven before I located Joe Riata. He worked in a small downtown brokerage. They told me he was out on client business, they didn't know when he'd be back. I thought about how Cynthia Rainey had described him, and went to his apartment in the old North Beach section. He was there, wouldn't open the door until I said I was from Shelly. He was tucking in his shirt when he did open up. The woman who had been lying on the couch with him disappeared into another room.

"What about Shelly, Mr. — ?"

"Fortune. I need you to tell me about her."

"Tell you? I thought —"

He was all dark Greek god and smoldering stud, but the god was tarnished and balding, and the stud had puffy eyes and wore stained pants.

"I hear you have a business deal she's interested in."

He brightened instantly. "Hey, yeah, the sweetest you ever saw." He brushed newspapers and a high-heeled shoe off one of two shabby armchairs in the seedy living room, waved me to sit. "Shelly send you to buy in too, Fortune?"

"She's that interested? Ready to buy in?"

He sat down eagerly on the old couch facing me. "She loves the deal. Prime stocks, undervalued as all hell, ready for the takeover I know's coming. She's going in all the way, and I can get you in too."

"She's going in on your deal? When she gets the cash?"

He laughed. "What when? Shelly's loaded, always has been. Sometimes I think I was crazy to toss all that, but ..." He shrugged, sighed, shook his head. "Hell, maybe we'll get back together yet. She still sends me cash when I need it, you know? A nice kid, Shelly, and with plenty of the long green."

"She didn't need her father's money to buy into your deal?"

His smile faded a little. "Her father?"

I told him. He stared at me for some time before he said what sounded like a long, slow breath, "Jesus."

"The Sheriff says she shut down the life support to solve her problems not Rainey's. That she really murdered her father to get free and get money for your deal."

Riata never moved from where he sat on the couch and leaned toward me, but everything else about him changed. His eager face and quick laugh, his confident manner, his bright eyes. The face sagged, the manner slid away, the eyes saw something a lot different. "Hell, she didn't need even her own money, Fortune. She wasn't interested in the deal. I was laying that trip on you to convince you to buy in. I never could con Shel, she knows me for what the hell I am. A two-bit flop who never said anything straight to anyone my whole life. I'm not going to change, but Shel plays straight no matter what, and she never thought twice about any deal of mine."

"Who else did you lay it on to get to buy in?"

His mind was something else. Probably himself.

"Who else?"

"Down in San Remo. Who else did you tell that Shelly was going to buy into your deal?"

He shrugged. "Hell, everyone I could get on the phone. It really is a pretty good deal, Fortune, and I tried all of them I still know down there."

"And told them Shelly was eager to buy in?"

"That sounds like me." He finally tried to grin again, but his eyes weren't in it.

★ ★

From John Shay's office in the ancient five-story high-rise in San Remo the early afternoon hills were more brass than gold, and the far off mountains were blacker, more menacing.

George Bates said, "I never wrote any letter to Shelly."

"The day after Memorial Day," I said. "A Tuesday. You'd spent Memorial Day with her, you couldn't believe you were writing the letter."

"You must be insane!" His mouth even hung open. "Who are you?" He looked at Shay. "Who is he, Shay?"

Shay told him.

"A detective?"

I said, "Last year in the same town was bad, what's it going to be like a thousand miles apart? Her father could live for years, a vegetable in constant pain. She had to make a choice. Let go and come with me, save us."

George Bates only stared at me.

"You're taking a job in another town?" Shay said.

"Retraining on new equipment at my company's head office for six months, that's all. Shelly and I talked it over. It's no big deal. For God's sake, we're grown up, we can be apart six months if we have to."

I said, "Do other people in town know it's only for six months?"

"I don't know what other people in town know."

"The letter was written on your typewriter."

I held the letter up for him to read. He paled.

"It is your typewriter?" Shay said.

George Bates nodded, stared at the letter that hung from my lone hand in the sun of the office above the small city.

"Where do you live, Mr. Bates?" I said. "A house? Condo? Apartment? How could someone —"

He looked from me to Shay and back again. Then his face seemed to go blank. "The Tuesday after Memorial Day? I wasn't at home the Tuesday after Memorial Day. I wasn't even in town the Tuesday after Memorial Day. I was —"

"Can you prove that, Bates?" Shay leaned across his desk in the silent office.

"I was at my head office. I flew there on Memorial Day. Shelly took me to the airport. I was there a week. A thousand miles away. I only got back two days after . . . it happened."

I said, "Who has access to your house while you're away?"

"Access?"

"Keys."

"Well, Shelly, of course. The cleaning woman. My regional boss. In case I take work home and get sick or go on a trip and he needs something. After they put Shelly in jail, she gave her key to her cousin Cynthia so she could feed my cats while . . ."

I said, "Get the Sheriff on the phone, Shay."

I was out the door before Shay hung up.

★ ★

In the evening sunlight there were no Margaritas on the redwood table of Cynthia Rainey's elegant patio. The slender blonde wore the same silk slacks and starched shirt that looked like a man's button-down but wasn't, only this time the slacks were pale green and the shirt was green striped. She probably had fifty of each, all in neat rows in her closet. She wouldn't be a woman to try anything different, change her ways.

I said, "Mr. Rainey took his insurance out himself years ago, nothing new happened since he became ill."

The Mexican maid or housekeeper appeared in the patio door with the tray. Cynthia Rainey angrily waived her away. We weren't guests this time.

"I never said there was anything wrong with Uncle Frank's insurance."

"You sure as hell implied it," Shay said.

The Sheriff said nothing. He had met us at Cynthia Rainey's big ranch house reluctantly. Only after Shay put on the screws. He sat with his weathered face impassive, his legs crossed, one booted foot swinging.

I said, "Joe Riata called you to try to get you to invest, told you Shelly was going in with him. In reality, she had no intention of investing, turned him down cold. But you didn't know that, built a whole fantasy to convince people Shelly killed her father for his money."

Cynthia Rainey sat silent. Shay shook his head with disbelief. The Sheriff's boot swung more violently.

"You went to feed George Bates' cats the day after Mr. Rainey died when Shelly couldn't, and you wrote that letter on Bates' typewriter. You put it in Shelly's house so the Sheriff would find it. He did, and jumped to the conclusion you wanted — that Shelly had killed her father to solve her problems not his. You thought or assumed Bates had left town the day after Memorial Day, but he left on Memorial Day, was already out of town that Tuesday night. He couldn't have written the letter then."

"Why?" John Shay said. "You had to know Bates would deny writing the letter, that Shelly didn't need her father's money. You knew there was nothing wrong with the insurance, that the coroner had already ruled Mr. Rainey died of cancer. Why?"

The Sheriff stopped his foot. Cynthia Rainey sat on the redwood chair like a stone statue. Her face grew red, her dark eyes manic in the evening sun, her thin mouth twisted into a grimace that was almost a snarl. But no snarl came out, no sound at all.

I said, "Because murder is murder, right, Ms. Rainey? Shelly Riata killed her father no matter what anyone says."

"She murdered him!" She was up on her feet. "I don't care what some stupid coroner's doctor says. She killed Uncle Frank and she has to pay for that. She murdered her own father. She took a human life."

"What life?" I said. "An hour, a day, a week, a month, all in helpless and hopeless pain?"

Her voice was almost a scream. "Life is life!"

"Is it?" I said. "Sometimes I wonder."

"That's blasphemy. Arrogance. Wrong is wrong. She killed her father. Murder is murder."

The Sheriff's men took her away. Shay went to tell Shelly Riata there would be no grand jury, no charges. The coroner's verdict would stand. I stood with the silent Sheriff outside the big house in the gaudy sunset of a rural California evening.

"What can you charge Cynthia Rainey with?"

"Obstructing justice, interfering with the police." He looked at me. "What do you want me to charge her with?"

I looked up at the purple sky that faded toward twilight, and then at his stone face. "You won't charge her with anything. You could have done everything I did, found the truth of that letter, the insurance, the business deal that never existed. But you wanted it all to be true as much as Cynthia Rainey. Murder is murder."

The Sheriff opened his car door. "The coroner's doc blew it, Fortune.

She's responsible for her father's death. She should be charged with first degree murder."

I watched him drive away. He was probably a good lawman, would probably have done his job sooner or later. Or maybe not. Shelly Riata was a murderer. She had to be punished.

As I'm pretty sure you've picked up on by now, during the Eighties and Nineties I wrote a short story only when someone asked me to — and offered money. When your entire income depends on writing, well — ?

This one was written for Deadly Allies I, *the collaborative anthology of Private Eye Writers of America and Sisters in Crime, edited by Bob Randisi and Marilyn Wallace. The impetus was the newspaper clipping of a pro athlete's rampage in a motel room. To me this told the story of what happens to human potential in a society completely dedicated to the bottom line and fast buck.*

No one escapes the devastation. Jake Butler's overt tragedy is the covert tragedy of us all. Even writers, as witness the first paragraph of this note.

ROLE MODEL

His voice shook so much it sounded far more than three thousand miles away.

"Brett Darcy, Fortune. They killed Jake. The cops just told me. Get here as fast as you can. All expenses."

It was 6:10 A.M. in Santa Barbara. In bed beside me, Kay rolled over and put her head under the pillow.

"Jake who?"

"Good God, Fortune, is there more than one Jake I'd call about at this hour? Jake Butler. Number 99. The Bonecrusher. They shot Jake Butler in some stinking alley."

Brett Darcy owned a football team that had played in more than one city, kept his main office in New York no matter where the team played. He was a lawyer, had a lot of other irons in the fire, New York was the place to be. But the team was the apple of his eye, and Jake Butler had once been the rock the team was built on. I'd worked for Darcy before, but New York has a lot of detectives.

"Why me, Darcy?"

"Because you know that Captain Pearce. I'll cry for Jake, Fortune, he was the best lineman I ever had. But I'd heard he was on the skids, and I don't want it to rub off on the team. I want our own man on the case so we have time to cover any slime."

It was honest. I gave my terms, including a week up front when dealing with billionaire businessmen in case things don't turn out right. He took my terms without a murmur. He's a sharp man, rich and educated.

The new breed of sports owner. I promised to be in New York by five or six, hung up and dressed.

"I suppose you have to go back once in a while," Kay said. "Just to keep me from taking you for granted."

"Don't pout, you're too dignified even naked. Get up, I'll cook breakfast."

★ ★

Captain Pearce's office gets more like old Captain Gazzo's every time I see it, especially now that I live out in California and don't see it that often. Messy and neglected as if he doesn't give a flying damn for such small things anymore. In perpetual midnight, shades drawn all hours. Maybe, in the end, it goes with the job.

"How do you like it in Tinsel Land, Fortune? La-La Town?"

"That's La-La Land and Tinseltown, Captain, and we don't live in Los Angeles."

"Whatever. Where do you live?"

"Santa Barbara. Ninety miles north. Warm days and cool nights. Mountains, sun and sea. Not too many people yet."

Pearce looked at the drawn shades of his dim and cluttered office. He's a college man, seemed to be wondering how he had ended up where he was. He sighed, opened a folder on his desk.

"Vice found Butler's body early yesterday morning in an alley behind a NoHo club. Shot once in the head, half the head blown away. Five bags of crack in his pocket. Wallet still in his jacket. No cash or credit cards, but everything else including his California driver's license. No jewelry, not even a watch, except his two super bowl rings. The —"

"They took his cash, credit cards, and his watch, but left his rings?"

"Left the crack too. Five good bags."

I looked at Pearce's covered windows that were like blind eyes. "It doesn't make much sense."

"That's not all that doesn't make sense," Pearce said. "The gun was in the alley next to his body. It traces out to a dead end. One of those 'specials' you buy in the right places."

"A gun to do a job like a robbery. The most valuable loot left behind, the gun left behind. Sounds like a plain robbery and the killer panicked, Captain."

Pearce studied his own blind windows. "Shot Butler in the mouth, wiped off his prints, put Butler's prints on the gun, and left it. Does that sound like panic in a dark alley, Dan? Only Butler's prints on the gun. The barrel would have to have been put into his mouth to blow the back of his head off. Then the gun wiped and placed neatly on the ground."

The silent office filled with the noises beyond his closed door. The voices and protests of the accused: outraged and angry, pleading and whining. The cool drone of the police.

I said, "Suicide? He didn't have any money, credit cards or a watch? Hooked on crack, broke, failed his fans? The tarnished role model?"

"The M.E. says he'd go for suicide ninety percent."

"Not you?"

"We have problems." He rocked in his chair. It creaked. "Who buys crack and then shoots themselves without smoking the crack first? Few suicides do it alone in a back alley without telling anyone or leaving a note." He continued to rock. "Then there's the blood and bone and brain tissue."

"Blood? Tissue?"

"Not enough, and he didn't walk far with half a head. Not even Jake Butler. Medical examiner can't explain it except by saying we'd had a heavy rain that maybe washed most of it away."

"But you think he was shot somewhere else."

Sometimes experience tells you as much as evidence.

"What else don't you like, Captain?"

"No word where he made the buy. No word on him at all. And we've pulled in a lot of markers. Not a word to place him in the area doing anything."

"They could be too scared because he was so famous."

"They could be."

★ ★

Darcy Enterprises, as befits a sports empire, was in a building not far from the new Madison Square Garden. Newly painted and carpeted in the team colors, blue and silver, the offices took an entire floor. The reception room and corridors were lined with action portraits of everyone who had played on the team. Famous, infamous or also ran. Larger and more often for the famous, and Jake Butler looked down at me life size at least a dozen times on my route to the executive suite.

"Sit down, Fortune."

The suite had an outer office, a kitchen, an antechamber with wet bar, and the inner corner office from where Brett Darcy ruled his empire. New Jersey, Brooklyn, the upper bay and the distant sea all visible in a wide arc through the windows.

"You know my wife?"

"Mrs. Darcy." I nodded to the tall redhead stretched on a dark green velvet couch that faced the windows and Darcy.

"Ms. La Luna. La Luna Cosmetics, you know? My real and business name. In public the business name. How did you lose the arm? The war?"

It was a long couch, but she filled it end to end. A whisper under six-feet, her long hair was a rich dark red between auburn and strawberry blonde. Her blue slacks were skin-tight without looking tight. A trick that had cost thousands of dollars she hadn't acquired by being shy. I didn't hit her with one of the snarling stories I have for the curious. She did that to you. You called it refreshing honesty and simplicity, and smiled.

"Something like that."

She was Darcy's third wife, and if she'd set her sights on him she'd gotten a lot more than money. Darcy was a trim six-foot-four, as handsome and athletic as Ted Turner. At forty-one, he wasn't more than two years older than Ms. La Luna. A Rhodes scholar and Harvard Law graduate. Maybe it was love. But love wasn't what Brett Darcy had on his mind.

"What did you get from Pearce?"

I told him the facts I'd gotten from Pearce. "The real kicker is that none of their pigeons or contacts know anything about Butler doing a buy or anything else down there."

"Suicide? Jake Butler?" He swivelled, scowled out his rows of high windows at the Brooklyn half of his view. "That's crazy. Christ, Fortune, he could lift a Honda and break an I-beam in his bare hands. An animal. Animals don't commit suicide. Right, Helen?"

Helen (La Luna) Darcy said, "He was too gentle, Dan."

"You knew Butler well, Ms. La Luna?"

"I know all of Brett's employees." She sat up, shook her head sadly. "Jake was the softest man I ever met. Even shy. I don't think he would be capable of any violence off the football field, especially not against himself. He was almost afraid of his strength. An overgrown boy, really."

She seemed to have as much interest in Jake Butler as her husband, but I had my doubts that boys of any kind would be high on her list of men. Except for that next-to-the-last line: Jake Butler afraid of his own strength, of what he might have done with that strength. Strength would attract Helen Darcy. It wasn't money that drew a woman like her to men like Darcy, it was power. In our society money is power, but not the only kind.

"There's got to be something else, Fortune." Darcy swivelled back to face me. "Five bags of crack. As I said on the phone, I've been hearing about Jake being in trouble. The scum down there could be too afraid of who Jake was to talk to the police."

"The police don't think he was shot in that alley."

Helen Darcy said, "On what do they base that, Dan?"

I told them Pearce's problems. Brett Darcy seemed to think about them.

Helen Darcy frowned. "It could have happened in a room ten feet away. In a car parked in the alley. In any of the buildings that back onto that alley."

"Helen's probably right," Darcy nodded. "But I don't like it. Could be a frame-up that might involve very bad characters. That could rub off on the team." Darcy gave me the exit line. "Cissie outside has your check. Find out what poor old Jake had gotten himself into. Remember, your first job is to keep Darcy Enterprises out of it as much as possible."

I sent the check to my bank express mail. Then I called Captain Pearce. They had thought of everything Helen Darcy had, were checking it all out, but it didn't look promising so far. Except maybe the car theory. A car had parked in that alley that night, left tracks in the mud after the rain.

★ ★

He talks to few people, his name doesn't matter. It's not real anyway. Not the name he has up here. In Colombia he has a name and a place. A powerful place. Up here he barely exists.

"It will fade away, your drug war. When your administration has a more visible demon. When the more notorious leaders of the cartels have been killed or incarcerated. When the epidemic of crack in your slums has diminished enough to be again useful. To those on top, yes?"

He is an educated man. An American university, our military training school in Panama. Prominent in old family Colombian politics on the side that happened to be out now, the business associate of both the Medellin and Cali cartels, and of other cartels we don't know about yet up here. He doesn't sell any cocaine or heroin, he supervises. If it wasn't drugs, it would be emeralds or another product. A businessman.

"But the trade will go on?" I said.

"As long as there is a demand, of course."

I had done him favors years ago through my old connections to Andy Pappas and the Mafia. In Colombia, where Side A and Side B of the same oligarchy have been warring and dividing up the wealth for two hundred years, favors are paid.

"Tell me about Jake Butler."

"There is nothing to tell. He appears to have been a most visible man, your Mr. Jake Butler. My people at all levels know of him, if I do not. But here, in the business, he is completely invisible, as I am sure the police have told you."

"They've been checking too?"

He smiled. "Of course they have been checking, which you know as well as I do. We all have our sources in the enemy camp, yes? It is an ancient game. One wins today, another tomorrow."

"But the people lose every day."

"It is their destiny."

The afternoon sun rested on the city outside. In the empty restaurant only thin shafts of sun through the closed shutters caught the dust motes. It wasn't open, we weren't there.

"No word on Butler buying the crack?"

"He did not buy it in that area, or anywhere in this city.   That I guarantee. If he bought the drug, he brought it with him."

"If he bought it? You think it was a setup?"

"The consensus on the street is against it. There seems to be no angle to a setup, no bottom line. No advantage, no profit."

Without an angle, a bottom line, who would set Jake Butler up as a junkie?

★ ★

Most slum families are large. There isn't much money, there isn't much work, and there isn't much fun. On what money they have they get drunk. Men and women. It's the cheapest escape from pain.

Jake Butler had six brothers and four sisters. Eight had survived to adulthood thanks to a mother who worked long and hard to raise them after her husband died in a street brawl. Only Jake's sister, Maddy, lived in the East.

"Jake, he come to see me maybe three times."

You get out of the slums how you can. For Jake it had been football. For one of his brothers it had been armed robbery. For Maddy it had been marriage to a man with a decent blue-collar job. The house was a semi-detached in Queens on a street that had seen better days. But Maddy Johnson, née Butler, had curtains at her windows, a color TV and comfortable furniture in her living room, food in the big freezer-refrigerator in her shiny kitchen.

"What did he talk about, Maddy?"

She shrugged, looked out through her neat curtains. "Jake don't talk much. Now I guess he don't never talk no more."

She started to cry. A solid woman with the soft face of a child and an expression that never changed even as she cried.

"You know what he's been doing since he left football?"

"Jake never done left football, Mr. Fortune. My Mom said Jake was playin' semi-pro out on the coast, helpin' out coachin' at his old high school, workin' nights down to the mall."

"The mall?"

She shrugged again. The gesture of the twentieth century. The shrug of resignation, of what's the use? The dream of the weak and poor to rise as one is gone. The dream now is to get yours. A dream of the aristocrat and the barbarian.

"What happened to all the money he made?"

"He don't make that much. Those was the days before the big bucks. I mean Jake done okay, give a lot to Mom and the family. The lawyers for Todd an' all. Mom say he lost money in a couple o' businesses don't pan out. Some pizza joints. A bar."

"What was he doing at the mall?"

"Security, I guess. He was tryin' to be a fighter, too. I heard some guys wanted him to do that wrestlin'. Jake he said it was all phony, but fightin' it was okay."

"You mean boxing? Professional?"

She nodded. That is the other gesture of the twentieth century. The shrug and the nod. As if there is nothing to say and even less desire to say it.

"He talked about taking up boxing when he visited you?"

"Some. He mostly come to borrow money. For his rent."

"He couldn't pay his rent?"

"He only come in from the coast a month ago, an' he just start workin' with his fighter friend. Walt Green, or Rashid Green. A gym over in Jersey. New Brunswick or maybe Trenton. Mario's Gym."

"Did you give him money, Maddy?"

"What you think? 'Course I give him some money. Ain't got much to give, but me'n Horace done what we could. Horace offer to try to get him a job drivin' trucks like Horace. Jake said he'd sure think about it, but he wanted to try fightin' an' maybe a couple other ideas first." The tears started again, dropping down her expressionless face. "Last time I seen Jake."

"Was he on drugs, Maddy?"

She was silent. "I been thinkin' about that. Jake done some grass back in California, before and after he was in football, but I never saw him use nothin' heavy. It wasn't drugs Jake got high on, Mr. Fortune, it was football. Sports. Just bein' in that there world, you know? The guys, the crowd, winnin'." She shook her head, shook away a tear. "Ever since he was a kid that there was all the high Jake he ever need."

★ ★

Brett Darcy had paid for the hotel without protest. The Cavendish is small, tucked away on the Eastside, and expensive. Darcy wanted to keep me happy. I didn't think he wanted me so happy he'd sent the lady who waited in the lobby.

"We need to talk," Helen (La Luna) Darcy said. "The bar."

Like everything else at the Cavendish, the lounge was small, quiet, elegant and expensive, but even it looked drab as Helen Darcy swept into it with me trailing behind. She wore a blue body suit and floppy top that was tres chic and took panache to wear. She had panache to burn. That's what gets the Brett Darcys. Then, a lot of men have money, it's the panache of a Darcy that gets the Helen La Lunas. Fair is fair.

"I like good white wine."

I ordered the most expensive white wine on the list. It was a Montrachet, Marquis la Guiche. Even her eyebrows went up.

"Can you afford that?"

"No, but your husband can."

She waved the waiter back, canceled the Montrachet for a good California chardonnay. "I don't want this to draw attention on your report or expense account. The Chalone will make Brett mad enough, but he'll accept it."

They don't serve that kind of wine by the glass. She watched the waiter bring bottle, ice bucket and glasses, pour my taste, get my nod, pour full, and leave. Her foot swung the whole time.

"Jake Butler was fixing fights out in California."

I drank. It's not Montrachet, but a great white wine. "How do you know, and why didn't Brett tell me?"

"Brett doesn't know." She drank. "It would kill him, Dan. He loved that man like a son. Jake was all of Brett's greatest moments. If he knew Jake had a reason to kill himself, and probably did, it would destroy him."

I had trouble picturing anything except the loss of a few billion destroying Brett Darcy. On the other hand, Jake Butler had been Darcy's greatest player at his greatest sports moments. Owners can come to think they're athletes and heroes too.

"How do you know?"

"A team scout out in California heard about it and told me. He knew what it would do to Brett. We kept it quiet, but you should know. It does give poor Jake a motive to kill himself."

"Or to be killed," I said.

"I suppose that too. Jake was basically such an honest man."

And knew too much. "You know any details?"

She stood. "The fights were all in L.A., the fixer's name is Reuben Huerta. I have to go. Remember, not a word of this to Brett. Maybe it's nothing, but —"

She let it hang as she swirled out of the elegant lounge leaving a vivid impression of flying red hair and a body made entirely of blue skin. She also left over half a bottle of the chardonnay. I was going nowhere until morning.

★ ★

Mario's Gym was in Trenton. The Metroliner got me there before noon, with only a light hangover after a decent breakfast. It took me another hour to find the gym in a rundown section of the grimy New Jersey state capital. As I walked in, a fight was finishing in the center ring.

A training fight — head guards, safety belts and pillow gloves. An older man was brawling a much younger kid. The older fighter was anywhere from thirty-five to sixty-five, his face battered but his body still taut despite an alligator skin that glistened with sweat. The kid 's face was red from some hard shots even the pillows had failed to soften, and as I watched he took a solid left that drew blood from his lip.

"Son-of-a-bitch!"

The kid picked off the old man's right, fired a real right of his own that missed by six inches as the older man moved neatly. Someone rang the bell.

"You see what the old bastard —" the kid yelled at a stocky man in a sweatshirt at ringside.

"I want a rematch," the old fighter said.

"Rematch?" the kid said to the sweatshirt.

"Get your shower," sweatshirt said to the kid. "You can't keep your face out of his glove, how you gonna fight someone real?" He turned to the older fighter. "Shower up, Johnny, an' come to the office for your dough."

"Sure, Mario."

Mario patted the older fighter on the shoulder, walked to me. He noticed my absent arm. "I can make a fighter out of almost anyone, but you're too old." He had a nice touch with human relations. "What can I do for you?"

I nodded to the older fighter who still leaned against the ring ropes. "What did he mean, a rematch?"

"What he said." He didn't look back at the older fighter, only at me. "Johnny's got some head damage, thinks every fight is for the money. Thinks he's still fighting for real. It makes him a hell of a spoiler, keeps these kids on their toes."

"Useful," I said.

"What else he gonna do to make a buck?"

What else was Johnny going to do? Shine shoes? Welfare? My guess was Mario paid him pretty well for making the macho kids work harder than they expected, and Johnny got to think he was still a fighter and a human being. Not a bad arrangement.

"I'm looking for Walt Green? Maybe Rashid Green?"

"Or Bucky Taylor or Ali ben Ali or Jack Dempsey the Fourth," Mario said. "Walt (The Salt) Green."

He was telling me that Green was an "opponent". One of that legion of fighters at the bottom of fight posters who fatten the wins of rising young hopefuls. They make it possible for twenty-year-olds to go on ESPN with 19-0 records, and compile 19-60 records themselves under ten names in fifteen states and five countries.

"When does he come in?"

Mario looked at the wall clock. "Should be here now. All depends if he can get his car to run."

There have always been "opponents." If a hopeful can't beat them, he isn't going far. You don't want kids with futures going around battering each other before either is ready, so where else are the fledgling Tysons to get their practical experience? Where else are promoters going to get cheap replacements for no shows?

"You want to talk to me?"

In ring trunks and headgear he looked like any other fighter. No more battered, no less. A solid middleweight. Taller, with a thick neck and bullet head, but longer, thinner legs. That was good for an "opponent," helped him fight at any weight from welter to light-heavy without looking too obvious a fraud.

"Tell me about Jake Butler."

He sat heavily on a weight bench. "Shit, that was real bad, man, real bad. They know who done it?"

"They don't even know why."

"Shit."

"How long had you been teaching him to fight?"

He shook his head and looked at the floor. "They suspends my license a couple years ago, I goes to L.A. Jake he a fight fan, you know? He come aroun', we gets to talkin'. He say maybe he be a fighter. I tells him any time he want to fight I manage him. He money in the bank. People they come to see The Bonecrusher fight. A couple, maybe three weeks ago he calls me."

"You were working with him here? Teaching him?"

"I work with him. Two weeks. Then I quit, I tell him to quit."

"That bad?"

"Worse, man. I mean, I could beat him in a round. Any round. An' I'm a middleweight. He was muscle bound, got a glass jaw an' no moves. He too old an' slow. Like, man, we tried. Maybe, a couple years ago he get good enough he lose without they throw garbage. Smart manager make a bundle on him. Not now, an' he Jake Butler, you know? No way I let Jake Butler be no freak."

"You told him to quit fighting?"

"He never start fightin', man. I tell him quit tryin' to fight. I got to knock the big guy down two, three times 'fore I makes him unnerstan'."

Playing semi-pro football on the Coast, doing what sounded like unpaid high school coaching, and working nights as a security guard at some mall. Money gone for his mother and lawyers for his brother. Money lost in some pizza parlors and a bar. Then he had to stop thinking about maybe being a fighter.

"How did he take it?"

"He don't kiss me. But he Jake Butler, he take it okay."

"He say what he planned to do?"

Green shook his head. He was itching to be moving, punching. That was what kept them in the ring, no matter how many fights they lost. The money, yes, what other way to make money did most of them have, but in the end it was the action. Even when they lost two fights in a single night, under two different names at two different weights. Whatever the promoter needed. They knew about the down side, the lies, the fix.

"You know a man named Reuben Huerta? Out on the Coast?"

"Shit, yeah. Who don't know that mother fucker? Slimy as a snake an' ten times 's crooked."

"There's word that Jake was involved with Huerta, fixing fights on the Coast."

"Jake never do nothin' like that. Jake he keep his name clean, you hear?

That why he got no eyes for that wrestlin', why he walk away from fightin' when I tell him all he be was a clown worse'n me."

He was punching the heavy bag hard when I left. If Jake tried to fight or wrestle, he'd be a clown. Had it made him look for another choice?

★ ★

Moving with the sun, the afternoon flight from Kennedy gets into LAX in the early evening. It gave me time to visit with Jake's mother in Oxnard, and still spend a night at home up in Santa Barbara.

A tall, spare woman with a thin mouth and steel eyes, Alice Mae Butler's gaunt face was suspicious and unfriendly. Raising ten kids alone in an L.A. ghetto, watching two die, does not make you especially loving or trusting of your fellow humans. The big house Jake had bought was dirty and ragged among the manicured lawns of an upper middle class neighborhood. Ghetto life doesn't foster middle-class standards.

"Jake's dead. What you care who done it?"

"Brett Darcy hired me to find out, Mrs. Butler."

"Ms. Butler. I earn the name, got no part o' that dead fool. What's that Darcy care 'bout Jake? He make a lot o' money, what more he want from Jake?" She might not care about middle-class values, but her ghetto suspicions were finely honed. "He figure Jake he got killed dealin' shit, don't want the good name o' the team dirtied up, right?"

"What do you figure Jake got killed doing?"

"How I know what Jake got killed doin', mister? He as big a fool as that old fool Butler hisself." Anger in her eyes at her son for dying and leaving her without yet another son as well as no husband. Leaving her without her meal ticket, the only man who'd ever made life sweeter.

In her anger and rage her voice had grown loud. A neighbor across the street glared from behind a lawnmower on his immaculate grounds. A young man and woman came out of the front door behind Mrs. Butler. They both had angry faces and surly eyes, the same slouching manner and ultra-mod designer clothes. The young woman smoked, her cigarette dangling arrogantly.

"What the fuck's all the noise, Ma?" the young man demanded.

"That honky botherin' you, Alice Mae?" the girl drawled, fixed her vacant gaze on my empty sleeve.

Alice Mae Butler turned on them, snarling. "You call me Ma, girl, an' you mind your mouth, Josh Butler! Get that filthy thing out o' your mouth Sarah Dee! Look at you, all dressed up. What you gonna do now your brother's dead? Where I gonna get the money so's you can lie aroun' all day?"

The daughter flounced back inside as much as a woman in tight pants and a sequined tank top can flounce. The son stood macho. Jake Butler's younger brother had been made to look like the kid he was in front of a stranger, a one-armed white honky at that, had to save what face he could,

"I don' need no Jake, an' I don't need you, old woman. I'm movin' out o' this dump, gettin' me a big job in L.A."

It's hard for a six-foot male in his twenties to flounce, but he did the male equivalent and followed his sister into the haven of the house that Jake had built and Momma kept. Slums don't necessarily build character. Alice Mae Butler watched the open doorway where they had disappeared.

"They my last two. I don't do 'em no favor lettin' 'em stay." She sat down on the front steps. "Jake he got killed tryin' to have some kind o' life. Like the rest of us."

"Why was it so hard, Ms. Butler?"

"Why what so hard?"

"Some kind of decent life."

She glared up at me, then looked away again toward the neighbor grooming his lawn. "Jake he got nothin' 'cept bad luck."

I said, "Was he selling drugs, Ms. Butler?'

The anger on her gaunt face had a mean look. She struggled to get up from the steps. Arthritis. I helped her. On her feet she pushed my hand away with bitter violence, "Jake he never sold no drugs, never done no drugs. 'Cept some grass in high school and that there college. Anyone says he done is a liar."

"Trouble with the law?"

"He got no trouble with no one!"

A man who is shot had some kind of trouble, and there is no way a boy in the ghetto, especially an oversized one, doesn't have some run-in with the police sooner or later.

"Was he gambling, Ms. Butler? Fixing fights? Maybe trying to fix football games?"

"You get out! Jake, he dead. What it matter how 'r why? Let it rest, mister. You let poor Jake rest."

★ ★

I got up late next morning, Kay was already gone. She'd had one of our special wine dinners waiting when I drove up from Oxnard.

"You that hungry?" I said.

"You had something else in mind?"

"It could probably be arranged."

"Arrange it then."

Dinner was late, and I overslept. I had to talk to Jake's old high school coach down in Watts, but decided to brace Manny Baum while I was in Santa Barbara. I got a bran muffin and coffee at Jeannine's, and walked along to Gold's Gym. Manny's there until noon to watch the kids spar in the hope of finding one worth coming out of retirement to manage.

"The hungry kids, the tigers, don't live in this town," Manny said. "Yeah, I know the Huerta. I wish I didn't."

"He's that bad?"

"Reu the Screw. They don't mean a former prison occupation or his sexual ability. Reu would cheat himself and probably has."

"Would he fix fights?"

"Would I eat lox for breakfast?"

"You know the name Jake Butler, Manny?"

"What weight does he fight?"

Next to thoroughbred racing, professional boxing is probably the narrowest profession.

"Where do I find this Huerta?"

Manny watched a junior bantamweight move with fluid grace. His eyes told me he wondered if the boy could take a punch. "Try Sammy Glick's gym in Venice. Don't mention my name."

Since anyone in their right mind who knows L.A. would do anything to avoid the 405 freeway, I took Highway One and the Santa Monica to Jake's high school. The Watts riots are twenty-five years ago. A lot has changed, a lot more hasn't. Failed shops are still boarded up, the morning bars full of men who have nothing else to do.

"Yeah, I heard about Jake." Coach Baines didn't notice my arm, looked past me at his own pain for Jake Butler.

"Was he selling drugs?"

"No."

"Then how did crack get into his pocket?"

"Somebody put it there."

"Why?"

"I'm not a policeman, and I'm not in New York."

"You are a coach, Jake's coach. He was helping you for free. Why not hire him?"

"I wanted to."

"Why didn't you? Gambling? Trouble with the law?"

"No."

We were in his office, and he wished I would go away.

"I've been told Jake was involved in fixing fights here in L.A. If he fixed fights, he fixed other events too. He —"

"Jake never gambled, didn't fix fights or anything else."

"Reuben Huerta. That's the name that says Jake was a fixer. You know that name?"

"I know that name. Jake wouldn't spit on that slime."

"Then tell me why you didn't hire him, coach. All I've learned tells me Jake needed money. Why not hire him here?"

He seemed to grow smaller where he sat, looked at his windows as if he wanted to look out at his playing field, his territory. But all the windows were too high in the basement office.

"He wasn't qualified."

"Jake Butler? Not qualified to coach a school team he —"

"Not qualified to teach. To coach high school in California you need a teaching credential."

"Why not help him get qualified."

"I tried, Fortune. I told him to go back to college, get his teaching credential."

"Why didn't he?"

"Too much work, I guess." He said it, but he looked away.

I said, "Jake wasn't afraid of work."

He had to have that window. He stood, walked to the high horizontal windows, looked out at the grass and the fence and the garbage-littered avenue beyond. He spoke without turning, "Bottom drawer. The manilla envelope."

It was a clipping from the *San Vicente Times*, dated a year ago: Jake Butler, former professional football great in town to apply for a coaching position with the San Vicente Broncos semi-pro football team, barricaded himself in a room at the Ramada Inn Friday in a tense standoff with local police.

Chief Mark Belden said that Butler, 38, told police he had a gun and held officers at bay for three hours while he shouted obscenities and tossed furniture from his third-floor window. He finally surrendered peacefully to Harold Baines, his former high school football coach.

Butler was charged with two felony counts of criminal damage to property, and a misdemeanor charge of criminal trespass. Chief Belden said no weapons were found in the room. Butler refused treatment at Sisters of Mercy Hospital. Baines, the Reverend Mr. George Ashe, and other community leaders from Los Angeles, posted bail and Butler was released.

It was later revealed that Butler had been arrested on Wednesday when he had been unable to pay his lunch bill at a local restaurant. Police stated that at that time it had taken twelve officers to subdue Butler.

A local story in a local newspaper. A story with a gaping omission in it.

"Jake Butler should have made AP, UPI, the works."

At the window his back was still to me. "The team kept it off the wires. The city cooperated."

"You mean Brett Darcy," I said. "It looks like Darcy kept a lid on something else too. What's missing, Mr. Baines. Why did it happen? Why did Jake go berserk like that?"

Baines turned from the window that looked out on his field and his city. "Jake couldn't read or write. He couldn't do basic arithmetic. He couldn't pass a test to get out of grade school. That day up in San Vicente to try for an assistant on a semi-pro team he hit rock bottom. They turned him down because even a semi-pro team couldn't hire a coach who didn't know how to read or write."

He paced his bare basement office. "He had gone to this high school and a major college. He'd been ten years in the pros, but had been educated nowhere. He had learning problems that were covered up so he could play. No one cared except that he play football. We all rationalized that it was his only chance to be someone. He graduated from here without learning anything. Four years in college he had a D average in bonehead courses like 'Theory of Football' and didn't graduate. It was a massive and cynical fraud on everyone, but mostly on Jake Butler."

He walked from wall to wall, anger and guilt on his face. "I don't know what happened in New York, but it wasn't about drugs, or criminal violence, or gambling."

★ ★

Venice is a raffish oceanfront community. A larger version of Summerland, mixed with some Coney Island and a lot all its own. It was late afternoon when I got there, the roller skaters out in force, the concrete walk alive with the first of the evening revelers and gawkers. Sammy Glick's Gym was on a street barely inside Venice. A cavernous building that had once been a warehouse. It was even more packed than the ocean walk.

There was no Sammy Glick. Only a manager whose glance swept his domain corner to corner like a prison guard watching the yard.

"Huerta comes around."

"When?"

"Who knows?"

"You have a home address? Phone number?"

"He just comes around."

"I guess I have to hang around."

"I guess." He yawned, looked away. "What you want him for?"

Casual, offhand. It told me he not only knew Reuben Huerta well, he knew exactly where Huerta could be found.

I said, "Tell you what, if he comes around tonight, you say Dan Fortune from New York wants to talk about Jake Butler. I'll be at the Marina Pacific Hotel."

If my hunch was right, Reu the Screw would be at the Marina Pacific to fill my ear with Jake's transgressions before the sun was down. The call came on the house phone after I'd unpacked and showered, but before I went down for the first beer of the night.

"Huerta."

"Room 220."

I slipped my old revolver between the arm and the first cushion of the couch, arranged the other chairs so they would face each other and I could see them all. However many Reuben Huerta brought with him.

★ ★

"You Fortune? From New York?"

There were three of them. The spokesman, who wore shades and a black silk suit, a monogrammed gray silk tie, pale yellow shirt, and jacket two inches too long, would be Huerta. The other two were smaller and trimmer, nervous in plain slacks, sport shirts and sport coats. Huerta looked at my empty sleeve without saying anything. He knew I had one arm before he saw me. Maybe the gym manager told him. I sat on the couch. Huerta took the armchair in the center, the other two sat on the edges of the straight chairs. They would be my aces.

I smiled. "So okay. Tell me about Jake Butler and the fights he fixed with you or for you."

He went through the act. "Who tell you Butler fix no fights? I don' know what the fuck you talk. You better —"

I said, "The guy who paid you to tell the story told me, for Christ sake. Who the hell else would know about something that never happened?"

"What the fuck you talk!" He began to sputter. "You want I show you the fights, the dates, the money I pay, the —"

One of the troubles with setting up a frame with small-time punks is that the people you have to use aren't too bright. He'd been paid to tell a yarn, but I wasn't playing right.

"Hell, no," I said. "I know you've got it all. Even those two to say they took the dives Jake 'fixed,' right? The clinchers to make me go home happy."

Huerta was on his feet. Confused, a little uneasy, he turned loud and nasty. "You callin' me a liar, man? What the fuck you come out here an' call me —"

"Did you tell the boys there Jake Butler got murdered?"

If an earthquake had buried us all, it couldn't have been more quiet in the room.

"Do they know they might have to tell their lies in a New York court? You ready for a murder trial, Reu baby?"

One of the trim ones said, "Hey, man, you don' —"

"Shut the fuck up!"

I said, "They found Jake Butler shot in a New York alley five days ago. The guy who paid you to lie about Jake tell you that?"

"Five day?"

"Before you even made the deal, right? That'll look sweet in court. Come on, no one's going to believe Jake Butler fixed any fights. Jake didn't know enough to fix a fight. You couldn't and wouldn't trust him. My guess is you never knew Butler that well."

The second trim one said, "I ain' goin' to no New York, Reu."

"Hey, you don' say no shootin' shit, man."

Huerta might have toughed it out, but the boys wouldn't. I gave him the coup de grace.

"You even knew I had one arm before you showed here. The man told you who'd come asking."

Huerta folded. "Shit, the guy don' pay me for no murder stuff. Okay, he come 'roun the gym, pay me I say Jake Butler help me fix fights. I got to tell on'y one guy. I know the guy 'cause he got one arm. Dates an' names an' bring a couple o' boys to say they took the dives."

"What man came around the gym?"

"I don' know. Latino guy like me. He pay cash, what the hell, hey? I do job, get same again."

"How were you to get the same again?"

"Phone call."

"Make it."

The number, of course, was out of service. He should have expected that, and so should I. It was his only contact. The unknown Latino would be from somewhere far away, and long gone.

"Shit man, what the hell, hey? I got paid good."

He grinned, herded his boys out. I went down for that first beer. I'd find a nice restaurant in Venice, get a night's sleep, be on the early plane out of LAX for New York and finish it.

★ ★

It took me a day to find what I knew had to be there, then I went to Captain Pearce. Next morning I made a phone call.

Helen Darcy wore a green tailored suit, green blouse, green shoes, when the maid ushered me into the living room of the penthouse condo the Darcy's called home when they were in New York. You could have put most of our Summerland house into the room, and the view over the city and Central Park was so vast I had the feeling that on a clear day you could see Pennsylvania.

"You're finished?"

She reached to take a cigarette from a bright green stone box on an antique coffee table, offered me one. I shook my head. She lit hers with a green table lighter. I wondered if she changed all the accessories in the apartment to match her outfits.

"All finished."

"Then why come to me? Brett hired you."

"Why did he kill Jake Butler, Helen?"

"I beg your pardon?" She didn't even blink. Smoked in the massive living room with its endless view.

"He sent you to me with that yarn about Reuben Huerta and fixing fights. Another smokescreen to go along with the crack and the back alley. Muddy the water, misdirect attention. Anything to keep the police and the publicity away from Darcy Enterprises."

"I don't know what you're talking about. If you have any accusations to make, I suggest you talk to Brett."

I didn't really have to hear the sound behind me to turn and see Brett Darcy in the room. He wasn't alone. The bodyguard had no visible weapon. As big as Jake Butler, he probably wouldn't need one to handle me. They were a team, Darcy and his wife. I had expected Brett would be around to see why I wanted to talk to her. It gave Captain Pearce more time down at Darcy's office.

"You think I killed Jake, Fortune?"

"Metaphorically," I said. "Jake shot himself in your office. In front of you. He took out that gun, stuck it in his mouth, and blew his brains all over your expensive walls."

"You're insane, Fortune," Helen Darcy said.

"You can't prove such an accusation," Brett Darcy said. "Why would I hire you to —"

"I already have proved it," I said. "I remembered the first day I got to your office. New paint and carpeting. The whole office. Must have cost you a fortune to get it done overnight, but how else are you going to hide the blood on the carpet, the bone and brains and blood on the walls? And what's a few bucks to Brett Darcy when it involves very bad publicity? You had to do the whole place, one suite would have stood out, looked different."

Darcy sat down on one of his antique Chippendale chairs, said nothing. Helen Darcy wasn't quite as smart as Brett, didn't know yet it was all over.

"How do you expect to prove —"

"There aren't a lot of people who could do the job on such short notice. I found them, Pearce has their statements, and he's checking the tires on all of Brett's and the company's cars right now. When he finds the tires that match the tracks in the alley he'll find blood inside the car. The crack you planted never did make sense. In that alley it should have been long gone. And the rings. You wanted to be sure the police knew who Jake was."

Brett Darcy said, "You told the police?"

"I told them."

"I hired you to work for Darcy Enterprises."

"They'd have figured it out themselves, sooner or later."

"No," Darcy said, "I don't think so. I made a mistake."

The bodyguard and Helen Darcy watched us, aware that something was going on, aware of Darcy's cold anger. And of mine.

"Why did he shoot himself?" I said. "Why in your office?"

"Because he was dumb and stupid and mentally ill."

"You covered up that time he went berserk out in San Vicente, kept it off the wires, out of anywhere but that backwater daily. That must have cost too. All those stringers and wire people to pay off, sweet talk, lean on"

Darcy said, "He snapped then, and he snapped again. Out of his mind."

"Jake Butler, sports hero, couldn't read or write. Four years of high school and four years of college and ten years in the pros, and when the money ran out he couldn't get a job as good as a security guard. Couldn't even coach at the high school that graduated him. He blamed you for it, didn't he, Brett?"

"He was crazy! What did I have to do with him being dumb? I don't run high schools, I don't run colleges. I run a business."

"Not dumb, Brett, uneducated. Jake wasn't dumb. Jake knew that behind it all was the money. All the money to be made on him by you and those like you, because of you and those like you. On his ability to play a game. That's all that mattered."

"I hired you to protect me and the company. You didn't do the job. Don't expect a check."

"Why do you think I get paid up front when I work for cheap tycoons?"

Now the bodyguard growled. He would do nothing without a command, and Darcy knew that Pearce knew where I was.

"He came to you for a job, didn't he? When? The day before? A week before?"

"Two days."

The day after Walt Green told him he wasn't good enough to be a professional boxer.

"Why didn't you give him a job?"

"I didn't have a job he could handle."

The doorbell rang. Helen Darcy went to answer it.

"He wouldn't take muscle work. What else could he do?"

Captain Pearce came in with three of his men. He looked at me. I nodded.

"I offered him some bucks, airfare back to the Coast."

Two detectives walked to Brett Darcy.

"Why the fuck did he have to shoot himself? In my goddamn office!"

I said, "He was a role model. An example to the nation."

They took Darcy out. Helen Darcy was already on the phone to the lawyers. It was clearly suicide, as the Medical Examiner had said. Brett wouldn't be held long. But obstructing the police would haul him into court, and the newspapers would get it all. Not that most people would give a damn.

Right now, I think "Angel Eyes" is the best crime story I've written. Few people seem to agree with me. Maybe it's the subject matter. Maybe it's the positions Dan takes on some of the incidents. Or the questions I'm asking readers to think about. I don't know, and I don't think I care. In the end, ivory tower or commercial writer, you have to write to please yourself.

This was another piece written on request for the second PWA/ SinC anthology, Deadly Allies II, *again edited by Randisi, this time with Susan Dunlap.*

ANGEL EYES

"When her child falls into a pond, what kind of mother waits half an hour to go to the police?" Sid Parker asked us.

We were in Elbert Walsh's law office in Placerville, California, in the foothills of the Sierra Nevada. Walsh sat behind his desk. I stood against a wall near the high windows. Sid Parker sat in a big armchair between us. The office was a second floor walk up in one of those old two story brick buildings from the Gold Rush days, carefully restored for the new gold rush of tourism across a rich and restless nation. I looked down at the main street, imagined the rough, violent miners and gamblers, thieves and brothel women, when they crowded these streets. The town had another name then: Hangtown.

"Motive, means and opportunity," Sid Parker said. "What more do you need?"

I had never been to Placerville or the Sierras, had taken the long way through the Mother Lode wine country. It was green after the winter rains, the odor of spring grass on the rolling hills. The high Sierras were off to the right, the farms and barns like a wilder New England. They haven't been here as long, the land is less tamed. A land of harsh weather for vineyards, hard-nosed people, and a wine grape, the Zinfandel, that is an immigrant like everyone else, but no one knows from where.

I said, "When the police say it was an accident, you need a lot more."

★ ★

It all began with a telephone call to my office in our Summerland house from Elbert Walsh. I'd worked for Walsh a few times in New York before I moved out to Santa Barbara. He'd left his New York firm, relocated to Placerville, gone into single practice.

"They don't have investigators up there, El?"

"Not as good as you." When a lawyer cites my abilities as his reason for hiring me, I file it under real-reason-to-be-determined-later and let him talk.

He had a client who accused his wife of murder. "Karen Watt came up from L.A. in the early Eighties, opened a woodworking shop, makes the most beautiful cutting boards you've ever seen. She married Sid Parker the second year. He's from a local old money family, works at the family winery. One child, a girl."

"Who did the wife murder?"

"The police say she didn't murder anyone."

That was when the stump of my lost arm started to tingle. Even for a lawyer it was a heavy evasion.

"What do the police say it was?"

"Accidental death."

"Who was it, Elbert?"

"Their daughter."

I knew why Walsh had called me. If he were going to try to prove that a local woman killed her own daughter, an outside detective was a wise move. It's an accusation that can inflame and divide a small community, and always clouds its judgment.

"What does the wife say?"

"The girl's death was a tragic accident. She feels guilty as hell, it was her fault, but it was an accident."

"No witnesses or evidence, but the wife could have done it. That the situation?"

"We'll talk when you get here."

"What about motive?"

"We'll talk."

That had been Walsh's second evasion, and after the long, all-day drive that didn't get me to Placerville and his old-fashioned office until after dark, he continued to evade the point while we waited for his client.

"Karen's a reserved woman, Dan. A war protestor in L.A., an environmental activist. Usually soft-spoken, but can get angry. Private and even melancholy. Maybe because her militancy failed to change people."

"Come on, El, why does her husband say she killed their daughter?"

A tall man, Walsh wore the same blue three-piece pinstripe suits he had in his New York office. A reserved Stetson on an old-fashioned hat stand in the corner and a pair of Western high-heel boots propped on his desk were his concession to The West. A craggy face and gray hair going to white. Independent and stubborn, Walsh. That was Hangtown too.

"The Parkers live out on Grizzly Pond. A week ago Monday, April 17th, Sid was at Debbie Burke's, Karen and Annie were alone in the house. At 6:35 P.M., Karen walked into the sheriff's office. She was scared Annie had fallen into the pond, wanted them to search the whole area in the hope she'd only wandered away. They got up a rescue team, finally found Annie in the pond up against the dam. From where they found her, and the condition of the body, she'd been in the water perhaps half an hour."

"Annie couldn't swim?"

"The pond is a dammed creek that runs into the South Fork. It's high in spring, the pond spills and has a nasty current."

"How old was she?"

"Nine."

"Nine?" What nine-year-old can't swim today?

He looked out his window. "She was retarded, Dan. Severely, with physical handicaps."

The voice spoke in the office behind me. "You wanted to know what Karen's motive was, Fortune. Now you know. She got rid of her problem."

Sid Parker walked past me and sat in a big armchair between both of us. He was a well-built man in his mid forties. Not tall, with dark hair long but neat above his collar, and a thin face with sharp features and prominent bones and hollows. A dark gray suit hung baggy, the collar of his dress shirt was loose.

"Your daughter was a problem for her, Mr. Parker?"

He found a package of cigarettes in his shirt pocket, lit one. "I didn't think she was." He made an angry gesture with his empty hand. "Annie was getting better. Doctor Grasselli was sure. The angel was a sign, I could feel that. Now ..."

"Angel?" I said.

Walsh said, "A spiritual happening. Sid went there that night. That's why he wasn't at home."

"Annie knew she was getting better all the time, but Karen never believed Annie could get better. She ..." He brushed angrily at his pale brown eyes that had a hard shine like amber. "The first few years she wanted to put Annie away in some home where she wouldn't bother us. I thought she'd stopped thinking that, but she never had. What she stopped thinking about was us. Only she couldn't leave a husband and a retarded daughter for another man. Not even today."

I said, "She has another man?"

"Without a doubt."

Walsh and I said nothing. That was when Sid Parker looked at me, said, "When her child falls into a pond, what kind of mother waits half an hour to go to the police?"

★ ★

Now, in the quiet office above the Hangtown main street, Sid Parker said, "She waited to get help to be sure Annie was dead, and the police won't even try to investigate. The whole town wants it to go away, to forget it."

"The police need real evidence, Sid," Walsh said.

"What about the teddy bear?"

I said, "Teddy bear?"

"Annie never went anywhere without it. If she'd fallen into the pond, the teddy bear would have been in the pond with her, or at the edge. Not on the picnic table inside the gate."

"What else?"

"Find something else! You're the detective!"

Loss, rage, another man and a teddy bear. It didn't seem enough for Walsh to have agreed to help Sid Parker. I looked over at Walsh, the question in my eyes. He frowned into his hands as he talked.

"Karen says she fed Annie about five P.M. that night. Annie wanted to go outside to watch the sunset colors. There's a fence and a gate between the yard and the pond, but Karen says they both sometimes got careless about locking the gate, right, Sid?"

Sid Parker glared at Walsh from the hard shine of his eyes.

"Karen stood out in the yard watching Annie," Walsh went on, "then went inside to get a drink. She admits she was drinking. There was a phone call, she won't say from whom. She —"

I said, "Why not say who called?"

"That's one of my questions," Walsh said. "She was inside about fifteen minutes. When she went out it was nearly dark, and Annie was gone. She ran out to the pond but saw no Annie. She searched around the pond from the dam to the creek before she went to the police. That's the half an hour."

"No one saw Annie fall in? No one saw anything?"

Walsh shook his head. "The neighbors aren't all that close. Those on their side of the pond can see only the front of the house through the trees. There are two houses on the far side of the pond where someone could see the Parkers' backyard, but they were watching TV and saw nothing."

I said, "No witnesses, no weapon, no physical evidence. Nothing except a possible motive and a block of time when only Karen knows what happened."

"A block of time filled with too many small things that were unusual. An open gate that's usually locked. A phone call she won't identify. A woman who doesn't drink much, then only beer and not at home, drinking that night. A woman who lives by a pond, but searches the land instead of the water for at least twenty minutes before she goes for help."

Sid Parker said, "She murdered Annie, Fortune."

★ ★

El Dorado is a rural county, the sheriff's department doesn't have many detectives. The one more or less handling the Parker case was named Randy Cansino.

"I can feel for Sid, Fortune. I hope I can feel for the kid too. But we have nothing to make us doubt Karen's story."

"The teddy bear?"

"Annie was retarded, for God's sake. She forgot it."

"Sid Parker says it was the one thing she wouldn't forget."

"She was distracted."

"By what?"

"How do I know? I wasn't there. No one was."

"Karen Parker was."

He swore. "I hate this case, you know?"

"I know. Where do I find Karen Parker?"

"In her shop, I guess."

★ ★

Karen Parker's woodworking shop was a few doors off the main street, with a hand-carved hanging sign so the tourists would know it was there. She worked on a wood lathe behind a cluttered counter, stopped when I came in.

"Mrs. Parker?"

She was a big woman whose short red hair was cut like a man's but more ragged. Round-faced, she wore little makeup, had deep creases of sun and wind. Her bones didn't show, and she had definite hips under tight jeans. The dark blue eyes that glanced up at me were full of pain. And something else.

"You're the detective." She didn't smile. "It's a small town. Word gets around."

Her voice was strong and clear, even musical, like the voices of women I'd heard once in Wales.

"I wasn't trying to hide."

She operated the lathe with steady hands. "You plan to prove that I murdered my daughter? For Sid?"

"Did you?" I had to shout over the noise of the lathe.

She shut it off, sat back on the stool, her back against the wall. "I was surprised a good lawyer like Walsh even listened to Sid."

"So was I."

"But you're here."

The shop was small and dark. The workshop of a solitary craftsman. There were bowls, and racks, and the cutting boards Walsh had praised. They were beautiful, made of many strips of different colored woods matched in a linear or geometric pattern, and oiled.

"Walsh thinks there were too many small things that night that were sort of unusual."

"What does he know about that night?"

"He knows your story."

"So do the police!" Anger flared like a quick flame behind her eyes, the stool fell over backwards as she stood. "Maybe you better get out of here."

"You're a little on edge."

"My daughter just died!"

There was violence in her anger and clenched hands, but it was pushed far back. I felt no threat from her, only a kind of deep frustration and despair that this world would ever be what she wanted it to be.

"Who called you that night? The call that kept you inside?"

"None of your damned business."

"The other man," I said. "You didn't want Sid to know his daughter died because you were talking to your sweetie. You didn't want the whole town to get down on you. But Sid can't get any angrier, and the town knows by now."

She picked up the fallen stool, set it on its legs, sat down again. "Brian feels bad enough about the call without having the whole town talking about us."

"That's his name? Brian?"

"Brian Engels. He's divorced. Owns the smallest bed and breakfast in town. It's all he got out of a bad marriage. He does his own cooking and tends bar. He's younger than I am. He likes the mountains and rivers and forests. That enough?"

"For now," I said. "You mind if I come to your house to look around?"

"The police closed it off until after the inquiry. Maybe it still is closed. I haven't gone back, I think Sid's with his parents." She looked at my empty sleeve. "Does the missing arm limit you?"

"I live with it."

She looked around her cluttered shop. "I know of a retarded boy who's seventeen now. He can sing some songs, read on first-grade level, sort and package nuts, bolts and pegs by size and color. That's what they call a wonderful success."

She was bent over her lathe again when I left.

★ ★

The rustic house was five miles out of town in the rocky, wooded valley of a large creek. A rambling one-story, it had been added onto over many years by many different owners with different concepts. Warm and more than pleasant in its diversity, it sat some fifty feet back from the long, narrow pond.

I walked the grounds aware of eyes that watched me through the trees from the neighboring houses. They had seen nothing on the one night they should have, were not going to make the same mistake again. The large backyard had two picnic tables, some benches, lawn chairs and a brick outdoor barbecue. In the pond I could see a strong current that flowed toward the dam. Across the pond I saw two houses in the spring afternoon sun. The closest showed flickering colors of a television set through a picture window. For many people in late-twentieth century United States television is the only world they know and relate to.

The back gate was still unlocked. A worn path to the pond revealed nothing. The water of the pond was clear and shallow close to shore, dropped off sharply to a vague bottom undulating far below in the sunlight and current. From the end of a narrow spit that jutted out into the pond, the moving figures on the distant TV were visible. Both houses across the pond were close enough for anyone to have heard loud cries or calls for help. They would certainly have turned to look out at the pond.

Off the path, the patch of torn grass and dirt with deep gouges in the rain-softened ground was a few feet from the edge of the pond. The depth and length of the gouges, the marks of what had to be rubber soles, suggested two people in some kind of struggle. The shoes seemed about the same small size, one with the deep grid pattern of a hiking boot, the other the smoother swirls of a running shoe.

Inside the house, the living room had a low ceiling with dark beams, a brick fireplace, and comfortable old furniture. A section was set off by bookcases as the dining room. Three bedrooms were down a crooked hallway to the right. I checked all three bedrooms, found no muddy boots or running shoes. In the living room, dinner dishes and cutlery were still dirty on the dining table. A bottle of Johnny Walker Black Label and a not-quite-empty glass stood on a coffee table. The telephone had a long cord, and had been moved to the coffee table.

The kitchen was to the right. Pots and pans were still on the stove, the blood-red water of beets in one pot. Some kind of rice casserole hardened in a baking dish, the red debris where the beets had been skinned was still in the sink, and a single glass drained in the plastic drain basket. It was the only dish or glass in the basket. There were water spots and an oily film inside. The outside was clean. The glass had been rinsed, not washed, and dried only on the outside. I smelled a faint odor that could be Scotch whisky.

★ ★

It was dark by the time Elbert Walsh met me at the sheriff's office. Detective Cansino didn't want to see either of us.

"Don't you think we should maybe give Karen Parker a break, counselor? Christ, her kid's dead, she feels guilty enough."

"We owe Sid something, Randy. And Annie."

I said, "When you went over the house and yard, how many glasses were on the coffee table with the scotch?"

"Shit, I don't remember. I'd have to get out the file." He didn't want to get out the file. "I've known Karen since she came here. The woman's suffering. What does Sid want?"

"The truth," Walsh said.

Cansino got the file. "Glasses? Okay, there was one glass, still some scotch in it. Karen's prints, no one else's."

"What about the glass in the drain basket in the kitchen?"

"It's noted here along with the rest of the dirty stuff in the kitchen. Clear as hell Karen forgot all about everything. Wouldn't you, Fortune? When you find your kid missing, you don't remember the dishes."

"The glass was rinsed," I said.

Walsh said, "One glass? Only that?"

"Someone carefully wiped and dried only the outside."

Cansino shrugged. "So Karen, or Annie, or someone used the glass earlier. It could have been any time."

"What about that torn-up ground out in the backyard? Did you check the sole marks, try to match them to what Karen and Annie were wearing?"

He read his file. "Nothing here about any torn-up ground. Sure don't remember seeing that myself."

"Maybe you better go and take a look."

"Torn-up ground could have happened anytime since the rain started in January."

"Anything could have happened anytime," I said.

"I'll take a look. At the glass too."

Outside, Walsh suggested some drinks and dinner. In the Sierra Tavern we sat in a booth. I had two quick Red Tail Ales, it had been a long day. Walsh had a martini, and watched me.

"You think someone else was there that night?"

"That's what I think."

"And you think Karen struggled with Annie in the yard?"

"I think someone struggled with someone in the yard."

Walsh thought about that. "She's protecting someone?"

"Or afraid of someone."

After dinner I went to my motel bar, had more Red Tails, thought long about Sid and Karen Parker before I went to bed.

★ ★

Sid Parker's parents lived in a large house on a hill that overlooked the South Fork of the American River. He was a short, broad man in a Western shirt and bola tie, had a strong face as craggy as his land. She was small, with short, matronly hair.

"The original house dates from 1860, Mr. Fortune," Ethel Parker informed me with the same voice a French Count would have used to announce that his chateau and lineage dated from the time of Charlemagne. "It's still our master bedroom."

"Sam Parker came around the Horn in 1847. He was sixteen," William Parker informed me. "Jumped ship in San Francisco, and was bang on the spot when they found the gold. Sold his claim the day before it ran out, went into business right here. When too many murderers and trouble-makers filled the town, he led the vigilantes that gave it the old name: Hangtown. We don't like troublemakers here."

"Actually," I said, "I came to talk to Sid."

"He's over in Napa. Winery business."

"I'm sure we can tell you anything he could," the mother smiled. "Would you like some tea, Mr. Fortune."

"Tea would be nice, thank you."

Ethel Parker went into the kitchen. I sat on a brocade love seat that matched a larger couch and armchair all set around a fine late-eighteenth-century English mahogany coffee table. One of three sitting areas in the giant living room, all with fine antique couches and tables and occasional

chairs. Mrs. Parker returned with a three-tiered plate of small sandwiches, muffins and petit fours. We all sat around it and drank tea.

"Does your daughter-in-law have any special friends? A relative,
maybe?"

"We wouldn't know," Mr. Parker snapped. "She's an irresponsible
troublemaker. We have as little to do with her as we can."

"We never liked that Sidney married her," the mother said. "It would
seem that we were right. Tragically."

"What do you know about the 'angel' Sid had gone to see that night?"

Ethel Parker smoothed her skirt. "It's a religious event in the town.
At Deborah Burke's house. Thousands of people came from all over the
country. I read about it in the newspaper."

"What did Sid want with this 'angel'?"

"You'll have to ask him," Mrs. Parker said.

She knew, but didn't want to tell me before Sid Parker told me his
version of whatever it was.

"How did you feel about your granddaughter?"

She went on smoothing her skirt and looked somewhere out the
windows. His craggy face was stone.

"We loved Annie," she said, "despite everything. She should probably
have never been born. But she was here, we wanted her to be as happy as
she could be."

"When she was born we took her to the best specialists, gave her
everything we could," Parker assured me.

"We wanted her to have all the special treatment she needed to get
better. Someone to be with her all day."

"Karen only wanted her to die, get her off her back."

"Now she has."

They were like a Greek chorus, their voices interchangeable. A
chorus that sang Sid Parker's song.

"Is Dr. Grasselli one of your specialists?"

"No," Parker said.

"He's a friend of Sid's," Mrs. Parker said. "Some kind of psychologist,
I believe."

"Does Dr. Grasselli have an address?"

"I'm sure it's in the telephone book. Joseph Grasselli."

I left them there in their giant living room, side by side and holding
hands.

★ ★

Dr. Joseph J. Grasselli, M.D., Ph.D., Psychologist and Radiologist in
Family Therapy and Advanced Spectral Treatment, had his office in a
house outside Placerville. His shingle hung from a post in the front yard,
but the office was in the rear.

"Sit down, Mr. Fortune." A small man with a narrow face and a neatly
trimmed beard, he sat behind his desk and smiled. "Feel free to tell me as

much or as little of your problem as you want. We won't rush you, will both learn as we go. All right?"

"Well, maybe you can sort of show me, like, I mean, what I can sort of expect?"

"Fine, fine. Why don't we take a brief tour of my office and facilities? As you can see, I have both a medical degree and a doctorate of philosophy in psychology."

Grasselli motioned toward the largest of the many framed documents on his walls. The medical degree was in German from St. Ignatius Hospital Medical School in Zurich. Certificates of internship from a hospital in Grand Forks, North Dakota, and residency from another hospital in Rolla, Missouri, were on either side. The Ph.D. in psychology was from Union University in Los Angeles. My missing arm started to throb like an abscessed tooth. Grasselli walked to a door on the right.

"In here is my spectral radiology room."

There were a lot of machines, one that looked like a fluoroscope, and others I recognized as autoclaves and an EKG. The largest had a chair and what looked like an X-Ray head mounted on a heavy arm. Grasselli patted this machine.

"This is my own development: a Spectral Radiochrome."

"What does it do?"

"How much do you know of Spectral Radiology?"

"Well, I heard of it," I lied. "Does it help family stuff?"

He almost rubbed his hands together. "That depends on the nature of the problem. If your problem is physical, impotence or infertility say, then we use one setting and bathe the area in blue or yellow light from the radiochrome. If, however, the trouble is mental, then we must use an entirely different setting and beam the brain with red light. Of course, the spectral rays are not simple light, but complex photon-neutron waves of vast therapeutic finesse."

I tried to look impressed. "What kind of mental problems? I mean, like, can it help if you see things that aren't there? Make you smarter? Stop you, like, maybe from beating your wife?"

Grasselli smiled. "Nothing comes easily, you understand. All cures take time, progress can be slow. But all of those problems can be helped with sound counseling and the Spectral Radiochrome, yes. Is one of those your problem, Mr. Fortune?"

I hesitated, looked nervous. "How about a sort of retarded kid? A friend of mine says you can make them better."

"Yes. There are no guarantees, but I have made special progress with the raising of intelligence levels. What friend told you — ?"

"Sid Parker," I said. "He says you made Annie better before Karen went and —"

He looked at my missing arm. "Who are you, Mr. Fortune?"

"Was Annie Parker getting better? Did you tell Sid that?"

He walked to the door. "You didn't come to consult me. I think you better leave."

"Was she getting better, Grasselli?"

He crossed his office, held the outside door open and smiled again. "Yes, and no one can say she wasn't."

"Oh, I'll bet a lot of people can say she wasn't. Like real doctors. You mean they can't prove she wasn't, especially now, right? The evidence is dead."

"Good-bye, Mr. Fortune."

"Are any of those diplomas and certificates real?"

He closed the door in my face.

★ ★

The South Fork of the American River runs northwest a few miles north of Placerville. Brian Engels had his bed and breakfast on a bank of the river. The South Fork Inn, five rooms and a small café and bar. In the early afternoon the bar was open, three men sat at a table in a noisy group. A solitary woman drank at the bar in silence. Brian Engels tended bar, and didn't think we needed to go anywhere else to talk.

"Not even about Karen Parker?"

"Especially about Karen," he smiled. "Half the town always knew, now I guess the other half will."

He was a big man, his darkening blond hair cut as ragged as Karen Parker's hair. In his late thirties, slender and bony for his size. The same deep creases of sun and wind, the same tight jeans behind the bar. He had a nice smile. I couldn't remember that Sid Parker had ever smiled.

"How long have you known each other, Mr. Engels?"

"Brian, okay?" He shook his head. "Do all you detectives pussyfoot around trying to fool people, Fortune? Karen and I've known each other since two days after she came to town and walked in here for a Sierra Nevada. But that's not what you want to know, is it? We've been in bed maybe two years, give or take a month or so. I never wrote down the big moment."

"Is it serious?"

"What the hell is serious? It's serious loving. It's serious friendship. It's serious human beings."

His voice had risen in the small, low-ceilinged barroom. The solitary woman at the bar turned to stare at us.

I said, "Is it serious, Brian?"

He washed dirty glasses in the sinks under the bar. "I hope it is. Maybe for my sake more than hers."

"Who do you doubt, you or her?"

He stacked clean glasses on the bar. "When a woman comes to you because she's lonely, because she needs a smile, because she needs some peace, you're never sure. Is it only comfort she needs? If the problem goes away, does she still love you? Does she still want you?"

"Does she still want you?"

"I don't know. She's upset, depressed, guilty."

"Annie's dead," I said. "Annie sent her to you, Annie could take her away. The problem is solved. She —"

The lone woman at the bar who had been staring at us, stood up. Sturdy, in her late thirties, she wore a plaid flannel shirt, battered cowboy hat, baggy chinos and running shoes.

Brian Engels said, "Annie? It wasn't Annie that sent her to me, for Christ sake. It was Sid. Her problem's Sid, not Annie. His goddamn obsession with Annie. Every waking minute put into believing the poor kid could get better, be normal. His quacks, witches, gurus, holy rollers, goddamn angels."

I said, "What about angels?"

The woman at the bar walked to us. "You want to know about our angel, Fortune? I'll tell you about our miraculous angel."

★ ★

For believers in galactic harmonic convergence, the weekend of Saturday, April 15, is one of the moments that will signal either a new age of peace, or the doom of mankind.

The Friday before, April 14, Deborah Burke, a believer, switches on the television set in her living room to enjoy her favorite soap opera. It isn't quite time, she changes channels to find the latest news of the harmonic convergence. A bright light seems to swell from the TV, and the angel appears on the screen. Deborah is transfixed, stares at the image that shimmers in all the colors of the rainbow.

She is beautiful, the angel. She smiles out at Deborah with a soft, gentle smile and eyes full of love. Deborah sits alone with the glowing image until her son and daughter find her.

Teenagers, they are even more dazzled by the image, must go at once to tell their friends, make them come and see the angel too. Their friends tell their parents, who also come to look. Word spreads all through town. The local newspaper sends a reporter. Its story of the angel on Deborah Burke's television is fed into the wire service.

By Sunday, six thousand people have made the pilgrimage to Placerville. They gather in meadows on the outskirts of the town and in the yard of Deborah Burke's house to meditate and watch the sun rise over the towering Sierras. Over five thousand of them come to Deborah's house to see the wonder of the angel on the TV screen. Psychics from across the country sit before the image and speak to the angel. The sick and the lame come from everywhere to look, wonder and pray that the miraculous angel will make them well.

"It's the harmonic convergence sign," one of the leaders of the movement declares. "The sign we've been expecting. It means peace and survival for the world, We're going to be all right."

Deborah Burke agrees. "The angel came to tell us we'd be okay. She's wonderful."

The police chief isn't so sure. He calls in a TV repairman to look at the angel. The repairman, Tom Whitney, identifies the source of the image at once: a bad capacitor and the set's low voltage power supply.

At first, at Deborah Burke's house, he doesn't say anything. "There were so many people praying in front of the set, and out in the yard. I didn't know how to tell them."

But Whitney goes to his shop and easily duplicates the image for anyone who wants to see it. He tells the Chief, who tells the town and everyone at Deborah Burke's house.

"Anyone who wants the truth, go on down to Tom Whitney's shop and see for yourself."

None of the six thousand who came to pray and meditate does.

★ ★

The woman in the cowboy hat said, "Sid took Annie to that TV set the moment he heard about the 'angel'. He took her over to Debbie Burke's that Sunday and sat with Annie in front of the set and talked to the 'angel.' He made Annie kneel in front of that 'angel' Tom Whitney could show anyone who had any grip on reality was nothing but an electronic malfunction. A glitch on a TV screen would make Annie better, make her normal."

The woman's eyes held the same anger and something else I'd seen in Karen Parker's eyes. It wasn't fear, not exactly. More like a dark shadow, a kind of internal agony. "When they didn't come home for dinner, Karen found them there. It was way past Annie's bedtime, no one had fed her. Her diaper was dirty, she was almost hysterical. Crying and moaning and trying to get closer to the screen to find the angel inside. Karen had to drag them out of there, clean Annie up at home, feed her and put her to bed. The next day Sid wanted to take her back to that phony 'angel'! Karen said no, but he said he damn well would if Deborah Burke would let him, went over there alone to ask her if Annie could come back."

Brian Engels said, "He grabbed at anything, even believed a couple who told him Annie was bewitched. They could free her from the witch, cure her, by putting a blessing on her while she stood naked on a hill when the moon was full and faced north."

The woman said. "The same couple killed a woman in San Francisco because she'd been a witch draining the wife of her beauty and religious powers. In court they described themselves as 'religious warriors in a holy war against witches.' Their religion authorized them to kill witches, they had acted reasonably against the imminent danger of attack by lethal supernatural powers."

Brian Engels said, "Outside of his work, it's all Sid thought about the last seven years. Karen watched him hurting that poor kid, and the rest of us watched him hurting her."

"Is that why she killed Annie? Because she decided Annie and her and even Sid would be better off?"

"Maybe they all are, Fortune," the woman said.

"Karen didn't kill Annie," Engels said. "If Karen was going to kill someone, it would've been Sid."

"How do you know what she did?" I said. "Were you there?"

The woman said, "Annie went out into the yard, the gate was open, Karen was in the house, Annie drowned."

I looked at Engels. "Who is this lady?"

"Sandra Gavin. Karen's best friend."

The sturdy woman wasn't my best friend. She didn't like me at all, and wasn't trying particularly hard to hide it. I looked down at her running shoes.

"Maybe you were there that night, Ms. Gavin?"

"No one was there except Karen and Annie."

I shook my head. "No, someone else was there. I don't know who or why, but Karen Parker wasn't alone with Annie. Two people drank scotch in the living room that night. That's why she was drinking at home: she had company. Whisky when she usually drank only beer, because she was upset by Sid, the 'angel', and Annie."

"She was upset," Brian Engels said. "That's why I called her, and why she was drinking. But she was alone."

"There were two glasses. She rinsed one so no one would see she hadn't been alone. But she forgot to put it away."

"She could have washed that glass anytime."

"It was an accident," Sandra Gavin said.

★ ★

Deborah Burke lived in a big white frame house on a back street. A native sycamore and two eastern maples shaded it from the late afternoon sun. Spiritual slogans and paintings hung all along the porch. When I rang, an ethereal woman in a flowing white robe opened the door and smiled up at me.

"Are you spiritual? A believer?"

She had big blue eyes that stared brightly with a beatific expression. One of those people who move in a world of their own, on some interior planet. Most of Placerville had to know by now a one-armed detective was in town trying to prove that Karen Parker murdered her child to be free of all her trouble.

"I doubt it," I said.

"You didn't come to see the angel?"

"No. I'd like to talk to you about Sid Parker."

"So spiritual, Sidney."

"And Annie."

"Poor child. No one understood."

"Understood what, Ms. Burke?"

"Why, that she was getting better all the time. Anyone with sensitivity could see that."

"How could you see that?"

"In her eyes, of course. They are the windows of the spirit. Annie's spirit was perfectly normal. A pure spirit trapped in that poor body. The spirit would triumph, we all knew that. We could see she was getting better all the time."

"Who's we?"

"Our spiritual group. We meet every week."

"Sid and Annie came to your meetings?"

"Sidney is a wonderful searcher."

"He brought Annie to see the angel?"

"Oh, yes. We knew at once there was something special between Annie and the angel. In their eyes, you see? She had the same eyes, Annie. Angel eyes. The way she looked at the angel. It was as if the angel came just to help Annie."

"They were here a long time?"

"Oh, yes. It was wonderful. Our spirits communing."

"Karen and her friends say she found Annie dirty, hungry and almost hysterical, moaning and trying to get closer to the screen to find the angel inside. Karen had to drag them home. Next day Sid was here again, while Karen was home alone with Annie."

The change was instantaneous. It could have been another person where she had stood in a kind of ecstasy seconds before. Her bright eyes clouded, her beatific smile became a scowl.

"Karen Parker is a woman without sensitivity! People say she is a sensitive artist, but they're wrong. She has no feeling for the Eastern wisdoms, for the world's holy places, for the harmonic convergence. She is afraid to feel the spirit. She rejects the pure foods, the mantras and karma. She wears clothes that bind the flesh and the spirit. She has no sensitivity."

"Was Annie crying, hungry and hysterical that Sunday?"

The beatific vision came into her eyes again. "What does the physical matter? Annie was joining her spirit to the angel."

★ ★

The woodworking shop on the downtown side street showed light. Karen Parker worked on a cutting board this time. She didn't look like she'd left the shop since yesterday.

"Living in the shop now?"

"I don't have rich parents to move in with." She put down her tools. "What do you want this time, Mr. Fortune?"

I leaned over the counter to look at her feet. She wore heavy hiking boots. The kind with thick lug soles.

"Someone else was there that night."

"No one else was there."

"There was a scuffle, an encounter. Outside near the pond."

"When Randy Cansino came around today, I figured that was your work."

"What did you tell Detective Cansino?"

"I used the other glass the day before. Sid and I horsed around out by the pond a week before. I drink scotch when I'm depressed."

"Alone?"

She went back to work. "Annie and I were alone. I was careless. She fell into the pond."

Her big hands moved delicately, quick and soft. The hands of an artist in wood.

"Depressed about your marriage? Sid's obsession with Annie? Cures, miracles, quacks? Not much of a marriage, I'd guess. A woman has to change something sooner or later."

"Not much of a marriage. Not for a long time. I did change something. I found Brian."

"That didn't help Annie."

She didn't look up. "I was drinking, talking on the telephone. I was careless. Annie drowned."

★ ★

After a chicken BBQ sandwich and milkshake at the local Carl's Jr., I drove out of town along the dark rural highway to the Parker house. There were lights in the neighbors' houses and in the two across the pond.

Outside the backyard fence, I looked again at the torn-up grass and soft earth with the marks of the running shoe and the boot. The marks weren't clear enough, or distinctive enough, to give identification. Across the dark pond the large television set in the nearest house was remarkably clear. From the edge of the pond, the faces and figures on the TV seemed almost real.

Out on the road I knocked at the closest house. A muscular man in work clothes looked at my arm.

"You're the detective Sid got to go after Karen."

"Dan Fortune," I said.

"Max Gerber. This is my wife."

The woman stood beside him in the doorway.

"You told the police you saw nothing unusual over there that night, didn't hear any cries. But did you hear anything? Maybe something brief, not loud. Voices, footsteps, a scuffle — "

"Scuffle?" Max Gerber looked at his wife. "You know, that's just what it could of been. A scuffle. I —"

"Start at the beginning."

They both looked off toward the shadow of the Parker house through the night trees. Mrs. Gerber said, "We was sitting out on the side porch. I mean, it was a nice night, we always have a drink before dinner, so —"

"We had drinks on the screen porch. Just about when it was dark there was this noise from somewhere. Hell, it wasn't much, didn't last more'n a couple of seconds, if that long. It —"

"Was like someone breathing hard, maybe a grunt, you know?"

"Maybe someone sort of jumping and sliding around. I mean, it couldn't of lasted more'n a second or so like my wife says."

"We figured a couple of kids somewhere around."

I said, "Could it have been Annie? Struggling?"

"Hell no," Gerber said. "When that kid made noise you could hear it to Sacramento."

"Especially if she was scared."

"Just getting dark? About five-thirty, six o'clock?"

"Closer to six, I'd say," Gerber said.

"Anything else?"

They looked at each other, shook their heads.

"No matter how small, unimportant, even routine."

The wife said, "Well, there was a car. I mean, just a car starting somewhere."

"Hell, there's always a goddamn car," Max Gerber said.

"This car was close?"

"Yeah, pretty close."

"Before, or after you heard the noise?"

"After," the wife said.

Gerber nodded. "Maybe ten, fifteen minutes. We was just goin' inside to eat. We always eat around six-fifteen, six-thirty. Star Trek reruns come on the TV at seven, right?"

★ ★

At the house on the far side of the Parkers, a tall angular woman answered my rings. She saw my arm, and half closed the door.

"Sorry to bother you," I smiled my polite and reassuring smile, flashed my photostat. "Dan Fortune. Private investigator working for attorney Elbert Walsh on behalf of Sid Parker. I'd like to ask you a few questions if it isn't inconvenient?"

She studied the photostat in front of her face. "He thinks she killed the child, doesn't he? Wouldn't put it past her. Kind of thing those hippies do."

The second woman was as tall, but neither spare nor angular. Forty pounds heavier, she had a round, pleasant face that smiled at me. "If anyone killed that poor child, May, it was him. Dragging the little thing everywhere and anywhere, never letting her alone, trying to make her what she could never be."

"The Parkers are a fine family! You wouldn't know anything about that, Maggie."

They faced each other across the gap of the open doorway like two lions on an Africa veldt. The glare of the thin one, the smile of the second, clashed in a struggle that had probably been going since they were teenagers. I coughed, got their attention.

"You told the police you saw nothing, heard nothing. But was there anything at all unusual, no matter how insignificant? Say between five-thirty and six? Something you barely noticed?"

The heavier, Maggie, looked past me. "There was this ..."

The skinny one, May, said, "This ... sound. I was in the kitchen peeling potatoes. Sort of low grunts, a bump —"

"I was outside," Maggie said. "I remember thinking they were perhaps tussling, Sid and Karen. You know, fun in their backyard. They used to do that a lot when they first moved in."

"Could it have been Annie?"

"Oh, no." In unison.

"What time would you estimate?"

Maggie always seemed to speak first. "Six o'clock?"

"Give or take ten, fifteen minutes."

I said, "What about the car?"

"Car?" Maggie said. "I don't remember —"

May said, "It went right past. Looked like a Ford Bronco. An old one. Red or dark brown. Six-fifteen or so."

"You heard it start next door? Looked out?"

"Heard some car start up pretty near, don't know if it was the same car," May said. "I had some garbage, took it out to the cans, saw the Bronco go past. Looked like Sandra Gavin's. She lives up the road that way."

At the South Fork Inn, Sandra Gavin had known my name before she joined us. Could she have heard Brian Engels say it from where she had been sitting, or had she already known who I was?

★ ★

On my way to the sheriff's office, I picked up Elbert Walsh. Cansino was off duty, wasn't pleased to see us at his home.

"I think I know who else was there that night," I said.

"We already went through all that, Fortune."

"I talked to the neighbors. They remember a brief noise about six o'clock. Hard breathing, some grunts and sliding in the dirt. They heard a car start somewhere close, one saw an old red Ford Bronco go past her house."

"They didn't tell me any of that."

"They didn't think of it again until I asked. They never thought it was important enough to talk about."

"Or they remembered what never happened when you put words in their mouths."

"Fortune didn't suggest anything specific, Randy," Walsh said. "Taken together with the glass and the scuffed ground, it at least opens the possibility Karen is lying when she says she was alone with Annie, and that makes me wonder what else she might be lying about."

"Why would Karen want to hide someone else being there?"

I said, "Why don't we find out?"

★ ★

The glass-and-redwood house looked like part of a modern art museum about to fall into the rushing water of the South Fork that surged white in the night. Sandra Gavin answered the door.

"Randy? What's up?"

I said, "Karen Parker wasn't alone that night. You were with her. At least until six-fifteen or so."

She ignored me. "Randy?"

"They want to ask some questions, Sandra," Cansino said.

Sandra Gavin walked inside her house. The living room ran the width of the small house. Skylights showed the stars clear above in the rural night, and a wall of glass stood between the room and the dark river with its bursts of white only ten feet below. Abstract paintings hung on all the walls, non-objective sculpture stood on the floor and most surfaces. Open double doors to the right showed an artist's studio and an unfinished sculpture. Sandra Gavin sat on a low leather-and-rosewood couch.

"All I know about that night is what Karen says."

I sat in a soft-leather Mies chair. "Two different sets of neighbors heard a brief scuffle about six o'clock, saw your car leave about fifteen minutes later."

"They couldn't have. I wasn't there."

Detective Cansino said, "Where were you, Sandy? From five-thirty to six-thirty? That's your drink time. Downtown at Matty's or The Sierra, or out at South Fork Inn. Which one was it that night? Will they cover for you?"

"I worked late. On a roll."

"That'd be the first time in five years. What do you always say? Take a break no matter how good it's going, or you'll lose your edge?" Cansino was in an old butterfly chair near me. "The other place you drink is with a friend. Usually Karen Parker."

Cansino heard her come in before Walsh or I did. Rural ears. She walked across the wide room to the glass wall that overlooked the rushing river, watched the night and the river.

"Funny, I always loved water," Karen Parker said. "Fast water, remote water. Rivers and lakes. Maybe because I grew up on the ocean."

Sandra Gavin said, "They don't know —"

"Yes they do, Sandy. Fortune'll keep digging, hammering at you, until it gets in the way of your work. He'll work on Randy until none of us has any peace."

Walsh said, "She was there that night, Mrs. Parker?"

Karen Parker still looked out and down at the rushing water that was like a giant shadow moving in the night. "It wasn't her problem. I didn't want her to be involved."

"Involved in what?" I said.

Cansino said, "You were covering for Sandra? It was — "

Karen Parker spoke into the window, into the night outside above the white-edged river. "I'm not covering for her, she's covering for me. I didn't want her to be part of it. To lie, or tell the truth and feel bad, or maybe even feel guilty."

Detective Cansino said, "If there's something you didn't want Sandy to tell us, I — "

I put my lone hand on his shoulder. Karen Parker wasn't listening. She didn't hear us, wasn't talking to us, wasn't even thinking of us. She was talking to the night and to herself. "I'd had to drag them home from that television set and its 'angel'. An electronic glitch, and Sid was off on his miracle chase again. First the doctors: pediatricians, psychologists, neurologists, brain surgeons, he did them all. Then the herbal healers, and faith healers, and the layers-on of hands. The priests and witch doctors, the star-gazers and the quacks."

Sandra Gavin walked toward her. "Karen — "

At the wide picture window, Karen Parker's face reflected in the glass against the darkness outside. She shook her head. "He never stopped to see what it was doing to us and to Annie. We had no marriage. Annie had no stability, no peace or rest. Dragged to one empty hope after the other. Prodded and poked and studied and dieted and analyzed. Annie didn't matter. Only the obsession — Annie could be, would be, a normal child. He never asked me, and he never asked Annie."

I said, "That Sunday night was the last straw. Annie was exhausted, hungry, in her own dirt. The next night, when Sid had gone to ask Deborah Burke to let Annie come back, you —"

She watched something large and black float down the dark river with its white teeth. "I fed my daughter dinner. I'd been upset by the night before. Sandra came over. I was still upset, we had a drink or two. Whisky, beer wasn't enough. Annie was restless, wanted to go out. I had left the back gate unlocked, I don't know how or why. We had another drink. Brian called. He asked how Annie was, if she'd recovered. I realized I hadn't heard a sound in ten, twenty minutes from out in the yard. I dropped the phone and ran outside. Sandra came behind me."

She turned, looked through and beyond the glass-and-redwood living room. "She was out on the little spit of land staring across the pond. I couldn't see why. There was still plenty of twilight, but there was no one and nothing on the pond or across it." Karen Parker's eyes searched for whatever was on the far side of the pond miles away behind her house. "Before I could even open my mouth to call to her, or yell, she walked straight out into the pond. It's shallow for a few feet, and then —"

Sandra Gavin said, "We were nowhere near her. She just stepped off into the damned water!"

"— it drops sharply. As I ran across the yard she went down. By the time I was near the pond she came up, sputtering and thrashing in the current. Then she stopped, lay back in the water, her eyes clear and very bright. She looked straight up at the last light in the night sky." Karen Parker turned again to the wall of glass above the fast-moving river, looked up at the night sky. "She was smiling. She floated in the water, and she smiled." She turned once more, looked at us this time. "She smiled and lay back and just slipped under the water."

The long silence in that sleek room with its giant abstract paintings and sculptures must have stretched a full minute before Detective Randy Cansino finally spoke.

"Could you have reached her?"

"I don't know. I'm a good swimmer, she wasn't far out."

I said, "You didn't try, and you stopped Sandra from trying. That was the scuffle."

"It was too late," Sandra Gavin said. "The current was too strong."

Karen Parker said, "Sandra was behind me. She tried to go past, jump into the pond. I stopped her. We fought for a second or two. I told Sandra to look at her eyes, at her face. She —"

"I saw her smiling like she was just lying in bed," Sandra Gavin said. "We both saw her smile."

"As if she knew it was all okay, she was okay," Karen Parker said. "In that moment she let go. And I let go."

"Perhaps it was you who was okay, Mrs. Parker?" Walsh said.

"Maybe it was, I don't know." She left the window, sat on the couch beside Sandra Gavin. "I don't know what I was thinking at that moment, Mr. Walsh. I know she was a pawn between me and Sid. I know she suffered being dragged around like an animal on show to fill her father's need for a miracle. Maybe I did decide she would be better off. Or maybe she decided she would be better off, and I let her go. There aren't any miracles."

I said, "What did she see across the pond?"

"I don't know that either. After she was ... gone, Sandra and I stood there on the shore for a while, holding hands and looking out, but there was nothing to see."

"Except the television set."

"Television?"

"In the first house across the pond. A big TV. You can even see the people on it. Was it on?"

"It sure as hell was," Sandra Gavin said. "Karen —"

"That's what Annie saw," I said. "A face or a figure on the TV. Like the angel. She walked out to get close to the angel the way she'd tried to at Deborah Burke's. So eager to reach the angel she even forgot her teddy bear. Maybe, in the water, she still saw the angel. Her father's miracle."

This silence was shorter, a few seconds before Karen Parker stood up again.

"Sandra and I went back into the house. She wanted to tell the police exactly what had happened. I said no, I didn't want her to be part of it. We argued, but I made her go home, rinsed and dried her glass, then went downtown."

Detective Cansino stood up too. "Let's go down there now, get it all on the record."

★ ★

The sun was too bright in Elbert Walsh's office, he'd drawn the shades.

"What will they charge her with?" Sid Parker said.

"Probably nothing," Walsh said. "She didn't kill her, Sid."

"She could have saved her. She let her die."

I said, "You don't know that, Parker. No one knows that."

"She stopped Sandra Gavin from saving her. She killed Annie as sure as if she'd pushed her in and held her under."

I said, "Annie walked into the pond toward the miracle you had offered her. Maybe she found her miracle."

"The most they can do," Walsh said, "is child endangerment, child neglect. I don't think they will."

"Annie was getting better. She would have been normal. Karen murdered my daughter. Nothing will change that."

When Sid Parker had gone, Walsh and I talked for a time about wine and fishing. He paid me, and I left. I drove out of Placerville. Sid and Karen Parker will divorce. Karen will go on with her work, Sid will always say she murdered their daughter who had been getting better every day. The town will split, different people will judge and condemn him or her. That is the nature of towns and people.

Me? I drove home down the edge of the Sierra Nevada, through the wonderful land toward the sea, and thought about Annie.

I wrote "Can Shoot" back in 1993, even though it wasn't published until 1998. I was paid in '93, of course, and when you're a pro that's supposed to be all you care about. That's what we like to say, anyway. But it's not, is it?

It was another that had its start in a small clipping from the inside pages of our local newspaper, but it resonated with a question I've carried in my mind all my life. It also has a certain close relation to another big question in modern America that, again, has been much in the news in recent years.

For me, writing is all about asking questions.

CAN SHOOT

The misery, greed and hate that breed most violent crime, and the vanity and arrogance that account for the rest, exist in Santa Barbara as well as New York. But Santa Barbara isn't New York, and out here walk-in trade is rare in my line of work.

"It's my brother, Mr. Fortune. He was murdered down here and the police won't do anything about it. They won't even listen to me. They just —"

"Slow down, Mr. — ?"

My office is in our house, the address is unlisted, and in Southern California nobody actually walks. So walk-in means a phone call from someone I don't know. A stranger with a problem who found me in the phone book under "Investigators — Private."

"Morgan Jones. My brother was David Jones. Mr. Bowan had no reason to shoot him. No —"

"Humphrey Bowan?"

Humphrey Bowan was one of Montecito's richest residents. He'd bought an old Dodge estate out on East Valley Road where the rich liked to build in the last century: away from the foggy ocean and not in the hot and dry mountains. Bowan lived there half the year, spent the rest of his time up in San Mateo County at his corporate headquarters — Bowan Industries, Inc., with interests in lumbering, mining, insurance, etc.

"He killed Dave right there on his big estate."

"Come out to my office."

When he came in the office door he looked exactly like his voice. A heavy man in his fifties, with a full head of thick dark hair going gray and a shy manner. He saw my left arm was missing, looked stricken for me, and tried hard to not look again.

"It's okay," I said. "I lost it forty years ago, give or take. And you can sit down."

Morgan Jones sat down. He took off his John Deere cap, held it in his lap. We sat there looking at each other.

"You can talk too. You said your brother was killed 'down here'. Where are you from, Mr. Jones?"

"Mendocino. Dave lived in King City. I came down to Santa Barbara to talk to the police, but they won't listen."

"What do you do, Morgan?"

"I run a farm. It's small. Dave worked with all kinds of big animals. He always liked the horses. That's why he went to college up at Davis, got to be a doctor."

"Doctor? You mean a veterinarian?"

"He was the smart one. That's why I know Mr. Bowan didn't have any cause to shoot him. I don't know what he was doing there, but I know for sure it wasn't to steal anything."

"Who says he was there to steal something?"

"Mr. Bowan and the cops. They say he had a gun, broke into the house, and stole some money and other stuff."

"Did he have a gun? Had he stolen anything?"

Morgan Jones was stubborn. "David never even owned a gun. And he didn't need any money. Vets do real good up in farming country. He had three kids in college, and he didn't owe a dime to anyone. He even left me money in his will."

"We don't always know everything about someone else, even our brother. How close were you?"

Jones looked at his hat in his lap. "We didn't see each other so much. I mean, him in King City, and me all the way up around Mendocino. But I knew Dave, and he wasn't on that estate to steal or hurt anyone."

"Why was he on the estate?"

He looked longer at the hat. "I don't know."

"Did he know Bowan? Anyone else on the estate?"

"I don't know."

What he really wanted was to know there had been a reason for his brother to die like that. He had to know, one way or the other. He wanted someone beside the police to tell him his brother had died because he'd been a thief.

"Okay, Morgan, I'll look into it. How did you find me, by the way? Yellow pages?"

"I told the cops I was going to get my own detective. That sergeant Koons said I should call you."

Sheriff's detectives don't usually send me business.

★ ★

Sheriff's headquarters is in Goleta out near the city dump and across from the county jail. In his office, major crimes detective sergeant Josh Koons pulled the file out of his desk.

"The lieutenant says if the brother was like him, no wonder he got shot. The undersheriff says it's a closed case."

"What do you say?"

Koons opened the file. "We got this call about midnight three weeks ago Thursday. Homicide in Montecito. When we got there, we found David Jones dead inside the twelve foot wall around Bowan's estate. He'd been shot once in the head with a high-powered rifle, died instantly. Bowan, his chauffeur and his head groundskeeper were waiting with the body."

He closed the file, recited from memory, "Bowan's up in his bedroom reading when he hears someone out on the grounds near the house. He looks out, sees a man in dark clothes outside french doors into his den. He keeps cash and valuables in a safe in the den, so he runs down. The den's empty, the french doors are open, one pane is broken. He grabs one of his rifles from the wall, shoves in a clip, runs out. The chauffeur, William Berra, hears the man too, comes out of the garage with the gun he carries because they drive around with large sums of cash. The head grounds-keeper, Anselmo Cortez, also hears someone and goes out to look. They all meet, hear the guy running through the trees and brush toward the wall. They chase him, and Bowan spots him. He fires a couple of warning shots in the air, and when the guy doesn't stop, shoots to wing him. The guy zags when he was supposed to zig, gets hit in the head. When we arrive we find a gun on him, cash and jewels from the safe in a bag. The guy's dressed all in black with a ski mask. We check Bowan's rifle, three shots are gone. Bowan is upset as hell, but the coroner's inquest takes ten minutes to bring in justifiable homicide."

Koons finished, put the file back into his desk.

I looked at the drawer where he'd put it. "That's it?"

"Tragic, but the guy was committing a felony."

I said. "If it had been me, and I'd shot a guy with clear justification, I'd still go to a grand jury."

Koons shrugged. Humphrey Bowan wasn't me.

"You trace Jones' gun?"

"An old Colt .45 automatic that disappeared way back in World War Two. Hadn't shown up anywhere since."

"Jones was in the service? Maybe his father?"

"Both of them were conscientious objectors."

"Jones has long burglary sheet?"

"No real sheet at all."

"What does 'no real sheet' mean? Does he have a record or not?"

"He'd been arrested three or four times."

"For what?"

"Damaging federal property. Resisting arrest." Koons looked out his window. "He was an anti-nuclear nut, a peacenik, an environmental activist back in the seventies."

"He was in bad financial trouble? Needed money?"

"Yearly income over a hundred thousand, half a mil in bonds. Three kids in college. A widower who owned his own house and had a steady girlfriend his own age who said he was solid as a rock. Didn't gamble, drink or chase other women."

I said. "Let me see if I've got this straight. You can't trace the gun to him. He's got no record of ever using a gun, in fact he's anti-war and weapons. He has no criminal record at all, when ninety-nine-point-nine percent of burglars are pros with sheets longer than Bowan's family tree. He doesn't need money, is an educated professional man and a solid pillar of the community. Have I got it right?"

Koons moved pencils on his desk. "He was dressed all in black with a ski mask. He had the gun, he had the loot. Even if the gun and loot were planted, I found no connection at all between him and Bowan or anyone else on the estate. And how could they have had a complete black outfit in his exact size, and a black ski mask, on hand to dress him in?"

"It's possible."

"The labels in the clothes were all from King City stores. I went up there to check the stores. Three different places remembered selling 'the Doc' the pants, the turtleneck and the ski mask. I was up there a week, and I found no connection between Jones and Bowan or anyone on the estate. All I found was he'd bought the clothes a couple of days before he came down here. That's when the lieutenant said it was my last trip on the case, and the undersheriff wrote closed."

We both sat there looking out his one window. There's a lot of noise in a police headquarters. All kinds of voices, laughs, whines, violent shouts, radios.

"It doesn't bother you a little?"

"It bothers me a lot. But look at it from the other angle. Bowan fired warning shots, then shot at an armed burglar and accidentally killed him. He has two witnesses who back him up. The dead man had a gun, the loot, and was dressed for burglary. He had a leather bag with him for the loot. An investigation found no connection between Jones and Bowan, and no reason to doubt the story told by Bowan. The sheriff said anything more would be harassing a man because he was prominent. Bowan puts money and time into the county and into the sheriff's campaigns."

"You traced the bag to Jones?"

"No. With the gun, it's the two things we can't trace."

I listened to the headquarter noises some more. "Bowan grabbed the rifle from his wall. Does he have a lot of rifles on that wall? Maybe pistols?"

"Rifles, shotguns, pistols. Trophy heads of all the world's large predators. He's a gun nut and a hunter."

"How far was he from David Jones when he aimed to wing him and hit him dead center of the skull?"

"Coroner says about fifty feet."

"Feet?"

"Feet," Koons said. "It was dark, the trees and brush are thick out there."

"How did Jones open the safe?"

"It's an easy safe. Bowan says he might have left it open."

"Jones's fingerprints on it?"

"He wore gloves. Black."

I listened to the sounds outside the office some more. "The two witnesses both work for Bowan."

"Why was Jones there that night? Dressed like a burglar?"

"They won't let you do any more on it."

"Not a prayer."

"Well then, it looks like I need to find a reason for David Jones to have been on the estate dressed like a burglar."

"I never said that. But somehow I feel I missed something."

It was closest I'd ever get to being told to investigate by the police.

★ ★

There are two ways to drive north from Santa Barbara. Both are beautiful drives, each takes the same time, give or take a few minutes depending on traffic. The longer freeway is faster and safer, the mountain pass is shorter, slower, and more varied. I told Kay, the lady who lets me live with her, I'd be back in a few days or less, and took the pass and back country route. It's more peaceful and relaxing.

The pass road rejoined the freeway beyond Los Olivos, and from Buellton north the drive alternated between the warm, dusty and brown inland valleys, and the cool, foggy, and green coast. With mountains always somewhere to the right or left or both. A pleasant land, Southern California, with gentle days and easy rhythms, where the only extremes are earthquakes, fires, floods and man. North of the Cuesta grade the day ended in a long twilight at Paso Robles, and by King City night had settled in.

King City is the dusty and brown interior. One of those small inland cities of California that seem to have no particular reason to exist except to provide fast-food stops and gasoline stations for the stream of travelers on the freeway. The real reason is in the two main features of the city: the restored and rebuilt Mission San Antonio De Padua, twenty miles southwest, founded by Fr. Junipero Serra on July 14, 1771; and the Monterey County Agricultural and Rural Life Museum right in town.

David Jones's house was two miles out of town on county highway G14 toward Jolon, the military reserve of Fort Hunter Liggett, and the wooded mountains of the Los Padres National Forest. A large, three story white frame Victorian, it had probably once been the mansion of a local ranch baron who married into the old Spanish land grant hidalgos, ended up with the girl and the land. His veterinarian's shingle hung out front, and his office, like mine, was in the rear. I rang at the front door.

The young woman who answered appeared to be in shock. Her eyes were glazed. She stood in the doorway without speaking.

"Ms. Jones? Can I talk to you about your father?"

"My father's dead."

She would have closed the door except she didn't seem capable of moving. Two youths appeared behind her. The oldest took a deep breath, knew he had to say something.

"Someone shot our father. We don't know why."

"He wasn't a crook!" That was the younger boy.

"Can we go inside and talk about it?"

The older one recovered partially from his paralysis, and led the way into a large living room. It had molding, hardwood floors, fireplace with a marble mantel, old-fashioned wallpaper and furniture, and green velvet drapes, but it wasn't a museum piece. Lovingly restored and cared for, it was also comfortable and even relaxed. The people who had put the room and the house together were determined, meticulous and gentle.

"Do any of you know what your father was doing on Humphrey Bowan's estate down in Santa Barbara?"

The three of them looked at each other, looked back at me, and shook their heads one at a time. They were normal young people, wrapped up in their own lives, needs and dreams. Without a mother, away at college most of the year, and not concerned about what their father happened to be doing except sending them money. They also didn't know what the future was going to be for them and they were scared. Abandoned and frightened.

"Do you know of anything he was involved in that might connect him to Humphrey Bowan or anyone who works for Bowan?"

I knew it was useless. David Jones had been their father, the source of money and support, and at their age very damn little else. Unless what I needed was obvious I wouldn't get it from them, and if it had been that obvious, Koons would have found it.

"Does he have an office in the house?"

Even that was a hard question for them. The youngest one realized he knew the answer. "No."

"It's in the house," the older boy corrected, "but you have to go outside to get to it."

"Could I maybe see the office then?"

They looked at each other, apparently decided that with their Dad dead and buried they had nothing to protect him from. The older one nodded. "I guess so. You need a key."

He told the younger boy to give me a key. He would get used to being the man of the family only too soon. Then the other two, especially the girl, would begin to rebel and tell him he wasn't their father.

★ ★

The office was another large, comfortable room with armchairs and side tables, a battered desk and daunting rows of file cabinets. There were three doors in addition to the outside door. David Jones had been primarily a large animals vet, few if any of his patients would have come to the office, but one door opened into an examination room with sterilizers and a surgical table for smaller animals. Another door was into a storage room and pharmacy. The last was a fully equipped darkroom made out of a closet.

Two walls of the main room were for the filing cabinets and bookcases. The other two walls were for the windows, and displays of diplomas and hundreds of framed photos of animals, protest marches, nuclear picketing and fine landscapes. Jones had been an amateur photographer, which was interesting, but he had certainly had the money to support a lot more expensive hobby than that.

I looked through the desk first, and after about an hour found nothing that looked in any way relevant. Then I tackled the files. Four hours later I gave up. Every file folder was for a veterinarian client, all local. None of them had any remote connection to Bowan, his estate, or Santa Barbara I could see. I had come directly to the house after checking into a motel, hadn't eaten, and after five hours was getting hungry. I drove to the motel, asked where I could get some dinner at the late hour, and was sent a block to a Denny's. King City.

In bed, the freeway still noisy outside even at midnight, and neon flashing in the windows of the room, I lay awake and went over it. Koons had done everything I had done so far, had talked to everyone in town who had known David Jones, and had come up empty. The people, none of whom believed David Jones had been a burglar, clothes or no clothes, were not going to tell me anything they hadn't already told Koons. If there were a reason for Jones to have gone to Santa Barbara and Humphrey Bowan, other than burglary, it had to be somewhere in his office.

★ ★

This time I had breakfast before I went out to the big old Victorian on G14. I still had the key, let myself in, and went around the office once more from the top. The desk, the files, every drawer and shelf in every room. By the time my stomach was rumbling for lunch, I still had nothing.

I was about to take care of my stomach before starting on the third go around, when the door opened and a woman came in.

"Who are you?"

I told her who I was.

"Morgan always did think far too much of Dave to accept that man's pack of lies as the police have."

"You must be Dave's lady?"

"I suppose I must. Do I gather you haven't accepted Bowan's blatant drivel either, Mr. Fortune?"

"Why would Bowan lie, Ms. —"

"Drusilla Barnes. Dave called me Drusie. I even liked it." There was more grief inside her than inside the dead man's kids, but she had it under iron control. "He lied because he killed Dave and needed an excuse to justify murder."

"Why did he kill him?"

"He had a reason."

"But you don't know it."

She sat down in one of the armchairs. A small, compact woman on the edge of being stout. In her mid-forties, brown hair cut short, wearing dark blue pants, a white blouse, and soft black medium-heeled boots. Not a wild swinger, but individual.

"You have no idea what he could have been doing on Bowan's estate? Dressed like a burglar?"

"No."

"Had he been involved in some environmental cause recently?" Bowan had interests in lumber, mining, and other fields the EPA and the environmentalists were hot on.

"Not for years. With the end of the Cold War he hadn't done any peace marches or protests either."

"He never mentioned Humphrey Bowan or his estate to you?"

"No."

"Santa Barbara?"

"No."

Every 'no' sounded like a shovelful of dirt falling on David Jones's coffin. I didn't really believe a third try would do anything to help. Drusilla Barnes looked around with something close to tears in her eyes. She fixed on the walls of photographs.

"He loved his photography so much. An art and a record, you know? He carried his camera everywhere."

I stared at the walls of photos. Then I stood up. "Look for it. Look everywhere you can think of."

"Look? For what?"

"His camera. Any camera. I've searched this office twice, and I don't remember a camera. You go inside and do the house. Every room. Get those kids to help, if they're still around."

I did my third search. There was no camera.

Drusilla Barnes came back. "It's nowhere in the house. He used an expensive mini-camera, a Minolta. I remember it very well, he nearly always had it with him. If he didn't take it with him, he left it here in the office."

"Let's say he did take it with him. That he went down to Santa Barbara to take pictures of something. Something he knew Bowan wouldn't want photographed. That would account for the dark clothes and the ski mask, for him sneaking onto the estate."

"But what, Mr. Fortune?"

"Did he mention anything about taking special photos?"

"No."

"Anything at all unusual? Anything he was upset about? Anything—"

"Well, he was disturbed one evening recently by an emergency call he'd made, but he was often upset after a call. He hated to see animals suffer."

"Why did you happen to recall this one time specially?"

She frowned. "I'm not sure. Perhaps . . . yes, because he seemed more angry than upset. We had dinner that night, and I asked him why he was angry. He said he didn't want to talk about it until he was sure."

"Do you remember who the client was?"

She shook her head. "No, I —"

"Think, Drusie!"

But she couldn't.

★ ★

I took Drusilla Barnes to lunch, coaxed and coached her the whole time, but no bells rang.

I tried the other vets in town. There were only three, and only one large animal. "Hell, Dave and I talked every day, but damned if I remember him being angry about any call he'd made."

I tried the feed stores and the Monterey County Agricultural and Rural Life Museum. They all knew Dave, none had a clue about anything disturbing him recently.

I tried the police. The sheriff's deputy at the local office knew Dave, but not all that well. "Like I told sergeant Koons when he come up here, Dave Jones was a real nice, quiet guy never had trouble with anyone I know. Never saw him get mad about anything."

After another not exactly sensational dinner at Denny's, I headed back to Jones's house to take one more look through his case files. This time I knew I was looking for something that had made Dave Jones angry, something out of the ordinary, something unusual, different, and I found it at once.

It was a single file folder. Not suspicious in itself, only . . . different. First, it was out of order. Second, it was at the front of the file drawer — as if it had been haphazardly dropped back in because Jones's mind was on something more important that the orderliness of his records. Third, it was empty except for an engraved business card, torn and dirty, with a name, Walter J. Bachman, and an address and telephone number in Bakersfield.

The label on the file read: Monterey Club Ranch.

I used the telephone. There was no answer in Bakersfield. I used the phone again.

On the other end, Drusilla Barnes said, "There's a Monterey Ranch out near Jolon. A big spread, and old. It's been in the same family since the last century. The Walkers. I heard they'd had some hard times, but I never heard of any club."

★ ★

The Monterey Ranch was past Jolon on the county highway toward the wooded mountains of the Santa Lucia Range that touched the ocean on the far side. A night so dark I almost missed the sign over the entrance to a narrow blacktop road: Monterey Ranch. A half a mile up the side road I was almost on top of it before the small white house emerged from the dark as well-cared for as a museum exhibit. I drove on past, and saw a single light at the rear of the house and a forest service pickup truck.

The blacktop road went on in the night past the house. Few rural ranches in California had blacktop roads leading to them, and fewer still had the blacktop go on to something else beyond. Another mile and a half in, the road curved around the shoulder of a steep slope in the night under the edge of the mountains. A large number of buildings lay directly ahead.

I parked, got out, and looked at the shadowy buildings. They didn't look much like those of any working ranch I'd ever seen. A central frame building in the center of a dusty dirt yard was ringed by smaller cottages under old oaks and other native trees I couldn't name. To the right were a series of low buildings with doors every ten feet or so. There were no cars. The central building and the cottages looked deserted, but I heard movement in the low buildings to the right, and some dogs were barking in that direction.

I walked through the night to the low buildings. The barking of the dogs grew louder and more agitated as I walked along the buildings. All the doors were locked with padlocks. I went around to the rear, and found the dogs. The buildings were cages. Most of the cages were empty, but the dogs barked and leaped inside some. In two others there was a fat old leopard who watched me with eyes that could have belonged to one of the hound dogs who wanted to be petted, and a feeble-looking Bengal tiger far back and frightened in the corner of its cage. As I walked closer, the tiger tried to get up but failed, and the leopard tried to lick me.

I didn't hear the footsteps until they were behind me.

"Put your hands behind your head. Now!"

I put my lone hand on the back of my neck. Someone made a sound, but patted me from shoulder to toe anyway, inside my legs and out.

"Turn around."

They were two sheriff's deputies with their guns drawn, and a man in a uniform I didn't recognize but could guess.

"What are you doing here."

I told them.

★ ★

The three men in the office were a Monterey County sheriff's lieutenant, an assistant district attorney, and a regional director for the U.S. Fish and Wildlife Service. The office was in the King City Division of the Monterey County Municipal Court, the subject was the Monterey Club Ranch. The main talker was assistant D.A. Marcus Delaney.

"The Monterey Ranch, Mr. Fortune, is a cattle ranch. It's run by Mr. Jackson Walker. Mr. Walker is well known here, the ranch has been in the Walker family for five generations, they tell me. It's a large spread in fairly remote country, with the forest and military reserve next to it. Some years ago Walker decided to increase his income by using the ranch for a sideline: hunting wild boar and deer."

Sheriff's lieutenant Tom Fierro wanted me, or maybe the U.S. Fish and Wildlife Service, to understand. "A lot of folks around here work as hunting guides. Deer, quail, doves, varmints like coyotes and such. Maybe fifty, seventy-five years ago, a rich guy over toward Big Sur imported these European wild pigs so him and his friends from back east could hunt 'em on his estate. They got loose, been running wild in Los Padres ever since. Tough damn pigs, and good huntin'. Jack Walker got a lotta land, plenty of wild pigs on it, so he got this idea to make some extra money. Ranching ain't been so good around here, and taxes keep going up on people's land."

"Monterey Club Ranch," the U.S. Fish and Wildlife Service man, Bill Mikoyan, took up the story. "Walker started advertising it down in L.A. and up in San Francisco. Even back east. A thrill for city people. Custom killing. Bring your gun, we supply the dogs and the targets."

He held a business card out for me to take. It had the name of the club, the embossed heads of a wild boar and a deer. It listed the hunting of the wild pigs, deer, dove and quail.

"The problem," assistant D.A. Delaney continued, "is that Mr. Walker didn't stop there. Two years ago, he —"

Lieutenant Fierro leaned forward in his chair in the quiet office, the moonlight bright outside now over the brown fields and distant mountains. He still wanted us to understand. "Five, six years of drought. People are hurtin' around here. The damned drought made Jack Walker sell off half his cattle, drove the pigs 'n deer deeper inside Los Padres when food and water dried up on his ranch. He didn't have enough grazing for his beef, lost his barley farming operation when he had a really bad crop, couldn't afford to buy even enough feed for the cattle he had left. He had to do something if he was going to survive and maybe not lose the whole ranch."

He looked around at all of them, pleading a case I hadn't heard yet, but could put together without a lot of trouble from what I'd seen and heard so far.

"Exotic animal hunting," I said. "Lions, tigers, leopards, jaguars. Old and toothless. Couldn't outrun a fat poodle or harm anyone over six. A 'can hunt'."

"An African or South American safari can cost over $20,000," the wild-life man, Mikoyan, said. "These kinds of sick operations are growing all the time. We must have ten other investigations going on right now across the country."

Delaney said, "Walker conducted five of these 'can hunts' in three months this year. Most of the animals come from zoos that no longer want them because they're too old and feeble. Some were pets people became afraid of or that grew too old to be fun. Some are raised specially in Mexico and Texas. Walker never kept them more than two or three days. It cost too much to feed them, I imagine. He only imported them when he had a 'hunt' lined up. These 'hunters' shot most of them a few feet from the cages, not that it mattered. Most of the animals didn't have enough teeth left to chew a chicken, or the strength to run a mile. Some wouldn't even come out, were shot right in the cages."

I said, "For trophies. Have you charged anyone beside Walker? Any of the clients?"

"We do if we can catch them with identifiable dead animals, the pelts, or the heads."

"What's the charge and sentence?"

Mikoyan, the Fish and Game director, shook his head. "Mostly violating endangered species laws and permit procedures. We don't respect animals in this country. This world, for that matter."

Delaney said. "Misdemeanors. One year in jail and a small fine on each charge. Enough to do damage to Walker's business, but not a lot more."

Mikoyan said, "Federal charges of interstate transportation and killing of endangered species could be filed. Those are both felonies."

"With a decent lawyer they'd get off with a slap anyway," I said. "Free enterprise carries a lot more weight than an old tiger. You have the names of the clients?"

"Walker didn't keep records. Under the table all the way."

"Then how'd you find any clients to charge?"

Delaney looked down at his file. He didn't have to, but he didn't like what he had to say. "Photos of the trophies. Those who supplied Walker had records of the animals. Sometimes the original owners had records."

"Photos? From where?"

"Anonymous," Mikoyan said. "They just came into my office in the mail with the names of the clients."

"The clients didn't know the photos had been taken?"

"No."

I thought about it for a time. "How did you learn about the can hunts at all?"

Mikoyan said, "Same way. Anonymous tip. We followed up, then brought in the sheriff."

David Jones had gone to Monterey Club Ranch to treat some lion or tiger, and seen something about the animals that made him angry and suspicious. He'd tipped the federal wildlife people, but that hadn't been enough. He wanted the hunters.

Mikoyan said, "There's something sick about shooting an old, feeble animal at short range and then claiming a trophy. The shooters even took photographs and videotapes."

"Sure, 'can shootin' ' is bad," Lieutenant Fierro said, "but I don't see nothing wrong with hunting the exotics if the chase is fair. What's the difference between that and lettin' folks go out and hunt deer and boar?"

Everyone looked at him.

"The difference," Mikoyan said, "is that the exotics aren't wild. They're tame animals, Fierro. Old and sick. They're goddamn pets!"

I said, "I don't really see all that difference myself, lieutenant. Except that deer aren't even as dangerous as pets, and damned few of us need to put meat on the table anymore."

Now they all looked at me.

★ ★

I sat in my Tempo outside the address in Bakersfield I'd found on the business card in the otherwise empty Monterey Ranch Club file. It was a storefront on a back street with houses all around and simple black-bordered gold lettering on the door: Walter J. Bachman, Taxidermist.

I guessed that David Jones, on an emergency call to Monterey Ranch to treat one of the exotic animals, probably told that they were 'caring for' the poor beasts in their last days, had been made suspicious by something, and had found the card too. He had called the number hoping to find a witness to confirm or deny his suspicions, and found instead Walter J. Bachman's trade. Why would somewhere that 'cared for' old exotic animals need a taxidermist? (It was obviously something Jack Walker and Walter Bachman had thought of too, hence nothing but name and address on the card.)

A sign in the window listed Bachman's hours as 8:00 to 12:00 and 1:30 to 5:30. It was like my business, not a lot of walk-in trade. I staked it out until the taxidermist locked up and went home for lunch. Then I broke in. David Jones had to have found the names and addresses of the can shooters somewhere. Walter J. Bachman, taxidermist, had to have records. He did.

Not in his regular account books, but in a special book in a locked drawer and coded. The drawer was simple to open, and the code was just as simple. Next to the names and addresses of the clients, the fees, and the delivery dates, were a series of letters: T, L, J. Maybe the taxidermist was proud of his skill, wanted to recall every exotic job he did. Whatever, he'd given David Jones his leads to find the clients and get his damning photographs, and next to Humphrey Bowan's name were three letters: T, J, and P.

I knew why David Jones had been on Humphrey Bowan's estate dressed all in black like a burglar. Now all I had to do was prove it.

★ ★

I got back to my Summerland hacienda before dark. Kay was waiting for me, and so was Morgan Jones.

"He's been here every day," Kay said, not pleased.

I shooed Jones away after telling him I might have an answer for him soon, be patient. I didn't shoo Kay away. What I had in mind to do on David Jones couldn't be done well at night. What I had in mind for Kay could. She agreed.

She slept in, I made my own breakfast, and considered the possibilities. David Jones had come down here to photograph Humphrey Bowan's illegal trophies, but no camera had been found on or near the body, or in his car parked on the side road. Either it had been found by Bowan and his people and probably destroyed, or it was still out there. Fifty-fifty odds.

I drove out to East Valley Road, parked on the same side street Jones had. It had been dark when he scaled the wall. I was going to have to do it in daylight. He had had two arms, I had one. Nobody ever said detective work was easy.

With the aid of a friendly low-hanging sycamore branch, I made it over the wall and located the exact spot where Koons had found Jones dead. It wasn't hard to spot even after three weeks. The thick brush had been trampled and flattened for ten yards around, there was even still a trace of blood. What there wasn't was a camera.

I worked outward in a circle, one eye alert for anyone who might spot me. The trees and brush were so thick the massive fifty-room imitation English manor house was invisible, but I still felt as exposed as a zebra in a pride of lions. As I moved closer to the house I heard voices through the trees, saw the chauffeur working on a limousine in front of the garages that had once been a coach house. But I didn't find a camera, and went back to the wall to think about it.

Assuming David Jones had gotten into the mansion and taken his pictures, as the broken french door panes indicated, and Bowan or the other two had spotted the camera, they'd have grabbed it. If I was going to find it, they had to have missed it. What would I have done with the camera if I were being pursued? Jones couldn't have imagined anyone would shoot him, so his main concern would have been to preserve the photos, his evidence against Humphrey Bowan, even if they caught him and turned him over to the police for trespassing.

He had been shot near the wall. If I had felt no one could see me, and I was at the wall, over the camera would have gone.

I used the same sycamore, went over again, worked my way through the brush between the wall and East Valley Road, and there it was.

A mini-Minolta that had landed in a thicket of manzanita, intact and undamaged.

★ ★

I took the film to one of those places where they claim to develop and print your roll in one hour, but always take half a day at best. It was late afternoon when I spread the prints out on my office desk. Fifteen closeups, from every angle, of three mounted heads on a wall between other heads and racks of guns. A grizzled tiger with a scarred eye, a jaguar with one ear bald and the other half gone, and a puma older than my grandfather after he was dead.

★ ★

The chauffeur, William Berra, came out of the gates of Bowan's mansion at exactly six P.M. He never slowed down until he got to the Miramar Hotel bar. A muscular dark-haired man with a thick neck and a battered, stubborn face, he wore narrow gray slacks that showed his slim waist, a sky blue sport shirt loose and wide over his muscles, and running shoes. Thirty-five or so, thick-haired and handsome.

He settled onto a stool at the piano bar, flirted with the waitress and eyed three women at the bar. Older women. Berra's smile said he expected them to appreciate his open attention. A confident man without a care in the world. He had two more Margaritas over the next two hours, looked at his watch, patted the waitress and left. I followed him back to Bowan's estate.

He didn't come out again for the next two nights, and when he did it was the same controlled ritual.

★ ★

Anselmo Cortez did nothing the first day. The second day he came out in mid-afternoon, went alone to a bar in the barrio of the lower eastside and drank for hours without a word. Brooding. He did the same on the third day, got drunk, and his wife found him and drove him home. When he came out later that same night, his dark face both angry and pale, I had my man.

He went to the same barrio saloon. I took a seat three stools up and waited. I was the only anglo in the place, but with one arm I didn't look like a cop. I didn't look like an easy mark for the macho young punks either, wasn't nervous, so they left me alone. When you're a minority, you tend to be wary of a member of the majority who doesn't fit the normal pattern.

On his third tequila, I moved next to Cortez.

"Women don't understand when a man's got trouble, amigo."

Cortez nodded gloomily. He was a tall, slim man with a worn and seamed face the color of saddle leather. Someone who had spent most of his life outdoors, and not always on the plush estate of Humphrey Bowan.

"The cops'll find out, you know that."

He nodded again, sorry for himself, and then the import of my words that echoed his own fears reached him and he froze.

"An honorable man like you shouldn't cover for someone like that. He's a coward, Anselmo, you know that."

Now he looked at me in abject terror.

"It's a good job, right? Your family? I understand that. But even the best job ..."

"Who ... who are you?"

"You didn't know he had a brother, did you? The man your boss killed. The murder you're covering up for him."

"I don' know what you say."

"He sent me, the brother. I'm a detective and I know what happened. It won't help your family if you go to prison."

He drained his tequila, didn't wave for another.

"Then I'll tell you. You heard someone outside, went out to look. You ran into your boss with his hunting rifle. Berra too, with his gun. You all chased the intruder. You all ..."

"Boss say we got big hunt. Boss —" He stopped. "You go. I don' talk to you no —"

"Hunt?"

A hunt! For a fleeing burglar! Bowan hadn't fired any warning shots. His first two shots had simply missed. Had they all missed until Bowan's fatal shot, or was the hunt only for Bowan? A hunt for the biggest game. A burglar, a criminal. Who would ask any questions? Especially when they put a gun with the body, and a bag of loot.

"David Jones wasn't a criminal, Anselmo. He wasn't there to steal anything. I know why he was there that night, and when I tell the police it's all going to come out. You —"

The other patrons in the bar were all looking at us. Even the bartender. Not a friendly look. It was one thing to let a questionable anglo alone, it was another to let him attack one of your own. I had to finish fast.

"I guess it comes down to this, Anselmo. You want to go down with your boss, lose your cushy job and your freedom, or lose just your job and feel ...?"

He pushed his empty glass away, walked to the door and out into the night. I sat and finished my beer. If I'd have tried to go after him, I wouldn't have reached the door.

★ ★

It was going to be a matter of timing.

Hair-trigger timing. But I didn't have much choice. Unless someone talked, all I had was conjecture. Nothing proved David Jones didn't take a gun as well as his camera, or decide to lift some loot on the side.

I borrowed the house from some friends of Kay's. It sat deep on a wooded acre off El Bosque Road two miles from Bowan's mansion. I waited until dark, and made the first call.

"Humphrey Bowan?"

"Yes. Who is this?"

"My name doesn't matter. What I know does. I know what David Jones was really doing on your estate that night, and you don't. When I tell the police, they'll know he wasn't any burglar. I know and they'll know what really happened. Now I'm a reasonable man. Dave's dead, what does he need, right? I'm alive, and I need a whole lot of things. So let's talk about what you got a lot of, right? I mean, it ought to be worth maybe six figures, right?"

"I don't know what —"

"One word, Mr. Bowan. Hunt. How's that? A hunt for a fleeing criminal."

The silence dripped with more venom than the voice when it finally came again. "Where are you."

"That's better. I'm at 184 El Bosque. It's pretty isolated, and I can see real good, so come alone."

"Half an hour."

He hung up. I sat and watched the grandfather clock in the borrowed house. He would need to gather the troops, make a plan, and drive the two miles. Say, fifteen minutes if he moved fast. I waited five and then called sergeant Koons.

"Koons? Dan Fortune. You want Humphrey Bowan, get out to 184 El Bosque, and fast."

"Fortune —"

This time I hung up. Fifteen minutes for Koons, twenty at the outside.

I left the lights on inside the house, drew the curtains, and went out to blend into the shadows of a grove of old oaks fifty feet from the house. They stood, thick and brooding, at a corner of the large yard where I could watch and see both the side of the property that bordered East Valley Road, and the front on El Bosque. It was a dark night, but the moon was coming up. So was what I hoped was the end of the game. I had my Sig-Sauer, and twelve minutes later I had them.

Anselmo Cortez parked his pickup at the front of the property on El Bosque. He got out and walked up the driveway toward the house. He had no gun, walked slowly and warily as if cautious. What he was doing was decoying the man they expected to be watching greedily from the house to see his money walking toward him. After all, the blackmailer on the telephone was only a dumb crook, right?

The chauffeur, Walter Berra, and Humphrey Bowan came through the brush from East Valley. They moved as silently as big cats, I'll give them that. After all, Bowan was a big game hunter. A tall, lean shadow that passed like a tiger in the night toward the silent house, and carried a hunting rifle ready to go to the shoulder or the hip.

I let them make their approach right up to the house. They signaled Cortez to climb the steps to the front door and knock. I heard the first distant siren, faint and still some miles away. When Cortez was on the porch, I stepped to the edge of the grove of oaks, half in and half out of the moonlight, my Sig-Sauer out and steady.

"Well now. Look who's trespassing, and with guns too."

Cortez recognized my voice. "That man is the —"

Berra came around with his pistol, got off two fast shots.

Too fast. He didn't come close. I shot twice, got his hand. The gun disappeared somewhere in the night, and he went down cursing and holding a broken and bleeding hand. Humphrey Bowan moved the rifle maybe an inch, and we faced off for maybe half a minute. Then he lowered the rifle.

"Yeah," I said. "You like it better when the target can't bite or shoot back."

"Mister, you better have a good explanation for this, or the police —"

I heard the car glide to a silent stop out on the road. I smiled to myself. I'd had a hunch Koons would come first and silent. Bowan was too busy intimidating me and planning a quick escape to notice the car. Berra was too busy with his pain to hear anything. I couldn't tell if Cortez heard the new arrival or not.

"Oh, I've got a good explanation. David Jones didn't steal anything from you, and he didn't have a gun that night. He was unarmed, and you shot him down in cold blood. Because you were sure you could get away with it. No other reason. A hunt, some sport. Another 'can shoot' just like up in Jolon. Only this time the quarry wasn't some scared and toothless old pet, but an unarmed human being who'd only come to your estate to help stop the killing of helpless animals."

And then I talked to Anselmo Cortez on the porch. "You're going to have to make up your mind, Anselmo. Are you going down with him, or are you going to tell us how he made you do what you're ashamed of?"

As if on cue, the sirens were suddenly close in the night, coming along East Valley Road. Cortez heard them.

"He tell us don' catch the man, on'y chase him. Make sure he don' get away. Make the man stay on the land so he, Mr. Bowan, can hunt the man like animal."

"The brave hunter," I said.

"He's a liar!" Bowan snarled. "You can't prove a damn thing. The sheriff won't listen —"

"I think he will. With Cortez talking, Berra will talk too. And with what I've put together, it should convince a jury."

That was when sergeant Koons stepped out of the trees. "It's convinced me."

★ ★

There were five of us in the lieutenant's office.

I said, "Morgan Jones didn't believe his brother could be a thief. Neither did Koons, and neither did I. So there had to be a reason for him to be on that estate dressed the way he was. That's what I found in King City. He was there to take photos of the trophy heads from the 'can shoot' up in Jolon. At first, I thought Bowan must have spotted him and the camera, known what he was doing, even though proving Bowan shot those helpless animals didn't sound like enough motive for murder. Not with the small penalties involved, but you never know. Some men, especially rich and arrogant men, would kill to keep from being humiliated, made to look small. If that had been what happened, the camera would be long gone. I would know what had happened, and so would you, but we could never have proved it. So when I found the camera I knew he had to have been shot for some other reason. Cortez told me the reason — a hunt."

Koons said, "They heard Jones, but they never saw him in the house, and they never spotted the camera. Bowan saw a chance to have a big thrill he'd never had. He'd never shot a man. He told Cortez and Berra to block Jones, shoo him back to where Bowan could get a clear shot. It took him three shots, the last at fifty feet. They planted the gun and the loot on the body and called us."

The lieutenant said, "That Berra better talk too. Or it's the Latino's word, and Fortune's story, against Bowan and his lawyers."

"Christ," the assistant D.A. said. "There's going to be hell to pay. Bowan funds half the goddamn charities in the county."

The undersheriff said, "The boss is going to shit purple."

"With Bowan's money he can appeal forever," the assistant D.A. groaned. "Jones was trespassing. He was wearing clothes that made him look like a goddamn burglar."

"Yeah," I said. "A real dangerous criminal."

The undersheriff glared at me. "Why the hell didn't that fucking Jones mind his own goddamn business."

"I think you'll all come out okay," I said. "Second degree, or at least voluntary manslaughter. The camera stuff lets you get the poor old animals in. Everybody cares about cruelty to animals if not to people."

Nobody seemed to think that was funny.

*Also in 1993, Elaine Chase asked me if I would participate in her
Partners in Crime anthology for NAL. Dan had never worked with
a partner. I thought about it, and realized that when he was in New
York, especially in the early books, the bartender Joe Harris had been
a sounding board, sidekick, and friend. What if old Joe were now a
successful club owner, a power on the Minnesota Strip, and Dan
needed his help for a case?*

*I guess it worked out pretty well. Elaine took "A Matter Of
Character," it was nominated for a Shamus award, and it was fun to
send Dan back to New York once more.*

*I also got to make fictional use of a bounty hunter who once
worked out of Santa Barbara, and tell distant readers that not all is
apple pie and palm trees even in paradise.*

A MATTER OF CHARACTER

He wore a suit and tie, sat alone at a table in the rear of the cocktail lounge
working on some ledgers. When he looked up, he smiled. "Hello, Dan."

"How the hell are you, Joe?"

"Older," Joe said.

The lounge was a long room on 48th street between Eighth Avenue and
Broadway. It had booths, tables, indirect lighting and a small bar at the
front where the bartender wore a red-and-gold jacket. I sat across the table.

"Classy place," I said. "How about a double Irish? On the cuff."

"You don't drink the hard stuff anymore, and I own the joint," Joe
smiled. "Cash on the line. Everything changes."

"Give some people power and they turn into Hitler."

We grew up together, Daniel Tadeusz Fortune, who had once been
Fortunowski, and Joseph Francis Harris. Down in Chelsea near the old
docks, and he knows how I lost my left arm. He was there the night two
seventeen-year-old thieves were looting a freighter and one fell into the
hold shattering his arm. Two juveniles, one whose cop father had run
away and whose mother brought home too many cops who hadn't run
away, and the other whose father and mother were both too drunk most
of the time to stand much less run anywhere.

"Nothing's free when you own the game," he said. "Especially for
tourists from cloud-cuckoo-land. I'll bet you ask for lemon slices and paper
umbrellas on your beer."

"Only the best now, Joe. Stuff you don't get back here."

"Like what?"

"Sierra Nevada, Red Tail."

People get busy, drift apart, move away, and it had been five years since I'd seen Joe. Longer. But there are some people who, when there's no one else, will always be there for you and you for them.

"I need some help, Joe."

"I told you that twenty years ago."

"Not mental this time, physical. I need knowledge, expertise, contacts. I need names, faces, and the word on the street. I've been away too long."

"Let's go back to my office." He called to the bartender, "Reuben, two Red Tails in the back." And grinned at me.

★ ★

It started in Santa Barbara when Samuel Armbruster came to my office, and I sent for the official New York Police Department record of the killing.

> *On the night of October 5, 1994, at 1:06 A. M., Roger Berenger, of 140 E. Pedregosa Street in Santa Barbara, California, was attacked in the corridor of the Emerson Hotel on West 41st Street, between Ninth and Tenth Avenue, while in the company of Ricky Franklin, 14, a male prostitute Berenger had picked up on Ninth Avenue, and was pronounced dead at the scene. Injured in the same attack, Franklin could not identify the assailants when questioned later in the hospital. There were no other witnesses. Gondolfo Godoy, hotel manager, found the victims and called the police. Autopsy by the medical examiner's office showed that Roger Berenger had died of multiple blows to the face and head. His money, watch, rings and shoes were missing.*

"Roger did not employ prostitutes, Mr. Fortune," Samuel Armbruster said. "He had neither the interest nor the need."

He was a tall man with thick gray hair and green eyes as fierce and determined as a hungry eagle.

"The evidence tells the New York police a different story," I said. "I'm afraid it tells me the same thing, Mr. Armbruster."

"Then either the evidence is wrong, or the New York police have the wrong evidence."

We sat in my office in the back room of the red-tile-roofed Summerland hacienda I share with my lady, Kay Michaels. Or I sat. Samuel Armbruster stood ramrod straight, legs slightly apart as if balancing on the deck of a rolling destroyer like the naval officer he had been. ("That was a long time ago, Mr. Fortune. During wars when they needed trained officers and didn't ask irrelevant questions," he'd told me the first time he'd come to the office. "They would probably toss me out of the service today.")

"It's not complicated evidence, Mr. Armbruster. There isn't much to question."

His friend Roger Berenger had been killed on a trip to a convention of violin teachers at the Sheraton Hotel in New York. As next of kin, Armbruster had gone to New York to identify the body, bring it back to Santa Barbara, and express his strong doubts. The New York police had been polite, but the case was open and shut, there was nothing they could do. Armbruster came to me. I still had good contacts among the New York police, especially now I was three thousand miles away. Captain Pearce sent me a copy of the case file.

"It could not have happened as they say it did. Roger would never have been with such a boy or in such a place."

He still stood like Farragut on his flagship at Mobile Bay. Damn the torpedoes, full speed ahead.

"You're saying Roger wasn't gay?"

He dismissed that with a wave. "Of course he was gay, we've been together for years. But Roger would not have gone near that area, such places disgusted him. He was far too fastidious, had far too much character."

"People can change," I said as gently as I could. "Sometimes we don't know everything about —"

"Spare me the homilies, Mr. Fortune. I am well aware of the possibilities and the psychology involved, probably far more than you in respect to the gay world, and I know what Roger would and wouldn't do."

He stood there like some tough old redwood that had survived a thousand years. We don't make life easy in this country for the different who want to stand tall and live like everyone else, do whatever anyone else can do. He was tough and strong and determined, but his life's companion had died, and he was trying to be all those things and somehow find out why. I wished he would sit down, not make me feel flabby and self-indulgent, but standing tall was part of what held him together. It probably always had been.

"Just how many years were you and Roger together, Mr. Armbruster?"

He didn't answer for a few seconds, probably looking for some hidden attack behind the question. We do that to the different in this country, too. He looked into my eyes, and looked at my empty sleeve, and whatever he saw in one or the other, he suddenly sat in my one armchair, his face no longer looking as tough or as hard.

"Twenty-six years." His voice was low, each word slow and distinct. "For twenty of those twenty-six years, we've lived in the same house. We each had a studio at the back of the house, we both composed and taught violin in those studios. We went to the same church, sang in the same choir, became deacons in the same church. Twenty-six years sharing our work, our pleasures and our troubles. Sharing our sex lives and our happiness. Now he's gone and I'm alone. My life essentially over as well as empty. But I will not let Roger's memory be a lie."

Not as tough or as hard, but just as determined.

"He was found dead in the corridor of that hotel, a fourteen-year-old male prostitute he had picked up injured beside him. If he didn't go there with the boy, how did he get there?"

"That, Mr. Fortune, is what I'm hiring you to find out, isn't it?"

"You're saying that someone took him there and killed him? Someone hired the boy to lie, beat him up, and somehow made him continue to lie in the hospital?"

"I don't know what I'm saying. I only know that Roger could not have died as the New York police say he did, because he could not have been with such a boy in such a place."

"You have an idea what a motive could be?"

"If I had, I wouldn't be here, Mr. Fortune."

His green eyes didn't flinch, but they did flicker. He might not know a specific motive for a specific person to murder Roger Berenger, but he knew a general motive for too many people to murder any man like Roger. Everyone in our country who dances to a different beat knows that motive.

★ ★

Over dinner, Kay watched me. "Are you going to help him?"

It was Saturday, one of our wine dinners. They're important, our wine dinners. The sharing of more than a house or a bed or even a career. She has her career and I have mine. Together we have the house and the bed. But on every Saturday we can manage we have more. A bottle of a good wine, a fine dinner, and time only for us.

"Do I have a devastated man groping for how to deal with the loss of the most important person in his life, a man who's come to a rational conclusion based on fact, or someone who knows more than he's telling me?"

"Does it matter, Dan?"

She knows me. I liked Samuel Armbruster, and when I like someone I tend to believe them, or at least go along with them until they prove they can't be believed. Most police departments wouldn't consider that a good character trait in a detective. It was one of the many ways I differed from most police officers, and most private investigators, for that matter.

"You like him too, Kay?"

"I like anyone who stands up for who and what he is," she said. "Mr. Armbruster is doing that. For his dead friend, and for himself."

"I'll probably have to go to New York."

"I'll live," Kay said.

"The woman of ice."

"You take good care of me. I can manage for a week or so."

I wasn't sure I could, and before I plunged back into the swamp of New York, I decided to find out a little more about my client and Roger Berenger.

★ ★

In a city and county as small as Santa Barbara you work with the same police, get to know some of them well, for better or worse. Sergeant Gus Chavalas, SBPD's favorite Latino detective, is for the better. He's actually Greek, but unless he is asked directly he keeps that information to himself in a city that is twenty percent Latino. Over the years we've come to trust each other, and he'll bend a few rules if no one will get hurt.

"I checked on your two old boys. All the way back to when they came to town. We've had some crank calls and a few inquiries from nervous parents thinking of sending their kids to them for violin lessons, but both Berenger and Armbruster always came out cleaner than the cranks. Not a whisper of trouble, sex or anything else, child or adult. They're both deacons in their church, serve on the board of the symphony society, volunteer one day a week for United Way. They're active, open and popular in the community."

"No gay bars, no cruising, no prostitutes?"

"Not on the record. No sheets on either of them, no arrests."

"They are gay?"

"Yeah, they're sure gay. They don't hide it, but they don't advertise it, if you know what I mean. You couldn't tell by how they look or how they act. At least not in public."

"So I noticed. Armbruster looks like a tough old guy."

"So was Berenger."

I heard the tone in his voice. We've gotten to know each other that well.

"You don't think Berenger died like that either?"

"Let's say from what I know about him it's out of character," Chavalas said, then shrugged. "But who knows what goes on inside someone who lives a kind of life you don't know anything about?"

"Someone different."

"Yeah. Someone different."

★ ★

You can be away from New York for a few months or too many years and still know where the streets are, but not what and who are on those streets. Especially not what and who are invisible behind those streets, hidden in the back rooms and the shadows, lurking in the sewers. For that only contacts could help, and after three years in California I had damn few. In the world of the permanent underclass that now populates those shadows and sewers, a month is a year, and a year is a century.

"There were two of them," Captain Pearce said. "No names, no faces, the meat-market kid never saw them before."

"You believe that?"

"Every word, and not a syllable."

He's a college man, Captain Pearce. In ten years he's aged thirty, and he stopped expecting to rise into the ranks of the brass long ago. Or even wanting to. Whenever I come back to the city now he stares at me as if wondering how I had escaped and he hadn't, and his face tells me he knows he never will.

"You've been out in paradise too long, Fortune. You know that down there you believe everything and you don't believe anything. Truth and fact are irrelevant."

"If they took his wallet, how did you identify him or know where he was staying?"

"They left his business card case, and a hotel bill."

"Convenient. You can sell a good leather card case."

Pearce looked at me as if I'd lost my mind. I was asking for logic from two grade-school dropouts, probably stoned, battering a man to death in the dim corridor of a flop house populated by a steady stream of hookers and nervous johns of all sexes. Maybe I had lost my mind.

"You never traced any of the loot?"

Pearce didn't even bother to answer that. The money would have been spent in an hour, the watch and rings would have been sold for ten cents on the dollar and be for sale in a flea market in Peru. Only the shoes might turn up someday — on the body of an overdose in an alley somewhere.

"Armbruster says he would never have been with that kid."

"He was."

"He had a hotel. Why the Emerson?"

"Ricky Franklin is fourteen and looks twelve. He's usually stoned and smells bad. He has purple spiked hair, pants he needs novocaine to put on. The pants are so thin his cock and ass might as well be purple too. He wouldn't get one foot inside a real hotel like the Sheraton if he was with Mother Teresa."

I watched him. "So it's open and shut. On the word of a fourteen-year-old drug addict male hooker."

"It's open and shot on probability. On where Berenger was and who he was with."

"And what he was," I said.

Pearce didn't flinch. "And what he was." He leaned forward. "Look, Dan, Berenger was a homosexual in a strange city. The boy was a male hooker, the hotel was a hooker hangout. You know how many muggings under exactly those conditions we get a year?"

"Have you talked to Samuel Armbruster?"

Pearce sat back. "I've talked to him."

"Can you see him with that boy in that hotel?"

"I never talked to Roger Berenger, not alive. And I can see anyone with anyone anywhere under the right pressure."

"If Armbruster were straight, and the hooker a fourteen-year-old girl, could you see him with her in a hotel like that? Would the pressure be right?"

As I said, Pearce is a college man.

"Probably not."

"Thanks," I said.

"But I still never met Roger Berenger."

"Neither did I, but, you know, Captain, I'm beginning to take Armbruster's word."

★ ★

I had checked into the same Sheraton where the violin teachers convention was held. This week it had a local association of security guards, and a national convention of police chiefs. I felt safe and secure. The hotel staff felt harried. None of the people on the desk, day or night shift, had any memory of Roger Berenger. The photograph Samuel Armbruster had given me drew nothing but blank stares from the desk clerks and the rest of the staff. If he had ever asked for his key they had no recollection of that. In fact, no one remembered him asking for anything.

No bellman recalled going to his room, the maids didn't remember ever seeing him, and the doorman swore he had never seen a man of his description leave the hotel.

The general consensus was that Roger Berenger had never done anything in his room and had never left the hotel. Which wasn't unusual for academic convention attendees. They never caroused, ate in the coffee shop, and tipped badly.

Using a list supplied by Armbruster, I called other violin teachers who would have been at the convention. They had all shared coffee shop meals with Berenger, had seen him often in the hotel. They all said he had attended every session until the night he was killed, played in many chamber music groups, been generally busy. He had been in good spirits, and had never mentioned going anywhere outside the hotel.

The manager, who talked to me only because Captain Pearce told him to be nice, looked at his watch more often than a drunk in a bar with a half hour to go before the last train home.

"You don't remember anything about Roger Berenger?"

"Mr. Fortune, really. A few thousand people pass through this hotel every week. I only became aware of Mr. Berenger as a guest when the police came to talk to me about his murder. I had nothing to tell them, and have nothing to tell you."

"Hang with me. I could have some different questions."

He sighed and looked at his watch while I asked all my questions, some of them maybe actually different. He looked at the watch with increasing frequency until I came to, "Did anything very special or unusual happen while Berenger was here? Something that involved him, or even that didn't?"

"My God, unusual things happen every minute in a hotel this size!

Especially when we have conventions, and we always have conventions."

Hotel owners like conventions, hotel managers don't. For the managers, conventions are a headache.

"I mean so unusual even you might have taken particular notice and remembered."

He shook his head. "No, there was..." His face went as blank as a computer screen reviewing its files while you sat and 'Please Waited'. "Wait... Yes... One of the bellmen... Some kind of argument, an actual fight in the changing lockers. Our security people had to be called. But I don't recall —"

★ ★

The head of hotel security, Chief Mazzoni, was a large man whose collar and tie were so tight they looked like a medieval neck iron. He wasn't someone who'd spent a great deal of his life behind a desk.

"Manager says Pearce sent word to help you out," Mazzoni said. "You an ex-cop like me?"

"My father was on the force. I lost the arm too young, so had to go private."

He nodded sympathetically. "So what can I do for you?"

"The manager says there was some kind of problem with a bellman. A fight?"

Mazzoni began to laugh. "Well, more like a mini Latin riot, you know? Not exactly a fight. But what's it got to do with this Berenger guy you're interested in?"

"Probably nothing. I'm grabbing straws."

He knew about grabbing at straws. "Well, it's the new kid we took on. Another damn Latino. Eighty percent of the staff is Latino now, a hundred percent in housekeeping, and it's getting bigger 'cause they all bring their cousins when a job opens up, you know? Anyway, this part-time kid was showering in the staff rooms to go off early because we were slow, and when he comes out all his clothes are gone! Street clothes, uniform, everything. There he was buck naked, in a hurry, no one else in the staff room. He's too scared we'll get mad to go out in a towel, so he waits until the regular shift comes off, accuses one of them of swiping his clothes to get him in trouble. They all deny it, but they laugh like all hell. Someone calls the bell captain who reads them the riot act about practical jokes, but they swear none of them did it. That's when the last guy on the shift shows up carrying the kid's uniform. He says he found it in a fourth floor stairwell, but no one believes him and the kids starts a fight with the guy. The bell captain breaks it up, tells the kid to calm down, lectures everyone again on practical jokes, and sends them home. The kid has to go home in the uniform. A maid finally finds his street clothes in the laundry room next day. And that was it. No one ever did find who the joker was."

"Maybe there wasn't any joker," I said. "What floor was Roger

Berenger on?"

Mazzoni picked up the phone, dialed three numbers. "What room did Roger Berenger have, Pete? The queer was killed the cops came asking about. Yeah, that one. Four-twenty-one? You're sure? How close is that room to a stairwell? Okay, thanks." He hung up, swivelled back to me. "Three rooms from the right stairwell."

"The one where the clothes were found?"

"Yeah."

We both thought for a time in the quiet office. I spoke first, "You have all your street exits and entrances under video surveillance?"

"Sure."

"You keep the tapes?"

He nodded. "Maybe a week, two."

It was a week and a half since the night Roger Berenger died.

"Have the police looked at them?"

"They never asked."

We started with the time between when the bellman's clothes disappeared and when they were 'found' in the stairwell. It was on the tape from the camera that monitored a small side exit. There were two of them. One was a skinny Latino in a black western hat, black suit that looked like silk, gray shirt and narrow yellow tie. The other was a short, muscular anglo with a heavy macho mustache, ill-fitting sport jacket and brown slacks.

The man who walked between them was Roger Berenger.

He did not walk well on the flickering, grainy video. His arms weren't free, his whole body resisted, and his feet seemed to drag. He wasn't leaving the hotel because he wanted to.

"Can I get some stills of those two men. Good full faces?"

"We can try."

★ ★

The still photos were blurred, but recognizable. My contacts on the Strip had no reason to talk to me. After three years I had no favors to give and no markers to call in. All I saw were a lot of blank faces, closed doors, shadows on dark streets and eyes watching me.

That was when I went to Joe Harris.

In his office we drank the Red Tail ales, Joe looked at the still photos, and I told the story of Roger Berenger and Samuel Armbruster. Joe had moved across Eighth Avenue into the higher rent district, owned a lounge that catered to people who expected boutique beers from California, but he was still a saloon keeper, and still on the Strip if only at the edge.

"You know how many times a year a guy like Roger Berenger comes to New York looking for what he can't get at home and ends up dead in a bed in one of those hotels with a Ricky Franklin? You ain't been away that long or that far, Dan."

"Captain Pearce already reminded me," I said. "Except Roger Berenger wasn't looking. He had all he needed at home. And if he had been looking, he could have found a reasonable facsimile of Ricky Franklin ten blocks from where he lived. Everything's up to date in Santa Barbara."

"He wasn't in Santa Barbara, and he was alone."

"He wasn't alone when he left the hotel that night."

Joe stared at the photographs spread out on his desk. "You think it was a setup?"

"As Sam Armbruster said, I don't know what I think. What I know so far is Berenger doesn't sound like a man who would be in that hotel with that boy. He didn't leave the Sheraton alone, and my hunch is he didn't leave voluntarily. I know if he hadn't been homosexual more questions would have been asked, and I'm wondering if someone counted on that."

Joe still stared down at the photos. Then he looked up, leaned back, and drank his ale. "What do you want me to do?"

"I need names, faces, connections, motives, clues. Anything I can get to help me convince the police it wasn't what it looks like, and maybe even lead me to the real killer. At least one fact to raise some doubt."

"I can give you one fact right now. What doubt it raises, I'm not so sure."

"What fact."

"The cool latin dude in the photo." Joe pointed to the skinny Latino in the silky black suit on one side of Roger Berenger.

"What about him?"

"His name's Belmonte. He's a pimp lives in the Emerson and specializes in boys."

"You think Ricky Franklin is one of his stable?"

"I don't know. But let's say it wouldn't astound me."

"I guess we better find out."

★ ★

I said 'we', but it was Joe who did the work.

I spent a day cruising Ninth, Tenth and Eleventh Avenues all the way from Gansevoort Street to Forty-Fourth, asking questions on all the hooker tracks, drinking too much beer, and getting the same closed doors and blank stares. Our theory was I would at least stir up the mud and maybe make the carrion eaters nervous enough to come closer to the surface.

Joe sat in his office and made calls. He asked questions and listened to answers. He sent out the radar and waited for the echoes. The first one's started to come in the second day.

"Ricky Franklin's in Belmonte's stable all right, and word on the street is that since little Ricky got out of the hospital he's been scoring the good white a lot bigger than usual."

"He's found some money?"

"That's how it reads, and Ricky wouldn't have money if Belmonte didn't have more, so I dug a lot deeper, called in some very big markers. You're gonna owe me for life, Dan boy."

"I already did," I said. "Tell me more about Belmonte?"

"It appears that Mr. Belmonte paid off a big bundle of debt he'd owed a certain party for a long time. The party isn't all that pleased. The loss of the vig Belmonte was carrying cuts into his weekly take, so he didn't mind talking some in the hope someone could dry up the pimp's source of sudden cash and he could get him back on the weekly rolls. Even offered to lean on little Ricky if we need help."

"No word on the source of all this cash Belmonte and Franklin are throwing around?"

"Not yet. But I got the name of the other guy in your still photos, and that may help."

"How?"

"He's a two-bit repo man and skip tracer named Zack Murfree. He did a couple of months on a misdemeanor with Belmonte a few years ago. Word is that since then he's supplied Belmonte with fresh meat from time to time. Sort of a recruiter of street boys he meets on his travels."

"How does that help us find the source of the cash?"

"Murfree works out of L.A."

Los Angeles was a lot closer to home. Roger Berenger's home.

★ ★

Ricky Franklin sneered. Cocaine courage. He sat on the filthy bed in his basement pad off Tenth Avenue, nothing on but his purple spiked hair and a sequined shirt dirtier than the bed, his legs splayed to display his wares.

"We know it was a setup, Ricky," Joe said. "Tomorrow the cops know. Dan here's a real good friend of Captain Pearce. You want the cops to know? You know how long you'll be inside? You know what happens to you inside?"

"Nothing ain't happened already out here." He rotated his hips and fluttered his fake eyelashes at Joe. "You want a taste, Mr. Harris? Maybe your friend?"

I said, "Who paid Belmonte to kill Berenger, Ricky?"

The sneer. "Who's Belmonte?"

"When the cops go looking for Mr. Belmonte," Joe said, "you won't live long enough to go to jail."

Ricky giggled. "No way, Jose. He likes my little ass too good."

I said, "He can get all the little asses he wants, Ricky. They're a dime a dozen down here."

"Screw you," the boy said, suddenly sullen.

He was still pouting when Joe's secret weapons came through the door. The friendly neighborhood loan shark and two of his larger collectors. The boy's pout turned into a grimace of horror, his sullen eyes wide with bottomless fear. A fear so strong the happy dust instantly boiled out of his veins. All the way down from his high, he cowered on the bed with his back trying to go through the wall, his skinny arms hugging his legs to his hollow chest. The loan shark enjoyed the effect he and his helpers had.

He smiled. "Tell the nice men what they want to know, boy."

Ricky shook and cowered, but he didn't speak.

"Maury."

One of the big collectors slapped Ricky across the face. Lightly. Just enough to split his lip. Ricky whimpered, wiped blood from his chin, said nothing.

"A tourist gets hurt, it's trouble," the loan shark said. "Trouble is bad for business."

"I don' know nothin'," the boy pleaded.

"Maury," the loan shark said.

Ricky screamed, covered his face, cowered. The big collector grinned, pulled the boy's hand away. He raised his fist. I caught his wrist with my lone hand. The big man scowled, pulled his arm away. Or tried to. My one arm is a lot stronger than I look.

I said, "Ricky, you want get out of here? Off the streets? Stop peddling your ass?"

The big collector got his hand free, forgot about Ricky. He looked at me as if I were a cockroach, and he knew what to do to cockroaches. Only not this time. His boss had the picture.

"Maury," the loan shark said.

I said, "Home, Ricky. Off the shit."

The boy stared. I was a man out of his mind.

"You get detoxed, a stake, a ticket to anywhere you say," Joe said.

Ricky looked at Joe. He knew Joe had money. Joe owned a cocktail lounge. Joe was a boss. The boy blinked, looked at the loan shark and his collectors with the big fists.

"Monte he kill me," he croaked through his bloody lip.

"Belmonte does nothin'," the loan shark said. "Take the man's deal, boy."

Ricky thought it over. Maybe somewhere inside he really wanted to get out, get off the white dreams, go home. Maybe. At least he knew the alternatives, and none of them were good. He knew what Maury and the silent collector could do to him. If the cops did come after Belmonte, he knew what the pimp would do. Nubile boys were a dime a dozen on Tenth Avenue.

"Monte got paid to set the john up. Him 'n Zack grab the mark over at his hotel, knock him aroun' in the Emerson, knock me aroun' so it looks good. We was s'posed to get picked up in the hall, you know? Only Monte and Zack hit the stupid fucking john too hard n' he croaks. Jesus, we's scared, but the cops don' even ask no questions." He smirked. "I gets a thousand bucks."

"How much did Belmonte get?" I asked.

"I don' know. Ten grand maybe. Him 'n Zack splits it."

"Who hired Belmonte?"

"Zack."

"Who hired Zack?"

The boy shrugged. "I don' know."

The loan shark said, "Maury."

"I swear!" Ricky shrieked, cowered again. "I don' know! I tell you all I know! Monte goddamn kill me! You get me out o' here like you say!"

I said, "Put your pants and shoes on."

The loan shark and his collectors left. They'd done what Joe asked, given Belmonte some trouble. All in a day's work. Ricky Franklin perked up the instant they were gone, looked like he was having second thoughts about going home.

"We'll get to Belmonte," I said. "And he has friends."

Ricky put on his pants and shoes. In the pants he might as well have been still naked. Joe would have to foot the bill for a new wardrobe too.

★ ★

I landed at LAX three hours later by clock time, and arrived at Zack Murfree's office an hour after that. It was in Hollywood, a three-floor walkup from the twenties. The new Hollywood. Where buildings were trashed and the streets dirty, traffic moved through at a brisk pace from somewhere else to somewhere else, and teenage hookers worked the doorways and streets. A Hollywood where the dreams had been trashed even more than the buildings.

Murfree's office had one of those old-fashioned half glass doors with his name stenciled on it in black with gold borders. The gold was flaking off. I went in expecting to see an outer room with a blonde in a perm behind a battered wooden desk. But there was only the single large room. The battered desk was there, but no blonde. A filing cabinet, sagging sofa, two wooden chairs, and Zack Murfree. Dead.

He had been shot in the shabby desk chair that creaked and squealed for oil when I moved it, fallen forward against the desk, and slid off to the floor, his head at a grotesque angle against a bottom drawer. There was too much blood, the exits wounds too big, to tell how many bullets he'd taken, but I saw two holes in the back of the desk chair. A big handgun.

I spent an hour going through his pockets, the drawers and the files. There wasn't much to go through. Half of one drawer in the filing cabinet, (the other drawers held his laundry and junk food); nothing but paper clips and rubber bands in the desk, not even a bottle; small change and keys in his pockets. If there had been anything about Roger Berenger it was gone. If Zack Murfree'd had a wallet or any other personal effects, they were gone.

I called Joe. The time difference put it early evening in New York. I told him.

"You think it's someone who hired Murfree?"

"I don't know what I think. What I know is we've lost our only lead. Unless Belmonte knows more than Ricky thinks he knows."

"He knows something," Joe said. "Word is he's gone to ground. No one's seen him for twenty-four hours."

"That's me asking questions."

"Or he knew someone was after Murfree, and maybe him."

"So maybe he does know more."

"That wouldn't shock me either."

"How's Ricky?"

"Scared shitless, but safe and in detox."

"I don't supposed he's remembered anything more?"

"I think he's trying to forget what he does remember."

Which left me with no leads at all to who had hired Zack Murfree. And probably killed him.

★ ★

Samuel Armbruster waved me to a high backed wing chair in his small, neat living room. The house was on a quiet Upper East street of big and small houses with front yards, trees and flowering bushes. It wasn't one of the smaller houses, but the downstairs front had been renovated into two studios, and that made the rear rooms smaller.

"I've just made a pot of tea. Roger and I always tried to have tea at four. People should take more time to simply sit and relax, enjoy the small things. Or would you rather have a beer? I have some good micro-brewery beers. Thomas Kemper."

Thomas Kemper Pale Lager or Pilsner are good beers. Over his tea and my beer I told him what had happened in New York and Los Angeles. He listened without comment or interruption in the comfortable room of the house he had shared with Roger Berenger. When I got to the video of Berenger leaving the hotel with Belmonte and Murfree, he leaned forward over his cup of tea and his eyes glittered with anger. When I finished he sat back, placed his tea cup on the coffee table, his face a mixture of rage and sorrow.

"Someone did murder Roger."

"Someone set him up, took him to the hotel. I'm not sure it was murder."

"What was it then?"

"I think an accident. They meant to beat him up, not kill him."

He leaned forward, poured milk from its small pitcher into his teacup, placed a silver strainer in the cup, took the cosy from his teapot and poured a fresh cup. He put in a sugar cube, stirred for a time before he sat back and sipped from the steaming cup.

"You're telling me they wanted Roger found by the police in that hotel with that boy so a public record would be made. They planned to beat him but not kill him. To compromise him, discredit him, but not to kill him?"

"That's how I read it. Who would want to discredit Roger that much? Probably both of you. Give you a bad name in the community? Someone who lives here. Murfree was too close to home to be a coincidence. Someone wanted to give you a bad name in this town in a very specific way."

"As faggot users of male prostitutes, the corrupters of little boys, frequenters of the slimy underbelly."

I nodded. "Any ideas now?"

I watched him as he sat there in his neat, comfortable living room, sipped his tea and appeared to think. But he wasn't really thinking. He wasn't a man who would think that ill of anyone. Certainly not anyone he associated with.

"No one I know would sink that low."

"That isn't what Sergeant Chavalas tells me. He says there have been crank calls and inquiries from parents before they sent their children to you for violin lessons. How recent were some crank calls? Inquiries by parents?"

"There are always some parents who question, and there are always cranks."

"That's not answering my question, Sam."

He smiled. "That's the first time you've called me anything but Mr. Armbruster."

"Don't read anything into it. Tell me about the recent crank?"

He shrugged. "We have a sad woman who rooms across the street. She is incapable of harm."

"Parents?"

"I don't know which parents might have been concerned about us, Mr. Fortune. They rarely tell us if they are."

"Dan," I said.

"Roger had twelve different pupils over the last year, Dan, and I had ten. I suppose you can check on all of them."

"Who else could have had a motive to discredit you and Roger?"

"I know of no one."

"No enemies?"

"None."

"Professional rivals?"

"Violin teachers don't kill each other."

"Sour business deals?"

"We had no business deals."

"A jealous lover?"

He snorted. "We were both too old for that kind of nonsense."

"Anyone at the church or the United Way?"

There was a momentary hesitation before he said, "No."

"Where was it, Sam? The church?"

He finished his second cup of tea, placed it carefully on the coffee table. "There were some rumblings when we were made deacons. It came to nothing."

His voice was angry. Not at the questioners or the rumblings, but at a society that made him have to talk about them, even think about them.

"How come Roger went alone to New York? You're both violin teachers."

"Normally we would have gone together and made a vacation of the trip, but this year an old friend of mine died of AIDS. I had to attend the funeral and memorial service in San Francisco."

"Who would have known that?"

He shrugged. "Almost anyone. The church, United Way, parents of the pupils. The neighbors who saw Roger leave with his bags."

I left the biggest question for last. "Is there anyone you know who's capable of murder, Sam?"

"You said it wasn't murder."

"It is now. Someone didn't want Zack Murfree to talk."

★ ★

None of the twelve families who had sent their students to Roger Berenger over the last year had made inquiries to the police. Two of Samuel Armbruster's had. One family had left town six months ago, the other had only good things to say about Armbruster and Berenger, was, as near as I could tell, genuinely shocked and saddened by the murder. Only one person in the last year had called the police to demand the arrest of the two dangerous criminals who lived in her decent neighborhood and lured small children into their house. The lady in rooms across the street. Mrs. Bithia Petit.

She peered at me around a door still on its chain. "The police won't do anything about those terrible men, but I see what goes on. Those children always going in and out. All the screaming and the crying, the parents dragging them in, and the police do nothing! It's so horrible."

"They give violin lessons to children, ma'am. The parents are only —"

"They may fool you and everyone else, but they don't fool me, not for a second. I know evil when I see it and hear it."

"Have you ever been to New York, Ms. Petit? Maybe recently? Hired anyone to go there? Maybe —"

"I don't dare leave this house until I know they're gone. And I must be back before they return or they'll catch me too. The devil never sleeps, young man."

"Tell me about what they do, Mrs. Petit. Tell me —"

The pale face in the narrow opening became terrified. "I know who you are! You're with them! You're the evil!"

The door slammed shut, and I was left alone on the front steps. I listened but heard nothing more inside. No movement, no sound at all, as if Mrs. Bithia Petit were standing motionless inside, hardly breathing, until the evil in the world walked away from her door.

★ ★

The Reverend Anthony Cartwright nodded me to a chair in the small sitting room of his rectory. "A tragedy, Mr. Fortune. I find it almost impossible to believe still."

"What?" I said. "That Berenger was killed, or that he was where he was killed?"

His blue eyes were steady. "Both."

"Armbruster tells me not all of your congregation would be that surprised."

The minister smiled. "I'm sure Samuel didn't tell you that, Mr. Fortune. He isn't a man to believe bad of anyone, to dwell on the past, or to harbor ill will. If he mentioned our problems, it was you who wormed it out of him. Am I right?"

I nodded. "Tell me about the 'problems'."

The pastor tented his fingers and looked ministerial. "Roger and Samuel made no secret of their life style, some parishioners weren't pleased. Not that they should have hidden anything, of course, and they certainly didn't flaunt . . . Still —" Reverend Cartwright hesitated, frowned, then, when I made no comment, hurried on. "It was really nothing. A few people asked questions about the compatibility of Christian belief and homosexuality, but we talked it out in open and honest discussion led by Roger and Samuel themselves. They are fine men. Then, one would expect that from a naval hero, of course."

He tried to smile, but it didn't come out right. He wasn't convincing himself about how 'nothing' it had been anymore than he was convincing me.

"It wasn't all that pleasant, was it, Reverend?"

He squirmed in his chair behind his desk, then sighed. "I'm afraid I may have made a mistake. I should have realized people can be pushed too far, moved too fast." He sighed again, rested his chin on his tented fingers.

"When you made them deacons?"

He nodded. "Those who had questioned them being with us at all became ugly, and many in the flock saw it as going beyond Christian toleration to approval, and they weren't ready for that."

"Became ugly how?"

His voice was a shade bitter. "They would have no 'homo' deacons. It was an 'affront to Jesus'. All Christian leaders must be 'pure', 'normal'. The worst declared it an outrage, even a sacrilege. Words like disgusting and filthy were used. Some said it turned their stomachs every time

Samuel and Roger passed the plate." He shook his head with a kind of horror. "It was unbelievable to me. Perhaps I've been too sheltered in my small world. But I was shocked by the vehemence, the flood of anger."

"But you didn't back down?"

He spread his hands with a kind of despair. "How could I? I believe in Christian love, in equality before God. I liked Roger and Samuel, even admired them. I couldn't give in to bigotry. Not in the church. Never."

"Where does it stand now?"

"I'm glad to say, while perhaps all the congregation isn't completely reconciled, the crisis has passed. Some people left, but most have returned, and the most violent objections have faded away. We're not home yet, but the violence has vanished."

Or had it simply taken a more deadly direction?

★ ★

On the phone Joe said, "Belmonte's a ghost, Dan. It's like he's dropped off the planet. Little Ricky's so scared of Belmonte he won't leave the detox center to go to the airport and fly home until he knows where Belmonte is."

"Belmonte's got to know more than Ricky says," I said from my office.

"And as scared of someone as Ricky is of him." Joe stopped as if to listen to the distant sirens at his end. The sounds of New York. "You figure it's someone at that church?"

"That's what I think."

"How would they know enough to arrange it all back here, Dan?"

"Maybe they hired it done."

"You have any leads about who?"

"With Murfree dead and Belmonte missing, not even a hope."

The sirens sounded again in the distance at the other end of the line. "Maybe we can find out. Smoke Belmonte into the open. Make him think we know more than we do and make a move."

"How do we do that?"

"Bring your Mr. Armbruster to New York, send him around the hooker walks asking questions. Make him act like Berenger told him more than he's told the cops."

"Who's going to believe that?"

"Belmonte, for one. And maybe the guy who hired Belmonte and Murfree."

"Why the hell would they believe it, Joe?"

"Because they couldn't afford not to," Joe said. "And maybe the guy who started it all might decide to try for your client too. Get rid of another queer."

★ ★

"You want me to be the bait in a trap," Samuel Armbruster said.

"You don't have to, Sam. It could be damned dangerous."

We were in his neat living room again. There was no tea or beer this time. I'd come to the point the moment he opened the door. Now he sat facing me across the coffee table.

"Yes I do," he said. "If I want to know what really happened to Roger and why. That's what you're saying."

"There could be other ways. Someone will crack, Belmonte will show up, they'll trace the gun that killed Murfree."

"You don't believe that, Dan."

I said nothing.

"When?" Armbruster said.

"The sooner the better."

"Tomorrow then. Go and get the tickets."

"All right."

"Now tell me what I have to do."

★ ★

For three days, Sam Armbruster talked to the young boys on Ninth, Tenth and Eleventh Avenues, walked below Houston and along the dark water of the river with Joe wandering around him playing a wino digging in garbage cans, and me staked and out of sight so my arm wouldn't show. Sam asked questions about Belmonte, implied far more knowledge of the death of Roger Berenger than any of us had. Until the scrawny, frightened and lost children fled when he came near them, those that hadn't vanished the moment he appeared on the street.

The twelve-year-old who didn't run or hide picked Armbruster up at 9:10 P.M. on Eleventh Avenue in the Thirties. Joe lifted his head out of a garbage can and went after them. I waited until Sam and the kid turned the corner toward Tenth Avenue, then ran for Joe's car. When I caught up with them, they were headed north on Tenth: the boy, Armbruster, and Joe staggering along far behind them. I pulled ahead, parked, and watched until they appeared in the rearview mirror. When they all passed and were a block ahead, I pulled out and repeated the maneuver until the boy reached home.

This time home was a flophouse hotel on West 40th Street between Ninth and Tenth Avenues. Criminals and pimps have no imagination. The narrow, seedy lobby was empty when I went in. The face of the night clerk was equally narrow and seedy. He looked shocked to see a man alone in his lobby.

"Three people just came in: a tall older man, a skinny kid you knew, and a short guy with dark hair. What room did you tell the short guy you gave the kid?"

"I didn't tell no one nothin'. Never saw no one like that."

"Yes you did, and I'm meaner that he is."

I smiled.

"Number fourteen, third floor."

"Which room's Belmonte in? And don't waste my time."

"Fifteen."

"Across the hall?"

He nodded.

I went up. The door to fifteen was open, and Belmonte wasn't inside. He was in fourteen. With a gun. I took it away from him. I didn't take the gun away from the big man with the beard.

★ ★

The clerk had told me about Belmonte in fifteen, but not about the man in twelve. He came through the connecting door between twelve and fourteen with a 10-mm Glock in his massive hand. Six-feet-four, 250-pounds, he had a trimmed full beard, a western hat, and cold eyes. He didn't say a word or waste a second. His first shot caught Joe, slammed him back against the wall. His second shot would be for me.

I knew, in one long, slow split second, that this man had killed Roger Berenger and Zack Murfree, and that he wasn't going to face a murder charge if there was any way out at all. He had no choice and neither did I. Both shots from my little Sig-Sauer took him through his left eye, so close together you could have covered the small black holes with a quarter. I'm a good shot by now, I learned to be, and with one arm I can't afford to wing a man twice my size who has his own gun and nothing to lose.

He hit the floor on his back before his Glock did. He didn't move again.

"Damn and damn," I said, my face feeling as pale as it could get, and ran to bend over Joe. There was more frustration in his eyes than pain.

"Shit," he said. He knew what I knew. "How do we get the goddamn guy who hired him now?"

"How do you feel?"

"Like I'd rather be dead," Joe said. "I'm okay. Those Glocks're too big for fast action, he only winged me. Nothing a week in the hospital won't fix."

On the bed Sam Armbruster was staring down at the big dead man, and the boy sat in a kind of trance. Nothing that had happened had reached him. He lived in some invisible world of his own where there wasn't any pain. Belmonte looked at the big man, at the blood oozing from under his head now. The pimp's face was so white it was green.

"What was his name?" I said to Belmonte. "The whole goddamn story."

Belmonte doubled over in a corner and threw up. When he finally stopped retching, he sat on the floor against the wall and couldn't stop staring at the big man dead on the floor. And he couldn't stop talking. The dead man was Matt Brunner. A bounty hunter who worked out of Santa Barbara. Someone there had hired him to discredit Roger Berenger. When he'd learned Berenger was coming to New York alone, he got Zack Murfree to hire Belmonte and frame Berenger with little Ricky. They beat Berenger up so the police would come and it would be on public record, and the client could reveal it and ruin both Roger and Sam Armbruster.

"The old guy don' got to go die, you know? We don' mean the old faggot got to croak!"

"Who in Santa Barbara?"

Belmonte looked like he would throw up again. "I don' know! I swear! Zack and Brunner they never done tol' me. I swear!"

On the bed, Sam Armbruster said, "Then we'll never find out."

"We'll find out," I said.

★ ★

We did.

It took some work by the NYPD, the SBPD, Joe and me, but two weeks later we faced all seven of them in the rectory of the Reverend Anthony Cartwright. Five men and two women. All over forty. All angry and outraged. One of them, Mr. Frederick Zackheim, demanded, "Who are these men, Cartwright? What is this nonsense all about?"

"My name is Sergeant Chavalas," Gus Chavalas said. "Santa Barbara Police. Mr. Fortune and Mr. Harris there are private investigators hired by Mr. Samuel Armbruster. That mean anything to you?"

They said nothing.

"It should," Chavalas said. "Since you all hired Matt Brunner to set Roger Berenger up with a New York prostitute he'd never have been anywhere near on his own."

There were seven explosions of protest. Or six. Mr. Fred Zackheim said only, "I know no one named Brunner. I'm not —"

I said, "Yes you do. He was a professional, Matt Brunner. Organized. He kept records. Even the Nazis kept records of all they did."

"None of our names would have been in his records," Fred Zackheim said.

"True, Mr. Zackheim, and the transaction was in cash, of course. However, unfortunately for you fine people, Brunner's records named where his client lived, what the deal was, and the fee: $25,000 in advance. None of you are rich, so I doubted anyone came up with the full twenty-five grand. That's —"

"That's where we came in." Chavalas said. "Only one of you had dealt with Brunner, and that had been in cash. But Dan figured the rest of you would have paid the spokesman by check. I mean, who would ever know? Reverend Cartwright told us which members of his congregation had objected most to Berenger and Armbruster being deacons, and we got a court order to open your bank records."

"And there you were," I said. "Six people who paid large chunks of money to the same man on the same day two days before Brunner was hired. Isn't that right, Mr. Zackheim?"

Fred Zackheim stood up. "That proves nothing. No court —"

"With Belmonte, Ricky Franklin, Brunner's records, and Dan and Joe's work," Chavalas said, "I think it does. And I think a court will too, Mr. Zackheim."

The gray-haired man's eyes flashed, "No court will blame us for trying to purify our church of that filth."

The silence was like an enormous weight on the small rectory room. Until one of the women began to talk. Her voice shook. With anger, but with fear too now. "He called a meeting, Fred did. He asked when were we going to stop talking about those perverts and do something? When would we show the Reverend, the whole city, what they really were. Expose them. We asked how we did that? How could we know what they did and when? He told us he knew a man who would make sure. We told him he was crazy. He told us to put our money where our mouths were. If he could arrange to get those two out of the church, would we pay for it? We were scared, but we wanted that evil out of our church. We wanted them to be exposed so no decent person would associate with such ... such ... obscene perverts."

A man looked at the floor, "We never knew what he was going to do."

"No," Joe said. "You just knew he was going to destroy two people you hated because they weren't like you." He walked out of the room past the two uniformed policemen outside the door.

I said, "Brunner learned of Roger's trip alone to New York. He knew Zack Murfree had plenty of contacts in New York of the kind he needed, and made his plan. Roger Berenger died. You didn't plan that, but it was okay as long as you weren't suspected. It wasn't okay with Sam Armbruster. He came to me. He knew Roger wouldn't have done what it looked like he had. It was a matter of character. Something none of you would understand."

They all glared at me. Anger and hate mixed with their fear for themselves.

"I want my lawyer," Frederick Zackheim said.

★ ★

On the next Sunday the church held a memorial service for Roger Berenger. The Reverend Cartwright delivered the eulogy himself. Joe and I stood at the back and watched Samuel Armbruster walk down the aisle to the altar rail to receive communion before passing the collection plate. Today he would pass it alone, no matter how long that took.

He walked slowly, with great dignity, a black armband on the sleeve of his impeccable dark gray suit.

The church was only three-quarters full, and some people left during the eulogy. More left when Armbruster passed the collection plate alone. Few shook his hand where he stood on the steps with the reverend after the service.

Joe and I stood beside him in the morning sun, wondering.

I had a story in Alfred Hitchcock's Mystery Magazine *in 1983, but it had been twenty-four years since I'd published in* Ellery Queen's Mystery Magazine *when, at the Omaha Bouchercon, Janet Hutchings asked why I never submitted to* EQMM. *(I'd submitted a story there in the Eighties before Janet was editor, but the subject matter was too hot for them. No crime magazine would take that story, so I suggested to Paul Bishop he publish it in his fanzine* The Thieftaker Journals. *He did, and it went on to be nominated for a Shamus and appear in the 1984 edition of Ed Hoch's* Year's Best Mystery and Suspense Stories. *But that's another story!)*

Anyway, I told Janet EQMM *had never paid enough to make it worth while. She said they did now, so I wrote this story and she took it.*

It came from two newspaper accounts of actual events. When I read the two news reports, I immediately saw the connection that would make a great story, and put them together in "Culture Clash."

CULTURE CLASH

Douglas firs grow thick down the final slopes of the coast mountains to the cliffs above the sea, and the cliffs plunge down to where the last rocks of the continent meet the surf of the Pacific Rim. The land is rock, and the wind cuts to the bone. It's a rugged coast at the edge of northern Mendocino County, where even the gulls have to fight the wind, their cries the only living sound. I hadn't driven this coast in a long time, and I wished I wasn't driving it now. I'm too old to be thrilled by the harsh realities of raw nature. Or maybe I've been in Southern California too long.

Sandy Ciaccio knew me from New York before she came west to Spanish Cliffs in Mendocino County to paint the rugged coast, and she tracked me down in Santa Barbara, "I don't know what really happened, Dan, but I do know that Setsuko isn't sick or crazy."

Her call came into my office at the rear of our hacienda in Summerland on a sunny Thursday in February. A friend of hers, a painter in the Japanese style and wife of a real estate tycoon, had been found stabbed and unconscious in the family den beside her two dead children. Now she was barely alive and in a coma in the hospital. The weapon was a sixteenth century *samurai* short sword. (Sandy used the proper Japanese term: *wakizashi.*) With the longer *katana*, the sword was one of a pair her husband had on display in an alcove in the living room. At first the police assumed the attacker had been an intruder. Then they announced that Setsuko Owada had murdered her two children and tried to kill herself.

They concluded that she had gone insane.

"But she's not insane, Dan. There has to be something we don't know."

"And you want me to find out what that could be?"

"That's what I want, and I can pay you."

"The art business is booming?"

"I'm cleaning up. Name your price."

And so I was driving along the wild northern Mendocino coast to find out why the local police were so sure Setsuko Takeda Owada was crazy.

★ ★

"Easy, Mr. Fortune," sergeant Tallich said, "there's no other reason, motive or explanation."

The sheriff's detective was a compact man in a neat dark blue suit and regimental tie. He readily agreed to see me, waved me to a chair, studied my empty left sleeve, then leaned back and shook his head. "We eliminated everything we could think of except that she intended a double murder and suicide, and we don't have any possible motive for that. If she or anyone else knew it or not, she's mentally ill and unstable. Her mind just blew. Pow!" He snapped his fingers, then looked out his window at trees and blowing sky. "It happens."

"It happens," I said, "but there's usually a reason, a trigger for a hidden illness."

"Okay, there's usually a trigger. But we can't find one. She's going to have to tell us what it was when she wakes up, if she ever does, or it dies with her."

"Murder-suicide while of unsound mind, case closed?"

"I can guarantee it."

"How?"

Tallich leaned forward, opened the file on his desk. "The first thing we suspected was a nut, some crazy intruder. It had rained hard all that day, there were no footprints, tire tracks, or any other marks around the house. No broken windows or doors, no signs of entry. Then we considered the husband, it was his damned sword. Only he was down in San Francisco. Witnesses saw him leave on the plane, he was with business people all day in San Francisco, and he was there when we called to tell him his housekeeper had found them. And there isn't a single person who knows her, and that includes her husband and your client, who can give us any reason for her to kill those kids and herself except that she lost her marbles and went ape."

"Someone was hiding in the house."

"And got out how?"

"After you arrived, in the confusion."

"There wasn't any confusion, we had men on all the doors and windows, and, again, no marks anywhere except ours. And he didn't slip out disguised as a deputy. We're a small office, we know all our officers. Oh, and I forgot to mention two other facts. Only her prints were on the weapon, and the den door and windows were locked on the inside."

Now he smiled.

"How'd the housekeeper find them?"

"Knocked, got no answer, tried the door, then went out and looked in through the window. We broke the door down to get in."

That was when I left his office.

★ ★

Sandy Ciaccio is tall, thin and angular, and she's a fine painter of expressionist landscapes that reflect the grandeur, and the consant war of land and water, on the rocky coast where she has chosen to live. She is, despite her last name, a dark blonde. Ciaccio was a long-forgotten husband. She's really a Scot. A stubborn Scot.

"I don't give one damn how it looks, Dan, she wasn't and isn't crazy. Hidden or otherwise."

"She killed her kids, Sandy, and tried to kill herself."

"I'm not saying she didn't. I'm saying there's more to it. If she did what they say she did, then she believed it was what she had to do, that she had no choice."

"Such as what?"

"I don't know!" Sandy got up from the couch where we were sitting, walked to the wall of windows that enclosed the living room in the one-bedroom cabin she had built at the edge of a cliff above the violent sea. "Setsuko comes from a *daimyo* family that goes back fourteen generations. They were the feudal lords the *samurai* served. In the sixteenth century wars the Takedas were almost the shoguns. She would do what she had to. She's neither weak, stupid, confused, nor insane."

"Then tell me where to look. Where do I start?"

"Hey." She turned from the window. "You're the detective. You tell me. Where would you start?"

It's not a large cabin — living room, studio, tiny kitchen and small bed-room. The living room and studio make up ninety percent of the cabin, with glass on every side and overhead. It was all she, or in her view anyone else, needed.

"The husband," I said. "Tell me about him."

"Hideki Owada, rich, smart, ruthless. He's from an old *samurai* family, only they served a lord who always guessed wrong in the old wars so they had a rocky road over the centuries and Hideki is even more touchy and proud. I'm surprised he's going along with the insanity idea for a second."

"How'd he make his money?"

"Real estate. He started when the old ancestral lands in the west coast snow country of Japan got valuable, then moved on into Kyoto and Tokyo. Finally he branched out to the States, and last year bought our famous local golf club, Spanish Cliffs. An old lumber baron's mansion went with it, and they live here."

"What does Setsuko do outside the house? Who are her friends beside you?"

"Nothing and no one."

"You said she painted. You're her friend."

"Her painting is all her outside activities, and that's done mostly at home on the golf course property. And I wouldn't say I was a friend exactly."

"What are you?"

"Someone who meets her maybe once a week because we like to paint the same view. Like Cezanne and Hokusai, we both make hundreds of sketches at the same spot on the coast in different lights and conditions. The spot happens to be on Spanish Cliffs property. We rarely speak, and when we do it's mostly about painting. I never see her anywhere else."

I walked to the window and the view of the wild and austere coast below. "How do you know so much about her, Sandy?"

"Because after it happened I found out everything I could about her and her husband." She came to stand beside me. "She never appears in public outside that house. In fact, except for her painting, and our chance meetings, she never seems to have gone anywhere or done anything around here."

"Her husband must go to functions, he has to give parties."

"She's the hostess at his parties at home, he goes alone to anything outside." She looked at me. "She's a virtual recluse, if not a prisoner. Dan, there's something wrong in that house, and it's not her mind."

"Yeah," I said, "and I can tell you what it is. Culture clash. You're describing the life of an old-fashioned Japanese *samurai* wife, and that's all. In the past, a *samurai* never even admitted he was married. His wife was 'the person from the north,' the direction where sneak attacks came from."

"Then maybe culture clash is where you better look for why her children are dead and she almost is."

As I said, Sandy Ciaccio's stubborn.

★ ★

"*Oyaku shinju.*"

His name is Harry: Professor of Asian History Harold Smith of the University of California at Santa Barbara. He's lived half his life in Japan. He's also a mean poker player. He's always in his office early the day of our weekly game, so I'd called him from Sandy's living room couch, where I'd spent the night with the surf pounding below, and told him the whole story.

"What the hell's *oyaku shinju*?"

"Very good," he said, "you got it right the first time."

"I'm talented. Now what is it?"

"Parent-child suicide," Harry explained from Santa Barbara. "It's

illegal now in Japan, but it's considered an honorable way to die, and is still
fairly common. Maybe 300 or so cases a year. Traditional Japanese
consider children an extension of their parents, together they form one
unit. In the traditional Japanese mind, when a parent commits suicide it's
more merciful to take the children along in death than to leave them
behind."

"So what happens if the parent survives and the kids don't?"

"The parent can be charged with murder, but it almost never happens.
A mother in particular is rarely punished. She's considered an unfortunate
victim of circumstances."

"Why would a mother do it, Harry?"

"Intense suffering, and an impossible situation. For a *daimyo* type like
your Setsuko Owada, an unbearable loss of honor would do it. An
honorable way to solve an intolerable problem."

"How would our police and courts act toward it?"

At the other end Harry snorted, "Badly, I'd expect. You see it a lot
these days. Korean refugees kill dogs for dinner, the Humane Society
screams for the police. Cubans sacrifice chickens in religious rites, they
get arrested. An Hmong steals a bride in traditional courting ritual, he's
charged with kidnaping and rape. On it goes. Culture clash, Dan."

"I guess it could work the other way too. The foreigner not understanding our ways."

"Every day," Harry agreed. "That all, Dan? We'll miss you at the game
tonight."

"You'll miss my money," I said, and asked the question I had a hunch I
didn't really need to. "What's the usual trigger for a Japanese wife to
commit *oyaku shinju?*"

"Could be many reasons, but I'd say most common would be adultery
by the husband. Especially for a wife from an old *daimyo* family."

★ ★

The lumber baron's mansion was an ornate three-story Victorian of
carved gingerbread with towers and turrets, gables and balconies.

A lean man in his late fifties, not much under six feet, Hideki Owada
met me at the door with a stiff bow, and led me through a half-Western,
half-Japanese living room to the den. He sat behind a desk in the room
where his wife and children had been slashed with his own *wakizashi*. He
was tall for a Japanese, and as expressionless as a Connecticut Yankee. His
eyebrows, eyes and mouth formed three narrow parallel slashes on a hard
face, except that the final slash of the mouth curved slightly downward.
A stone face.

"You wish to speak of my wife, Mr. Fortune?" His eyes never even
flickered toward my missing arm.

"I expect a lot of people have spoken to you about your wife, Mr.
Owada."

"Americans have a fascination with violence, death."

"Japanese don't?"

"For us death is another part of life, a private matter."

"Even *oyaku shinju?*"

The parallel lines on his stern face became thinner, but he said nothing.

"Why didn't you tell the police it was *oyaku shinju?*"

"Because I would lose honor at home."

"And lose business?"

"Yes."

"And that's more important than your wife's honor? Better to let the world think she's insane?"

"My wife is insane," Owada said. "She must be."

"Why?"

"Because *oyaku shinju* is not possible."

I knew what he was telling me, but I asked anyway, "You're not having an affair? Seeing another woman?"

"My wife has not been dishonored."

"I can find out, Mr. Owada, believe me."

He bowed slightly. "In Japan, the word of an Owada would be sufficient. But investigate as you wish, Mr. Fortune."

"There are other reasons for *oyaku shinju.*"

"My wife is a Takeda, only I could dishonor her enough."

We sat in silence for a time. The old mansion wasn't as close to the cliffs as Sandy's cabin, but close enough to hear the distant pound of the waves on the rocks, and feel the wind that with the cliffs and surf make Spanish Cliffs the spectacular and world-famous golf course it is.

I said, "Then maybe she thought she had a reason."

"How could she think what has no basis?"

I stood. "Does she have some room of her own?"

"She has a studio for her painting."

"Okay if I look around it?"

It was a large room with a northern skylight, sunny and warm even on these days of cutting winds. Setsuko Owada's paintings were Japanese, yet they weren't classical and they weren't delicate. There was a modern Western influence, and the rocks and cliffs, clouds and winds, fogs and storms, were harsh and powerful. The room was Spartan. A single narrow cot could have been in the garret of any struggling Western artist. The only other furniture was a wooden table full of paints, and a straight chair. The room of someone who would do what had to be done.

The notebook was in the table drawer. It was filled with notes and sketches of the views and scenery from many parts of Spanish Cliffs, comments on paintings, records of conversations with other painters especially Sandy, all apparently taking place at spots where she and the others painted. It was written in English.

"My wife is well educated," Owada said.

"The university? Away from Japan?"

"Privately in her father's home."

"She does everything in English?"

"It is my wish while we live here. Even when we are alone."

"But a private notebook?"

"To do otherwise would dishonor me."

I looked at the notebook again, read the last few pages. There was nothing personal or gossipy, all strictly about painting, until I found the woman's name. A single name, written down, underlined. Written down again. And again. It was in the book twelve times.

"Emily Foster," I read to Owada. "You know the name?"

"She is a local woman I must do business with."

"At her house?"

"Yes. She often prefers to do business in her home office."

"Has she been here to your house?"

"Yes. At parties." His eyes did flicker now. "Sometimes alone. On business."

"Does she flirt? A brash woman, bold as brass. Very American, very forward?"

Owada said nothing.

I said, "Your wife wrote this woman's name in her painting notebook too many times. If Emily Foster isn't a painter, I wonder why?"

★ ★

Sergeant Tallich said, "Not a whisper, Fortune. As far as we can find out Mr. Owada's as pure as the snow. No scandal, not even a hint, and around here now even a hint would be used as an excuse to run him out of the town and the country."

"Why?"

"He's pushing a business deal that's got the locals pretty damned annoyed."

"What kind of deal?"

"Something to do with Spanish Cliffs and a club. I don't play golf, don't know the details."

"Would Emily Foster know the details?"

"I expect she might."

"Could it have had anything to do with what Setsuko Owada did, Sergeant?"

"How?" Tallich shrugged. "She cut her kids' throats, stabbed herself. If she did that over some business deal of Owada's, she's even crazier than we think."

★ ★

Emily Foster turned out to be Mrs. Courtney W. Foster IV of 14 Cliff

View Drive — a house not quite as big as Buckingham Palace in a gated community cheek to jowl with the Spanish Cliffs Golf Club. In fact, Hideki Owada's lumber baron's mansion was in clear sight through a high fence.

Mrs. Foster received me in the sun room. In her early forties, not tall and no more than 110 pounds, she radiated confidence. With short red hair, she wasn't beautiful, but she wasn't ugly. She was sitting in a white wicker lounge chair with a book and a bottle of white wine in an ice bucket, and she saw my empty sleeve. She shivered as if she'd touched something unclean. Then her good manners took over. Or maybe it was compassion. I like to give people the benefit of the doubt.

"It must be a horrible tragedy for you, Mr. Fortune, I'm so sorry. Was it Vietnam?"

"Another war. No need to be sorry, it was only indirectly your mother and father's fault."

That confused her. She didn't know if I was insulting her parents, excusing them for something she didn't understand, or making fun of her. She didn't like being confused, so changed the subject. "What possible interest could a private detective have in me? Or in Spanish Cliffs, for that matter?"

"That depends on why your name is in Setsuko Owada's sketch book about a dozen times, Mrs. Foster."

"My name?" She had no confusion over that question and all its implications. "May I ask who hired you, and exactly why? I was under the impression that tragic matter was settled."

"A friend of Mrs. Owada's doesn't think so."

Her green eyes studied me more carefully. A careful, analytical stare. I suddenly realized Mrs. Courtney Foster was a heavy hitter, an important woman in the community.

"I didn't know Mr. Owada had a friend left in town, and the wife doesn't leave that house enough to make any."

"Sandy Ciaccio."

"The painter? How did they — ?"

"Setsuko painted too. They met on the cliffs."

"Surprises never end." She still studied me as if trying to assess exactly how important this all was to her. "But I have no idea why my name is in her sketchbook."

"You don't know her well?"

"I met her twice, both times at Owada's house, and the only words she spoke were 'hello' and 'good-bye.' No one here knows Mrs. Owada."

"How about Mr. Owada? You know him very well, Mrs. Foster?"

I put an obvious insinuating emphasis into my voice and she didn't miss it. The compassion for my missing arm, if it had been that, vanished. The green eyes turned to a stone a lot harder than Owada's face.

"I think that is your last question unless you want to be sued for slander."

Threats make me push harder. "No affair with Hideki, Emily? You're above that sort of thing?"

Coldly, "If I were to indulge in an affair, Mr. Fortune, it wouldn't be with a Jap, and certainly not with one who wants to sell our American rights to his countrymen."

"You dislike the Japanese, Mrs. Foster?"

"I like them in Japan. I don't like them in my backyard and certainly not in my bedroom." She shivered delicately. A Jap was as bad as a cripple. "Now —"

"Selling our American rights? Is that the business deal the community is against?"

"Yes. Now, if you —"

"Are you involved in this deal?"

"You could say that."

"Financially?"

"Politically," she said. "Sergeant Tallich forgot to tell you I'm a county supervisor. Mr. Owada's plan is up before the Board of Supervisors for approval. Without that approval his project will never get off the ground."

"Do I take that as meaning you intend to vote against the plan, whatever it is?"

"You can take it any way you like. My vote is, of course, confidential until our next meeting. As for what it is, that's quite simple. Owada bought the Spanish Cliffs complex about a year ago for a great deal of money. Far too much, as it turns out. The income from the hotels and golf courses can't pay off on the interest of the debt he acquired. Whether or not Owada knew that in advance, and planned all along to use the threat of his company's insolvency as a lever to get our approval for this proposed project, is one of our questions. Whatever the truth of that, he is using the problem to justify selling memberships in the golf courses for as much as $700,000 each to solve his cash problem."

"Are there enough buyers for something like that?"

"Oh there'll be plenty of buyers, Mr. Fortune. However, that's not the county's concern. What does concern us is that the club members would get exclusive preferential treatment on what is, after all, the county's coastline. There is a serious problem of public access."

"To a private golf course?"

"To a part of our public coastline."

She was a good politician, nothing much showed on her face.

"Just how serious is this threat to 'public access' being taken in the community, Mrs. Foster?"

"That would depend on who you talk to."

"Anyone you know taking it particularly seriously?"

"Not that I can think of," she said. She poured herself another glass of the white wine. She didn't offer me a glass. "You're suggesting a connection between what happened to Mrs. Owada and her children, and Owada's business proposal?"

"It's the first hint of a motive I've had."

"Except the real one: She was unbalanced and her mind snapped."

"With no previous record of mental instability whatsoever."

"She intended to commit a suicide-murder, Mr. Fortune."

"She tried to commit a known Japanese ritual murder-suicide: *oyaku shinju.*"

Emily Foster drank her wine. "Does that make some kind of difference?"

"It does to the Japanese."

"We're not in Japan. Their barbarous customs don't especially interest me." She put her glass down, looked me in the eye. "If there's nothing else?"

I was getting a strong hunch there was very much something else, but it was still too much only a hunch to talk about to Emily Foster.

★ ★

Hideki Owada was working in his garden.

"When I am tense, Mr. Fortune, I find working in the garden can bring much peace."

"What do you think of your chances of pushing through your club membership idea?"

"I am optimistic."

"You know there's a lot of opposition."

"I am confident they will understand my problem and see the long-range potential for the community."

"You mean the supervisors?"

"Yes."

"How about the rest of the community? The short range?"

Owada said nothing, continued to dig at a particularly stubborn weed.

I said, "Prejudice and insularity are one thing, but not enough to commit what could be essentially murder. That would take something more important, more critical. Like money."

"Murder?" Owada sat back on his heels, looked up at me. It was a look I expect the enemy had seen on many hard *samurai* faces in sixteenth-century Japan. "In Japan, my wife would not be charged with —"

"I'm not talking about your wife," I said.

His face went behind an invisible wall. "You are talking about what, Mr. Fortune?"

"Call it a hunch," I said. "Can you think of anyone your club could cause to lose a lot of money?"

Sitting on his heels in his garden, he thought for some time. "There are many who perceive they will lose, but that is because they do not see the large opportunities of the future."

"How about someone who doesn't think he'll survive to the long run?" He shrugged. "I cannot say."

★ ★

Sandy Ciaccio said, "Half the community is against Owada's plan, Dan, although I'm not sure why. Is it important?"

"I think I know what happened to Setsuko Owada, and Owada's club project is the only possible motive. I need a suspect who isn't just against Owada, or even violently against. I need someone who could lose a short-range fortune. Someone who could go down the tubes if Owada gets his club."

We were sitting again in her one-bedroom cabin at the edge of the cliff above the sea. In the large room with more glass than wood or furniture. Sandy believed in open space, bringing the outdoors inside. At the moment the outdoors was gray becoming black with the wind blowing hard and the gulls fighting to stay in one place above the cliffs.

"I can't imagine how the club would do that to anyone. Nothing would really change."

"Okay," I said, "let's narrow it. What does Owada's plan do? Basically, it sells the course to the rich who can afford to pay $700,000, plus yearly fees and assessments, for a lifetime of playing golf on a great course. According to Emily Foster, the problem is that'll give them exclusive preferential treatment on what is the county's coastline, and limit public access. What access to the coastline on Spanish Cliffs Golf Club does the public have now?"

"It's open to anyone who wants to play golf, or stay at the hotel."

"What else?"

"As far as I know, that's it. It's fenced and gated. There's no way in without paying, and no reason to go in except to play golf."

"No public beaches? No public pool? No fishing? No camping? No RV parking?"

"The hotel has a pool and riding paths, but they're for hotel guests only."

"For how much?"

"Three-hundred-and-fifty a night to start."

"And the golf course?"

"One round costs $200, and I hear the best tee-off times are booked months in advance by locals and regulars from as far as Los Angeles."

"So when Emily Foster says 'public access,' what she really means by the public are people who can afford $200 to play a few hours of golf, and pay $350 a night for a room."

"I guess that's it."

I looked out through her walls of glass at the black sky and gale winds of the rugged coast and thought about public access at $200 a round. And a private golf-and-hotel-club at $700,000 down and yearly fees. What would those club members get? What would club membership mean?

It was then I remembered what Emily Foster had said about the Japs belonging in Japan, and knew what the objection to Hideki Owada's proposed club was, and what trouble it could cause some local businessman.

"Americans don't buy high-priced memberships in golf clubs, Sandy. The Japanese do. They have the money and the love of golf. And the club members would always come first. That's what no one wants to happen." I could see it as clearly as the violent wind blowing the gulls out there through the wall of glass. "Owada is selling first crack at everything at Spanish Cliffs, including the restaurant and all the best tee-times. Americans would be lining up behind the 'Japs' to hit a ball at Spanish Cliffs, if they got the chance at all." I looked at Sandy across the Spartan living room. "That's the 'public access' they want to preserve; the rights of $200-a-round American golfers over $700,000 membership Japanese golfers."

She was silent for a time. "But what does that have to do with Setsuko committing *oyaku shinju?*"

"I think someone counted on her doing it, Sandy, set her up to do it."

"How could anyone do that, for God's sake?"

"By telling her Owada was having an affair and naming the name of a woman he met with often — in her own home and in his. A woman Owada spent a lot of time with, often at her house. A woman who's bold, brazen, forward, and familiar around Owada. Like a whore in Setsuko's eyes. A geisha. Worse. A geisha wouldn't be so brazen and public about it."

"That would be murder, Dan."

"At least accessory before the fact."

Her silence was longer this time. "Because he was going to lose money if the club deal went through?"

"The American way," I said. I stood and began to pace, feeling like those gulls outside battling the murderous wind. "It's going to be hard to prove or even pin down. It could take months even to figure out who had the motive, but I don't think we'll have to."

"You've got a better way?"

I watched the struggling gulls. "Someone in Spanish Flats told Setsuko her husband was having an affair with Emily Foster. Whoever it is has to be worried because Setsuko is alive, could regain consciousness at any time and tell what happened. Let's give him more to worry about."

★ ★

Sergeant Tallich said, "You're grabbing at straws, Fortune. No one in Spanish Cliffs would do anything that crazy. Hell, it'd never work anyway. The first damn thing she'd do is confront Owada, for Christ sake."

"That's the last thing she'd do, Sergeant," Sandy said. "It would be too much shame to speak about."

"I think she was already suspicious," I said. "The way Emily Foster acted around Owada. To Setsuko there would have been only one possible explanation — Foster wanted her husband. All she needed was someone to tell her Owada had succumbed, and she assumed the worst. That's why she wrote Foster's name over and over in her book. She was deciding what she had to do."

"She didn't understand American culture," Sandy said.

Tallich was still unconvinced.

"If we're wrong," Sandy said, "Dan's plan can't hurt. If we're right, there's a really sick person around Spanish Flats."

I said, "Setsuko could recover consciousness any time and tell us the truth. But it could be too late. If the killer gets to her first."

He didn't like it, but couldn't take the risk. "We'll try it for a week. I probably should have my head examined."

The local newspaper editor smelled an exclusive even the wire services would pick up, was more than eager to cooperate. We cleared it with Hideki Owada, and the newspaper announced next morning that Setsuko was out of danger and expected to regain full consciousness any day.

Each day we upped the pressure. Setsuko had made another step on the road to full recovery. She was off life-support. She was beginning to respond to questions. She had asked to speak to the sheriff.

It took three days.

He wasn't a killer, not even a criminal. Only a businessman afraid of financial ruin. Inept, feeble and almost pathetic.

Sandy, staked out at the staff entrance to the hospital, spotted him the moment he arrived — in his own car, dressed in green surgical scrubs under his own tweed topcoat, and wearing common street shoes. Tallich's hidden men tracked him all the way up to Setsuko Owada's room. There was no guard on the door, why would anyone want to harm a poor insane woman? He walked into the room, stood building his courage, then moved stiffly to the bed and reached for a pillow with trembling hands.

He had the pillow over her face, his own face chalk white against the ill-fitting scrubs, when sergeant Tallich took it away from him. His face turned from white to the green of abject terror as the rest of us walked into the room, and he collapsed into a chair with his head in his hands and his whole body shaking.

"Who?" I said.

"George Chattaway," Sandy said.

Tallich said, "He owns a new upscale multimillion-dollar gated development half a mile from the golf course. The close availability of the course is one of his biggest selling points. I guess he got worried about what might happen if the club went through and the Japanese froze everyone else out."

As we all watched him, George Chattaway looked up at us in the dim room. "It would ruin me. What else could I do?"

★ ★

It turned out that George Chattaway had lived for two years in Japan, knew all about *oyaku shinju* and ancient *daimyo* and *samurai* families with their excessive sense of honor. He had every penny of his own, and a lot more he'd begged and borrowed, invested in his development, and was so overextended he had to sell the million-dollar houses fast to stay one jump ahead of creditors. The club would ruin their appeal. Or that was what he thought.

So he told Setsuko that Owada was having an affair with Emily Foster, knowing she would almost certainly commit *oyaku shinju*. He was sure that shame would make Hideki Owada give up and go home. But if by some chance that didn't happen, then he was equally sure the horror of the barbaric Japanese culture that allowed such a thing would convince the Board of Supervisors to turn down Owada's whole project and save his investment.

The county attorney charged Chattaway with conspiracy to commit murder for the deaths of Setsuko's children. "We may only get accessory, but that'll put him away a long time."

The Board of Supervisors voted three days later. They still turned Owada's club project down flat.

"Public access comes first," Emily Foster told me. She even kept a straight face.

Hideki Owada wasn't all that upset.

"Won't you have to sell out now?"

"We will see what the future brings, Mr. Fortune."

"How can you meet your debt payments without the club?"

His stern face almost smiled. "I will return in a few months with a new proposal. One they will not refuse."

"Like what?"

"Perhaps a development. Three or four hundred fine houses set discretely around the golf course. Very upscale."

"The supervisors'll never approve —" But I stopped. Of course the supervisors would approve. The houses would be for Americans, not for Japanese, and a businessman had a right to protect his investment. Hideki Owada understood Americans a lot better than his wife.

Setsuko eventually recovered, but remembered little of what had happened. If George Chattaway had been tougher he might have gotten away with it all. But, as I said, he wasn't a killer, only a weak and scared businessman.

Setsuko went to trial. The judge listened to the Japanese experts, said she would suffer enough the rest of her life, and let her off with probation.

She returned to Japan. Perhaps she will find some peace there, some way to come to terms with the deaths of her children, the tragedy of her clash with a foreign culture.

Maybe "A Death In Montecito" comes out of simply getting older. People love to talk about the wonderful past, the quieter, simpler, better world we used to live in. But if we think about it honestly, the good old days were never that good, not for anybody. We tend to remember an idealized past, not the way it really was.

I liked what Janet Hutchings was doing with EQMM *so much that I wrote this story for her too. I'd like to do more, but time and the exigencies of the marketplace have kept me too busy, alas.*

A DEATH IN MONTECITO

The house was a two-story white Colonial with blue trim, unusual for Southern California. Deep in the shadows of western oaks and sycamores, it stood on the bank of a creek that was dry for eight months even in a good rain year. This had not been a good rain year, and the creek and ground were thickly littered with brown leaves under the dusty trees.

"It was built by an easterner nostalgic for home," Deborah Urban, legally Urbanski, said. "The perfect house for my father. He's an overage hippie. He just had to buy the opposite of what people expected. It's the only one like it in Montecito. That kind of thing's important to him."

There was anger in her voice when she spoke of Gus Urbanski, and I realized I knew her. At least her face and the feature stories in *Parade* and *People*. Two movies I could recall: a big spy thriller, *Fog of Terror*, or something like that; and a teenage drug flick I can't put a name on but the director was important. The magazine stories had been all about her men and work. An early marriage to a violent ex-jock with grown kids, and a second to the kid co-star of the teen angst flick. That one broke up in less than a year over his drug habit. Or hers. Or both.

"It could be just right for me too," I said.

Tree forts decayed high in a big old holly oak and an even bigger sycamore. Swings hung from thick tree limbs that jutted out over the dry creek. One, made of an old automobile tire, was festooned with spider webs and old leaves. The other was a real swing with a clean wooden seat. Down in the creek bed a deflated rubber raft lay half buried under leaves and debris.

She said, "What makes you think the house is for sale, Mr. Fortune?"

"My real estate agent told me. He said it wasn't listed, but he figured it was coming on the market."

"Ghouls, all of them!"

She was dressed for a night in Hollywood — a sleek white sheath that barely covered her from nipples to crotch, left a vast expanse of very firm, very smooth, very tanned flesh. But it wasn't night and she wasn't in Hollywood. She was in the dim late afternoon shadows under thick oaks and sycamores looking at the house where her mother had been murdered.

"I'm sorry," I said. "Lawyers and real estate agents. They read the papers and see money. You were close to your mother?"

"As close as I could be from Malibu or whatever godforsaken part of the world I have to go to. Closer than Sarah. She likes my father."

"I guess you don't."

"A man who walked out on his wife and children? No, I don't like my father." Her hands pulled at a wadded facial tissue she'd found hidden somehow inside the tight white sheath. "You were sent on a complete wild goose chase, Mr. Fortune. I expect mother...left...the house to my sister and me. Sarah'll want to live in it. She likes this town. The quiet life." She laughed. "A rent-free house would've sounded good to me a few years ago."

"Not now?"

"Rent isn't my problem, and the quiet life isn't in the picture for a long time. In Hollywood you're on and there twenty-four hours a day." She smiled. A devastating smile: girlish, wistful, sexy, enticing, warm and melting all at once. "Besides, I think I'd like to know the house was here for me when I burn out. And I will, everyone does down there." The smile blended almost magically into a hard face of sheer willpower and determination. "But not yet. Not by a long shot."

"The real estate agent told me your mother had been planning to sell the house and move away before..."

"That man in Santa Fe? She'd never have done it. My mother thought about as much of men as I do."

I smiled. "You're young to give up on men."

Her face went cold. She was a chameleon, mercurial. Maybe you have to be to succeed in Hollywood.

"How old do you think a woman has to be, Mr. Fortune?"

"Sorry again, none of my business. I'm not usually that insensitive. The house is just so attractive."

She softened, seemed to see my empty left sleeve for the first time. "Look, Mr. Fortune, we haven't even thought about what to do with the house, I'm sorry."

She turned to go inside.

"If I could take a fast tour, I wouldn't bother you again."

★ ★

Out of the sun, the interior was cool. I walked from room to room studying the layout of the furniture.

In the living room everything was clean and untouched, except a grouping of a love seat and armchair around a coffee table and a color TV set. The armchair lay on its side, and there were two coffee-stained coasters on the coffee table. An irregular stain had dried dark on the carpet.

Deborah Urban nodded to the color TV. "Mom set that up for when she and my father had company, not that he cared about any company at home. Coffee houses and bars was his speed."

The family room was a glassed-in porch at the rear. A shabby blue futon couch sat directly on the floor in front of another color TV with a blue-painted coffee table between. A massive leather recliner stood in a far corner, its footrest raised, a narrow side table beside it.

"Your mother always had the furniture arranged like this?"

Deborah frowned. "I haven't been in the house in years, but it does look different." She continued to glance around as we walked, and seemed puzzled. "She'd moved things, but I can't say what. Does it matter?"

"Just wondering what other arrangements might look good."

A chandelier hung in the center of the formal dining room, but the dining table and chairs had been pushed against a wall between two windows where the sunlight came through the trees. Sideboards and a china cabinet were in normal positions against other walls, leaving a large open space covered by a rug.

The master bedroom was arranged for a single occupant.

"I really would like to be alone now, Mr. Fortune. I have to go to a cocktail party, and — ?"

"Of course. I've bothered you enough."

★ ★

She emerged less than an hour later. A chauffeur held the door of a black stretch limousine. She climbed in, the limo drove off. I got out of my car and walked back to the house.

There were no footprints in the hard dirt, but a path had been crushed through the dry leaves from the blacktop driveway to the steps up to the rear door. On the door the lock had been literally torn out of the frame. I got down on my knees and examined the lock and frame. There were no dents, no marks, and the frame had been broken before: repaired with screws and paint. It had broken again at the same places, the screws torn loose. I wondered if someone had expected it would do that?

Back inside, the two coffee cups the police had found drying in the kitchen basket that day were still there. The two other bedrooms had become storage rooms stacked with dusty boxes. In each, shelves were full of toys, dolls and children's keepsakes. In the rear one, rows of stuffed animals gathered dust on a top shelf. The three bears seemed lonely without a Goldilocks. The stains on the floor of the rear bedroom were blood.

I got my camera and went to work.

★ ★

Gus Urbanski studied the series of color snapshots sadly. "Yeah, that's the house. Where'd you get these?"

"Real estate agent," I said. "Told me the house would come on market soon."

"I wouldn't know," Urbanski said. He stared at the photos of each room. "Twelve years since I set foot inside the house. Sarah was still climbing trees and riding rafts down the creek, much to her mother's horror. Debbie'd never heard of Hollywood."

"It's hard to be thirteen in America and not know about Hollywood, Mr. Urbanski," I said.

He laughed on the rickety deck, his chair tilted against the cabin wall. "Truth is in the image not the facts. Debbie was as far as Jupiter from imagining the life she has now. Big bucks, magazine covers, two bad marriages before she's twenty-five. The movie star."

He was short and wiry, with a ragged gray beard and skin the color of cordovan from years of fierce suns. Early fifties, he looked like a man who could outlast a mule, and sounded like one who didn't care a damn about anything but his own views.

"What did she imagine?" I asked.

"A nurse. She was going to be an angel to the sick. Sarah was going to explore the universe. Now Deb's cruising the world jiggling her tits, and Sarah's running a boutique shop in town."

"Is that bad?"

"Not if it's what they want. That's what counts: doing exactly what you want. Self-sufficient, and never do what you don't want to do. That's why I had to get out of that house and what went with it." He looked at the photos. "Too bad, too. I liked the house. Seeing it inside again, I remember."

"Sounds like you had good times there."

His rustic cabin was on the first steep slope above Mountain Drive, and the unpainted deck had a view of the city below, the sea and Channel Islands, and half the world in all directions.

"The kids and I did." He looked out at his view. "When I went off on a trip, I brought something exotic from wherever the hell I'd been for Sarah, and one of those stuffed animals for Debbie. She loved those animals."

"How did the back door get broken?"

He shrugged. "Kicked it down one night. One of the things made me realize I had to leave. Split the goddamn door, and had to replace it. Too expensive to replace the frame, so I put it back together with glue and screws and painted it."

"Looks like that's how the killer got in," I said. "Broke the door open at the weak spot, grabbed the kitchen hammer, hit her in the living room. Some vagrant, the police say. Tragic."

He stared at me. "You don't want to buy the house. You didn't come here because you thought I still owned a share in it. Who the hell are you?"

"Just someone interested in the house, Mr. Urbanski."

"Get the hell out of here!"

★ ★

Santa Barbara Polo Field is an expanse of grass on the east end of Montecito surrounded by trees and condominiums. It's used for dog shows, classic auto rallies, and even polo on weekends and special occasions when princes, kings and South American millionaires come to ride their ponies and swing a mallet.

Most of the time it's an exotic front yard for the condos.

Kevin Moore lived in a second-floor unit in building number 12. The smallest and cheapest unit they sold — no garden, terrace or second bedroom. I found Carol Urbanski's brother out front polishing a classic old MG.

Moore put my snapshots on the hood of the car. "Who told you Carol left me part of the house?"

"Didn't she?" I said. "The real estate agent must have made a mistake."

"Hell, I don't know. Haven't heard anything about the will yet. Could be she did."

A slender man an inch under six feet, he wore white flannel slacks, a flowing navy blue shirt, and an ascot. A tennis sweater was tied around his neck by its arms. The MG had a vanity plate — GO NAVY 3 — and a naval reserve sticker.

He studied the photos, maybe willing the house to be his. "A goddamn officer's pension doesn't go far these days, and our old man left her most of the money. 'The poor abandoned woman' and all that shit. Maybe she decided she owed me, you know? What were you thinking of offering, Mr. Fortune?"

"I'm not sure. Those photos don't really tell me a lot."

Kevin Moore picked up the snapshots again. "They don't do it justice, that's for sure. And the furniture's all moved around. Looks terrible. Why the hell do that when she was selling the place? Look at the dining room table. Awful."

I said, "Maybe she didn't move the furniture."

"What? Who the hell else could — ?"

"Maybe whoever killed her," I said.

"What the hell for?"

"Looking for something?" I said. "Hidden money, jewels, or just something important to someone."

"But how would a vagrant — ?"

"He wouldn't."

Kevin Moore stared. "You're saying the police are wrong? Some damned nut didn't kill her?"

"Seems like a possibility. The furniture, the door with the broken lock, nothing stolen..."

He blinked into space, appeared to be thinking hard. "No, no way. The police would know if it wasn't some crazy, right?" Then he licked his lips. "I'm sorry...I've got to go. An appointment..."

He went into the building leaving the MG half polished.

★ ★

The patrol car picked me up at the Polo Field and escorted me to sheriff's headquarters across from the jail in Goleta. Deputy Sergeant Max Marquez pointed to a chair.

"Gus Urbanski wants to know what you're doing, Dan. So do we. Why the undercover act?"

"I'm working for Ronnie Dawes. It's the way he wanted it."

"Carol Urbanski's lawyer? What's he think he knows."

"The furniture in the house was moved around, rearranged."

Marquez waited. "That's it? Someone moved the furniture?"

"And what didn't happen."

"What didn't happen?"

"Nothing was taken, she wasn't raped, and no vagrants or even strangers were seen near the house."

"Nobody was seen near the house. Vagrants have been around Montecito the last two months. The kitchen door was broken, the weapon was the hammer she kept in the kitchen. He broke in, she surprised him, he killed her and ran before he could grab."

"Dawes says none of the neighbors had coffee with her. He didn't have coffee with her. Who did she have coffee with?"

"Christ, Dan, maybe it was the milkman."

"In the living room? She didn't use it three times a year. The kitchen or family room, maybe. But not the living room, and the odds say not with some casual stranger who killed her."

"Odds aren't proof."

"They raise a doubt."

"Not to me," Marquez said. "The leaves were walked through, the back door lock was broken. Everyone except Gus Urbanski had a key, and Gus has the only decent alibi."

"What?"

Marquez looked up at his ceiling. "He was in San Luis. He was seen there early and late. He could have driven down and back, but he sure wouldn't have had time to move furniture."

"The others?"

"Sarah, the younger kid, was in her shop. She did lunch and errands and there are big gaps. Ms. Hollywood was on location in the Mojave, went back to L.A. for a photo session, karate class, and shopping errands. No one can say for sure she was at the karate class or did any shopping. If she cut the class she had time to squeeze in a murder and make it back to the Mojave when she did. The brother was out sailing alone, and the cowboy lover was in Santa Fe."

He leaned back and looked at me. "They could all've killed her, or they could all've been doing exactly what they say. Just about normal for alibis." Now he leaned forward. "But no one saw any of them near the house, we didn't find any evidence, and all but Urbanski had keys."

"The furniture didn't rearrange itself."

"Then she rearranged it."

"What sense would it make to move a dining table and a reclining chair from their normal spots to crazy places when you planned to sell the house?"

Marquez chewed a pencil. "You think the killer rearranged the furniture?"

"Yes."

"Why?"

"Maybe to find some item and take it away before she sold the house. That means someone who'd been in the house before."

Marquez looked out his windows. "Forget about no witnesses and no evidence. And say one of them is lying about the alibi. You've still got a big problem."

"Motive?"

"Bingo. We couldn't find a smell of one. Hell, we couldn't even invent one."

★ ★

A compact woman of twenty-two, Sarah Urbanski had the look of an athlete. Her blonde hair was short and ragged. She wore stained jeans, running shoes, and a green cotton blouse where she stood on the edge of the dry creek behind her dead mother's house.

"The raft was mine. The tree forts and swings were both of us. We had great times. I loved to climb in all the trees. I used to stay up there for hours. I especially loved the creek in a rainy winter. I'd send paper boats down to the sea, and go down myself on the raft. God, did I get in trouble for that. Twice the cops pulled me out and brought me home. Mom and Debbie were mad as hell. Gus, that's my Dad, was already gone."

She continued to stare down into the dry creek. "Always doing something, that was me. Dirt biking, running, climbing in the mountains. Debbie was the stay-at-home. Pets and stuffed animals. Now I'm still here, and Deb's all over the world."

She appeared to think about still being in Santa Barbara while her sister was all over the world. "We haven't even started to think about the house, Mr. Fortune."

"Of course. It must be a shock, your mother murdered."

She looked at my empty left sleeve, as if maybe she'd seen me around town, knew what I really did. "You're sure your real estate agent said the house was for sale?"

"Agents aren't very sensitive. But could I bother you just another moment, and take a look inside? I mean, in case you do decide to sell?"

In the living room the armchair still lay on its side in front of the color TV, and the two coffee-stained coasters were still on the coffee table. The irregular stain had darkened more on the carpet near the fallen armchair.

Sarah Urbanski touched the TV. "Carol set it up here for her and Gus. Kids weren't supposed to clutter up the living room. But Gus liked us all to watch in the family room."

I walked through the other rooms. "Is this the way the furniture has always been?"

We were in the family room. She looked around. "I haven't been in the house for a year. Maybe it's not exactly..." Then she stopped looking at the furniture. "You weren't told the house was for sale. Who are you? What do you want here?"

"What a private detective always wants, Sarah. Answers."

"Answers? About what? Who sent you?"

"Your mother's lawyer doesn't think a vagrant killed her."

"He's wrong! Now you get —"

"The furniture was moved and put back in all the wrong places. Dawes thinks the killer was looking for something."

"Is that what you think?"

"I think that's one possibility."

Surprised and angry, she calmed down fast. A thoughtful young woman, or maybe she had more on her mind than me. "Looking for what?"

"That was going to be my question."

She went to stand at the expanse of windows that faced the mountains. "I didn't get along with my mother, Mr. Fortune. But I didn't kill her."

"How did everyone else get along with her?"

"Debbie got along fine. She lives in another town. Dad got out. Uncle Marty sponged off her. I don't know about the cowboy except she was hot to sell the house and fly off to Santa Fe."

"What did you think about that?"

"I was ecstatic. Mom would be a thousand miles away. Maybe we could even really talk to each other."

"Who killed her, Sarah?"

She returned to the futon, sat and didn't look at me. "A prowler. That's all it could be."

"Then who moved the furniture?"

"Mom must have moved it herself. Mr. Dawes is wrong."

★ ★

The mountains towered north and east of Santa Fe, snow on the highest peak as white and startling in the hot sun as Edgar Bowers' hair. He held the photos and looked out and up at the peaks from the shaded patio of his old Spanish-style house.

"This isn't how the house was arranged the last time I was there. I never saw the furniture that way."

"You were there less than a month ago?"

"Three weeks. It was when Carol agreed to move here and give it a try. Us and Santa Fe and away from Santa Barbara and all she was carrying since Gus left."

"Were you surprised, Mr. Bowers?"

He glanced back at me, then returned to his peaks. "A little. I told her all along she was dying there, not living, but she couldn't seem to let go. I wasn't sure she ever would."

He put the pictures on a bench, but still looked up toward the snow peaks. "You're from the police, Mr. Fortune? You've decided it wasn't some unknown intruder after all?"

"Private," I said. "An unknown intruder is still the official opinion."

"Who has an unofficial opinion?"

"Her lawyer."

"On what does he base this opinion?"

"The rearranged furniture. He thinks someone was searching for something."

He looked down at the photos again. He was a tall, slender man in well-worn jeans, denim shirt, cowboy hat and boots, inlaid silver belt buckle, and drooping mustache as white as his hair. But he was no aging cowboy. A full professor at the University of New Mexico. The clothes went with the geography, not the work.

"Because she was planning to sell the house?"

"That's what the lawyer thinks. Did she say anything to you about any of them not wanting her to sell?"

"As far as I know she hadn't informed them yet, but she expected all of them to oppose her." His voice grew angry. "I told her it proved she did have to get out."

"Did she mention anything one of them might want?"

"No."

"Did she ever say whose idea it was for her and Gus Urbanski to break up?"

"No. I think it was simply two people with absolute ideas of what life should be no matter what the other wanted."

"But they kept in touch?"

"Only through the children, as far as I know."

I said, "You were surprised when she agreed to leave Santa Barbara. You never expected her to sell the house. Where had you expected to live with her?"

His dark blue eyes didn't flicker a hair. "Nowhere. Here, or nowhere."

★ ★

The house wasn't a mansion, or unusual, or especially beautiful. One of thousands of beach houses in Southern California. It was the location that made it extra desirable and therefore extra expensive. Malibu. The best part. On the beach. With important neighbors. Important in Hollywood, anyway.

The maid let me in.

"I never met a private eye before," Debbie Urban said, and laughed. "Especially one who suspects me of evil deeds."

Sarah Urbanski said, "What do you want this time, Mr. Fortune?"

They were in a living room the size of my whole hacienda in Summerland, with so much glass you felt you could walk straight across the beach into the ocean. Coffee cups and Irish whisky. I didn't drink it anymore, but I could still remember and miss the smoke and fire. The bottle was half empty and I didn't think they'd been laughing a lot.

"Same thing: answers. You know who gets the house yet?"

"Yes," Sarah said.

"Oh, Sare, we can tell him. Why not, for God's sake? Come and sit down, Mr. Fortune. Coffee? A drink?"

I sat on the beige leather and steel couch. It felt like sitting on air and butter. "The coffee looks good."

She poured the coffee. Sarah wasn't happy.

"Does Gus still have a stake in the house?"

"No," Sarah said.

"Take the cash and run, that's my father," Debbie said. "A long time ago."

"How about Kevin Moore or Edgar Bowers?"

"No," Sarah said.

Debbie laughed again. "Uncle Lush and the cowboy are out in the cold."

"She left everything to us, Fortune," Sarah said. "Which means the house, okay? That should clear up any idea of our moving furniture to look for something."

"Not necessarily," I said.

"Wonderful!" Debbie said. "Detective work is fascinating!"

"Mostly plodding, listening, and checking. For example, your karate teacher isn't sure you were in the class that day, Debbie. Can you prove it somehow?"

"Why I talked to him, for God's sake!" She frowned. "If he doesn't remember, I'm not sure I can. I was in a hurry to get back to the desert, didn't stop to talk to anyone else."

Sarah said, "Karate class? So you finally got to take one. Good for you."

"Finally?" I said.

"We both wanted lessons when we were kids, but Mom said no. Too masculine. I never did take a class."

"I don't remember that, Sare. I need it for a movie. Hey, maybe that's why I want the movie."

I said, "How about you, Sarah? Can you fill in the time you were away from your shop that day?"

"You know damn well I can't. I told the police."

"So you did. What about the house? Going to sell it?"

"Of course not," Debbie said. "We had wonderful times in that house, we couldn't sell it."

Sarah said, "We haven't decided yet, okay?"

"Sarah! You'll live in it, for God's sake. Free rent. I'll pay the mortgage."

"I don't want to live in it, Deb."

"Then we'll rent it. When we both burn out we can live there together."

"Renting is a big hassle. Tenants trash a house. We can keep anything we want from the old days, Deb."

Debbie's exotic Hollywood face broke into that devastating smile: girlish, wistful, sexy, enticing, warm and melting all at once. "Well, I guess you're right. But we'll talk about it."

Sarah looked at me. "Is there anything else, Mr. Fortune? Deb and I don't get together all that often."

★ ★

"All right," I said. "The motive was triggered by her decision to sell the house. One of them killed her, moved the furniture to look for something, and put it back wrong."

Lawyer Ronald Dawes is a small, skinny man with weak eyes and a shy manner. This fools people. The weak eyes come from damage he took leading a platoon in Vietnam. When he came back he was top man in his class at Harvard Law, and in court he goes for the jugular and gets it.

"That's what I think," Dawes said.

We were in his office. All the windows are on the south side overlooking an ocean of red tile roofs that slope away down to the real ocean and the distant Channel Islands.

"She had coffee with the killer in the living room," Dawes said.

"To tell whoever it was about selling the house?"

"The final decision," he said.

"One of them trying to talk her out of selling."

We both sat and thought about what had happened when Carol Urbanski wasn't talked out of selling.

That was when I remembered.

★ ★

Gus Urbanski sat again on the rickety deck, his chair at the edge where he could admire his panorama of sea, town and sky. I held the snapshots out to him.

I said, "When you saw these, you said, 'I liked the house. Seeing it inside again, I remember.' As if nothing had changed in twelve years."

The wiry and muscular outdoors man let his gaze move all across his vast view from his rustic cabin.

I said, "The killer knew about the broken back door frame."

He stroked his gray beard, almost tenderly, and reached for the photos. "It's different, but not all that much. I shoved the dining room table over under the windows so we could look out at the trees and creek, and the kids had a big space to play in. I bought that old futon couch and set it up in front of the TV, painted that blue coffee table myself. But that big recliner I never saw. We had a lamp and table over in that corner."

"When you brought the three bears back for Debbie, did you buy a Goldilocks with them?"

He nodded.

I said, "The killer didn't want your ex-wife to sell the house, but the furniture wasn't moved to look for anything."

"Why was it moved?"

"Let's go find out."

★ ★

Four dilapidated palms towered over a ragged brown lawn in front of the shabby gray three-story Victorian on the Westside.

Sarah Urbanski didn't answer our ringing. Gus Urbanski had a key.

"She and I always got along," he said.

We went into a living room furnished with rugs, chairs and cushions from half the world, and up a series of narrow corkscrew stairs. The apartment was more vertical than horizontal. The living room and a kitchen were the entire first floor, a dining room the second. An office/den/TV room was a half-level between the second and third floor. Two bedrooms under low eaves were the third floor.

"She says it's like living in a tower," Urbanski said. "Her own castle. Where is she, Fortune?"

There was no sign of Sarah Urbanski in the apartment. No Sarah and no struggle. The apartment as neat and orderly as if she'd just walked away.

"Look around," I said.

He found the Goldilocks behind an armchair down in the living room.

I found the telephone. "Give me whoever handles Debbie Urban. Damn it, this is urgent. Fred Merkur? Where? I don't care how private it is, if he wants a live client, you better give it to me fast!" I took down the unlisted number, and dialed again. "Mr. Merkur? Debbie Urban's in bad trouble. Really bad, yes. I have to know about her karate class. What movie is it for? You're sure? All right, I'll get back to you."

I hung up and headed for the door. Gus Urbanski was close behind.

★ ★

The house showed light under its old oaks and sycamores. I motioned Gus Urbanski to be quiet. We went into the lighted kitchen through the broken door.

There was fresh blood on the kitchen floor, and a sound in the dining room. Faint, like something heavy trying to move.

Under the dining table, he lay on his back like a giant beetle trying to turn over, a deep gash on his forehead.

"Kevin?" Gus Urbanski said. Too loud.

I clamped my lone hand over his mouth. We listened. There was no other sound in the house. I felt the semi-conscious Kevin Moore's pulse. It was there, but weak. He was going nowhere for a while. Gus Urbanski's face was white.

The living room was empty. As we stepped softly along the hall toward the lighted back bedrooms, I heard it. A soft, slow sound like a distant chant, or a mother crooning over her baby.

The first bedroom was alight, but empty, the boxes unmoved, the rows of toys untouched on the shelves.

As we turned to the second back bedroom, the low, rhythmic crooning changed to a high, bright voice.

"Everything has to be exactly as it was, don't you see? We'll live here again the way we did. Before . . ." The voice stopped as if confused. "Everything's in the same place it was. The table against the wall so Mom and Dad can see outside and we can play on the floor. The futon and the table and the TV and the whole family room the way it was so we can all watch . . ."

"Not the recliner," another voice said. A steadier voice. "We didn't have a recliner. All that was a long time ago. We're not kids . . ."

"Let's go and climb the school steeple! The way we did every year, you remember?" And the voice changed again to the low dreamy sing-song like crooning. "Mom never liked me doing that. I was going to be a nurse. Mom cried when I didn't want to be a nurse anymore. I never wanted to make her cry."

I had reached the bedroom door. Sarah Urbanski sat on a chair, blood in her hair. Her hands were tied to the chair. Debbie Urban sat on the floor against the wall under the shelves of stuffed animals. Where her bed had been all those years ago.

"You didn't make her cry," Sarah said. "She just wanted you to feel guilty. She was good at that. She . . ."

"I made her cry!" Hard now, a fierce rage. "She hated what I was. Hollywood, the slime, the men! Sick and dirty! All Mom wanted was for me to be what I used to be. For all of us to be what we were before . . . Before we changed . . . Before Dad . . . Before you . . . Before I . . ."

Over coffee in the formal living room, her mother tells her the house will be sold. The safe walls, the happy days, will be gone forever. On the edge for who knew how long — the constant pressure, failed marriages, drugs — her mind snaps. The hammer is there. Or she goes to the kitchen for coffee and the hammer is there. One manic blow and she regains her lost childhood behind the secure walls where everything will always be the same.

Gus Urbanski walked past me straight toward his daughters. "Debbie, it's okay. We'll all help you..."

I reached Sarah, cut her ropes.

Debbie lunged at Urbanski. She had the hammer. He took two hard blows on the shoulder before he could catch her wrist. She struggled like an insane animal, raging and crying. It took all three of us to hold her, take the hammer from her.

Suddenly she stopped, smiled. The girlish, wistful, sexy, enticing, warm and melting smile.

"I know! We'll all go hide in the tree houses!"

★ ★

In his office, Sergeant Marquez sighed, "Moore figured one of them did it and was watching them both. Planning on some easy blackmail, I guess, but she spotted him and belted him."

I said, "I think it started all the way back when Gus left her mother. Then, when the pressure built in Hollywood, and things went bad, her 'happy' childhood became a final haven. That's why the karate class. There wasn't any movie that needed karate."

"She rearranged the furniture," Marquez said, "went in and out, past and present. She washed the coffee cups, but left them in the basket and forgot the coasters. She broke the door where it was weak, but took her Goldilocks and rode her swing down there over the creek. She's still in and out. Sometimes knows, sometimes doesn't."

I said, "By the time she drove home to Malibu, she'd blacked it out. Until I appeared and she had vague memories, but wasn't sure what they were. Then Sarah wanted to sell the house."

The younger girl nodded. "She called me to meet her at the house. When I walked in she hit me and tied me to that chair. She couldn't let me sell it. We were all going to live in the house together." She shook her head, looked at both of us. "The thing is, our childhoods in that house weren't all that happy or even safe."

"They never are," I said. "We just want them to be."

Or need them to be, at least the memory of them. But most of us don't have the desperate need to make the illusion real.

"Family Values" is my first Dan Fortune since 1995. I've written a few non-Fortune stories in the interim, including one for a cat crime anthology! But for those who, after the cats and "A Death In Montecito," thought I'd mellowed, I guess you can't teach an old dog new tricks after all.

This one was written specially for this collection, had its origin once more in a newspaper clipping. It treats another question much in the news today.

FAMILY VALUES

She leaped into the path of my old Tempo with the bold freedom of a yearling deer.

I slammed the brakes, and shuddered to a stop a few feet in front of her. She leaned in my open window.

"Hey, you only got one arm! They let you drive that way?"

I closed my eyes. "When did you notice you'd gone insane?"

"Hey, sorry. Most folks they just speeds up they see a hitchhiker, and I got to get into Three Rivers." She grinned at me.

If there's one thing no one ever accused Dan Fortune of it was being speechless, but this woman came close to doing the job. Jumping in front of a moving car seemed to be her idea of effective hitchhiking.

A girl, really. Eighteen tops, and I suspected younger. Her grin revealed crooked teeth white against darker skin. But the grin disappeared as fast as it had come, and I saw tension in the oval face with its thin, prominent nose under wary eyes. Her coarse jet black hair was loose and long on her shoulders. The hair needed combing and probably washing, her jeans and frayed flannel shirt were dirty, and her faded denim jacket was missing more than half its buttons. The watchful eyes had a faint epicanthic fold. A Native American.

A nervous and worried Native American. No, it wasn't exactly nerves or even worry. More like anger mixed with apprehension.

"Dan Fortune," I introduced myself. "You have a name, or did you forget it when you went crazy?"

"Della Keane." She added helpfully, "I'm Modoc."

"I'm Polack," I told her, "and I'm mad. You always do stupid tricks like that?"

"Hey, so people don't stop. Twentieth-century paranoia."

"College course?"

"My Dad." The battle of anger and uneasiness deepened in her dark eyes. Anger won. "Do I get a ride or not, mister?"

Her speech was a curious blend of big words and not much education, and her manner was abrupt and mercurial. A girl living on a high edge.

"Climb in."

★ ★

The stringer's call from Visalia had been my second lead to Dolf Stam in the two months I'd been after the fugitive witness. The first had been a bust.

Up in Tulare County, for about fifteen miles after the freeway exit, Highway 198 is another good divided four-lane highway through Visalia. But near Lincoln it narrows to two lanes and turns abruptly northeast through Lemon Cove. It skirts the south shore of Lake Kaweah and parallels the Kaweah River toward Three Rivers. The thick forests and high peaks of Sequoia National Park rise ahead. Mount Whitney, the highest point in the contiguous U.S., is only a few miles away, and Death Valley, the lowest point in all the United States, only 82 miles beyond that.

A state of extremes, California, and the girl who'd jumped in front of my car was another kind of extreme.

★ ★

Her anger lasted all of two minutes as I drove with one eye on the massive mountain scenery of Sequoia National Forest and the southernmost peaks of the Sierra Nevada.

"Hey, you a salesman? Horse buyer? Beef inspector?"

"Not a local?"

She nodded to my empty left sleeve. "You're kind of easy to remember. Anyway, that's a L.A. street map in the door slot."

"Why not just a tourist on vacation? Up here for the fishing? Maybe a rock climber?"

"Hell, tourists don't come back here. And you're too old for rocks 'n hiking. Maybe fishing. That what you're gonna do?"

"No," I said. "What about you? Modoc country's way up on both side of the Oregon border."

"My father worked on a cattle ranch in the foothills here 'fore he got killed. My boyfriend grew up in Three Rivers, so we stayed around."

Driving with my knees, I fished a photo of my quarry from my pocket. "You see this man recently? Name's Dolf Stam, but he's probably using something else."

She stared at my knees driving the car, didn't look at the photo. "Wow, look at that."

"Old salesman's trick so he can read his notes before a call. What about Stam? Big guy going to fat, has a torn-up left ear?"

She reluctantly looked at the photo. "Never seen him. Half the guys around here look like that. What you want with him?"

"He's a witness in a big case down south, and a lawyer wants him to testify."

"That what you are? A cop?

"Private."

She lapsed into another silence, stared out the car window in the warm noon summer sun. In early June the excessive inland heat hadn't begun in Tulare County, and it was pleasant driving with my window open as we entered the outskirts of Three Rivers. Mostly faded frame houses and shacks, some auto repair shops with their yards full of battered pickups, and a feed lot or two.

She continued to watch outside. "You work for anyone asks?"

"Anyone who pays." Her silence continued as the town grew more tangible. "Trouble?"

"I always got trouble," she said. "You're a Indian, you got trouble."

"The kind that needs an investigator?"

If she heard me, she didn't answer. We were approaching the main business district when she suddenly grabbed the door handle. "My stop. Thanks a lot, mister ... I forgot your name."

"Dan Fortune. Here, take my card."

She held the business card as if it were hot as she climbed out. On the sidewalk, she hesitated. "That guy? The one you're looking for? You could maybe try North Fork Tavern."

★ ★

I watched her walk toward a young man who paced and looked at his watch in front of a post office. One of those thin hollow-chested youths with patchy face hair too scraggly to be called a beard. He scowled and fidgeted — eager, nervous, or impatient. I couldn't read him, but I had a hunch fidgeting was his normal condition. From too little eating, too many drugs, too many schemes, and too little work. When the girl reached him he flashed a sincere smile, looked concerned for her, and began to talk fast as they turned up a side street.

Out of curiosity, I followed. They stopped in front of a gray frame house. The boy held her arm, talked earnestly into her face. A motherly woman in an expensive black dress and sensible low heels came out of the house and down the porch steps to meet them. She had severe blue-tinted gray hair and spoke sharply to the boy. He released the girl. The woman put her arm around the girl, spoke quietly and calmly as she gently guided the girl up a brick walk toward the house.

Suddenly, the girl twisted away and stalked off. The scraggly boy hurried after her, pleading. As I drove on past I had a glimpse of her face, sullen and close to tears.

★ ★

I checked into the Holiday Inn Express: sauna, whirlpool, color TV, and laundry facilities. Three Rivers' idea of the best place in town, but, hell, Barry Yorke, the lawyer in Santa Barbara, was paying for it. I skipped all those great amenities to pay the mandatory call on the local sheriff's sub-station.

Deputy sergeant Ryan Giggs was in charge. He checked my bench warrant on the California Law Enforcement Teletype Service and NCIC, and suggested some places to look.

"Matt Blomquist over at Sierra Construction hires a lot of transient labor when he's got too many projects, which is all the time. And Jack Berg's feed lots always need unskilled muscle."

No one at either place recognized Stam's picture, or remembered hiring anyone who answered his description. It was still early afternoon, so I canvassed the motels, apartments, rooming houses, grocery and liquor stores with my photo, and came up equally empty. At the last motel I asked for directions to North Fork Tavern.

As I drove north on the county road, the bald peak of Mt. Kaweah rose to the east. Evergreen valley oaks and tall Western sycamores were scattered across the hills of hay-colored wild oats. The hills and valleys were like a step back in time and a dislocation in space.

When people say California isn't really part of the "Old West," they're talking about the urban coast and the agricultural central valleys west of the Sierras. But the part of California east of the Sierra is as much cowboy country as Montana or Wyoming, and despite the last of the Sierras to the north and east the Three Rivers area belonged east of the mountains.

Exactly 2.4 miles out of town, the isolated roadhouse nestled deep into the shadow of a mountain. Thick pine forest reached past it to the banks of a roaring tributary of the Kaweah River. Because of the angle of the mountain, the sun didn't reach into the gloom of the steep valley. Cars in the parking lot were protected from rolling into the torrent by nothing but some logs laid on the blacktop at the edge of the tributary. A wooden bridge crossed the stream to the roadhouse.

There were only ten vehicles in the parking lot when I turned in, and every one was a well-used pickup or four-wheel drive SUV. It looked like a tavern whose clientele was largely local, and in rural areas there is a tendency to resent outside law picking on one of their own, or even one who wasn't especially their own but happened to be among them. Cowboys, lumbermen, miners, oil workers, sailors, or any other rough male in a rough job. It's a populist thing, individual rights and distrust of any authority they can't call by its first name.

That meant it was better to stake out rather than go in to show the photo or ask questions. I got on the cell phone and called my stringer in Visalia. Ed Green was a New York PI who'd moved west like me. Unlike me he'd retired. He picked up extra cash by doing occasional leg work for friends. He said he'd be at the tavern in two hours.

The sun was nearly down, and Stam hadn't appeared, when Green's old but mint-condition Mercedes pulled up next to my Tempo. He already knew what Stam looked like. I'd relieve him at dawn if Stam didn't show tonight.

"I got plenty of coffee and sandwiches," he said, and settled in for the night.

★ ★

In town, I circulated through the bars, motels, and restaurants showing my photo of Stam.

I was considering dinner when I spotted Della Keane at the Far West, a pricey upscale steak house, with an older man. He was expensively casual and rustic in a leather vest, slim jeans, and button-down tattersal shirt that flowed in soft waves every time he moved his arms. A shearling jacket hung over the back of his chair like an emperor to her plebeian buttonless denim. They were eating high off the beeve: steaks, side dishes, a bottle of wine. The man was intense and solicitous, almost fawning over her like a salesman with a hot prospect.

I went about my business, showing Stam's photo to the various bartenders and waiters, and had turned to leave for my next destination when the fidgety post-adolescent I'd seen her with on the side street stormed into the steak house and up to their table yelling and gesticulating wildly at the man.

Della Keane was furious. "Don't be such a jerk, Randy."

The man tried to mollify Randy. "Why don't you sit down, Randy, have something to eat with us. We can work this all out if we..."

"Fuck you!" Randy raged, his patchy whiskers like the mangy fur of a spastic rat. "Fuck you, you hear!"

Della jumped up and stormed out of the restaurant, leaving her denim jacket behind. The man grabbed the jacket, brushed a still-shouting Randy aside like an inconvenient cobweb, and ran out after the girl.

Randy took after the man.

I completed the parade by following them into the dark night of the mountain town. The only one left in the night was Randy. The skinny youth was swearing at the top of his lungs at the deserted and silent street.

A big black Cadillac appeared from nowhere to stop beside the furious Randy. A rear window rolled down. Randy instantly calmed and walked to the big car. He leaned in to listen to someone. Then the door opened, and the scrawny youth climbed inside. The door closed, and the Cadillac glided away, turned the first corner, and was gone.

I wrote the license in my notebook, and went back to work.

When I finished showing Stam's photo in every saloon, eatery and motel, I returned to the Far West for my own dinner. None of them had returned. By midnight I gave up.

In the motel room I read and watched TV. When I finally went to bed, I lay awake wondering what was going on with Della Keane. Was it all part of the "trouble" she'd thought of hiring me for?

★ ★

Dawn found me in the deep umbra of North Fork Tavern parking lot. A lone man arrived to open up about 6:00 A.M. By eight, one other car and a rusted pickup had arrived for breakfast, or for a badly needed morning drink. At eight-thirty a rusted Ford Escort screeched into the lot, and Dolf Stam climbed out and crossed the bridge. Della Keane knew more than she'd told me.

At nine Stam came out alone. I popped the holster strap off my Sig-Sauer, waited until he was on the bridge, and went to meet him.

"Stam! Hold it right there!"

When he saw me, his body leaned back toward the roadhouse and the woods. Up on his toes like a deer about to flee. Then he saw my empty sleeve and well-aged face, and knew he could handle any crippled old man. He was just dumb enough.

We met on the bridge.

"Dan Fortune," I announced over the rushing water. "Barry Yorke needs your testimony. I'm carrying a bench warrant. You can come back to Santa Barbara easy or hard."

His grin was a sneer. "You think you can make me, old man?"

"That's the plan."

The grin became a snarl. "Get the fuck out of my way."

He swung his arm to sweep me out of his path across the bridge. I caught the arm below the elbow, twisted my body, bent the elbow backwards against my hip as a fulcrum, and kicked his feet out from under him. He howled as the elbow ligaments ripped, and flew on his own momentum over the railing into the torrent of the creek below.

Flailing with one arm, bouncing off boulders, gulping water and gasping for air, he was carried fifty feet downstream into the relative calm of a deep pool. When I got there he was bleeding, gagging, and crawling his bruised and drowned body up on the sandy bank of the pool.

I pulled him to his feet, and half dragged him hopping on his unbloodied leg to the parking lot and across it to my car.

"I'll send someone for your Escort later," I told him.

He was still trying not to stand on a bloody left leg, and holding the elbow I'd ripped up, when I shoved him into my Tempo, handcuffed him to the stanchion I'd had rigged there for the purpose, and drove to the sheriff's sub-station. Deputy sergeant Giggs locked him up and sent for a doctor.

"You can take him soon as the Doc says it's okay," Giggs told me, "or I can hold him if you want to get help."

He'd seen my advanced age and empty sleeve too.

"I need some breakfast," I smiled; "he had his. After that I can take him down alone. Right, Dolf?"

Stam sullenly swore at both of us from the cell.

"Mother Lode Café puts out the best breakfast." Giggs said. "Try the Hangtown Fry."

★ ★

Mother Lode proved Giggs right. Eggs and oysters were fresh, shrimp plump, onions sweet and brown, and peppers hearty. A great Hangtown Fry. Coffee was fresh and strong.

It was over the second cup I looked out the window and saw them hauling Della Keane out of a patrol car and pushing her into the sub-station. People stopped on the sidewalks to watch. The owner of the café walked out to talk to them. When he returned he announced to the other breakfasters, "That crazy Della Keane killed her damn boyfriend."

Someone laughed. "Now ain't that a big shock."

"Never was no good, that girl," a woman decided.

While the Mother Lode customers were all agreeing with each other about Della's bad ways, I paid and walked across the street to the sub-station. Inside, the sheriff himself was there and too busy to talk to me. I cornered the friendly Sergeant Giggs.

"Any problem about me taking Stam out of here?"

"Jesus, I forgot all about him. I still got to do the paperwork." He checked his watch, glanced around the small sub-station office that was packed with civilians and deputies. "Gimme an hour, things oughta calm down in here by then. Maybe two hours, okay?"

"Okay," I agreed. "What's the commotion about the Indian girl?"

"Murdered her boyfriend. Says it was a fight."

"She say what they were fighting about?"

"Who knows? Hell, she's been in trouble around here since she could walk: drinking, drugs, stealing, whoring, ripping off welfare, you name it. That shifty boyfriend wasn't much better. We all knew she was gonna grow up and get in real trouble. Now she's done it. Not that the town's gonna miss Randy Butt."

Before I could ask more, the sheriff yelled for Giggs, and I went back to the motel to pack. I'd liked to have heard exactly what happened, maybe help Della Keane, but Yorke needed Stam in Santa Barbara tonight, and I didn't see much I could do.

★ ★

In the motel room I packed in ten minutes, considered an hour in the whirlpool and sauna, but decided against it. In the sub-station breathing down Giggs's neck I had a better chance of getting back to Santa Barbara today.

The knocking was so soft I didn't connect it with my door for over a minute. A lot of hesitation, tentative, almost afraid.

He stood outside under the overhang, short and broad. Five-foot-five, the shoulders of a bull, the legs of a tree trunk, and the belly of a beer barrel. A high-crown black Stetson in both hands, the wide brim of the hat flat and straight. Black hair in a braid down his back, Rob Roy flannel shirt, and loose jeans.

"Mister..." he glanced at the business card he held in one of the hands that also held the hat "...Dan Fortune?"

I'd given out only two cards in Three Rivers. I didn't think he'd gotten this one from deputy sergeant Giggs.

"Come in." He followed me back into the room as tentatively as he'd knocked. A man who'd learned it was best to not move the air as he passed. "Della Keane sent you?"

"My brother's daughter," he said. "She don't send me, they don't let me go to her. She tells me about you yesterday. A nice guy gives her a ride and he's a detective. She's surprised, you know? Cops ain't nice much. My own idea I come here. I figure you help her. Scare 'em. Show 'em she ain't no walkover Indian."

"I don't think I'd scare them much, Mr. Keane."

"Maybe, maybe not. They say she's a bad kid. Wild an' no good. We's Indians, you know? She been in trouble."

"Is she a bad kid?" I remembered her leap in front of my car. Reckless, thinking of herself, not giving a damn what might happen to me.

He sat down in the motel armchair. Sat silent. I waited. For a long moment, the street sounds were the only noise in the room. I felt it was a hundred and fifty years ago. In a rawhide tepee, or a bark wigwam, or a hogan, or whatever the Modoc had lived in up on the Oregon border.

"She's eight." He spoke in a measured voice, careful in the only language he knew but that wasn't really his own. "My brother 'n me hears they's good jobs down here on a ranch for horse trainers. We gets the jobs, he brings Della down."

"What about her mother?"

"She runs off long time ago." I'd broken his train of thought, and he had to fight inside to get it back. "She's eight. We's at Lazy F two year. Good jobs. Two white horse guys shows up. Foreman says no jobs, sorry. All other guys on ranch goes to boss, say they not like they got to sleep with Indians if they's white guys can do job. Foremen tells 'em shut their faces, we do good job. Owner says, 'Wait a minute, not fair to all the white guys. Let's see who best, they get jobs.' I say to boss, he want to give my job to white guy, go ahead. I don't want to work for him no more. Sammy, he got Della. She's in school, all that. He say, okay, see who better with horse. They get this bad horse no one ride. Toss quarter. Sammy rides first. For a while, he hangs on good. Three minutes. Foreman looks at boss. Boss he says nothin'. Four minutes. Sammy gets tossed, hits head on fence, is dead. Boss says terrible thing, but got job open now."

I could almost hear the wind blowing hard out of the lava beds up on the Oregon border. See Captain Jack dragged from the lava beds by artillery, cavalry. Not so very long ago.

"Della she's ten. I work any job I gets, long hours. They give Della to foster people. She runs away. She keeps runnin' away. She lives on her own, gets in trouble. Drugs, stealin', men. Sleeps around. Bad kid."

The wind was still blowing, but it was today's wind. He looked at me. "She's sixteen. She kills Randy, he got to of done somethin' bad to her. You find out."

I said, "I'll talk to the sheriff."

★ ★

The sub-station had calmed. Only the sheriff, deputy sergeant Giggs, and a single civilian from the prosecutor's office were left in quiet conversation.

"Papers are all ready, Fortune," Giggs announced, standing up and reaching for the jail keys.

"Could I talk to the sheriff before you get Stam?"

The prosecutor's man stood. "I'm finished anyway. We'll go for man-one, agreed?"

The sheriff nodded, and waved me to the chair at his desk. A big man, he gave the impression of moving slowly, deliberately. Like a thoughtful bear. He listened patiently to my story, but at the end he shook his head. "If Butt did something to her that made her hit him, something that might justify her, she's not telling us."

"What is she telling you?"

"The Butt kid was beating on her, so she grabbed a hammer and brained him. She didn't mean to hit him so hard, but she was afraid he'd kill her, it was self-defense."

"You don't believe her?"

"Believe her or not, it's still manslaughter."

"Not if she feared for her life. Then it is self-defense."

"Okay, I don't believe the self-defense." He ticked off the fingers on his left hand. "One, Randy Butt wasn't strong enough to kill a mouse with his fists, sure as hell not a tough kid like Della Keane. Two, there wasn't any blood at the scene except his. She was only bruised up. Three, Butt was hit at least twice. Four, after she killed him she packed all her stuff, grabbed her uncle's keys and car, and ran. A neighbor found the body, and when we picked her up she was already the other side of Visalia."

He shook his head more emphatically this time. "It was just another of their nasty fights the whole town knew about. This time it got out of hand, and she whacked him too hard. That's manslaughter in my book." He leaned toward me. "You think I like it? Sixteen years old? But she's a bad kid, and so was Butt, and that's all there is."

He stood up. The interview was over.

I signed the papers, and Giggs turned Stam over.

I again handcuffed him to the stanchion in the Tempo.

He was in a surly mood, and I had plenty of silence in which to think as

I drove out of Three Rivers. I'd liked Della Keane the brief time I'd seen her, and even more after her uncle told me about her father. She'd had a hard life, yet there was a kind of freedom about her we all should have. An unfettered humanity that only needed a path. A determination that would sustain her once she found a way she could accept, and a world she could live with.

But, reluctantly, I had to agree with the sheriff. If she didn't have a better reason to have killed Randy Butt, it looked like a certain man-one conviction.

"Stam? You know Della Keane?" She'd been right about looking for him at the North Fork Tavern. I wondered if Stam had something to do with her 'trouble.'

"That Indian whore killed her boyfriend? Wish I had. They tell me she's a hot number. I sure knew the sorry-ass boyfriend." He laughed a nasty laugh. "A two-bit punk from the word go. With a fucking big mouth."

"How did you know him?"

His eyes got cunning. "You gimme back my fucking cigarettes?"

I stuck one of his cigarettes in his mouth and lit it for him. He was only a witness, I didn't think he'd risk his neck to escape from a moving car, but I wasn't about to take chances. He blew a long stream of smoke.

"When he had any cash, Butt played in a regular crap game we had at the Lazy F. Bastard was always braggin' about his schemes. Last time he played he says we was gonna need a new player 'cause he and the whore was gonna make a real big score and split." That nasty laugh. Mean and humorless. "In a pig's ass they was."

I remembered how the ragged youth had pleaded with Della, tried to pull her into that house on the side street. How the well-dressed woman had calmed her and urged her toward the house. How the older man had fawned all over her in the Far West. How mad Randy Butt had been. How she'd walked out furious and close to tears.

And I remembered the Cadillac that had picked Butt up.

★ ★

We reached Bakersfield about two P.M. I drove to the airport, and got lucky. A commuter plane was leaving for L.A. in fifteen minutes. It was half empty, and stopped in Santa Barbara. I parked my Tempo in short term parking, flew down to Santa Barbara, turned Stam over to Barry Yorke, and was back in Three Rivers by nightfall.

The house on the side street was dark. I parked and walked up the brick walk to the porch and the front door. A small brass plaque next to the door read: Family Values Society. The door was locked, but had a stained glass insert, and a card was affixed to the inside of the glass: *In Emergencies, Call 657-9989.*

The woman who answered was cautious. "Yes?"

"Hello," I tried. "My name's Dan Fortune, Ms. — ?"

"What do you want?"

"I'd like to talk to you about Della Keane's visits to your —"

She hung up.

★ ★

At the Far West Steakhouse I was more careful and more diplomatic. I lied.

"I was here for dinner last night, and I met this man at the bar. He said he could help me with a business problem, gave me his card. Damned if I didn't lose it. I had the feeling he was a regular here." I described the man who'd been with Della Keane.

"I'm sorry, sir," the maitre d' apologized. "I do not know the man you describe, saw no such a man with a young woman."

"I'll bet you didn't even see Randy Butt storm in and cause a big ruckus either?" So much for caution and diplomacy.

"Ah, yes, I do remember a young man. But I did not know his name, and didn't see who he was angry with. Is that all?"

There was no point pushing it. I wasn't getting a name from the restaurant. But I'd gotten enough. From the way the maitre d' protected the man I was pretty sure he was someone important in Three Rivers.

★ ★

The public library was open, and had the last six months of the local weekly newspaper loose in the periodical stacks. It took less than twenty minutes to find my man. The two-column photo showed him on some kind of panel at the local high school: Dennis Irwin, CEO of Sierra Enterprises, Inc.

But he wasn't the only familiar face on that panel.

At the other end of the long table a woman looked an awful lot like the motherly woman in the expensive black dress and sensible low heels who'd tried to get Della Keane into the Family Values Society house. The same severe blue-tinted gray hair, a pale wool dress the twin of the black dress: Mrs. David Beckham, wife of county supervisor David Beckham.

★ ★

When Dennis Irwin opened the door of his enormous stone house built on a long rise at the far end of a mountain valley, he was dressed very much as he had been leaning earnestly toward Della Keane in the Far Western Steakhouse: Levi jeans, beaded leather vest, a soft flannel shirt, and wearing the shearling coat as if about to go out.

"Hello," he said cheerfully. "Can I help you?"

"You can tell me about Della Keane."

His eyes retreated behind the hard CEO stone wall, but his voice remained calm if not as cheerful. "Tragic thing. That poor girl. And Randy Butt, too, of course."

"Of course," I said, "but that doesn't tell me about you and Della, does it?"

"Me and—?" He tried hard to act totally surprised. It didn't quite come off.

"Della Keane," I finished for him. "Last night at the Far West? The tete-a-tete? Remember?" My meaning was pretty clear.

"You better come inside."

He took me into a small study. Shelves lined the entire room, and the books looked real and read. A gray corner desk of Formica and black steel tubes held a computer, printer, moveable keyboard shelf, and a steel rack for file folders. An Office Max special, simple and efficient. He waved me to a single leather armchair, sat at the desk facing me.

"Can you tell me why you want to know about Ms. Keane, Mr. —?"

"Dan Fortune. I'm a private investigator hired by her uncle to find out why she killed Randy Butt." It was only a small lie.

He sat for a time, obviously thinking. Serious thinking, but not panicky. Careful and thorough, deciding that if I were there I could find out sooner or later no matter what he said.

"I'm this year's president of Family Planning, Inc., a local organization to counsel and assist women about pregnancies, wanted or unwanted, planned or a reality. Della is two months pregnant."

Now I had to think. It could explain her hurry to get into town, Randy Butt's solicitude and pleading, even a violent fight that went wrong. But why was Butt so mad in the restaurant, why was Irwin wining and dining and fawning over Della?

"Is the Family Values Society another family planning group?"

"You might say that."

"Led by Mrs. county supervisor David Beckham?"

"You investigate well."

"Okay. Now tell me why you had a private dinner with Della, and why you were trying to sell her something?"

"The girl needed to talk more with us. She was hungry, and I wasn't trying to 'sell' her anything, as you put it."

"Why was Butt so mad about that dinner?"

"I don't know that he was. Perhaps they disagreed about the baby. Couples do. I assume he was the father."

"You don't know for sure?"

"It's not a question we usually ask."

"Why was she also going to Family Values?"

"You'll have to ask her or them."

His voice never changed, remained calm and casual, but I smelled the wall rising, a curtain coming down. The show was over. I would get nothing more without knowing more.

★ ★

The phone number on the card in the door of Family Values Society

turned out to be Mrs. David Beckham's private home number. It was in the
telephone book, and so was her address. Small towns don't like unlisted
numbers, especially for county supervisors and their wives.

The Beckham house was in town on a shady back street. Not as big as
Irwin's stone mansion, but big enough. A white frame Victorian with
turrets and cupolas and a stained glass fanlight over the door. Here, a
maid answered the door.

"Mrs. David Beckham, please." You never know how many Mrs.
Beckhams there might be in a house. Especially a rich house.

"Who shall I say?"

"Dan Fortune. Tell her Dennis Irwin sent me."

The maid was back in ten seconds. "Follow me, please."

This, too, was a study or office, but simplicity wasn't the *leitmotif.*
Twice the size of Irwin's, with heavy burgundy velvet drapes, dark wood
paneling, one solitary Victorian bookcase and a giant leather-topped desk,
it was a sterile imitation of a nineteenth-century English gentleman's
study with none of the warmth and eccentricity of most originals.

"Whatever Irwin told you is probably a lie."

Mrs. David Beckham didn't believe in warning shots. She was wearing
what seemed to be her everyday uniform: black dress, single strand of
pearls, low heels, and short blue-gray hair curled tight to her head like a
helmet. She radiated antagonism like the suit of armor that matched her
hair helmet.

"Della Keane isn't pregnant?" I said.

"Sarcasm won't get you far, Mr. Fortune. By the way, what kind of
name is that? Fortune? It doesn't sound —"

"It was Fortunowski," I told her. "Polish. My father changed it so as
not to alarm the natives. My grandfather never forgave him."

She let that hang between us. "I see. Yes, well, what else did Dennis
Irwin tell you?"

"That Della came to his organization for advice when she became
pregnant. I guess he took a personal interest in her."

She didn't rise to the bait. "We both take a personal interest in our
clients."

"She came to you for advice, too?"

"Yes."

"What did you advise her?"

"That all babies are created by God, that abortion is murder and a sin.
That children are the light of a woman's life, her reason for being. But
that, if absolutely necessary, adoption is always possible."

"Did she listen to you?"

"If you mean what did she decide to do, you'll have to ask her. Is that
all?"

It wasn't. Something was missing. Like the central piece to a giant puzzle. Here and with Dennis Irwin.

★ ★

Only deputy sergeant Giggs was in his office working at his desk. The silence of the late night was broken by an occasional car on the main street outside, and distant sounds from the jail above: a cough, a drunken song, footsteps of the guards.

Giggs didn't look up. "What are you doing back here?"

"Can I talk to Della Keane?"

"Not this late. All locked up."

"I think it's important."

"It'll keep till tomorrow.

"I'm not sure it will."

He finally looked up, and frowned. "What's up?"

"Can I see her right now?"

Giggs continued to watch me. Then he stood. "Okay, follow me."

She didn't greet me with open arms, but she didn't refuse to see me, either. The jail deputy hadn't been too happy, but Giggs had persuaded him. I sat on the toilet under the single dim bulb of her narrow cell. On the bunk she stared at the ceiling.

"Didn't Randy want the baby?"

"I didn't want the baby."

"Randy and Mrs. Beckham were trying to talk you out of an abortion?"

"Hey, you're a good detective." But her heart wasn't in the sarcasm. Her edge of wild exuberance was missing.

"If you were going to have an abortion, what was Dennis Irwin trying to talk you into?"

She laughed. "What the hell you think?"

I didn't believe her. Irwin didn't act like a womanizer, and certainly not of underage women.

"What was going to make you and Randy's big score?"

"What big score?"

"The one that would get you out of this town, this county."

"Someone's smoking bad pot." She turned to stare at me in the feeble light. "Go back to Santa Barbara, okay?"

"No," I said. I leaned toward her, hands clasped and arms on knees. "Not okay. If you don't tell me why you killed Randy, the real reason, I can't help you, Della."

"Don't need your help. Don't want your fucking help."

"Your uncle does."

"Hey, that's his problem."

"You thought about needing help when I gave you the lift. Trouble, you said. With who? Randy or someone else?"

She turned her back to me, lay facing the wall. A wild, free animal locked in a cage. A confused animal, scared and without hope. What was scaring her?

"You want to have your baby in prison?"

"Why not? You get three meals and a roof every day. That's more'n I had since my Dad got killed."

"You going to let his death poison your whole life? You think he'd want that?"

"My Dad was a stupid jerk."

She started to cry. Silent tears. Her back turned to me, knees up to her chest, shoulders heaving, curled in a fetal position. Child and mother.

"Tell me why you killed Randy, what the fight was really about."

She lay curled and silent, back heaving.

"There's got to be more. You and Randy fought before. This time was worse, and you ended up killing him. Why not tell? You afraid of something or someone? Is that it?"

She suddenly rolled over again to face me, her eyes fierce and her voice cold, "Something *and* someone. Now get out of here."

"Who drives a big black Cadillac and knew Randy?"

She sat up on the bunk. "Guard! Guard!"

A guard appeared at the cell door. She pointed at me. "Get him out of here."

★ ★

I lay in the motel bed trying to think. Two cars passed. Once there were unsteady footsteps on the sidewalk, like a fading memory. Pink and blue neon tinted the shades in bizarre colors until somewhere near two A.M. when the motel sign went off.

What was I missing? She was two months pregnant, not something you want to broadcast to the town, not when you're sixteen with her reputation. But why hide it now?

I was finally near sleep when I began to hear the voice whispering to me. My own voice. Whispered words that wouldn't go away. Like overheard conversation carried from far across one of those high mountain valleys. Whispering words I wasn't sure I wanted to hear. Not in my world.

★ ★

In a gray three-piece pin-stripe suit, Dennis Irwin sat stiff and formal in his large corner office in the Sierra Industries, Inc. main building five miles out of town.

"You said Della Keane hadn't decided if she'd have an abortion or not. She says she wanted an abortion. You ready to tell me the real story."

"There's nothing to tell, Mr. Fortune. If you'll leave quietly —"

"No," I said. "No, I won't leave. Quietly or any other way. Della and Randy Butt were expecting a big payoff. Who was going to supply the money? I've got a hunch, and when I've got a hunch I find out the truth sooner or later. But Della's in jail, and I want it sooner."

He studied his nails for a time, then clicked his intercom, "Celeste, hold my calls. I'm out for ten minutes." He clicked off and sat back. "It won't help Ms. Keane."

"Let me judge that."

He contemplated his tented hands this time. "She came to us for an abortion. She had no idea what that entailed. She knew nothing of the cost, and had no money anyway. A private doctor would be too expensive, but there was a clinic near Fresno that cost about $500. We told her to go home and think about it for a few days, and if she wanted to proceed we would find a donor who would pay the fee."

"You always pay for people's abortions?"

"No. It wouldn't be ethical." He studied a fine Motherwell in blacks and yellows on his wall. "Children raising children is always a disaster for society. But this child was a worse candidate than most. Alone, wild, on drugs, unpredictable, and almost certain to have to raise the baby alone. The fathers are usually ne'er-do-well adults, or children themselves, and they bolt if the girl decides to have the child. Randy Butt was both a child and a ne'er-do-well."

"Did she come back?"

"Yes. She had Butt with her." He was back to contemplating his fingernails. "He said he wouldn't let her go to Fresno alone. They'd both lose at least a week's earnings. They had no car. They'd need more money or she'd have to have the baby. I pointed out that it would cost much more to have the baby." He looked up, but his eyes focused somewhere past my shoulder. "He said Medi-Cal would cover that, and, besides, they'd been offered a thousand dollars if she had the baby."

I think I licked my lips. I know my throat was dry. The whispering voice I didn't want to hear last night came back, carried on the silence of the big corner office. "What did you offer to top the thousand?"

He flinched in his chair, as if I'd torn out a fingernail. "The counselor advising Della called me. She wanted me to authorize paying for transportation and treatment and after care, with a small stipend for living the first few weeks after the procedure. She said it was bizarre that a legal procedure even middle class women could get privately with no problem, a poor Indian girl had to beg or steal to get. I said the organization couldn't do that, but I'd try to find a generous donor."

"Did you find a donor."

"Yes.

"For how much?"

"Two thousand dollars."

"Who offered her the first thousand dollars?"

"I think you'll have to ask her that."

But I didn't really have to. My whispered voice had already told me.

★ ★

Mrs. David Beckham's office at the back of the Family Values Society house had once been a maid's bedroom. Small with a single window. Her suit of armor this time was a navy blue dress and she looked me straight in the eye.

"Yes, we have a program to aid indigent young women who wish to have their babies."

"With a thousand in cash?"

"I wish we had the facilities to clothe and house mother and child, but we don't."

"What was your next bid to Della? Or was it to Randy Butt?"

The blue dress seemed to turn into actual steel. "I beg your pardon!"

"I've talked to Dennis Irwin, Mrs. Beckham. The bidding was up to two thousand for Della to have an abortion. I expect he can give me the figure of your next bid. If not, Della can."

The steel armor cracked like thin foil that released a red and molten core. "Abortion is murder and sin, Mr. Fortune! All life is God's will and sacred! Whatever is necessary to prevent the loss of God's life is what I will do!"

"So you're against capital punishment?"

"Don't mock me. I know what is moral, and I know what is immoral."

"You don't even know what the word morality means," I told her. "Neither did Randy Butt. How high did you have to go? Or did Irwin and his Pro-Choice people win this one?"

Her armor may have cracked, but her righteousness hadn't. She didn't flinch or blink. "We found a source in New York that would give her ten thousand dollars, and an organization in Texas who located a couple who would adopt her child if she wanted."

"The complete package," I said. "How high did Irwin's outfit go in the next round of bidding?"

She almost smiled. "Fifteen thousand. Some shyster legal group in Los Angeles."

"But you topped that."

"Twenty-five. Our donors are generous."

"That where it ended?"

She did smile. "They don't have our resources."

"So Della was going to have the baby?"

"Of course."

Of course. Twenty-five thousand would be a fortune to Randy Butt. But more would be better. A lot better.

★ ★

In the jail cell I told her everything I knew. She listened in silence. Then I asked, "Who was in the black Cadillac, Della?"

The silence continued for a minute, maybe two. Finally, she raised her hand. "Gimme a cigarette."

"I quit years ago. You should too.'

"Yeah, hey?" She stood and peered down the jail corridor. When she saw no one, she dug under her mattress and pulled out a flattened pack of Virginia Slims. She lit one and started to walk the diminutive cell with the caged energy of the free yearling deer I seen when she jumped into the path of my Tempo.

"When I found out, I said, Hey, Della, no way, you know? I mean, I'm fucking sixteen. Real truth? Fifteen another three months. I work for anyone pays me, sleep anywhere I can. Randy, now there's a responsible old man, right? So I go to this Family Planning place. They tell me, sure, we can fix you up, even pay for the deal, but first you go home and think about it some more."

She waved the long cigarette. "So I go home. I think, and all of a sudden I ain't so sure. I mean, it's a real baby, you know? My baby. I still ain't told Randy. So I tell him. A baby, he says, like I'm crazy, and then he kind of likes the idea. I think it makes him feel like a real man. Mature. His kid, you know. So we go to the other place."

"The Family Values Society."

She walked and smoked. "This uptight old lady tells me all abortion's murder and a sin. Randy says, yes ma'am, he sure knows that for a fact. Then I tell her the other guys're going to pay for everything. She ups the ante to a thousand bucks if I'll have the kid."

She stopped to take a long drag on the cigarette, then paced again. "That's when I see Randy's wheels start turning. He backs off the polite act, says we'll think about it, and when we leaves he says to me let's go back to the other guys. So we do. Randy gives them a dance, and they go up to two thousand if I get the abortion."

Pacing, the cigarette forgotten. "Now Randy's real excited. He's smelling a big score. We play the two philanthropists against each other, and you know the rest. Hey, they was both so eager, you know? So sure they were doing right."

"They were doing right for themselves."

She shrugged. "Whatever."

Suddenly, she sat down on the cell floor, the cigarette limp in her hand. I saw tears on her face. "After a while I couldn't stand it no more. We was selling our baby to who paid us the most money. Money was gonna decide if my baby lived or died! So I told Randy we had to get out of here and then decide what to do. What we *wanted* to do. But the money'd got to him, he couldn't let go. He said the Family Values people'd bid the most, so I had to have the baby and let it get adopted."

Her silence stretched, the small tears. Too tough to really cry. Too abandoned for too long to lower her defenses, to know how to lower her defenses. I finished the story for her.

"You decided the only way out was to have the abortion. No baby, no money. That's why you jumped in front of my car. You'd made an appointment to meet Dennis Irwin in that fancy steakhouse so Randy wouldn't know. But Randy must have suspected, and followed you. When he got home the fight started. You —"

At first I thought I was still talking, but it was Della from the floor of the cell, "— he'd made this other deal. He'd found out about this gang who bought and sold babies for adoption by people who couldn't get them the legal way. I told him no way! No! He grabbed me, said I didn't understand. I started hitting him. I'm almost as strong as him. He hit me back. I was screaming and hitting, and then he said I *had* to have the baby or they'd kill us both. He'd already taken their money. Another twenty-five thousand. We'd be rich. It was only a lousy baby."

She looked straight up at me, her face wet but no longer crying. "He said, it was a gold mine, we'd keep doing it. Me getting pregnant and selling the baby for a bundle every time. I grabbed the hammer, and I hit him."

★ ★

They'd already heard about the baby-buying gang, and started an investigation. With the license plate number I gave them, the sheriff picked up the entire gang. The boss's name was Hector Viera, and he refused to admit he even knew Randy Butt. With my deposition, that didn't matter. They were out of business in Tulare County, at least for a time. Where there's a market there'll be a supplier. It's called capitalism.

"It doesn't get her off, Fortune," the sheriff said. "She still killed Randy Butt in a fight. That's still man-one."

He had us all in the sub-station office. Sergeant Giggs, the assistant prosecutor I'd met earlier, Dennis Irwin, Mrs. David Beckham, and me. Irwin and Mrs. Beckham had already admitted what they'd done. Irwin reluctantly, Mrs. Beckham defiantly.

"You'll never get a conviction," I told him. "She was afraid for her life and for her baby. She had to 'sell' her baby, or Viera would kill her. If he didn't, an enraged and desperate Randy Butt would. Both Irwin and Mrs. Beckham will testify she was going to have the baby, even though she'd first decided she couldn't. When she changed her mind again, Butt attacked her and she had to defend herself."

"Self-defense?" the assistant prosecutor wondered. "I don't think that'll fly, Fortune. He wasn't armed, and the sheriff tells me she's as strong as he was."

"He was armed, counselor. With the threat of Viera's muscle, and his own fear and greed, against her and her baby."

"Damn it," the sheriff exploded. "She *killed* a man with a hammer!"

"Maybe she was the instrument." I faced Irwin and Mrs. Beckham. "But *they* killed Randy Butt. Irwin's zealotry for his cause, and Mrs. Beckham's fanaticism for her beliefs, gave Randy the idea. They turned the most basic, private, sacred concern of a human being into a cash auction. Their obsessions led them into a frenzy that created the opportunity for Randy Butt's scheme. They set it all in motion."

Dennis Irwin said, "I did what I thought was right, Fortune. She was a child, she drank, she was promiscuous, she took drugs, Butt would abandon her sooner or later. Who knew what damage she'd already done to the baby, and what she'd do when it was born? She's wild and immature. Society —"

"They would have murdered that child!" Mrs. Beckham cried. "In God's eyes they're worse than that poor girl. I apologize for nothing I did to save that unborn child."

I said, "You don't care about the child. You care about your God. You care about your own salvation." I swung to Irwin. "And what you care about are your principles. About society. You're pro-choice, but it became *your* choice, *society's* choice."

I turned to the sheriff. "And you only care about the law."

The sheriff sat back in his desk chair. "And I guess a jury'll decide who's right."

"I don't think it'll get to a jury. Not even a grand jury." I nodded to the assistant prosecutor. "Will it, counselor?"

"I'll have to discuss it with my boss," he said. He didn't sound too optimistic.

★ ★

It did go to a grand jury in Visalia. Two days later they returned a verdict of justifiable homicide and Della walked out. Her uncle and I were waiting.

"Hey," she said cheerfully, "how about that?"

There wasn't much cheer in her eyes. We found a coffee shop. She thanked me, and thanked her uncle for coming to me. Then she sipped her coffee and gazed past both of us out the front window at the busy street. "Poor Randy. It was more money than he'd ever seen, you know?"

"I know," I said. "What are you going to do?"

"Get to be sixteen." There was a hint of bitterness. Then she shook her hand. "Hey, sorry. I'm pretty lucky, you know?"

"And the baby?"

She still watched the street as if waiting for Randy Butt to walk past. "In jail I decided if they let me go I'd have the abortion. Not for any damn principle, for me. It's too soon. I can't raise a kid. Not yet." She swirled the coffee cup, held it in both hands. "But, you know what? Since I got out, I'm thinking maybe I ain't too young. Maybe I can raise a kid. But not alone. Maybe I go home with Uncle, have my baby, make a life with the tribe."

"Which one, Della?"

She drained her coffee, stood up. "I ain't made up my mind. But whatever, it'll be for my own reasons. It'll be *my* choice."

★ ★

I drove south alone. She'd done some hard thinking over the last few days, and I knew whatever choice she made would be the right one for her. A yearling deer, bold and free, with her own life.

A DAN FORTUNE CHECKLIST

Novels

Act of Fear. New York: Dodd Mead, 1967.
The Brass Rainbow. New York: Dodd Mead, 1969
Night of the Toads. New York: Dodd Mead, 1970.
Walk a Black Wind. New York: Dodd Mead, 1971.
Shadow of a Tiger. New York: Dodd Mead, 1972.
The Silent Scream. New York: Dodd Mead, 1973.
Blue Death. New York: Dodd Mead. 1975.
The Blood-Red Dream. New York: Dodd Mead, 1976.
The Nightrunners. New York: Dodd Mead, 1978.
The Slasher. New York: Dodd Mead, 1980.
Freak. New York: Dodd Mead, 1983.
Minnesota Strip. New York: Donald L Fine, 1987.
Red Rosa. New York: Donald I. Fine, 1988.
Castrato. New York: Donald I. Fine, 1989.
Chasing Eights. New York: Donald I. Fine, 1990.
The Irishman's Horse. New York: Donald I. Fine, 1991.
Cassandra in Red. New York: Donald I. Fine, 1992.

Collections:

Crime, Punishment and Resurrection. New York: Donald I. Fine, 1992.
Fortune's World. Norfolk, VA: Crippen & Landru Publishers, 2000.

Short Stories:

[* = A story collected in *Crime, Punishment and Resurrection*; + = a story collected in *Fortune's World*.]

* "No One Likes To Be Played for a Sucker," *Ellery Queen's Mystery Magazine,* July 1969.
+ "Scream All The Way," *Alfred Hitchcock's Mystery Magazine,* October 1969.
+ "Long Shot," *Alfred Hitchcock's Mystery Magazine,* July 1972.
* "Who?" *Alfred Hitchcock's Mystery Magazine,* August 1972.
* "The Woman Who Ruined John Ireland," *Alfred Hitchcock's Mystery Magazine* (as "Dan Fortune and the Hollywood Caper"), November 1983.

* "The Oldest Killer," *The Thieftaker Journals*, November 1983.
+ "Eighty Million Dead," *The Eyes Have It*. New York: The Mysterious Press, 1984.
+ "A Reason To Die," *New Black Mask Quarterly, No. 2*, September 1985.
+ "Killer's Mind," *New Black Mask, No. 6*, June 1986.
* "The Motive," *A Matter of Crime, No. 2*, 1987,
* "Black in The Snow," *The Eyes of Justice*. New York: The Mysterious Press, 1988.
* "Crime and Punishment," *A Matter of Crime, No. 3*, 1988.
+ "The Chair," *Justice for Hire*. New York: The Mysterious Press, 1990.
+ "Role Model," *Deadly Allies*. New York: Doubleday, 1992.
* "Big Rock Candy Mountains," *Crime, Punishment and Resurrection*. New York: Donald. I. Fine, 1992.
+ "Murder is Murder," *Constable New Crimes 1*. London: Constable, 1992.
+ "Culture Clash," *Ellery Queen's Mystery Magazine*, November 1994.
+ "Angel Eyes," *Deadly Allies II*. New York: Doubleday, 1994,
+ "A Matter of Character," *Partners in Crime*. New York: Signet, 1994.
+ "A Death in Montecito," *Ellery Queen's Mystery Magazine*, April 1995.
+ "Can Shoot," *Private Eyes*. New York: Signet, 1998.
+ "Family Values," *Fortune's World*. Norfolk, VA: Crippen & Landru, 2000.

FORTUNE'S WORLD

Fortune's World by Michael Collins is printed on 60-pound Turin Book Natural (a chlorine-free and acid-free stock) from 10-point Century Old Style for the text and Bodoni for the titles. The cover design is by Deborah Miller. The first printing comprises two hundred copies sewn in cloth, signed and numbered by the author, and approximately one thousand softcover. Each of the clothbound copies includes a separate pamphlet, *The Dreamer, a Slot-Machine Kelly Story* by Michael Collins. The book was printed and bound by Thomson-Shore, Inc., Dexter, Michigan, and published in August 2000 by Crippen & Landru Publishers, Norfolk, Virginia.

CRIPPEN & LANDRU, PUBLISHERS
P. O. Box 9315
Norfolk, VA 23505
E-mail: CrippenL@Pilot.Infi.Net
Web: www.crippenlandru.com

Crippen & Landru publishes first edition short-story collections by important detective and mystery writers. Most books are issued in two editions: trade softcover, and signed, limited clothbound with either a typescript page from the author's files or an additional story in a separate pamphlet. As of August 2000, the following books have been published:

Speak of the Devil by John Dickson Carr. 1994. Eight-part impossible crime mystery broadcast on BBC radio in 1941. Introduction by Tony Medawar; cover design by Deborah Miller. Published only in trade softcover.　　　　　　　　　Out of Print

The McCone Files by Marcia Muller. 1995. Fifteen Sharon McCone short stories by the creator of the modern female private eye, including two written especially for the collection. Winner of the Anthony Award for Best Short Story collection. Introduction by the author; cover painting by Carol Heyer.
　　　　　　　　　Signed, limited clothbound, Out of Print
　　　　　　　　　Trade softcover, fifth printing, $15.00

The Darings of the Red Rose by Margery Allingham. 1995. Eight crook stories about a female Robin Hood, written in 1930 by the creator of the classic sleuth, Albert Campion. Introduction by B. A. Pike; cover design by Deborah Miller. Published only in trade softcover.　　　　　　　　　Out of Print

Diagnosis: Impossible, The Problems of Dr. Sam Hawthorne by Edward D. Hoch. 1996. Twelve stories about the country doctor who solves "miracle problems," written by the greatest current expert on the challenge-to-the-reader story. Introduction by the author; Sam Hawthorne chronology by Marvin Lachman; cover painting by Carol Heyer.　　　　　　　Signed, limited clothbound, Out of Print
　　　　　　　　　Trade softcover, second printing, $15.00

Spadework: A Collection of "Nameless Detective" Stories by Bill Pronzini. 1996. Fifteen stories, including two written for the collection, by a Grandmaster of the Private Eye tale. Introduction by Marcia Muller; afterword by the author; cover painting by Carol Heyer.
　　Signed, limited clothbound, Out of Print; a few overrun copies available, $30.00
　　　　　　　　　Trade softcover, $16.00

Who Killed Father Christmas? And Other Unseasonable Demises by Patricia Moyes. 1996. Twenty-one stories ranging from holiday homicides to village villainies to Caribbean crimes. Introduction by the author; cover design by Deborah Miller.

Signed, limited clothbound, $40.00

Trade softcover, $16.00

My Mother, The Detective: The Complete "Mom" Short Stories, by James Yaffe. 1997. Eight stories about the Bronx armchair maven who solves crimes between the chicken soup and the *schnecken*. Introduction by the author; cover painting by Carol Heyer.

Signed, limited clothbound, Out of Print

Trade softcover, $15.00

In Kensington Gardens Once... by H.R.F. Keating. 1997. Ten crime and mystery stories taking place in London's famous park, including two written for this collection, by the recipient of the Cartier Diamond Dagger for Lifetime Achievement. Illustrations and cover by Gwen Mandley.

Signed, limited clothbound, $35.00

Trade softcover, $12.00

Shoveling Smoke: Selected Mystery Stories by Margaret Maron. 1997. Twenty-two stories by the Edgar-award winning author, including all the short cases of Sigrid Harald and Deborah Knott (with a new Judge Knott story). Introduction and prefaces to each story by the author; cover painting by Victoria Russell.

Signed, limited clothbound, Out of Print

Trade softcover, third printing, $16.00

The Man Who Hated Banks and Other Mysteries by Michael Gilbert. 1997. Eighteen stories by the recipient of the Mystery Writers of America's Grandmaster Award, including mysteries featuring Inspectors Petrella and Hazlerigg, rogue cop Bill Mercer, and solicitor Henry Bohun. Introduction by the author; cover painting by Deborah Miller.

Signed, limited clothbound, Out of Print

Trade softcover, second printing, $16.00

The Ripper of Storyville and Other Ben Snow Tales by Edward D. Hoch. 1997. The first fourteen historical detective stories about wandering gunslinger Ben Snow. Introduction by the author; Ben Snow chronology by Marvin Lachman; cover painting by Barbara Mitchell.

Signed, limited clothbound, Out of Print

Trade softcover, $16.00

Do Not Exceed the Stated Dose by Peter Lovesey. 1998. Fifteen crime and mystery stories, including two featuring Peter Diamond and two with Bertie, Prince of Wales. Preface by the author; cover painting by Carol Heyer.

Signed, limited clothbound, Out of Print

Trade softcover, $16.00

Renowned Be Thy Grave; Or, The Murderous Miss Mooney by P. M. Carlson. 1998. Ten stories about Bridget Mooney, the Victorian actress who becomes criminously involved in important historical events. Introduction by the author; cover design by Deborah Miller.

Signed, limited clothbound, Out of Print; a few overrun copies available, $30.00

Trade softcover, $16.00

Carpenter and Quincannon, Professional Detective Services by Bill Pronzini. 1998. Nine detective stories, including one written for this volume, set in San Francisco during the 1890's. Introduction by the author; cover painting by Carol Heyer.

Signed, limited clothbound, Out of Print

Trade softcover, second printing, $16.00

Not Safe After Dark and Other Stories by Peter Robinson. 1998. Thirteen stories about Inspector Banks and others, including one written for this volume. Introduction and prefaces to each story by the author; cover painting by Victoria Russell.

Signed, limited clothbound, Out of Print

Trade softcover, second printing, $16.00

The Concise Cuddy, A Collection of John Francis Cuddy Stories by Jeremiah Healy. 1998. Seventeen stories about the Boston private eye by the Shamus Award winner. Introduction by the author; cover painting by Carol Heyer.

Signed, limited clothbound, Out of Print

Trade softcover, $17.00

One Night Stands by Lawrence Block. 1999. Twenty-four early tough crime tales by a Grandmaster of the Mystery Writers of America. Introduction by the author; cover painting by Deborah Miller. Published only in a signed, limited edition.

Out of Print

All Creatures Dark and Dangerous by Doug Allyn. 1999. Seven long stories about the veterinarian detective Dr. David Westbrook by the Edgar and Ellery Queen Readers Award winner. Introduction by the author; cover painting by Barbara Mitchell.

Signed, limited clothbound, Out of Print

Trade softcover, $16.00

Famous Blue Raincoat: Mystery Stories by Ed Gorman. 1999. Twelve detective and crime stories by the author described as "great, possibly one of *the* greats ... never a word too many, never a word too few, never a word that doesn't come from the heart." Introduction by the author; cover design by Gail Cross.

Signed, limited clothbound, $42.00

Trade softcover, $17.00

The Tragedy of Errors and Others by Ellery Queen. 1999. Published to celebrate the seventieth anniversary of the first Ellery Queen novel, this book contains the lengthy plot outline of the final, never published EQ novel, six previously uncollected stories, and essays, tributes, and reminiscences of EQ by family members, friends, and some of the finest current mystery writers. Cover design by Deborah Miller.
Limited clothbound, Out of Print
Trade softcover, second printing, $16.00

McCone and Friends by Marcia Muller. 2000. Eight of Muller's recent mystery stories—three told by Sharon McCone and four by her colleagues, Rae Kelleher (including a novella), Mick Savage, Ted Smalley, and Hy Ripinsky. Introduction by the author; cover painting by Carol Heyer.
Signed, limited clothbound, Out of Print
Trade softcover, $16.00

Challenge the Widow Maker and Other Stories of People in Peril by Clark Howard. 2000. Winner of the Edgar for Best Short Story and five-time winner of the Ellery Queen Readers Award, Clark Howard writes about ordinary people who have to find the strength, the humanity, to survive. Introduction by the author; cover painting by Victoria Russell.
Signed, limited clothbound, Out of Print
Trade softcover, $16.00

The Velvet Touch by Edward D. Hoch. 2000. Fourteen stories about Nick Velvet, the choosey crook who steals only the seemingly valueless, including all the tales in involving "The White Queen," who claims to be able to do impossible things before breakfast. Introduction by the author; cover painting by Carol Heyer.
Signed, limited clothbound, $40.00
Trade softcover, $16.00

Fortune's World by Michael Collins. 2000. Fourteen classic private-eye stories, including one written for the collection, about Dan Fortune, the one-armed op who investigates cases involving major issues of our times. Cover painting by Deborah Miller.
Signed, limited clothbound, $40.00
Trade softcover, $16.00

Forthcoming Short-Story Collections

Tales Out of School by Carolyn Wheat.
Long Live the Dead: Tales from Black Mask by Hugh B. Cave.
Stakeout on Page Street and Other DKA Files by Joe Gores.
Strangers in Town: Three Newly Discovered Stories by Ross Macdonald.
The Celestial Buffet by Susan Dunlap.
Adam and Eve on a Raft: Mystery Stories by Ron Goulart.
Kisses of Death: Nate Heller Stories by Max Allan Collins.
The Reluctant Detective and Other Stories by Michael Z. Lewin.
Nine Sons and Other Mysteries by Wendy Hornsby.
The Dark Snow and Other Stories by Brendan DuBois.
The Spotted Cat and Other Mysteries: The Casebook of Inspector Cockrill by
    Christianna Brand.
The Adventure of the Murdered Moths and Other Radio Mysteries by Ellery Queen.
Solving Problems by Bill Pronzini and Barry N. Malzberg.
Kill the Umpire: The Calls of Ed Gorgon by Jon L. Breen.
One of a Kind: Collected Mystery Stories by Eric Wright.
Cuddy Plus One by Jeremiah Healy.
The Old Spies Club and Other Intrigues of Rand by Edward D. Hoch.
The Iron Angel and Other Tales of Michael Vlado by Edward D. Hoch.

Crippen & Landru offers discounts to individuals and institutions
who place Standing Order Subscriptions for its forthcoming
publications. Please write or e-mail for details.